A
WICKED
MAGIC

A
WICKED
MAGIC

SASHA LAURENS

RAZORBILL

RAZORBILL

An imprint of Penguin Random House LLC, New York

First published in the United States of America by Razorbill,
an imprint of Penguin Random House LLC, 2020

Copyright © 2020 by Sasha Laurens

Penguin supports copyright. Copyright fuels creativity, encourages diverse voices,
promotes free speech, and creates a vibrant culture. Thank you for buying an authorized
edition of this book and for complying with copyright laws by not reproducing, scanning,
or distributing any part of it in any form without permission. You are supporting writers
and allowing Penguin to continue to publish books for every reader.

RAZORBILL & colophon are registered trademarks of Penguin Random House LLC.

Visit us online at penguinrandomhouse.com

LIBRARY OF CONGRESS CATALOGING-IN-PUBLICATION DATA
Names: Laurens, Sasha, author.
Title: A wicked magic / Sasha Laurens.
Description: New York : Razorbill, 2020. | Audience: Ages 14+.
Summary: When their feelings for the same boy cause a rift in their friendship,
Liss and Daniela, who practice witchcraft on California's northern coast, must work together to
rescue him when a misguided spell makes him a prisoner of an ancient demon.
Identifiers: LCCN 2019051802 | ISBN 9780593117255 (hardcover)
ISBN 9780593117262 (ebook)
Subjects: CYAC: Friendship—Fiction. | Witchcraft—Fiction. |
Magic—Fiction. | Demonology—Fiction. | California, Northern—Fiction.
Classification: LCC PZ7.1.L3822 Wi 2020 | DDC [Fic]—dc23
LC record available at https://lccn.loc.gov/2019051802

Printed in the United States of America

1 3 5 7 9 10 8 6 4 2

Design by Rebecca Aidlin

Text set in Arno Pro

For Ash

Prologue

The May before Johnny Su kissed her, Dan and her best friend, Liss, rolled back the rug in Liss's bedroom. Dan marked straight lines with white chalk on the hardwood, while Liss compared her work to a drawing in a musty book.

"The angle should be ninety degrees." Liss drummed her fingers against the book's cracked black cover. "We need to get this exactly right."

Dan sat back on her heels. The symbol was two feet wide and looked something like an asterisk, or two *K*'s stuck together back-to-back. "Is this okay?"

Liss scrutinized the page, then Dan's work. "Better than okay—perfect," Liss declared. "Now the candles."

Dan sat on Liss's bed and rubbed chalk from her hands, while Liss went about positioning the six candles: two red, two white, two black. They had worked all week carving other symbols copied out of the book into the wax. Neither of them knew what the symbols meant, and they weren't exactly something you could type into Google.

"Should we be doing this outside?" Liss looked up from the book with a conspiratorial smile. "What if we unleash some crazy power, and there's like, a magical explosion and we craterize all of North Coast?"

"Then I don't think being outside would help."

"That was a joke, Dan." Liss shot her a look that said *Don't ruin my fun.*

Liss had started talking about doing the spell the minute they found the book. Of course it wasn't actually a spell, because that kind of thing wasn't real, but the book made it easy to pretend it could be. The book had this fetid, mushroomy smell that was clearly gross, but was also so alluring that Dan had once stopped herself from burying her nose in its spine. Even weirder, most of its pages—which numbered in the hundreds, after the spell at the beginning—were blank, except for water stains and the occasional smear of ink. Dan had the uneasy feeling that the book *wanted* them to do this spell, which was definitely creepy and definitely not something she was going to admit to out loud. But creepy or not, there was next to nothing to do in sleepy, foggy North Coast, California, and Dan and Liss had a whole weekend to kill.

Why not cast a spell to turn themselves into witches?

"You still want to do this, right?" Liss asked. It sounded like an instruction.

Dan fiddled with the backing of a pin from her jean jacket, running the sharp part across the pad of her thumb. "Obviously," Dan answered.

Liss compared her work to the open page beside her. Across the top, neat cursive letters spelled out "A Spell for the Making of Naive Witches." Then she looked up at Dan. Liss's blue eyes were hungry and sparkling. She flicked the wheel of a lighter, springing a tiny flame to life. "Then let's do some magic."

Dan sat on the floor across from Liss. The white candle she had carved stood in front of her, the red to her left and black to her right. She grabbed the other lighter, and they began.

They spoke an incantation as they first lit their red candles, then their black. Already Liss's bedroom felt strange and somber, darker than it had been moments ago despite the light from the candles. Dan shivered, and the feeling lingered in her fingers and toes and deep in her chest, as if some energy in her body was waiting, trembling.

Magic wasn't real, Dan reminded herself; nothing bad was going to happen. Nothing was going to happen at all. She and Liss took up their black and red candles, and brought them together to light the white.

The white wicks caught.

Immediately the air in the room was moving. It started as a slow churn, then kicked up into vicious gusts of wind that snaked around them. Adrenaline punched Dan's heartbeat into high gear. The wind roared in her ears, her mouth, her nose, heaving like the waves of the nearby Pacific Ocean. Across from her, Liss's eyes went wide with fear. The wind pressed against them, ropes holding them in the whirlwind, yet somehow neither of them broke off the words of the spell, as if something beyond them were pushing them on, pushing the very words into their mouths.

The candles blew out and an absolute darkness filled the room.

The ground slid out from under Dan. She was careening, falling, then borne up by that wind, raging and playful and thunderous. She was a leaf carried by a gust, she was a bird in a storm, she was dust in the air. She was carried off in darkness, deeper and deeper.

Something was changing inside her, growing and blooming, expanding until it pressed up against the boundary of her skin from within. It squeezed the air from her lungs, the blood in her veins and arteries throbbed against it. It was *too much*—too much power, more than she was built for, and if she couldn't contain it—

But just in time it was retreating, the pressure collapsing. Whatever it was that had been growing was now folding in on itself, smaller and smaller, as if this new strange force was concentrating itself inside her. The wind was dying too, and everything began to still.

Dan was afraid to open her eyes. When she finally did, she was sitting on the floor in Liss's bedroom, the rug rolled back. Her heart was racing and jaw clenched, and Liss was there, out of breath. It was moonlit dark in the room, but the world felt stinging and bright, distilled in a way that was almost nauseating. Dan was sure, all at once, that every star in the sky was staring right at them, that the world was paused for them, its breath held, waiting and watching for what they would do.

Between them, the book was splayed open. Its pages turned lazily, petals from the head of a dying flower caught in the waning wind. They had been blank but were now crammed with text, diagrams, lists. Dan turned to the first page. Where the text of the spell they had just done should have been, it read *The Black Book—IIV*.

Dan raised her eyes to Liss. Slowly, they both began to grin.

"That might have actually worked," Dan whispered.

All summer, Dan waited for magic to change her life. She and Liss had transformed themselves, together, so Dan expected to feel different—better. As the long days went by, if anything she felt worse.

Then, the first week of September, Johnny Su kissed Dan in the parking lot of 7-Eleven. Pressing her up against the dull silver paint of his thirdhand Volvo, Johnny smelled like weed and Doritos and a particular kind of shampoo, and Dan wondered if she could learn to like that strange combination, or the strange feeling of his tongue in her mouth. It was her first kiss. It lasted only a few moments, but as they pulled apart and he laughed his bashful, charming laugh, Dan wondered if maybe it wasn't magic that would change things. Maybe it was this.

She had been halfway right.

By the middle of October, Liss was dating Johnny.

Four months after that, Johnny was gone, his car abandoned where Hare Creek Road crossed Escondido in a perfect X. The police called him a runaway or maybe a suicide.

Dan and Liss knew better. Johnny wasn't just missing. He'd been taken into the cold February night by something the girls didn't understand. But magic gone wrong wasn't the kind of thing you explained to the police, or to anyone else.

Not when you didn't know what kind of creature had stolen him away, where they had gone, or whether Johnny was alive or dead.

Not when you'd just stood there and let it happen.

And especially not when everything, in the first place, was your fault.

ONE

Dan

The singer howled into the mic, and a strange body slammed into Dan's shoulder. She careened into a set of unfamiliar hips, shoved herself off a sweaty back, until someone else crashed into her. Their bodies churned against one another, and Dan let them carry her.

Arms up.

Watch out for your face, nose especially.

Fists up at the chorus. And always, always singing, until your throat was dry and vocal cords wrecked, but it didn't matter, because you couldn't hear yourself anyway, not over the music, the music, the music.

The guitars groaned out into silence as the singer shouted his thanks to the crowd. The lights came up and Dan found herself undeniably at the Fort Gratton Teen Oasis, which was not cool at all. The sweaty, bruised kids made the wall-size mural of a tropical island look even more pathetic than it usually did.

Dan pushed her hand through the snarls of her wet hair, tied it up into a bun, and pulled her sticky T-shirt away from her skin. Her heart was beating all over her body, keeping time to the now-vanished song as her breathing came back to steady. This was only some band from an hour inland. Dan didn't even really like them. It didn't matter: at the end of each show a part of her that felt alive and vibrant with the pulse of the music and the sheer *here-ness* of throwing herself against others darkened.

She shrugged herself together, stretched her shoulders, and turned toward the emergency exit at the back. She navigated through the couples holding hands and past the tiki-themed hut selling water and juice (no soda; parents had protested), and made her way to the pool of red light under the exit sign.

Her mouth pulled into a smile at the short girl in cat-eye liner and round glasses.

"Have fun up there?" Alexa held out Dan's sweatshirt to her. "You look like a total wreck, so I'm guessing yes."

Dan yanked on the sweatshirt. When she looked up, Alexa was grinning at her. "What? Did you meet a cute girl or something?"

"You know I never *actually* meet cute girls, right?" Alexa laughed.

They walked out to Alexa's car. The fog was lying heavy, casting a halo around the single orange light in the parking lot. Alexa pulled her oversized cardigan closer around herself.

"Did you have a good time?" Dan asked. "I mean, their songs are kind of dumb, but it was fun, right?"

"Yeah, I've never been to a show like this before," Alexa answered. "You got *so* into it."

Dan pulled her sleeves over her hands against the chill in the air and shoved them into her pockets, then glanced at Alexa, unsure. This was Alexa, Dan reminded herself. There wasn't any malice in it. "I just like it, you know? It's like it helps you forget, for a while."

"Forget what?"

Dan shrugged. "Everything. Yourself."

Alexa cocked an eyebrow at her but nodded as she unlocked the car. She leaned across to let Dan into the passenger side, then dug around in her bag for Dan's phone. "By the way, your phone's been ringing. The same number's called like six times."

Dan slid into the car and grabbed her phone. She glanced at the screen, then shoved it into her pocket. "Whatever."

"Whatever," Alexa agreed sternly.

The engine shuddered to life. Dan flipped through the CDs she'd burned for Alexa when she found out her battered Toyota had no digital input. Dan slipped a CD into the player and the car filled with music.

"God bless The Cure," Dan said as Alexa steered the car onto Highway 1, back toward Dogtown.

The coast road unwound before them, just a few feet at a time of white and yellow lines caught in Alexa's feeble headlights. There were places where the road ran inland, the sharp turns smoothing and solid ground on both sides, but for most of the way from Fort Gratton back to Dogtown, the asphalt clung to the cliffside in near-switchback turns so sharp the headlights illuminated barely anything of the road. To the right, there was nothing but the flimsy guardrail, crumbling sienna and ochre rock, and a long, steep drop into the ocean. Tonight the fog was thick enough that Alexa flipped the wipers on every few minutes to clear the mist.

"I hate these roads at night," Alexa said. "Especially going south."

"Want me to drive?" Dan's feet were perched on the dash, her head resting against the window.

"Lorelei says I have to get used to it. When we moved out here, she gave this little speech. *The most important thing about living in a small town is being able to get away.* I think she got me the car because she felt bad. No more buses for you, she said."

Dan snorted. "There *are* no buses out here."

They crested a hill and Dan looked out at the Pacific, or what would have been the Pacific if there had been any light to see by. It was beautiful during the day, but at night, she'd never liked the ocean. So much darkness, the water the same black as the sky. Some nights it was like a curtain had been drawn closed around them, separating the tiny, scattered towns of North Coast from the rest of the world.

Then the road veered inland, away from the cliff, and they hit a pocket of cell coverage. Dan's phone lit the car up white.

Call me Dan seriously please

She shoved it back into the pocket of her hoodie.

"That's the same number?" Alexa asked. "What do they want?"

"Your guess is as good as mine." Dan pulled her knees in to her chest, catching the heels of her sneakers on the seat. It wasn't comfortable, but it stopped her from checking her phone every few minutes.

She wasn't going to answer. Even if you were asked nicely, you didn't have to do everything you were told.

The Dogtown exit wasn't marked—just a hard turn off the highway onto a narrow road. A year ago, some magazine anointed Dogtown the quintessential California coast town: a little grocery with the Free Box on the porch where Dogtowners left stuff they didn't need for whoever wanted it, a few artists' studios, an old nondenominational church (now decorated with a peace sign for the Winter Solstice). But Dogtowners weren't interested in entertaining tourists. Signs marking the exit turned up in the Free Box. Now, you either knew the turn or you kept driving south to the fancy waterfront mansions of Marlena Beach, which was what you probably wanted anyway if you needed a sign.

Alexa made a left at the old church onto a one-lane road, unlit under a dense canopy of trees. At the end of it, she turned onto Dan's gravel driveway.

"Whose car is that?" Alexa asked at the exact moment that Dan said, "Motherfuck."

A red Range Rover was parked at the end of the long driveway. In the driver's seat, a girl with long blond hair was frantically tapping something into her phone. The screen cast her face in a blue glow.

Dan squeezed her eyes closed and took a deep breath. For the first time in months, Dan wished she still had anything to do with magic: she'd make the Range Rover vanish.

"Who is that?" Alexa asked again. Dan heard the door of the Range Rover open and shut, footsteps crunching against the gravel. "Is that—"

"You should go home, Alexa. I'll see you at school tomorrow."

Before Alexa could protest, Dan was out of the car and slamming the door behind her.

"What is *wrong* with you?" the blond girl hissed. "Don't you ever check your phone or are you the one young person on earth who's above that?"

"Hello to you too, Liss."

"I've been texting you all night—I called a million times and you know I *hate* calling."

"I deleted your number," Dan said as coldly as she could, which wasn't very cold at all, because she couldn't stop herself from softening the truth with a lie. "My phone kind of broke and I lost a bunch of numbers. It doesn't matter—what do you want?"

Liss folded her arms. One hand still clutched her phone, but with the other, she was touching the pad of each finger to her thumb, as if she were counting up to four and back again. Liss did this when she was nervous, Dan knew, which was basically all the time. "I need to talk to you. *Alone,*" she added, jutting her jaw toward the little white Toyota.

Alexa was standing against her door, one arm thrown up on the roof. She was glaring at Liss with such derision that her lip practically curled. "So you're Liss? Nice outfit."

It wasn't necessary, Dan knew, and that made it mean, which made her love Alexa fiercely.

"Kudos, you've correctly identified that I'm wearing a school uniform. Where did you find someone with such amazing powers of observation, Dan?"

Dan soured. Being around Liss gave her a dizzy, nauseous feeling—the collision of how much she'd loved her before with how much she hated her now. For so long they had been almost a single unit that even now, Dan found it hard to resist Liss's pull. Liss could ask anything of Dan—and she had—but it was another thing entirely to go after Alexa.

Dan took a long look at Liss. She'd never seen her in her new uniform. Dan hadn't seen her at all, in fact, since she'd started school at St. Ignatius. There was something fractured about her, a vision of the old, perfect Liss with spider cracks running through. Her hair was frizzing in the fog, and even in the dim light, Dan could see the dark circles under her eyes. Her kneecaps and cheekbones seemed sharper, as if she'd lost weight—at least her mother would be happy about that.

Strangest of all was the dirt. The white uniform shirt was smeared with it, her hands and knees were grubby, and her tennis shoes were crusted with mud. That wasn't like Liss at all—she hated being dirty—and it raised a lump in Dan's throat. She forced herself to say, "I don't want to talk to you."

Liss's fingers counted to four and back, but she didn't move.

She'd never taken well to people saying no to her.

"Go home, Liss, I'm serious."

"Don't be stupid, Dan. I'm telling you we need to talk."

"Do people usually do what you want after you insult them?" Alexa snarled.

Liss's mouth was half open, but Dan spoke first. "Just say whatever you came here to say."

Liss shook her head. "Not in front of her."

Dan bristled. "*Her* name is Alexa. And I guess you'll be leaving, because this is the only way we're having this conversation."

Dan met Liss's eyes. She could tell Liss was burning, and she willed herself to take some pleasure in it.

"You're going to regret that decision," Liss said through her teeth, then closed the space separating them in a few steps. The air between them seemed to turn staticky, crackling with energy, although Dan didn't know if it was magic or just mutual animosity. She reminded herself that Alexa was behind her, ready to defend her if she needed to, and she schooled her features to a look of indifference.

Then Liss took a breath and said, "I talked to Johnny."

Liss

Liss didn't expect to feel as gratified as she did to see Dan speechless, but she also hadn't expected her to put up such a fight. And she hadn't expected to get this other girl—Alexa—involved. Dan's new best friend was still leaning against her dingy little car like an emo James Dean in a thrift-store sweater. It was funny that Alexa thought she could protect Dan from Liss.

As if Liss was the danger Dan needed protection from.

"That's impossible," Dan finally said in a small voice. "Johnny's gone."

"Who's Johnny?" Alexa asked.

"A guy we used to know," Dan answered.

Liss held out a flat hand. "He's my boyfriend."

Dan darkened. "Don't be pathetic. You don't get to call him your boyfriend after all this."

"You can't *still* be jealous."

"I was never jealous of you, and you aren't dating Johnny. Johnny is—he's gone."

There was something frantic in Dan's dark brown eyes. Liss wondered if she thought Johnny was dead, if she thought he died right away or if it was drawn out, long and slow. She wondered if Dan thought Johnny might make it back without her help—*their* help.

She wondered if Dan still thought about Johnny at all.

"Let me get this straight," Alexa cut in. "Johnny is some guy you used to know—past tense—and your present-tense boyfriend, and no one knows where he is?"

Dan bit her lip, her shoulders curled in. It was no surprise that Dan didn't talk about Johnny to Alexa, but everyone had heard what happened to him. Had this girl been living under a rock?

"Johnny Su," Dan said carefully. "He went missing at the end of February. Before you moved here," she added for Liss's benefit. "No one's heard from him since."

"I have," Liss said emphatically. "Understand what I mean? I can tell you what he said, but we should be having this conversation in private, don't you think?" Liss glared at Dan, trying to convey the significance Dan was obviously missing. Dan should have at least been happy that Johnny was alive, even if she couldn't muster any enthusiasm over reuniting with her old best friend. Instead Dan looked like she wanted to hide under her bed.

"She said she didn't," Alexa snapped.

Liss ignored that. "Dan, you promised."

Dan's eyes went glossy and wet, like she was getting ready to cry, which would be a very Dan thing to do. She opened her mouth, then closed it again, then opened it again and finally said, "You talked to him? How?"

Just like that, Liss had burned through her patience. "*That's* what you want to know? *How?*" Liss exploded. "I called him on the fucking phone, Dan. Why didn't I think of that sooner? He's at some guy named Kasyan's house and he needs a ride home. But don't worry, I can manage it myself."

Dan recoiled as though she'd been slapped, but Liss didn't wait for her to pull herself together. Her blood was on fire as she stalked back to her car. How dare Dan be so ungrateful for everything Liss had done to make this right for both of them? Liss let the force of her anger and exhaustion crush the mislaid faith she'd put in Dan's help. She would not let herself be disappointed. True, her fingers practically curled for the Black Book, but she'd been getting by without it, hadn't she? Liss gritted her teeth and reached for the Range Rover's door.

"Kasyan? Like Lord Kasyan?"

Liss and Dan both trained their eyes on Alexa.

Liss kicked herself. The last thing she needed was this aspiring art school dropout on her case. She chose her words delicately. "That's what I said. Kasyan. What do you know about it?"

"Nothing. My aunt Lorelei told me a few scary stories about him when I was a kid. You know, the Lord of Last Resort." Liss narrowed her eyes at Alexa—her choppy bob, the bitchy slant to her mouth. Alexa held her gaze. "They're fairy tales."

"Thanks for that incredible insight." Liss yanked open the door to the Range Rover. "Dan, if your phone gets fixed, undelete my number and let me know if you want to help."

As Liss pulled out of Dan's drive, she looked back. Dan was standing in the feeble yellow glow of the porch light. Even from this distance, Liss could see her huddled posture, as if she were steeling herself against some pain that hadn't yet come.

Liss set her mouth in a firm line. Dan would text her if she knew what was good for her—which she almost never did without Liss telling her.

"See you soon, bestie," she whispered as she left Dogtown behind her.

Liss took Highway 1's switchbacks on the drive from Dogtown down to Marlena Beach with the same mechanical precision with which she punched in the security code at her house's gate and guided the red Range Rover into its parking place beside the two white BMWs (one sedan, one SUV).

Liss did not get out of the car.

She checked her phone for texts she might have missed in the spotty coverage between Dogtown and Marlena, but there was nothing from Dan. So she spent a few minutes checking her social accounts, not even concentrating enough to register what was going on in the little videos she was liking, then checked her texts again, as if the little videos had been a ritual that would make new texts appear.

No new texts appeared, specifically no new texts from Dan, which was mainly annoying because it was only a matter of time until Dan texted her, because Dan was Dan and she was Liss and it was the natural order of things that Dan would text her back.

Especially about this. Dan had promised.

Liss went to rub her eyes, then remembered how filthy her hands were and stopped herself.

She was so, so tired.

She tipped her head back against the headrest and closed her eyes. Liss took a heavy breath and let it out, using her diaphragm the way a therapist had taught her once as a holistic anxiety management technique. But focusing on her breathing made all the other stuff that wasn't her breathing—all the stuff that focusing on her breathing was meant to quiet—even louder and hotter and brighter. They were the fires that caught in the dark, burning your retinas so you saw them even in the blackness.

That afternoon, the sun had already been low as she half slid down the bank of a creek in Digger's Gulch State Park, which meant her spell had been done nearly in the dark. She had laid her mirror on the leaves at the bottom of the crevasse and carefully pooled water like mercury on the mirror's surface. Then she dug her hands into the mud on either side, locked eyes with her own harried reflection, and whispered the words of the spell. She fought against the chill in the December air, the worsening ache in her back, the ever-more-intrusive voice in her head calling this a lost cause.

Then the water began to change. Something milky white bled into it. Similar things had happened before—oily shimmers or puke orange; once ice crystals had formed. Soon Liss's reflection was obscured, and all at once she knew this time was different. The energy of a correctly executed spell had an inexpressible feeling of alignment that melded profound perfection with absolute relief. If Liss hadn't forced herself to focus on the words of the spell, she would have stopped breathing entirely.

When she felt the connection, it was like a phone that had been answered before anyone spoke. Liss had expected Johnny's face to appear in the fluid on the mirror, but it wasn't that at all. He was in her mind, his face so gaunt and gray she barely recognized him.

Liss? Oh my god, Liss, get me out of here.

Liss didn't know if he was speaking aloud or just thinking to her, but his words sounded reedy and thin.

Out of where? she'd pleaded. *Where did she take you? Who was she?*

Her name is Mora. We're underground, I think, I don't know where. But she's not the one keeping me here. He had been trembling then, his heart racing, mouth dry—she had felt his fear in her own body.

Who?

Kasyan—he's a demon or something. He's trapped here too. It's some kind of prison. Help me, Liss. It's a fucking nightmare down here. The words stumbled out of him like they'd had nowhere to go all these months. *I don't want to die here . . .*

The spell had fractured then, before she'd been able to promise him she was coming, and she'd been left gasping and shaking and alone.

A fucking nightmare.

A fucking nightmare.

A fucking nightmare.

A fucking nightmare.

Liss made herself count to four and back, to four and back, to four and back, tapping out the familiar rhythm that helped her feel still even when she couldn't stop moving, stop working, stop thinking.

Liss opened her eyes. Some of the dirt caked under her nails had loosened and fallen onto her already mud-streaked skirt.

She grabbed her backpack and got out of the car.

Liss was toweling her hair dry, bathrobe cinched around her waist, when her mother opened the door to her room.

"You promised to knock!"

"You think I care about seeing you in a towel?" Her mother tapped a manicured nail against the bulb of her wine glass.

"*I* care."

"Where were you tonight? It's a school night."

"At Dan's again." Although tonight it was true, this was a lie Liss had been telling for months. Thankfully their parents weren't close.

"There are so many good connections at St. Ignatius. Would it kill you to make some new friends?"

"It might."

Her mother seemed to be considering whether Liss's possible death was worth good connections. Liss suspected she'd decided that it was, but she hadn't had enough wine to admit it. She always drank less when Liss's father was home. "That's charming, Elisabeth. Now, I heard from the college consultant today. He had a cancellation, so he's fitting you in for a session to go over the final draft of your essay next Monday."

"Amazing," Liss said. "Now, can I change?"

Liss closed the door behind her mother and listened for the door of her parents' bedroom to close too, and then a few more minutes to be safe, before she opened her laptop and pulled up a password-protected file: "AP Chem Notes Winter Final."

It was not notes for her upcoming chemistry final.

She scrolled to the bottom of the document and entered the date, December 8. Johnny had been gone nearly ten months. She typed out the word *success*, then modified it (*success?*), then deleted it altogether and wrote instead *made contact* and entered the necessary details: coordinates of the creek bed where the spell finally worked, atmospheric conditions, time, the birds she'd observed.

Liss had long since memorized the spell, but still she scrolled back to the top of the document to her first entry from early August, where it was transcribed. Not for the first time, Liss congratulated herself for having the foresight to take meticulous notes on any-thing the Black Book gave them. Obviously, she hadn't predicted that Dan would hold the Book hostage, but the Book was unreli-able. It was almost impossible to find the same page twice, so when it gave you something good, you copied it down.

Liss had meant to review the spell's steps, but instead her gaze snagged on the text at the top of the page: *The Araxes Process for.* A knot tightened deep in her stomach. She'd deleted the second half of the spell's name months ago. Every time she'd seen it, it had taunted her—reminding her of all the things she'd done that couldn't be reversed, things that would probably disqualify her from using the spell altogether.

But today it had worked. At the top of the page, Liss typed in the missing words: *The Araxes Process for Speaking to Lost Love.*

Just below was her first entry.

How much love is enough?

Now she knew the answer, at least in part. The spell had worked, and it had worked on her and Johnny. That meant irrefutably—verified by magic—that they loved each other and their love was, on a technical level, enough. Which, of course it was, Liss told her-self. She'd been stupid to doubt that.

Liss realized she was frowning at the computer so intensely her chin was getting sore. She forced herself to smile, although there was no one there to see her. After all, she was supposed to be happy now, or slightly closer to happiness than yesterday.

Liss moved on through her notes of the last four months. The Black Book had given her and Dan this particular spell over a year be-fore Liss first tried to use it on her own—back before she even knew who Johnny was. That summer, the singer of Dan's favorite band, IronWeaks, had gone missing. Dan insisted they ask the Black Book for help; she wanted to talk to him and ask him to come home. That seemed a little invasive to Liss, but Rickey IronWeaks constituted at least 50 percent of the contents of Dan's brain and around 90 percent of her heart. Then the news broke that Rickey had died by suicide, and they abandoned the spell before they'd made much progress.

This spell had been terrible to figure out. The right location for it depended on auspices. Liss had done enough auspicious spells to know the basics: the spell gave you a set of auspicious conditions and you found them. You might need wind speed, the level of the tides, the phase of the moon. Most of that information was online, or at worst, at the library. But this particular spell relied on the auspices of birds. Liss had never taken those before but knew they had to be observed directly—and she had to do it with no help from anyone. She'd looked for those stupid birds all over North Coast. For months, her evenings were spent hiking into redwood forests on barely marked trails or scrambling down cliffs during low tide, clunky binoculars hanging from her neck. All the while, her brain ground against the thought that she had set herself to an impossible, futile task.

She stopped on an entry from a few weeks ago.

I have to believe I am getting closer. But North Coast is huge, California is bigger, and after that, the world. How long can I keep looking for him alone?

Liss slammed her laptop shut and spun her chair away from the desk. It was the second question that had been answered today. She had a spell for speaking to a lost love, but not a spell for finding him, or rescuing him from an underground prison, or defeating whatever Kasyan and Mora were. She couldn't carry on alone. She needed the Black Book. She needed Dan.

She could still hear Johnny's voice saying her name, with such terrible relief and desperation, it had almost sounded like *please.*

Liss would not give up now. Johnny was out there, waiting for her, and she was going to save him. Dan would text her tomorrow, Liss was sure of it, and if she didn't, Liss knew every one of Dan's weak spots. What good was that knowledge if you didn't put it to use?

Dan

Up in her room, Dan slammed the door and collapsed onto her bed.

It was as if she was being crushed very slowly by some very great weight. That was the Liss effect: she operated with a gravity that dominated everything in her world. You didn't move unless she let you.

Dan took a shallow breath.

She wasn't in Liss's world now, Dan reminded herself. She hadn't seen Liss in months. They'd barely talked over the summer, and starting in September, Liss had been commuting inland to St. Ignatius with the other rich kids from Marlena. Liss's parents claimed she transferred to spend her senior year at a school with a stronger college admissions record, but that wasn't the whole story. Everyone at North Coast High was sure that Liss had something to do with what happened to Johnny and that whatever happened to Johnny had something to do with her. Liss's parents had barely tolerated Johnny; they would not permit his disappearance to damage their daughter's reputation.

In all those months of silence, Dan thought about Liss more than she wanted to admit. Mostly, she'd imagined Liss trying to apologize. She had played out ten thousand conversations where she told Liss in the cleverest possible way exactly how she'd been hurt. Imaginary-Liss would defend herself, but Dan would be strong against her—also witty, coming up with perfect little retorts, until

Imaginary-Liss was begging for her friendship back. She couldn't have it. The friendship had been ruined beyond repair, and it was Liss who did the ruining.

Tonight had not gone like that at all. Dan had forgotten all her sharp comebacks and practically broken into tears, remembering what they did to Johnny. Liss had done nothing but roll her eyes, like usual.

Liss said she wanted Dan's help to find Johnny, but Dan knew better.

What Liss really wanted was the Black Book.

They had always kept it at Dan's house, because her mom didn't snoop like Liss's did, but Liss definitely hadn't meant to leave it with Dan permanently. Without the Book, Liss had no hope of doing real magic. No more real magic meant that instead of being a witch, Liss was just someone who *used to be* a witch. Dan was perfectly happy with that, but Liss absolutely could not bear being un-special. Magic made her special. Her disappeared-but-almost-certainly-dead boyfriend made her special. It was actually sort of pathetic how Liss clung to those two things, desperately enough to lie about talking to Johnny, when it was basically impossible that she could have done that spell on her own.

Dan would have thought Liss made up Kasyan, if Alexa hadn't been around to say he'd come up in Lorelei's stories.

Lord Kasyan.

Goose bumps prickled down Dan's arms. He certainly sounded like something out of a story, even if Dan had never heard of him. That wasn't surprising: Dan was raised on stories about schools of fish celebrating diversity or happy foxes taking care of the environment. The creepiest things her parents told her related to the vibrancy of her aura and the overwhelming probability of extraterrestrial life, nothing about any kind of Lord of Last Resort.

But the Black Book had taught them fairy tales were often based on nuggets of truth. If Kasyan was real, that could mean Johnny— no, Dan stopped herself. It meant nothing about Johnny, definitely not that he was alive.

Still, to be sure, Dan typed *kasyan fairy tale* into the browser on her phone. The results page flashed a list of links, then went white and froze. Dan reloaded the page, but it crashed again, then again. Dan chewed her lip. That didn't mean anything. The internet was always going down, although it wasn't actually down at that moment, since all her other apps were working and the search results for just *fairy tale*, no *kasyan*, loaded just fine.

She eyed her closet, which was vomiting a pile of clothes out onto the carpet.

In all the months she'd had the Book in her possession, she'd never been tempted. Liss always thought that if they learned the right rules and recipes, magic would be predictable, controllable. Dan knew she was wrong. Magic wasn't science. It wasn't bound by laws and regularities that could be memorized. It ran on its own unknowable and treacherous pathways, and Dan had already come close enough to getting lost. She didn't want anything badly enough to risk that again.

But the idea tugged at her: Surely, the Book would know about Kasyan. She would only need to ask it the right way.

Dan rolled off her bed and kicked aside the mound of stuff on the closet floor until she could reach a plastic bin wedged into the corner on the highest shelf. It was full of keepsakes—birthday cards and yearbooks and participation ribbons from the Marlena Beach Fourth of July Games. Underneath it all was an unremarkable shoe- box that Dan eased free and carried back to her bed. Scrawled on the lid in thick marker was DAN + LISS TOP SECRET. Dan frowned. She'd written that a lifetime ago, right when they'd found the Book in the Dogtown Free Box and magic felt like an inside joke between them, before they'd even done that first spell that would change them forever.

Dan had promised herself she wouldn't try to use the Book without Liss. It hadn't been hard, after what happened the night Johnny was taken. But now, running her fingers along the edge of the lid, she could taste the metallic tang of witchcraft within. It carried the Black Book's distinctive scent, so stilling and satisfying. It was nothing she could describe—the space between leaving home and returning, between losing yourself and being found safe.

But suddenly Dan was back at the crossroads, an eerie, fierce wind riffling the pages of the Book as it lay on the pavement, and that creature looking at the three of them like she couldn't wait to gnaw on their bones, the moment her black gaze narrowed on Johnny, the way terror can burst like a nuclear bomb in your chest—

No, Dan told herself again. If she let herself go back there, she might not survive it. She forced out the breath she was holding and shoved the box, unopened, under her bed. Her hands were shaking as she stripped off her sweaty T-shirt and turned the light off. Under the covers, she settled her headphones over her ears and pressed play.

It was a ballad by her all-time favorite band forever, IronWeaks. This song almost never failed to make her cry, and tonight, tears felt appropriate. Dan turned the volume up to drown out the tinny ringing in her ears from the concert.

Most of the song was given over to Rickey's dirty velvet voice repeating, "Let me go, don't you know, I'm never coming back?" In the days last year when she and all the other IronWeaks fans had just thought Rickey was missing, she listened to the song hundreds of times. She'd hoped so hard for him to come home that it felt like magic—an energy her body could barely contain.

It had made no difference. Rickey was never missing. He had

been dead the whole time. A few weeks after the band announced Rickey's suicide, they broke up. "Without Rickey, the poetry's gone out of the music," they said.

That was how Dan felt about magic after Johnny was taken. She didn't have proof he was dead, but any hope that he wasn't blew out so fast, it was like it had never existed. Dan felt horrible to think it, but things were better that way. If Johnny were alive it would mean that he'd spent all this time—nearly ten months—suffering, waiting, trapped, and Dan couldn't live with herself if she'd done that to him.

She could barely live with herself as it was.

The song ended. Dan wormed her hand out of the covers and set it to repeat. "Let me go . . ." Rickey whispered. His face looked down at Dan from a poster taped above the bed. Even in the dark she could see his eyes rimmed in black, full lips, skin hugging tight to his collarbones and the curve of his jaw. Dan's heart stuttered to think of a world without him.

Dan had moved on from all of it—slowly, but she had. Of course, Liss hadn't. Liss never put anything behind her or let anything go. She was precisely the kind of person who would wait in your driveway for hours, to remind you of the exact thing you were fighting to forget. The sooner Liss accepted that they couldn't reverse what they'd done, the better it would be for both of them. And if Liss didn't want to do that, well, she would have to respect that she wasn't going to drag Dan back into the past with her.

If Liss wanted to talk, they could talk. That didn't mean it had to be the conversation Liss was expecting.

Dan reached for her phone.

TWO

Dan

Johnny was gone.

One minute there had been three of them at the crossroads, then there were four. Johnny's eyes had gone black and unseeing, his ears deaf to their screams, and he was taken into the night.

Now they were only two, Dan and Liss.

Something had gone sideways about the world, which was what happened when you saw an impossible—*totally impossible*—thing.

Dan's breath came in short bursts as she looked behind her, then behind her again, because Johnny had to be somewhere, he could not just be *gone*. Dan rubbed her eyes and looked behind her again, and she knew she was spinning around like a total idiot.

"Shit, I broke the line," she said, falling to her knees on the asphalt where they'd drawn a circle of salt. It was hopelessly scattered and bore the imprint of the sole of her Converse. In the middle of it, the Black Book lay splayed open, its pages fluttering in the wind, and Dan was hit with a wave of nausea.

"Forget the line," Liss snapped. "It didn't work anyway and it can't help us now."

"Are we going after him? We should find where that—that *thing* is taking him, right?"

The crossroads was just over the border of a state park. The coal-black silhouettes of trees hemmed them in at all sides, clusters of redwoods stretching dagger-like into the moonless sky. Every direction looked the same. The idea of going into the woods to look for Johnny made Dan's eyes literally go wide with fear, which was something she'd always thought was made up for movies, which made her think of fight-or-flight responses, and she absolutely could not remember what you were supposed to do in each of those responses, because what she was actually doing was kneeling in the middle of a road, shaking and trying not to vomit, which was not a plan at all and definitely not going to *fix this horrible thing she'd done*—

"No." Liss grabbed Dan's arm. "We're getting the hell out of here. Right now." Dan gaped at her: Liss's fingers digging into Dan's flesh as she heaved her off the ground; the firm, even tenor of her voice; her cold rationality in the face of a world that had just revealed itself to be far stranger and more dangerous than either of them had ever imagined. "Get your car. We're going to my house."

Liss released Dan's arm and began gathering the remains of the failed spell.

"I should never have—"

"Later, Dan! Car. *Now.*"

Liss knew what she was doing, she always did, and although Dan sometimes hated her for it, now relief washed over her. They didn't have to go into the woods. They didn't have to pursue the strange old woman, or cast the spell again and hope she'd return to let Johnny go. Dan didn't have to think about what she had done, or why Johnny had been chosen, not one of them.

Dan put her fate in Liss's hands.

Dan grabbed the Black Book off the pavement and found her keys, while Liss tossed any evidence of the spell into Dan's trunk. Dan got into the driver's seat. In the quiet of the car, Dan could hear the blood rushing in her ears. She was clutching the Book in both hands and all of a sudden it felt *wrong*. What *was* this thing they had been following—an enchantment, a distraction, a murder weapon?

Liss slammed the trunk closed.

Dan hurled the Book into the back seat and started the car.

Dan took the curves toward Liss's house as fast as she was able, but the drive was still over a half hour. "My parents are at a party in Gratton. They'll be back around ten," Liss had said. "We have to get there first."

But when they crested the hill that led down into Marlena, it was ten minutes till, and both their hearts were hammering with adrenaline. Dan turned onto Kingfisher Drive toward the beach, then into Liss's drive and punched the key code into the gate. As the wooden gate swung inward, neither one of them breathed, waiting to see how many white BMWs were parked out front.

No one was home.

Liss sent Dan up the enormous curving stairs to her bedroom. Liss came up a few moments later with a bag of banana chips and two seltzers.

"You seriously want a snack right now?"

Liss dropped the bag of chips on the white carpet, then sunk down beside it and leaned against the bed. "Of course not. I'm one wrong move away from puking." Liss yanked a textbook out of her backpack and flung it onto the bed toward Dan.

"Liss, what are we doing?"

Liss looked up at her with cold eyes. "We need an alibi. When my parents get home, we'll say we've been here all night studying. I got some dishes dirty and left them in the sink so it'll look like we had dinner here too. We hung out with Johnny after school for a while, then we got here around seven and we've been studying ever since, which they will see when they get home. Johnny said he was going on a drive. Sometimes he liked to drive around and get high, and I always gave him a hard time for that, because it's dangerous. At around nine thirty, I texted him to check in and got no answer. Got it?"

"Liss," was all Dan managed to say, but that one word carried all of Dan's concerns: Wasn't this callous, wasn't this wrong?

"This is the plan. If you can't do it, tell me right now," Liss answered, and suddenly, Dan was afraid of her. She wasn't sure if this driven, calculating Liss was all that different from the Liss she was best friends with, who helped her mourn Rickey and IronWeaks, who she confided in after Johnny kissed her. The Liss in front of her was dangerous. This Liss, Dan could tell, would accept nothing short of compliance with her plan.

Dan pulled the textbook toward herself. "I can do it," Dan said.

With that, something about Liss softened. She was allowing herself to be scared, just a little. There was a needful, uncertain note in her voice when she said, "We're going to survive this, right?"

Dan said something she didn't feel but that she wanted badly to be true. "Everything will be okay. We'll be okay. I promise."

It was a promise she didn't know how to keep.

Johnny's mother filed a missing person report as soon as she could, but the cops didn't address the case with any particular urgency, so it was a few days before a police car pulled up at the entrance to North Coast High. Dan alerted Liss that she'd seen the cops on campus, and Liss pulled her into the Range Rover at lunch. They rehearsed their story again, until Liss realized they might sound too practiced once they were questioned and ended the session.

"We just have to get through this," Liss told her as she tapped her fingers against her thumb. Up to four and back. "Then we'll try to find him. But we can't do anything when the cops are around. You understand that, right, Dan?"

She did. If Liss wanted to wait, she would wait. Maybe if they waited, it would not be so raw, so painful. The gnawing, black feeling inside her didn't seem to be weakening with the passing days. Actually, the opposite was happening. It would wash over her like a wave of ice, bringing with it horrible little memories she didn't want to know were hers.

Like now, sitting next to Liss, who was watching a cop car across the parking lot and doing that nervous thing with her fingers, Dan remembered this:

The way Johnny's hands seized up into rigid claws the moment that the strange woman they had summoned chose him and how Dan had watched those same hands slip into Liss's only a few minutes earlier, their fingers laced and palms pressed together.

She remembered the absolute, void-like blackness of the woman's eyes; her too-long, thin fingers and their thick yellow nails; how the night air swirling around her suddenly carried the scent of decay.

Tears stung Dan's eyes. She'd cried so much in the last forty-eight hours she thought the swelling around her eyes might never go down.

"Jesus, I wish I could cry as easily as you," Liss said as Dan yanked down her sleeve to wipe her eyes.

And so Dan sat beside Liss, trying to hold back her tears as Liss tried to muster her own. "My boyfriend disappeared," Liss whispered to herself. "My boyfriend disappeared," over and over until her eyes were watery and she was sniffling. Then they got out of the car, which Liss locked three times in a row, took a few steps, then locked it three more times, like she always did, and went to the cafeteria so Liss could cry in front of an audience.

———

They found his car the next day: a beat-up silver Volvo pulled off the road into the grass beyond the shoulder, at an intersection near Hare Creek State Park. There was talk of a candlelight vigil at the school, or at the North Coast Community Center, but it never came to pass. Liss told the police her story of Johnny's plan to get high and go for a drive, and Dan told hers about doing homework at Liss's. Johnny's friends were cagey around the cops but agreed that that sounded like Johnny. They didn't know if he was unhappy, if anything was troubling him, if he ever talked about hurting himself. He hadn't been hanging around with them much since he started dating Liss. They didn't know what he had been up to.

The police labeled Johnny a "voluntary missing adult," given that he was already eighteen, and marked his case low priority. By that time, an understanding of Johnny Su's fate had emerged in Fort Gratton, in Dogtown, down in the mansions of Marlena. People went missing in the North Coast. Drifters floated in and out off Highway 1. Weed farmers operated in thousands of unmonitored acres of redwood forest. Local kids hitchhiked down to San Francisco or up to Portland, then called home when their money ran out, and middle-age parents moved into Buddhist retreats for weeks-long vows of silence. North Coasters lived off the land, wired solar panels to their camper vans, and microdosed hallucinogenic mushrooms in one of the thousands of pockets along the coast where cell coverage didn't reach but the gray mist of fog did. Usually, they turned up again, though sometimes it was just their bodies, or worse, bones picked clean by the animals that called North Coast their home.

Everyone knew Johnny was gone, at least for now. If he was coming back, it wasn't because anyone could find him.

THREE

Dan

The day after the show, Alexa and Dan set up at their regular lunch spot at the back corner of the cafeteria, far from the soda machines (decommissioned by concerned parents) and the girls who giggled and shrieked at the boys throwing fries at one another. Dan examined her Tupperware without enthusiasm.

"Yesterday's quinoa with yucca," she told Alexa as she doused a whitish chunk with hot sauce. "I thought it was impossible for Mexican people to make food this bland, but my mom's under the impression that yucca's an undiscovered superfood. And also under the impression that superfoods are a thing."

Alexa took a bite of her PB&J sandwich, which was a little smushed after spending the morning in her bag. "How are you doing, after last night? I thought you would text me."

"I'm fine," Dan said mechanically. "I was super tired."

"Oh, good." Alexa swallowed a mouthful. "Was worried for a second you might be upset by the whole nemesis-waiting-in-the-driveway-to-talk-about-her-boyfriend thing. But. Happy to hear you're fine."

Dan let herself smile a little. She always said she was fine. It was a habit she couldn't break, even when it was the furthest thing from the truth. She said it even as her eyes stung from holding back tears, and when her face felt like a hard mask, because she had somehow managed to sink to a place below feelings, where nothing reached her but sadness and the urge to sleep. Sometimes she said it with a savage desperation that others mistook for anger—that she had to be fine, because if she admitted to being something else, she would crumble.

The funny thing was, Dan was never exactly sure if it really was a lie. Wasn't she fine? Maybe sad was a bad way to be, but life was like that. It seemed foolish to expect more. After all, wasn't that why everyone heard her say it—*I'm fine*—and whether they believed it or not, they accepted it? Even Liss, who had to have known when Dan felt so low it was like she had burned away to ash, never pushed her to say what was wrong.

I'm fine was an agreement. It meant: I'll never mention this, and you'll never ask.

Or that's what it used to mean, until Alexa.

Alexa never let her be fine. The first time it happened had been mid-September, only a few weeks into their friendship, and Dan had been so miserable and bleak, she'd been stabbing a paperclip into her thigh through her pocket to get through her morning classes without crying. At lunch, Alexa made it clear with an arch of her eyebrow that she didn't buy Dan's deflection. "But seriously?" she'd asked, her hazel eyes searching and her forehead a little tight with concern. "You seem down. What's bothering you?"

It was as if Alexa, with one glance, had seen through the person Dan pretended to be—the person everyone agreed she was. "Yeah, I guess," Dan mumbled. "Kind of down. It's just . . . stuff."

Alexa sighed sympathetically. "Stuff. I've got that too."

And even though it shouldn't have made any difference at all, it was as if Alexa had found some back door to her heart by seeing her and not wanting to look away. It made Dan feel better, just a little. The feeling didn't last, but a few hours of feeling close to okay was enough to get through the day.

Now, Dan prodded a pale yucca-chunk and admitted, "It was weird to see her again. She didn't expect you to be there."

"What, the Lizard thought you'd never make another friend?"

Dan rolled her eyes. "Probably."

"You're not going to text her, are you?" When Dan didn't answer immediately, Alexa's eyes widened. "You are *not*." When Dan didn't answer at all, they went even wider. "You already *did*? Jesus, Dan, not to put words in your mouth, but you literally told me you hate her."

"I don't *hate* her."

"You said you wished you'd never met her and you called her a total garbage monster. All I mean is, you don't have to do whatever she's asking you to. You can just go on living your life."

"It's not that simple."

"Yes, it is." There was a sudden hardness in Alexa's voice. "She doesn't care about you, Dan—she just wants to use you to get what she wants and then she'll get rid of you."

"You don't even know her."

"From what you've said about her, I don't need to. I've known enough bad people to recognize it when someone only cares about themselves, and that's how Liss is. Fixing her damage is none of your business."

That Alexa hated Liss with iron certainty entirely on Dan's behalf gave her an all-over warm feeling that seemed pretty similar to happiness. It made her want to promise Alexa that she'd never talk to Liss again, if that's what Alexa thought was best. It made her want to trust Alexa with every secret.

But not this one.

This, Dan didn't want Alexa to understand. She didn't want Alexa to have to accept that Dan had messed around with magic, until she made a disastrous, unfixable mistake. She didn't want to explain that feeling of transformation on the night that started it all in Liss's bedroom and how it turned into something toxic.

She wanted to go back to being the person she was before all that, the person who Alexa thought she was now: someone who didn't know that there was magic in the world, real magic, and that it wasn't a good thing.

To call it magic didn't even seem right. The magic most people knew was a lie, either magicians and card tricks or the fantasy novels that Alexa loved to read. What she and Liss had tapped into was more than that—not a deception at all, but the opposite, a tide of power that ran through the world totally unseen, a current that they could never understand, that had crashed over them when they had their backs turned and nearly dragged them under.

Magic wasn't friendly. It amazed you with its power to destroy, the same way the salt waves of the Pacific hammered cliffs into rubble, broke boats, annihilated beaches. Magic gave you gifts, but it took from you too, and although it had seemed fantastic and fun when she and Liss first tasted that world, they had learned better.

Or at least Dan had.

"It's not about being friends again. We're just going to talk one last time, for closure, and then we'll be done, forever." Dan stabbed another piece of yucca. "Anyway, I don't think Liss's damage is the kind that can be fixed."

Still, Alexa didn't seem satisfied as she walked Dan to English class.

"Tell Liss to be careful with this Kasyan guy, okay? Those stories Lorelei told me never ended well. They call him Kasyan the Unmerciful for a reason. Only a real weirdo would name himself after the Big Bad Wolf, right?"

Liss

That afternoon, Dan's mom greeted Liss with a long, cozy hug. "You've stayed away too long! I missed your energy," Graciela said. She pulled back and beamed at the girls, apparently failing to see that one of them was sulking and the other, with a bit more pressure, would snap entirely in two. "Beautiful. The power of female energy. It's always such a strong presence in you girls."

"Seriously. Mom." Dan's cheeks flared.

"Do you want some hot chocolate?" Graciela asked as she swept aside a piece of Liss's hair that had come loose. "I just picked up some fresh goat milk."

"Mom!" Dan groaned, but Liss smiled. She loved Dan's mom, but it hadn't occurred to her to miss her until just now. Graciela was always there with a warm hug, a hunk of macrobiotic dark chocolate, or an unsolicited but shame-free talk about safely embracing sexual pleasure. Graciela always seemed shocked by their beauty and their maturity, not in the trivial way men sometimes admired Liss, but in a way that was rich with wonder and made her feel proud, as if she were on the brink of becoming someone amazing.

Dan didn't know how lucky she had it, to have a mom like that—a mom whose qualifications for wonderful you met by simply existing exactly as you were.

Liss would have stayed there, safe in that warm kitchen with Graciela, even if it meant drinking goat milk hot chocolate, but Dan's embarrassment was about to cause her to pass completely out of existence. They went up to Dan's attic room, which was still the same old chaos of half-read books and IronWeaks posters and dirty laundry. Liss shoved aside a pile of Dan's clothes and pulled her legs up under herself in the armchair by the window, the same way she'd always done. Dan climbed onto her bed and slumped against the pillows.

Liss waited for a feeling of stillness and alignment to settle over her, now that she and Dan were both where they belonged again. Dan's cozy room held more than memories of studying the Black Book, its magic pulsing in their fingertips. It was marathons of Brat Pack movies and sleepovers spent watching K-Pop music videos and stalking the social media accounts of all the boys Liss thought were cute. But still Liss felt that frizzing anxiety in her chest, as if every beat of her heart was a whispered *not yet, not yet, not yet.*

She counted to four and back on her fingers and hoped that Dan didn't see her do it.

"So?" Dan asked.

"Graciela won't hear us?"

Dan shook her head. "She'll be in her pottery studio in the back. Tell me about Johnny."

So Liss told her: the spell she'd used, the birds, the weeks and weeks of failure until, finally, she reached Johnny.

"So you saw him."

"That's not really how it works. You don't really *see* anything, it just gets into your head. I know he looks bad, like he hasn't seen the sun since he was taken. He said he was underground somewhere."

"Where?"

Liss rubbed her eyes. "Don't you think I would have led with that information? He didn't know, but he can't get out of there by himself."

"So you're saying he's a prisoner."

"Kasyan's prisoner."

"Do you know why they call him Kasyan the Unmerciful?"

Liss made a mental note to add *the Unmerciful* to her notes. "Not yet. I've only just started the research on him. For some reason I haven't had much luck online." Liss paused and licked her lips. "But tonight we can start with the Black Book."

The Black Book. Like a sudden craving, Liss was aware of it, somewhere, in the room. In just a few moments she'd once again have the Book in front of her, its delicious electricity buzzing in her stomach and its crumbling pages promising to give you exactly what you wanted. This was the real reason Liss had let the Book stay with Dan: she didn't trust herself around it. Her hunger for the Book was huge and inexplicable, like she wanted to devour it and for the book to devour her in return. She saw it in her dreams and woke up panting and desperate, her face screwed up in frustration. Liss knew she sounded like one of those people addicted to eating couch cushions—or she would have, if she had ever told anyone about it.

Dan had been picking at a cuticle with rapt attention, but now she looked up. Liss wondered if Dan could see her trembling.

"I don't know," Dan said.

Liss flinched. "*What* don't you know?"

"The last time we used the Black Book, things didn't exactly go as planned."

"This time will be different."

"You don't know that."

"I know we can't get Johnny kidnapped twice. Therefore, different."

"That's not what I meant. I think we should try to move on and—"

"Don't you think I want to move on?" Liss snapped. "This is what we have to do to make that happen."

"This is what *you think* we have to do."

Dan rolled her eyes, and a sick bubble of desperation burst in Liss's stomach. "Yes, I *think* we have to save Johnny. I *think* we owe it to him to try with everything we've got, Black Book included. But it so happens that what I *think* we have to do is *what we actually have to do.*"

Dan glared at her. "You always have to be the one who decides."

Liss counted to four and back on her fingers. She would not lose Dan—she had been sure that Dan would throw herself at this, especially when Liss had already done so much on her own.

Just then, she felt it like an open wound: she wanted her old life back. She'd lost the only person who knew the truth about Johnny, who had seen the oily eyes and long, loose neck of the old woman who took him. Dan had been there in the moment they let magic tornado into their lives. She had to be there to find Kasyan too.

But worse, Liss missed the time before Johnny had changed everything between them, when she and Dan would read each other's tarot cards, trying to forecast their futures and fantasizing about the sprawling, bold lives they would live. They used to laugh at the idea of promising to be friends forever, because what ran between them was deeper than a promise—it was something that couldn't be broken.

She missed Dan.

Liss forced herself to bring her tone back to something less acid. "You promised."

"Yeah, well." Dan broke her gaze. "I made that promise because I trusted you."

"You don't trust me anymore?" Liss sniffed.

Dan made an incredulous, open-handed gesture around the room that seemed to capture everything between them, everything that had been said—that all of it was evidence of the answer to Liss's question.

"I can't do this alone. I need your help with the spells. And I need the Book."

"Or, you could just not do any more spells."

Liss knew her voice was rising, but she couldn't control it. "If that's how you feel, give me the Book. It belongs to me too. I can do the spells myself."

Dan would know that wasn't true where the Black Book was concerned: it needed the two of them there to tell them anything at all. "Why can't you just let it go?"

"Let it *go*?" Liss spat. "We can't let it go when Johnny needs us. How can you say that when the spell was your idea in the first place?"

Dan crumpled a little at this, but she pushed back. "It was your fault Johnny was there *in the first place*."

"Seriously? We were *dating*," Liss said.

"I know, Liss! You were *dating*, so he had to go everywhere you went. You were *dating*, so we couldn't do the spell with only the two of us, without him. You were *dating*, so you got to be a part of this great tragedy of the missing boyfriend for months after he disappeared. Did it ever occur to you to leave him alone?"

"You said you weren't interested! You don't kiss a boy once and own him forever."

"I know what I said, but that didn't mean you had to—"

"When are you going to learn to actually tell people what you're thinking? I'm not psychic. I can't just magically guess your true feelings. We had that whole love spell lined up for you and you called it off. I asked if it would bother you if I went after him and you said it was fine. How was I supposed to know you meant the *exact opposite of fine*?"

"Because you were my best friend!" Dan exploded. "You were supposed to understand and you never even tried."

There was a voice screaming in Liss's head, warning her to bite her tongue. If she had to leave without Dan, she couldn't leave without the Book. It was practically crying out for her, her only hope to find Johnny.

Liss couldn't bring herself to listen.

"You don't want to be understood, Dan. You want an excuse to be miserable." Liss stood and marched to the door. Dan wouldn't even look at her, her head in her hands. "We were in love. Did you know that?"

Dan tilted her head, parting her dark hair. Her eyes glinted with tears. "You didn't love him. You slept with him for four months then destroyed him. It's not the same thing."

Speeding away from Dan's house, Liss curled a fist around the steering wheel and cursed Dan—with conventional profanity, not magically—then cursed herself for being stupid enough to have left the Book with her in the first place.

So Dan was still jealous over Johnny, but was she willing to let him *die* just because he wouldn't date her? It wasn't anyone's fault that Dan met Johnny first, and no one could help it that he'd fallen for Liss. Liss had honestly tried to help Dan, but Dan hadn't been hungry for it, not like Liss was.

That was what Dan never understood: Liss needed Johnny, and Dan didn't.

Thinking about Johnny, before they were together and he was just the object of Dan's crush, made Liss feel empty and starved. She'd barely known him then, but she knew he had something that would satisfy that feeling. She tasted it when she first caught him in the hall at school looking at her instead of Dan, when she read the captions of the pictures he posted, when he held the door for her once as she dashed across the parking lot and out of the rain. Out of all these little pieces of Johnny's attention, she was convinced that she could assemble something like happiness. And it would be better than it had been with boys in the past, who'd failed to stop that same hunger, because Dan had seen something in Johnny too. She liked him too, and Dan rarely had crushes.

When you felt that kind of hunger, you couldn't just sit there and do nothing about it.

Liss hadn't.

Had it been worth it?

Johnny did make Liss some kind of happy, with the moony look he got when he told her how pretty she was and how he always asked permission before he kissed her and the way he'd smile that lazy, lucky smile at her when they were pressed skin to skin in the back seat of his car. She knew he loved her; he had to.

Liss clenched her teeth remembering how she always wanted more from him. The hunger never really stopped, sometimes even got worse, as if he was teasing her with satisfaction just out of reach.

When she tried to talk to him about how her parents were fighting or how she worried that she'd never get her SAT scores where they needed to be, Johnny would mumble "Don't be stupid," then pull her in for a kiss or start packing a bowl. Every time he responded to one of her texts with *haha nice*, she felt desperate and miserable. One night she'd had to check that every light in her house was off, that the stove was off, and that her curling iron was unplugged so many times that she was an hour late to meet him and they'd had to catch the next showing of the movie. She could barely focus on the screen, her every muscle tense and the acid of anxiety moving through her guts, and he'd never asked her what was wrong, never noticed that she felt like she'd been twisted into a pathetic knot, tied so tight she could barely breathe. But then they'd parked the car in the empty high school parking lot and taken off their clothes.

The way he looked at her, shamelessly wanting her, made Liss feel very far away from herself, from the Liss who was anxious and real. She could let herself be the Liss that Johnny was looking at, and it made her feel good enough that she unraveled around him. It never lasted as long as she wanted.

She had told Dan that she loved him, and magic had proved it wasn't a lie. Right before Johnny was taken, things had been changing between them for the better. He had been so sweet to her on Valentine's Day, she'd nearly cried for real. He drove her all the way to Santa Rosa, where they had dinner in an Italian restaurant with candles on the tables and walked around the downtown eating ice cream and made out frantically in the middle of a park, high on the idea that they didn't know anyone there, not like in North Coast where anyone passing by could be a friend of your parents or your elementary school teacher. On the way home, she fell asleep in the passenger seat holding his hand.

Then two weeks later he was stolen from her by something that wasn't even human, and Liss was left wondering what they might have been—if their love could have fixed her, or if she would have given him permission to kiss her, then let him go.

FOUR

Dan

One thing about running at night in North Coast was that the road unspooled obsidian and silky before you, more and more of it around each turn, and you could smell the salt the wind carried off the black ocean—you could lick that salt off your upper lip, where it mixed with your sweat.

This was the second thing about running at night in North Coast: it wasn't safe. The roads weren't made for it, all blind turns and soft shoulders that fell off into the sea or cut into the cliffs so there were only a few spare inches where Dan's feet found the tarmac. The streetlights were few and far between, and Dan didn't have a headlamp as some other runners did, so if she ran on the coast side, there were places where she knew she risked slipping in the roadside gravel and over the edge into the nothingness below. She'd leave no trace—no one knew where she was, where she was going, and this struck her as dangerous.

After Liss stormed out, Dan felt wild and small, so after dinner she'd pulled on her running shoes. As usual, her mom didn't ask where she was going and Dan never offered up the information. If her dad had been home, he might have called out "Be safe" from his spot on the couch, and Graciela would have swatted at him with her pottery magazine. Graciela believed that safety was the enemy of experience, that girls were told too often to be safe and boys were told too rarely. "I'd rather you be strong than safe," she always told Dan. But Dan's father wasn't in front of the TV because he was driving back from a job somewhere inland, so Dan left her mother engrossed in a complicated crochet project in the incense-smogged living room.

Dan pushed herself further into the darkness: the wicked beat of IronWeaks blaring in her ears, the wind stinging her eyes, her chest tightening around each breath as it fought to get away.

She'd begun running only a few months earlier. When school started, without Liss, Dan barely spoke to anyone. It wasn't exactly difficult—she'd been spending all her time with Liss for so long that the kids she'd grown up with hardly seemed to remember her. She didn't want them to. She had changed, and explaining how felt impossible and terrible, an effort that could only end in them seeing her for the worthless, destructive thing she'd become. She joined the cross-country team because she'd heard long-distance running was a solitary sport, but then quit when the coach emphasized the team dynamic and suggested running with music wasn't allowed in competition.

So now she ran alone, the cold mist of the fog chilling her skin while her muscles blazed with pain.

That was the point of running: that if you pushed yourself hard enough, it hurt, and if it hurt enough, you could give all your thoughts over to that pain. The same way, alone in her room at night, she dug long scratches into her thigh where no one would see them and listened to IronWeaks loud enough to damage her hearing. If it hurt enough, it satisfied that empty thing inside you enough so you could have a little peace.

The relief was only temporary. The punishment never truly erased the crime. The guilt was always there. It filled her, sluggish and thick, as if were she cut, she'd bleed something black and putrid—although repeated experience demonstrated this wasn't true. The guilt always came back just as savage.

But tonight, although she was running harder than usual and her quads already felt filled with liquid fire, her mind wouldn't quiet. She felt Johnny's name in the rhythm of her stride; she heard the whisper of Liss's name with each of her breaths.

She should have been happy—no, happy was too high a bar. She should have gotten some kind of satisfaction from resisting Liss's influence, but now Dan could barely remember what she'd said, only that she'd gotten what she wanted: Liss had driven off feeling abandoned.

It was only right that Liss got to taste that feeling too.

It was true that Dan had promised to go along with her plan, but Liss hadn't held up her end of the bargain. She'd made a promise to Dan too—that they would help Johnny, but they had to wait for the right time.

Dan had waited. She kept quiet and lied when she had to and trusted Liss to tell her when the waiting was over. Neither of them liked talking about that night. Plus, Dan felt for sure Liss was mad at her for wanting to do the stupid spell in the first place, and it was only a matter of time before that anger exploded in her face. Now, Dan remembered the day in June, more than three months after Johnny had vanished, when she finally asked Liss what the plan was, because once school was out, they could focus on getting Johnny back. Liss had grimaced and admitted that she would be in Guatemala all summer. Her parents had signed her up for a program to generate content for her college admissions essays. She was leaving a week after school ended.

That was when Dan knew: promises weren't binding forever, and the clock on theirs had already run out. Dan was ashamed to admit it, but it had come as a sad relief. Part of her had always known that the time would never be right, because Johnny was gone.

That summer, Dan had been afraid for what it would mean for

her to be Liss-less. Dan had expected to miss her, but distance made it easier not to have to pretend that whatever once made them inseparable had turned bitter and broken. It made it easier to try to forget what they'd done.

Dan rounded a turn onto an uphill slope. The road clung to the cliff, then turned sharply at the top of the climb. She forced herself on, although her legs felt heavy as lead and the air kept slipping from her lungs. One foot, then the other, then the other again.

Obviously Liss would have no problem making Johnny's death about how much she'd sacrificed to try to find him, then bulldoze back into Dan's life just to rub it in her face. Had she expected Dan to thank her, after everything she'd done? It was as if nothing at all had changed between them: the more Liss demanded of her, the more Dan resented her—the kind of anger that was only possible when you really, truly loved someone—and the more Dan resented her, the more Liss demanded.

Why had Liss needed to get involved with Johnny in the first place?

Dan's foot came down funny, and she stumbled over to the very edge of the road, gasping for air. She pulled out her earbuds and set her hands on her hips. "Fuck," she gasped.

This hill was too steep for her. It beat her every time. Her legs turned to deadweight, her muscles seized. She heaved in air and spat on the ground and looked back the way she'd come. She still had to make it home, and anyway, she was almost at the Black Grass Spiritual Advancement Center, which had a severe gate that always gave her the creeps. Up ahead, she could barely see where the road curved around the hill. It was a blind turn, she knew, from the thousands of times she'd driven it on the way from her house to Liss's in Marlena.

On the road's narrow shoulder, Dan kneeled in the sharp, cold gravel and pressed her fists into her stomach.

In her mind, she saw a road not unlike this one, not so far from here. She saw the scattered salt of the broken line. Johnny's pupils blown out black, filling his eyes, as the woman took him, and Dan herself standing there, doing nothing to stop it.

Thinking of Johnny opened a cavern inside her, a gnawing abyss that made her want to fold herself in two. The abyss took whatever she could give it, and never went away, never shrank, never healed.

Dan wanted to scream.

Instead, she stepped back onto the road. Her heart was beating in her ears—a quick, monotone thud—as she lay down on the asphalt. Above her, fog obscured the night sky. Below her, the ocean curled against the cliffs with a quiet purr. The road was cool against her sweaty shoulders and back. Gone was the heat she'd burned with while she ran. She shivered.

Dan could barely breathe.

If a car came, would she hear it? Could she, if she wanted to, move in time? Or would she let it crush her, alone and unprotected out here on the road?

She held her hands open to the sky and ground her knuckles against the rough pavement until they stung. She pushed harder. She hoped they would bleed.

If Alexa asked about her knuckles tomorrow, Dan would have to lie to her.

Alexa somehow saw a person in Dan who was worth discovering. Dan ached with how badly she wanted that to be true.

Alexa would tell her that she shouldn't give Liss this power over her—shouldn't hurt herself because Liss had already hurt her.

Dan took a breath. She flipped her hand over and pressed her palm onto the road.

This was the final thing about running at night in North Coast:

the roads were empty. You might run for miles, never seeing another car or another person. You might lie down in the street just beyond the edge of a blind turn and wait, and a car might never come by.

Dan got up and ran home.

Dan

They both should have stayed away from Johnny Su. He had black hair that fell in slashes across his forehead and a collection of actual records and a sheepish way of smiling the tiniest bit when you caught him looking at you with those rich brown eyes and eyelashes out of a mascara commercial. He played the guitar and loved surfing in the freezing Pacific and spoke Chinese, he said, like a five-year-old who loved to swear. He was a year older than Dan and Liss, so that he gave the impression of a better-formed version of the boys their age. He lived on the outskirts of Gratton and could be spotted skateboarding to school on the sunny mornings that were so rare in North Coast.

Dan met Johnny in Spanish class—she had been the only sophomore in Spanish 3—but she didn't get to know him until she got a job at Achieve! that spring. Johnny had been working at the tutoring service for a year already, so he trained her in how pull up the right math or reading program for each kid on their assigned computer and what to do in the nightmare situation that one of the younger ones had an accident. Most of the job was standing around in khakis and an unflattering red polo while the kids tapped away at their keyboards with headphones on, handing out stickers, and taking their parents' credit cards.

Dan didn't like working with children. She didn't know how to behave around them. When they had questions, she couldn't find answers simple enough for the younger ones, but the middle schoolers would tell her they weren't little kids anymore. The embarrassing fact was that she really wanted them to like her, but kids had a way of seeing right through you, of finding you boring almost immediately, and they didn't have any interest in pretending otherwise.

Johnny, on the other hand, was a natural. He got the elementary schoolers to sit still and convinced the tweens to put their phones away. The parents beamed at him as their kids grabbed onto Johnny's leg and whined that they didn't want to go home. When he was on shift, Johnny was the glowing center of Achieve!

At first, they barely talked over closing—whose turn it was to take out the trash, whether the keyboards had been cleaned yet. Dan assumed that if he wanted to talk to her, he would, and anything else would probably be bothering him. But then he asked her for help on when to use the imperfective in Spanish and commented approvingly ("Nice") of the IronWeaks patch on her backpack.

After that, it was all music all the time—classic punk, new wave, indie rock. Liss wasn't really into music, and now Dan realized there was a special thrill in discovering new bands cool enough to tell Johnny about and listening to his recommendations. When he heard Dan didn't have a record player, he invited her over to listen on his, because everything sounded better on vinyl, although they never actually made plans to do it and Dan never found the nerve to follow up. Once, they stayed late after closing to watch videos of the Germs on the computer in the back office. She only half watched the clips—pale bodies covered in sweat and convulsing with rage—and instead her gaze wandered to Johnny, shards of black hair bouncing along with the frantic beat as he tapped out the drum line to "Lexicon Devil" on his thigh.

He ran his fingers through his hair in a totally unselfconscious way that snagged Dan's brain, and she blurted, "You don't seem angry enough to listen to music like this." Johnny looked at her from the corner of his eye. "Sorry, I shouldn't have said that."

"Don't apologize." He brushed his hair back again, but it was silky and long and always falling where it looked perfect but didn't belong. The lights of the rest of Achieve! were already switched off, and when he turned to her, Dan felt sharply how alone they were. "You don't have be angry to listen to punk. It makes me feel alive. All that energy. It makes me want to . . ." He spread his hands wide.

"Yeah, I know," Dan said. "It makes you want to escape your whole life."

Johnny shook his head. "Not even close. This music's angry, but I guess it makes me feel happy to be alive enough to be angry or happy or bummed or whatever. That sounds so dumb."

"No, it doesn't. I totally get that," she said, although she definitely didn't.

Johnny cleared the browser search history. "We should get out of here. Get home safe, okay, *Daniela*?" He called her by her full name with a Spanish flourish to tease her around Achieve! Dan was never sure if he knew that was actually how it was pronounced. He never said it like that in Spanish class, where he never said her name at all.

"You too, *Juan*."

Dan didn't know what to think. She was sure she was one dumb comment away from making him realize how annoying she was. It didn't help that at school he basically ignored her, sometimes throwing her a nod in the hall when he was with his friends. Once he overheard her complaining to Liss about her period cramps, and she was so embarrassed she'd nearly skipped work that afternoon.

Then other times, she could barely bring herself to care about him. It was a crush, that was all, and of course, he didn't like her back. Why *would* he? Lately she felt heavy nearly all the time, and no one wanted a girlfriend who couldn't get it together enough to smile. Dan was looking forward to summer, so she could stop pretending she wanted to do anything other than sleep all day.

But then they let magic into their lives, and things felt brighter, here and there. Liss was always looking for spells that would fix something: a goal at her soccer game, a nasty zit to clear. Liss approached each with the same serious excitement, like every spell was bringing her life that much closer to perfection. It felt like magic every time they cast, and magic felt like *something*, at least, but Dan struggled to think of what to ask the Black Book. She rarely knew what needed changing, and when she did, she didn't want to say it out loud to Liss.

Then summer started and Achieve! moved to eight-hour shifts. It was exhausting work, not interesting enough to fight off boredom, but there was too much going on to completely zone out. Watching the summer days go from socked in with fog to sun-blistered blue and back to foggy again in the evening made Dan feel she was watching her life slide by. Liss still asked her about Johnny, but the more she did, the more he felt like an impossible problem: something she was supposed to want, although she hadn't figured out exactly how wanting worked.

When Rickey IronWeaks died in July of that summer, Dan felt something in her come unmoored and sink, stone-heavy. It hadn't changed by the time school started at the end of August. When she wasn't slogging through junior year, she spent more and more time curled up in bed, although most of the time she wasn't sleeping, not really—just existing. She felt the same way when she was at her classes, at work, or sneaking out onto the roof of her house with

Liss to do a spell. Like she was always half asleep, part of mind float-ing in some melancholy place, far away from the strange and useless anchor of her body.

"Same as Darby Crash from the Germs," Johnny said, shaking his head in disappointment. It was the end of their first shift together since Rickey's death. "They gave too much to the music."

Dan glared at him, a blister of anger bursting in her throat. "Darby Crash died of a drug overdose, so it's totally different. And anyway music is supposed to make things better."

After work, Dan crawled into bed and listened to the saddest music in the world.

The kiss happened two weeks into school. Dan's car broke down. She managed to get the car to an auto shop, cursing the whole way there that all her savings would be gone. She showed up late to Achieve!, flushed with frustration as she explained to Johnny what happened.

He put his hands on her shoulders. "Hey, relax. Don't worry about being late. You need a ride home?"

It took her a second to reply. It was the first time he'd ever touched her on purpose. "Dogtown's forty-five minutes away."

"So it's too far to walk."

But they didn't go home after changing out of their red Achieve! polos. The sun was setting, and they went to watch it at the overlook south of Gratton, where the Pacific had carved jagged monoliths out of the cliffs. They smoked a bowl, then went to 7-Eleven for snacks.

They leaned against his Volvo watching the sky light itself on fire and eating Doritos. The weed made Dan feel warm and sweet and empty, and also anxious that her mouth was covered in powdered Cool Ranch.

Then Johnny put his arm around her. Probably just in a friendly way, Dan told herself, even as she let herself sink into him. When he asked, "What do you want to do now?" she tilted her face to his. The moon was rising clearly over his shoulder, above the jagged edge of the distant trees, and he was looking at her shyly, as if they were a secret. She was caught on the ocean wind, drifting away. He could kiss her, he could not; what did any of it matter? She answered, "I don't know, what do you want to do?"

Johnny grinned. "I don't know. What do you want to do?" he parroted back to her, and all of a sudden they were laughing, and Dan was curled against him now, both their bodies trembling and taut, her face buried against his neck.

He kissed her.

Dan was out of breath, her heart already racing, and she forgot entirely that she was supposed to close her eyes. His lips were soft against hers, moving in an unfamiliar way, yet somehow her own lips knew how to move against them. He tasted like Doritos, and she could smell the conditioner in his hair and the wet sucking sound their mouths made was more strange than sexy. Johnny's eyes were shut tight, and she didn't know if she wanted him to open them or not, to see her there kissing him or not.

So that's how kissing is, Dan thought as Johnny broke away from her, and then, *I can't wait to tell Liss.*

Dan slept over at Liss's exactly eight days after The Kiss, and Liss was treating it like the event of the century.

"So you like him, right?" Liss pressed. They were lying on her bed scrolling through Johnny's social media. "I can tell you really like him."

"Come on, Liss!" Dan protested.

Dan had no idea how Liss could tell when Dan still couldn't bring herself to say it out loud. True, in the first days of the Post-Kiss Era, she had no appetite, and a smile crept across her face whenever she thought about the way he smelled (who knew Doritos could be romantic?) and how when he was deeply tanned from surfing, his skin was nearly the same color as hers, when it seemed like everyone else in North Coast was white. All that definitely pointed in the direction of liking Johnny. But she'd also checked her phone approximately every fifteen seconds and he still hadn't texted her, which annoyed her intensely, as if all she wanted was for him to just text her to get it over with already. She'd reminded herself that if he didn't text her and somehow he fell off the face of the earth and she never had to see him again, she could deal with that—ignoring how totally unromantic that sounded and how it definitely did not point to liking Johnny.

Dan had imagined, before, that if "something happened" between them, afterward she wouldn't be so hopelessly awkward, and he would—he would what? Johnny had always treated her perfectly fine. He'd told her a million bands to check out and offered a ride home without her even asking. But he had this careless way with her, ignoring her at school even now that they were Post-Kiss. Maybe that was because he liked her, because you didn't just kiss people you didn't like. But that kind of logic made it seem like everything he did was a part of some elaborate strategy to win her over, a strategy that looked the same as what he would do if he didn't care about her at all. Maybe he didn't know how he felt about her, just like she didn't know how she felt about him. Then again didn't that just mean they didn't really like each other, and how could that be when they had kissed?

"I can't believe I have to see him on Monday," Dan said. "We're scheduled together at Achieve!, so there's no way I can avoid talking to him."

"Why would you want to?"

"I don't know, I just . . ." Dan began. Thinking about it turned her stomach a little, but that was probably just part of having a crush. "He makes me nervous, I guess."

Liss tossed her phone aside. "I know what we have to do!" Her blue eyes narrowed. "A love spell. I'm not saying he doesn't like you back, but what's the point of being witches if we're going to leave things to chance?"

Dan pushed herself up against the pillows. "What would that even do?"

"Make him fall in love with you, obviously!"

"Like, forever?" Dan squeaked.

"That would be super romantic!"

"That would be kind of fucked up."

Liss swatted at Dan's shoulder. "What if you guys get separated for like fifteen years, and then he sees you on TV interviewing a band or something and he'd be like, I'm still so in love with her, I have to find her! That would be *so* romantic."

"Oh my god, Liss!" Dan laughed. "We're not trying to *curse* him. Plus I think that would be stalking."

"Fine, he can love you very respectfully," Liss said. "We'll ask for that to be part of the spell."

"Love in moderation only!" Dan said, mimicking Liss's stern tone, and then they were both laughing again. It felt better to be curled up under a down comforter with Liss, talking about Johnny, than it was to actually be with him.

That's why Dan agreed to ask the Black Book for the spell.

The next day, they sat on Dan's bedroom floor in the only circle that was clear of stuff. The Black Book lay between them, holding the focus of all the energy in the room, like it was a slice of chocolate cake and Dan was starving but had to wait for her first bite.

It wasn't always easy to search the Black Book. For one, it was long: hundreds of pages, and they weren't numbered. There was no index or table of contents. More importantly, the pages had no fixed order. It was almost impossible to find a page you'd seen before, even if you flipped back to its general whereabouts. You might remember seeing a spell near the middle, right after a memorable section on how to sacrifice a goat, but when you'd turn the page, you'd find something entirely different, like an even more unpleasant section on how to sacrifice a cat. Other times, the Book practically opened to the spell they were looking for, as if it just decided to let them have what it knew they wanted. At first, Liss had thought the book made your memory play tricks on you. Then Dan pointed out that whenever they tried to leave sticky notes to mark the pages, they fell out, or ended up directing them to something totally pointless.

Eventually the two of them developed a way of asking the Book for what they wanted that was almost a spell in itself. Now, they placed their hands on the cover. Static electricity crackled over Dan's skin: Liss, the Book, and herself completing some circuit, current running through them.

"We need a love spell for Johnny Su," Liss said in a low voice.

"But nothing too extreme," Dan added. "Like a moderate, respectful love spell."

Liss rolled her eyes. "We can't actually ask for that. The Book won't know what it means."

"It knew what you meant when you asked for a spell to mess up your mom's Botox."

Liss relented, and they fell silent. Dan focused on what they needed from the Book, feeling that need channel into the depths of its dingy pages. It was like shuffling the cards in a tarot reading: you meditated on your question, so the cards would hear what you needed to know.

A love spell for Johnny.

Dan opened the Book to a random page and skimmed it, but it wasn't their spell—it was something about banishing an incubus. Now it was Liss's turn to flip to a new page.

A love spell, Dan thought. *A love spell for Johnny.*

Suddenly Dan imagined herself sitting shotgun in Johnny's Volvo as it took the turns of Highway 1. He'd pull over in some remote spot and lean across the center console to kiss her. Did you take your seat belt off first? Or would that send a signal—kissing's not enough for me, I'm ready for more? Would they get into the back seat? Would they talk first, or maybe it was better not to, in case she said something stupid? But how did you decide whether to get in the back seat if you weren't going to talk first?

Dan turned a page to a diagram of the constellation Aquarius.

A love spell.

The point of the spell was to simplify things, Liss had said. Dan understood that to mean that once Johnny fell for her, she wouldn't need to worry about why or how much, or when to hold hands, or him seeing her with her top off, or him seeing her scars, or how humiliated Johnny would feel once he realized he'd been tricked into dating a sad gremlin of a person. But how could she ever stop worrying about those things, when she knew she didn't deserve his love, and she wasn't even sure if she wanted it?

"Liss, I think we should—"

"This is it," Liss breathed. The page she had just turned to was titled "An Incantation for Love."

"That's kind of vague, isn't it?" Dan ventured.

Liss was hunched over the Book. She'd already read through

the steps. "It's so simple! Just a charm you say on the bank of a body of water—easy—and then you say his name three times and ring a bell."

"Wait a second—it doesn't say what it exactly does. Like, just love in general? What does that mean?"

Liss grabbed her backup Black Book notebook and was copying out the spell. "We could totally do it tonight—didn't your mom bring back a bunch of bells from her trip to Tibet?"

"Liss, stop!" Dan burst out. "I don't want to do it, okay?"

"Borrow one of the bells?"

"The spell! I don't want to do the spell."

Liss had already finished copying it. She sat back on her heels, her lips in an annoyed pout. "Why not?"

"It's not fair to him. Or me. If this isn't meant to be then it just isn't, I guess."

"I thought you liked him," Liss said. Her tone was cagey, testing.

Dan sighed and flipped the Book shut. "I want to give it more time, that's all. We have the spell now, we can do it whenever, right?"

"Right," Liss agreed, and closed her notebook.

FIVE

Alexa

It had taken nearly all of English class, but Alexa had drawn a pretty comprehensive map of Flintowerland that plotted the lairs of three different mythic beasts, which Alexa needed to know before she could write a story about the badass gang of girl-warriors dead set on defeating them. Or on doing something more cooperative, like befriending them, she wasn't sure. She was wondering about the position of the River Gnoss relative to the Aeryl Mountains when she realized Mr. Aquino was saying her name.

Mr. Aquino repeated, "An example of irony?"

Alexa didn't hesitate. "The whole situation with Lydia and Wickham is ironic because it's supposed to be this disaster for Lizzie, but it actually brings her and Darcy even closer together."

Mr. Aquino's nostrils flared, then he moved on to his next question, and Alexa went back to her map.

English bored Alexa half to death, which was also ironic because she liked reading the most of almost anything. The problem was, when you'd been to three high schools in three different cities (the first two years in Tempe, junior in Los Angeles, and now senior in Fort Gratton), you read *Pride and Prejudice* three times, and you could practically fall asleep in class and still be able to answer any question the teacher lobbed at you. That was a super-effective way to get teachers to hate you.

Her second reading of *Pride and Prejudice* happened not long after Alexa had gone to Los Angeles to live with Lorelei. Alexa got to wondering what she'd missed in her literary education in order to realize once again that Darcy was Lizzie Bennet's dream man. (Actually Alexa thought Lizzie would be happier running off with Charlotte Lucas. Maybe she'd write a fic.) To make up for it, she'd made a syllabus of must-reads for her own education, with Lorelei suggesting contemporary classics she couldn't skip.

Reading was an escape to a different world, a different life. Plus, it was very cheap, and back in Arizona, Alexa could usually get to the library without her mother's help. But like most things, with Lorelei it was different. Lorelei never made fun of her for reading too much, or warned her that she'd give herself wrinkles, or resented her as if having an intelligent daughter made a parent look stupid—although Lorelei was really her aunt and would only be her legal guardian until she turned eighteen in May. Kim, Alexa's mother, told her that boys didn't like a girl who read so much, and men didn't like them either—which was messed up advice in the first place, and in the second place, drove Alexa crazy because Kim seemed to think Alexa's queerness was a phase. If it was a phase, Alexa was pretty sure it began when she was born and would end when she died. So Alexa would spit back that Kim didn't really seem to know what men liked, because she couldn't keep one, and Kim would hit her with a wooden spoon. It hurt a lot more than it seemed like a spoon should, but then again Alexa had known that was coming and decided it was better than keeping her mouth shut.

Mr. Aquino was saying something about marriage and romance, which felt about as remote from Alexa's life as Mars.

Alexa yawned. She'd stayed up texting Dan about her meet-up with Liss—how Liss had just assumed Dan was going to help her, like Dan didn't have any of her own opinions or thoughts or anything about that, and then basically freaked out when Dan stood up to her, which she totally deserved. It wasn't unusual for them to text until one of them fell asleep, but Alexa made a special point of it when Dan was in a dark mood. Last night, even after Dan fell asleep, Alexa couldn't. Alexa didn't know the full story of what went on between Dan and Liss. She did know that when Liss came up, Dan got this look like she was nauseous from a gut punch and expecting another, and Alexa hated to think of her alone with her thoughts in that little attic room.

She first guessed that Dan was depressed not long after they met. She could tell from the way Dan always said she was *doing good* or *having a chill weekend* or just *fine*, with this strange and perfect lightness that made you want to believe her. Growing up with Kim, Alexa learned how to tell lies like that—lies that presented a reality a lot nicer than the one everyone knew you were in, lies that rolled off your tongue without hesitation because you needed them. Four months into their friendship, Dan had still never talked outright about it. If there were rules about when and how to confront your best friend about her depression, Alexa didn't know them. But she was beginning to think she should find out.

Alexa was so lost in thought that she almost didn't realize class had ended. Half the kids had left and she was still packing up, which meant she heard it when the post-class conversation shifted from controlled chaos to something quiet and covert, the kind of half-whispered voices that meant only one thing: gossip.

Normally, she would have ignored it. Alexa almost never knew who they were gossiping about. She hadn't made any friends at North Coast outside Dan, mainly because Alexa rarely tried to be friendly, and when she did, she didn't quite get to *friendly* friendly. Just sort of like, not glaring at you, which wasn't for everybody. But today there was the hiss of something in their voices that made

Alexa turn to the group of girls at the back of the room and ask, "What're you talking about?"

One of the girls gave Alexa a look that did not entirely conceal her excitement. "A girl from St. Ignatius disappeared last night."

"What do you mean disappeared?"

"You know, like, poof, gone? She's missing. They found her car by the side of the road a few miles south of Gratton. They don't know if it's a kidnapping or whatever. Super scary."

Alexa didn't wait to hear their theories about who it was. She grabbed her stuff and went to look for Dan.

Alexa decided to play it cool. That would be the best way to make it seem like Dan's fears were unfounded, because Alexa hadn't leapt to the exact same conclusion.

Although naturally she had. Alexa only knew one student at St. Ignatius, but that student was on a solo quest to locate her runaway boyfriend. Liss's disappearance had the potential to unravel Dan completely, and Alexa didn't know if either of them would have the capacity to put her back together.

She could *not* let that happen. Dan was her first real friend—someone who would spend a weekend with her watching a *Buffy* marathon or go to midnight showings or laugh at her whining about how sore her boobs got before her period. Sometimes they would actually sit around talking and painting their nails, like they'd stumbled onto the set of a movie about teenagers. All of it was silly to care about, but only if you could take it for granted.

Alexa said the name under her breath like a curse: *Liss.*

Dan's locker hung open, exposing its innards to the world: a photo collage of Dan's favorite bands (so many boys in eyeliner), old lunch containers she forgot to bring home, piles of papers and broken binders that she'd managed to amass with astonishing speed as soon as the semester started. Dan was standing in front of this mess, clutching the locker door hard enough that the metal edge was probably digging into her hand; there were fresh scabs on her knuckles. She wore the sick, desperate look she always got when she was unhappy, but she was furtively scanning the hallway, straining for any overheard shred of information about the missing girl.

"What's up?" Alexa asked breezily.

Dan released her death grip on the locker and crossed her arms. "Did you hear that a girl from St. Ignatius went missing last night? Everyone's talking about it."

"They'll find whoever it is. Don't worry."

The look she got from Dan was a flash of misery so unvarnished, Alexa's breath caught in her throat. She pulled Dan into a hug. Alexa could practically feel the tightness in Dan's chest, pressed against hers. She would definitely need those rules, soon. "You're okay," she whispered. "It'll be okay."

She felt more than heard Dan's reply. "How do you know?"

Alexa pulled back. She didn't know what to say.

"So it's Liss?" A husky voice interrupted from behind Alexa. She turned to see Sierra Nagler wearing leggings so expensive the price of them could have fed a family of four for a week, and a look of unrepentant curiosity.

"What are you talking about?" Alexa growled.

"You know, the girl from St. Ignatius. Jocelyn's dad's a cop, and she texts with one of the younger guys on the force." Alexa sneered at this, but Sierra rolled her eyes and continued. "They aren't releasing the name yet. Anyway, Dan, we thought you'd know if it was Liss."

Dan's gaze shifted between Sierra and Alexa, like a snared animal unsure if it should lie down or fight.

Sierra carried on, "Because she goes to St. Ignatius now? And she was basically destroyed over that stuff with Johnny last year, so we thought—"

Alexa focused very hard on breathing properly. "Sierra," she said as calmly as she could. "You need to get the fuck away from us right now and reassess everything about your life."

"Jeez, Alexa, you didn't even know her."

"Right now. As in immediately. Away."

Sierra smirked, but there was no satisfaction in it. She turned on her heel and went back to her identically dressed friends, shrugging dramatically.

When Alexa looked back at Dan, Dan had arranged her face into something resembling keeping it together.

"I do not like that girl at all." Alexa frowned.

"Really? I was worried I was about to be knocked out of the number-one best friend spot," Dan answered, and Alexa smiled, barely, because Dan was trying to be brave.

"I bet the Lizard's fine," Alexa said.

"You're probably right," Dan said, but Alexa could see she didn't believe it.

Dan

After lunch, Dan excused herself from Chemistry, locked herself in a bathroom stall, and balled her hands into fists. She stood there, with her eyes shut tight and the scabs across her knuckles splitting, trying to shake the images in her head: Liss finding some secluded spot off Highway 1 where the vibes were right, ignoring that it was dark and dangerous and she was alone. Liss, with her dirty-blond hair falling into her eyes and that pinched look her face had when she was concentrating, casting another spell gone wrong and that horrible woman with her shuffling gait and hunched shoulders coming out of the night. There were so many ways to end up lost in North Coast.

Alexa said the missing girl had to be someone else, but Alexa didn't know Liss. When Liss undertook a project, she gave herself to it entirely. She would let nothing stop her, let no one dissuade her, even if she couldn't possibly do it on her own because it was a thing that could not be done.

Dan knew this about her, and when Liss had come to her for help, she'd said no. Dan had been stupid to think she could convince Liss to just *give up*. Liss had been in a rage when she'd left Dan's house yesterday. Who knew what she could have done next?

Even as Dan pulled her phone from her pocket and typed out the text—*are you ok?*—she felt certain of the answer. Liss wasn't okay. Liss was gone. And it was Dan's fault, again, same as before—another stone to lay on her conscience, Liss alongside Johnny like she always wanted to be.

All the way back to class, Dan stared into her phone, which wasn't strictly speaking allowed, waiting to see the three dots that meant Liss was sending a reply.

But fifth period ended without word from Liss, then so did sixth. Dan couldn't put her phone down in seventh, not even waiting for Liss anymore, but for someone to let her know that Liss was gone.

When the last bell rang, Dan hurried out to her car, the tightness in her chest unbearable. She would drive all the way to Liss's house, she would talk to Liss's parents and—and tell them what? That being a witch was a lot more complicated than it looked? That demons might be a safety risk they'd never considered when raising a teenage daughter?

Then her phone buzzed.

What's that supposed to mean?

Dan slumped forward to rest her forehead on the steering wheel. Her breath came in quick little gulps. She waited for the leaded, dark feeling of guilt to ease. Liss was safe—everything was fine.

Wasn't it?

Then why couldn't she shake the feeling that it *should have been* Liss? This was the fate Liss was racing toward—lost on the side of the road somewhere, and Dan the only one left alive who knew what really happened and the only one who could have stopped it.

Liss's plan was stupid, pointless, dangerous. Johnny was dead, and he wasn't coming back. But even if she hated Liss, Dan couldn't let her lose herself to figure that out.

I'm in, she texted Liss.

Liss sent back an emoji of twin girls dancing.

Alexa

Alexa was halfway through a new novel, her feet curled under her in a knit blanket on the couch, when Lorelei's headlights flooded the living room of their little cottage. Alexa yawned and stretched and headed into the kitchen. It was after nine, which meant frozen pizza, which Alexa knew without looking at the box meant an oven temp of 425°F. She turned the knob and heard the gas catch as Lorelei spilled through the door and collapsed promptly onto the couch, the strap of her bag still looped around one wrist and the other arm flung across her forehead and her legs kicked up carefully so her shoes didn't dirty the already-stained couch. Domino, the black cat Lorelei had had since college, jumped up on her stomach.

"Ugh, Alexa, I'm literally dead," Lorelei moaned. "And I'm also literally dying of hunger."

"You can't be dead and dying at the same time."

Lorelei grinned and said, "There you go being all *intelligent* again," in a way that made Alexa feel fluttery and warm. She loved it when Lorelei did that—teased her without being mean, in a way that made Alexa feel treasured. It was almost enough to make her forget all the times Kim had told her to *quit it with that smart mouth.*

"Oven's on. Cheese?"

"Do we have any pepperoni? I want to eat something that's very bad for me. All they eat up there is buckwheat groats."

"What even is that?"

"It's a grain. Tastes like cardboard, but . . . nubbly-er."

"Nubbly-er?"

Lorelei opened one eye. "I'll smuggle you some out tomorrow. Grab you a pocketful. It's probably better with lint."

"You could try it with some fingernail clippings for crunch."

"Brilliant." Lorelei laughed. "Brilliant."

They ate the pizza at the big table in the living room, which also served as both of their desks. It was stacked on one side with textbooks and on the other piled with documents related to Lorelei's investigation into Black Grass Spiritual Advancement Center for *The Wardens* magazine. They both agreed that eating dinner surrounded by work wasn't good for their mental health, but every time they cleared the table off, it was only a matter of days before Alexa had a test to study for or an essay to write, or Lorelei ended up spending all night researching this or that thing for her story, and the piles of books and notes reappeared and they found themselves wondering which papers were fine to put their plates directly on top of.

As Alexa sliced the pizza, Lorelei fiddled with the evil eye charm on the necklace she always wore. Lore hadn't been sleeping much. To get the inside scoop on Black Grass, she'd posed as a member— a seeker, as Black Grass called them. Lately, she'd had to report to the campus just down Highway 1 earlier and earlier, and stay later into the evening, which meant she had less time to write up her notes from the day and talk to her editor and work on the story.

"Did you get anything good today?" Alexa asked.

Lorelei's eyes refocused on Alexa, as if she'd forgotten she was there. She rubbed her eyes and grabbed her slice. "Not enough. Keith's trying to get me to move up there. All this bullshit—sorry, I mean BS—about how they really need me and I really need them, that I can't really get enlightened if I'm off campus. I've told him so many times that I can't, but he keeps pushing. He knows I have you."

"But he wishes you didn't."

"That used to be his tune. He acted like you're something I can 'advance' myself out of, with all his iterative desires and needs crap. Like you can't be fully *spiritual* if you actually care about other people, which is absolute bull—BS. Now he's been saying that you ought to move up there too, which is *so* never gonna happen. He even tried to get me to bring you up there to visit last week."

"I can do that, if it would help."

"You are *not* going up there," Lorelei said firmly, then sighed. "Honestly, I can't believe I managed not to punch him. I can't look at that man's face anymore."

She flipped over a pamphlet for Black Grass from the top of one of her stacks.

Alexa knew the face well. It was always slipping out of Lorelei's papers, emblazoned on nearly every Black Grass document. Always the same headshot: tanned, apple cheeks under an overgrown shag of scruffy brown hair; eyes, a photo-retouched polar blue. He was wearing red prayer beads and two necklaces that were basically only thin strips of leather over a white linen shirt. He wasn't quite smiling, but his mouth was open, exposing teeth as white and regular as chewing gum Chiclets. Keith Levandowski had made a fortune in Silicon Valley, his bio said, but he had always been seeking something more—until he heard the calling from some higher power he called his Lord. He founded Black Grass Spiritual Advancement Center to teach his philosophy and practice of transcendental meditation to his "seekers." Under Keith's headshot, the words EMPOWERED GROWTHFUL ENERGY were written in oversized letters.

Lorelei had been working on her exposé on Black Grass for months. She suspected the organization was involved in some kind of financial fraud, and on top of that, was probably a cult. Midsummer in LA, Lorelei had sat down with Alexa and told her that her editor wanted her to move out to North Coast to investigate Black Grass's new center; the whole campus had been set up in a remote spot in the hills virtually overnight, and it was definitely fishy. Lorelei promised Alexa that they would do whatever Alexa thought was best: she knew it wasn't fair to make her move again, especially when she'd only been in LA for a year and North Coast was so far from Arizona.

But far from Arizona was where Alexa wanted to be, she'd said. She didn't mention that she would have agreed to anything Lorelei wanted, because she was pretty sure living on the moon with Lorelei would have been better than living anywhere with Kim. Alexa still didn't understand how she'd gotten so lucky, and she wasn't about to blow it by making Lorelei stay in LA. So they'd packed up the Koreatown apartment and driven up to Dogtown, the whole way practicing Lorelei's new identity as a graduate student alienated by modern life ("Why do things make us who we are, when we make things?" Lorelei would ask. "If phones are meant to connect us, why do they make us so lonely?" Alexa would answer). Five months later, Lorelei had leveled up enough that Keith had finally given her access to Black Grass's offices, which he called his "inner sanctum." But Lorelei was frustrated; she needed more.

Alexa eyed the photo of the little white bungalows on the back of the pamphlet.

"Maybe you should move up there. You can come home on weekends." Alexa chose her words carefully. "If that's what the story needs."

"I can't," Lorelei said around a mouthful of pizza. "Can't miss dinner, otherwise we aren't a proper family-thing."

"You can't ruin the whole article so I have someone to eat dinner with. I'm perfectly capable of eating frozen pizza all on my own."

"I told you, I'm getting a pizza stone and then we can make pizza from scratch and it'll be delicious," Lorelei said, the pointy end of her slice drooping toward the floor. "You know dinner's non-negotiable. That's our only rule, got it?"

Alexa nodded. Although she sometimes complained about it, Alexa loved that Lorelei insisted that they eat together. Whenever she asked if she could skip and meet up with Dan instead, part of her always wondered if this was finally the time when Lorelei would stop caring. But every time, Lorelei would say *nope* so it sounded like she was popping a bubblegum bubble and suggest that Dan come over to their place for dinner instead.

"Besides, I doubt they'd give me weekends away. I couldn't leave until the article's done, and who knows how many weeks of sleeping in those creepy bungalows that would take. I'm not going to leave you to go join some cult in the middle of college application season." She punctuated this last point by stabbing the air with her slice. "So tell me how school was."

Alexa shrugged. "All anyone wanted to talk about was that missing girl."

Lorelei set her pizza down. "What missing girl?"

"The girl from Marlena. They found her car a few miles north of here."

Alexa told her everything she knew. The last few hours had been fertile with gossip. Kids from St. Ignatius took rumors home to Marlena or Dogtown, text messages circulated unrestrained by no-phones-during-school-hours rules, the police department issued a statement, and everyone overheard parents whispering into their phones.

The missing girl was Zephyr Finnemore, seventeen, of Marlena Beach. Her father was a tech entrepreneur, which meant no one really knew how he'd gotten rich, and her mother was returning as fast as possible from a trip to Palm Springs. It was suspected that Zephyr disappeared on the way to meet up with her boyfriend, who was a darryl—North Coaster slang for derelict (Dan had explained), which referred to the dudes and occasional lady who traveled up and down the county looking for odd jobs, a place to crash, and a friend to share some good herb. There were good darryls and bad darryls, but everyone thought Zephyr's darryl, whose name was Brodie, was basically an all right guy. Alexa had no idea how that consensus had emerged, since he was thirty-one years old— fourteen years older than Zephyr, which was super disgusting and for sure illegal—and he slept on a massage table he carted around to construction sites where he worked as a carpenter. Apparently being okay with that kind of situation was a North Coast thing (Dan had explained), although Alexa still thought it was extremely nasty.

Zephyr's car had been found a mile past the turn to Brodie's current home/work site with her phone still in it. The police were looking for tips on Zephyr's whereabouts and wouldn't say if Brodie was a suspect. Most people seemed to believe this wasn't his kind of thing, which made Alexa wonder *whose* kind of thing people thought *this* was, if not a full-grown adult who was basically homeless and got down with high school girls.

Lorelei's face grew increasingly drawn as Alexa recounted her gossip, with a deep wrinkle slicing between her eyebrows. When Alexa was done, Lorelei got up and lit the small candles in the altar she had set up in the defunct fireplace. It was a quirky array of precisely positioned items that Lorelei often reconfigured: chunky crystals or dull rocks, dried plants or fresh flowers, candles in any color of the rainbow. Alexa never asked why; she assumed Lorelei's spirituality was private.

Kneeling on the floor, Lorelei blew out her match. "I'm going to finish this assignment and then we'll get out of here, okay? We'll go back to LA. It was better for you there, right?"

Alexa thought about North Coast's too-damp weather and how the nearest actual nonfrozen-pizza place was forty-five minutes away and the strange reality that it was almost impossible to find food that wasn't organic. Sometimes the yellow sun of LA felt like a liquid gold dream. But then she thought about Dan, and crawling out onto the roof from her bedroom window and singing along to the music in her car during the forty-five-minute drive to that pizza place and how Dan could with just one look make Alexa crack up entirely during history class.

Maybe Alexa's life in North Coast wasn't quite *normal*. It certainly wasn't a life she could have imagined for herself when things with her mother had gotten so bad that Lorelei suggested Alexa come stay with her. But North Coast was the first place Alexa didn't feel like an afterthought—a place that finally felt something like *home*.

"I don't know," Alexa said. "Dogtown's growing on me."

Lorelei leaned against the fireplace lintel. She seemed more relaxed with the candles now flickering, but Alexa could tell she was a little surprised. "Then we'll talk about it. I'll finish the story as fast as I can and we'll figure it out. But until then, just . . . be safe, okay? Stay away from creepy darryls—stay away from everything creepy. Promise?"

"You're sounding awfully maternal."

"I'm not kidding, kid. You're too smart to go around doing stupid things. Promise me?"

"I promise," Alexa said.

SIX

Dan

Thursday's block schedule meant Dan had her last period free, and today she spent it holed up in the library, logged in to the most out of the way computer she could find. She was meeting Liss after school to try to recast the spell that had reached Johnny, as soon as Liss could get from St. Ignatius to Gratton. Dan didn't know how to feel. She couldn't ignore the tremors of excitement she felt at the prospect of doing magic again, even though the Black Book was still hidden under her bed and she hadn't gotten up the nerve to look at it.

Then there was Liss. Dan had practically promised Alexa she would keep the Lizard at arm's length. She had definitely not been honest about the fact that she was seeing Liss after school. As much as Dan dreaded seeing her, there was a part of her heart that still answered to Liss, that had never stopped missing her.

Plus, if she was honest, she was curious too.

The magic Dan knew had always been about spells, charms, and incantations. Dan didn't know how they worked, only that they did. But magic wasn't *creatures*—or it hadn't been, until that terrifying woman who stole Johnny away. Now Liss wanted her to believe there was a demon-lord-whatever named Kasyan hiding underground and keeping Johnny captive. She wouldn't have believed at all if Alexa hadn't mentioned the fairy tales. Was Kasyan made up or not?

It was time for some research.

Dan opened an incognito browser. It had been months, but she still remembered the URLs and her log-ins. Of course, the witchboards all looked exactly the same. Most of the message boards had never updated their original aesthetic of purple and black, that hideous basic-HTML blue for every link, and clipart that was older than Dan was. She checked all the usual sites: Occultists Anonymous, Spellshare, ~*~The Unknown~*~. She could practically hear Liss sneering, "Why does everyone on the witchboards have to be *so lame*?"

There wasn't much of anything on Kasyan. On the first board, the few threads on him had been wiped by the moderators. All that remained were cryptic subject lines.

Kasyan Lord of Last Resort—seeking any info!!! [7 replies]

Question for an occult lexicographer on Kasyan/Cassian/Kashus [23 replies]

lord kasyan + blood plagues [4 replies]

U will NOT believe this! **Kasyan** [46 replies]

Dan frowned. It didn't seem that the posts violated the community guidelines, but if they'd been deleted anyway, she had to move on.

The other witchboards were no better. On one, searches for *Kasyan* and all variant spellings turned up exactly zero results, which was unusual.

Dan typed the name into a regular search, hoping for better luck. This time they loaded, but even ten pages deep into the results, all she'd done was scribble down a half dozen conflicting interpretations that had the feel of rumors. Dan chewed the end of her pen. You didn't usually come across hard facts when researching the occult, but typically knowledge and experience congealed around a consensus.

Kasyan wasn't like that: there was barely enough information to bring together at all.

Dan was about to give up when she followed a link to a site that collected "dark popular beliefs." She didn't know what "dark popular beliefs" were, but the site had pages on everything from Cthulhu to the Tunguska Event to the Knights Templar, combining things that were obviously made up with things that had actually happened, and lumping in outdated superstitions and folklore with real religious beliefs. Dan rolled her eyes. She didn't expect the site to be helpful, but she clicked onto the page for Kasyan anyway.

KASYAN
* * * PROCEED WITH CAUTION * * *

Also Known As: Lord Kasyan—Lord of Last Resort—Kasyan the Unmerciful—Kasyan the Merciful

Type: Trickster, Wish-Granter

Kasyan is famous for misguided kindness.
He grants wishes to serve himself more than the wisher.

Dates Associated: February 29

Sightings: None recorded

One tale survives of a village that worshipped Kasyan, in exchange for good harvest, until Kasyan abducted all the village's unmarried girls. Villagers moved his Saint's Day to the leap day in retaliation, a tradition that spread when

The entry cut off. Dan reloaded the page, but the missing text never appeared. She even navigated to a few others (La Llorona, Bigfoot) to check that they loaded just fine.

Dan glared at the page. Kasyan couldn't really grant wishes—nothing could do that. *Probably* nothing could do that.

But the date was right.

"Is that an assignment for Coding?"

Dan jumped at Alexa's voice behind her and hurriedly closed the browser window. Unfortunately, behind it, she'd left ~*~The Unknown~*~ open in all its garish royal purple glory. The page was decorated with rough jpegs of hexagrams and black cats, which was cheeky and stupid when Dan was alone, but totally humiliating for someone else to see.

"Are you on a *message board*?" Alexa asked.

Dan closed the window and flipped her notebook shut, but she knew she was blushing. "Uh, yeah, it was . . . about IronWeaks. There's a rumor about some unreleased songs."

Alexa dropped into the chair at the computer next to Dan and began to spin herself in slow circles. "Want to do homework at SmoothieTown? I don't have to be home until dinner."

"Actually I think I can't today?" Dan's voice edged upward, like she was asking Alexa's permission. "I mean I definitely can't, I have to stop by Achieve! My old manager wanted to talk to me."

"I can wait while you do that, no problem."

Dan's face wrinkled up in a way that certainly didn't make her lie any more convincing. "It could take a while, I don't know? You can go home. If you want to."

"Good to know that I can go home. If I want to," Alexa said.

"I just meant I can't hang out, that's all." Dan shoved her notebook into her backpack and signed out of the computer. "But I have to run or I'll be late."

Her cheeks on fire, Dan headed out of the library, leaving Alexa slowly spinning in a computer chair alone.

Liss

When Liss walked into Aroma Café on Main Street in Gratton, it took her a minute to find Dan. First, Mad Mags was occupying the front of the cafe, pacing back and forth in front of the window so that bits of newspaper and little feathers and a whole lot of odor swirled in her wake.

"Hi, Mags," Liss mumbled.

"I'm waiting, I said I'll wait, I'll wait right here." Mags chattered nonsense in reply. "He's the very best at what he does!"

Mags was a North Coast fixture, spotted anywhere from Jenner up to north of Gratton, where civilization petered out. She'd been around for as long as Liss could remember, wearing the same long and ratty skirt, which Liss hoped was as Victorian as it looked, because then Mad Mags would have a petticoat under it, rather than a large volume of stinking newspaper. Her hair hung down to the small of her back, in greasy, gray-brown hanks that seemed to contain their own ecosystem. But as unclean and mentally unsound as Mags might be, she was a North Coaster. She was welcome in almost any business, and there were a number of homes where she had standing invitations, in case of bad weather. Dan once told Liss that kids in Dogtown had a superstition, that it was bad luck not to say hi to Mad Mags when you saw her. Liss thought that was ridiculous, but then couldn't help herself from doing it.

Second, Dan was sitting in a corner all the way at the back of the coffee shop, slurping the whipped cream off a coconut mocha and casing the place like she was about to rob it and needed quick access to the exits. There was only one reason why Dan wouldn't want to be seen at a coffee place she went to literally every week. Liss pursed her lips against her smile and wondered what Dan had told Alexa she was up to.

"Let's get out of here," Dan said the minute she saw Liss.

"Hello to you too," Liss said. "Why are you in such a hurry? I want to get a chai."

They followed the swing of the road north in the red Range Rover. It was a half an hour's drive, but they barely talked. Dan was curled into a ball with her feet on the dash (which was not a clean or safe thing to do, but Liss decided to ignore it). Whenever Liss glanced at her, Dan looked away or had her eyes glued to the window. Sure, the drive up Highway 1 was psychotically beautiful, with the slate-gray Pacific and deep green pines shrouded in a fairy mist of fog, every switchback of the road revealing a little inlet where the waves crashed into the cliffs or washed up on narrow beaches. It was beautiful, but Dan had seen it before, thousands of times, and what she had not done in weeks and weeks was talk to Liss, her best friend.

Once Dan texted her, Liss put the fight behind them. She'd assumed Dan had done the same—thus the texting. Liss hadn't really wanted to *hurt* Dan, but the rules of the game were different when you were fighting: the *whole point* was to hurt the other person. Then later, you got over it and forgave them. So she'd already forgiven Dan for the cruel things she'd said about her and Johnny. If Dan hadn't done the same, why had she agreed to help?

Liss took her eyes off the road and peeked at Dan. She couldn't tell if Dan was sulking or only tired. Liss didn't know how she'd expected Dan to be. She would have said something like *normal*, but Dan was never exactly a ray of sunshine.

It was one of Dan's best qualities.

The fight probably went differently for the winner (herself) and the loser (Dan). After all, she'd gotten what she wanted: Dan gave in. Liss was sympathetic—giving in was a feeling that she especially hated, and she knew its sour taste could linger. But *giving in* to trying to save someone's life didn't earn you a lot of pity points.

Liss rolled her eyes.

"You're being taciturn," Liss said.

"The SATs are over."

"Put some music on." Liss tossed Dan the cord.

They parked on the shoulder about a hundred feet from the trailhead into Digger's Gulch State Park, and Liss threw open the back of the Range Rover.

"You came prepared," Dan said.

"Yeah, well, if I have to spend all my time hiking out into the middle of nowhere, I don't want to die out there too."

The trunk was crammed with a mix of backwoods survival gear, magical equipment, and Liss's school stuff: Mylar blankets and first aid kits alongside a plastic case Dan recognized as Liss's crystal collection and a chemistry textbook. An eyeshadow palette had cracked open and glitterized a copy of the *St. Ignatius Jesuit*, the school's newspaper, with two huge pictures of Zephyr Finnemore on the front page: her senior class portrait and a candid, celebrating a victory with the softball team she captained.

Liss tossed the paper aside to rifle through her stuff. She grabbed two flashlights with extra batteries, two bottles of water, a whole box of wet wipes, and a rope, along with some candles and a lighter, and last, the mirror, and shoved it all into a backpack that she slung over her shoulder.

Liss locked the car three times in a row.

"Ready?" she asked Dan.

Dan nodded, Liss locked the car again, and they headed into the park.

The hike wasn't long, but it was dismal on account of a fire last summer that had burned through a hundred of the park's acres. They hiked out through nature that was either half dead or half living, depending on the angle you looked at it. Tiny, hardy plants began staking their claim to the place not so long after the fire, but it would be a long while before they obliterated the burnt-out husks of trees. It looked like the world with the scab picked off, which is why Liss had thought to check its auspices in the first place. That, and it was unpopular with hikers and joggers, which made the place creepy in a "life after people" way and therefore perfect for uninterrupted magic.

Dan followed Liss in a silence that meant that she was always one step closer to complaining about how far it was. Dan hated hiking, an outcome of Graciela's idea of quality family time and the uncool look of tall socks and hiking boots. Liss told her they were almost there three times, one of which was definitely a lie and one sort of a lie and the last one she quickly followed with, "I can literally see it from here," which to Liss's relief was basically true.

Dan peered over the edge of the bank. "Jesus, Liss, how'd you get down there?"

The banks of the gulch were steep, and although there was barely a trickle of water running through the bottom now, one good storm here or farther inland could raise the water level quickly, flooding the gulch with a fast-moving current seeking an outlet to the ocean. But Liss was fairly confident, based on her reading of the Doppler radar in that particular moment, there was low risk of a flash flood. The banks of the gulch were all exposed roots, rocks, and earth the color and texture of red clay, with few obvious footholds. Dan chewed her lip, eyeing the descent into the gulch uncertainly, and Liss knew what Dan was thinking: it wasn't safe for her to have come out here alone, to have slid down into the gulch by herself and hoped she could scramble out again, in an empty state park where the cell reception was spotty at best and nonexistent on average. She could have gotten hurt, she could have gotten lost or stranded, she could have been just another North Coaster who dropped off the map.

It felt good to see Dan like that—realizing how scared she was to lose her.

Liss shrugged and dug around in the backpack for the rope. "Yeah, it was dangerous, but I was careful. What was I supposed to do, *not* go down there when the auspices were right? Someone had to." Liss knotted the rope around a sturdy-looking tree on the bank and tossed the loose end into the gulch. Dan peered over the edge of the gulch. "Climbing down's the easy part. It's not *that* steep. The rope's to make sure we can get out."

Dan looked at her like she was crazy, and Liss glared back at her. Dan had no right be upset that this was dangerous when she'd outright abandoned Liss, and now she was about to benefit from everything Liss had learned in her time alone, every risk she'd taken.

"I did this by myself," Liss reminded her. "You'll be fine." Then Liss slipped the backpack on and stepped over the edge of the gulch. "Unless you fall on me, and then we're both screwed."

They stumbled and slid to the bottom of the gulch, then Liss led Dan down a few paces. The trickle of water running out to the ocean was only deep enough to soak their sneakers and coat the soles in clay-thick mud. They stopped at a place where the creek bed widened a bit. Here, the mud formed a kind of flat shelf next to the water, but it would be easily submerged after a good rain.

The momentary widening of the creek bed carved out space in the sky as well. Liss pointed it out to Dan: the ashy remains of the tree branches on the banks above them bordered a perfect circle of light blue.

"The other important thing is redwood." Liss consulted the compass on her phone, turning her body to orient properly. "Over there."

Dan looked where she pointed, which was roughly directly into the muddy bank. It was taller than both of them combined. "I don't see it," Dan said.

"That's the thing. It used to be one of the tallest in North Coast, but it fell after the fire, and it's a half-mile away. That's why it took me so long to figure this place out. But you feel it, right?"

Dan frowned in the general direction of the nonvisible redwood tree. Liss counted to four and back and tried not to think about how much she needed Dan to feel it. Liss mentally added that to the checklist of things she needed Dan to do: to be her gut check when it came to magic; to look at her with well-deserved appreciation and tell her that she'd worked so hard for good reason; to give her the Black Book; to say she'd abandoned this stupid grudge she was holding about Johnny and they could just be *friends* again, simple as that.

"You have to feel it," Liss pressed.

"It's been a long time," Dan faltered. "But yeah, something feels right here. Like . . . things coming together."

"Exactly," Liss said. "I *knew* you'd feel it. This stuff comes so easy to you, but it took me literally months to find this spot."

Dan glared at her. "I learned all this from scratch, same as you did."

"That's not what I meant! I've just always had to work harder at magic than you, that's all. I'm trying to say something nice."

"About who?" Dan asked. "You always have to be the best at everything."

"I do *not*," Liss said, although it was definitely true that she did. She had a wild drive in her that kept her up at night, that curdled her stomach in fear of failure. "It doesn't matter which of us is better"— another lie—"*I'm* the one who put in the work for all those months while you sat on your ass and felt sorry for yourself. So I don't care if you're better or not. *You weren't there.*"

"You never asked for my help," Dan protested.

"Yes, I did. The other night. It went super great. Anyway, why would I have asked when you would rather pretend none of this ever happened than talk to me?"

Dan opened her mouth, then closed it again. Her arms were folded over her chest. Was she going to cry? That would be extremely Dan of her: Dan was additionally lucky that she'd grown up without learning that crying left you open to attack.

But to Liss's surprise, Dan hardened herself and said, "I'm here now. Let's get this over with."

Liss shrugged the backpack off. "Since you've worked so hard, can you still draw a mercuriad, or do I need to show you how?"

Dan tied her long hair back. "Where do you want it?"

It was not at all gratifying that Dan completely did not need help marking the circular symbol that would confine the spell into the mud, and actually did a surprisingly efficient job of clearing gulch-y debris from the vicinity of their work. That had never occurred to Liss but was stupid obvious once Dan pointed out that natural material like old leaves and rocks could cause interference.

"Especially if we're going down," Dan added.

"Dark. I know you're not sold on this yet, but jeez."

"I mean the direction of the spell." Dan eyed the ground beneath their feet. "You said Johnny's underground. So that's where the spell needs to project, yes?"

"Oh, right. Yes."

"That's probably why you got lucky with the gulch, too. We're practically underground already."

A smile spread across Liss's face. She hadn't thought of that either, and immediately it felt right—another tiny piece of the puzzle settling into place. She set the circular mirror down in the center of the symbol and poured a little water onto its surface. Dan stood across from her, watching with her brow furrowed. The mirror captured both of their faces, Liss's framed in light hair and Dan's in dark. Then they broke away and sank to their knees in the mud, facing each other with the mirror between them.

"How long has it been?" Liss asked.

Dan exhaled. "This is the first time, since Johnny."

Liss could feel how nervous Dan was. It was the kind of nervous that named an inseparable mess of excitement and fear over a thing that was probably good but could also be terrible.

"Too long," Liss said. "Let's do some magic."

Everything was perfect—exactly the same as last time, if not better, stronger, because Dan was there, but they still kneeled for what felt like hours, their hands buried in up to their wrists in mud, whispering the words of the spell from Liss's notebook over and over, each syllable synchronized. They kept their voices in time with each other with only the exchange of glances, kept each other focused when attention wandered with a jut of the chin, managed to convey that it was taking too long with the arch of an eyebrow, an eye roll, a quirk of the mouth—and not once did either of them stumble over the words.

It was perfect.

And it didn't work.

Eventually the spell began—a prickling sensation that ran up from the mud, into their hands, up their arms and over their skin.

But also: a staticky feeling that blossomed from the air and not from the ground at all, and grew into a bolder charge that made their baby hairs stand on end. Dan's eyes grew wide and focused on Liss as each wave of sensation passed over them, perfectly in time. A pressure against their bodies, like a very serious hug, the feeling you get when a plane takes off and your ears haven't popped, the heavy lead blanket they made you wear getting X-rays at the dentist. Goose bumps all over, all at once.

And then the feeling fissured and snapped and the water pooled in the mirror began to change.

Dan's breathing hitched, but she didn't lose the thread of the words. Her eyes darted to Liss's, and Liss popped her eyebrows in an answer that said, *See? Look what I managed to do without you?* even though she instantly knew it was different from what she'd seen before.

A black-brown substance like old blood was seeping into the water, but instead of mixing, the substances seemed to repel each other. The blackish stuff kept leaking in and out of view, and its energy felt feeble. Last time, the mirror had been obscured entirely, but now she could clearly still see her reflection. Worse, the feeling wasn't there, of someone on the other end of the line. Liss put extra force into her words and thought of Johnny. She had planned out what she would say if they connected again: *I'm coming for you, you'll be safe, I love you.*

Three truths—two truths and a guess.

But he never came.

Liss raised her eyes to Dan's and nodded, and in the same moment, they fell silent.

Liss wrenched her hands from the mud and pushed herself unsteadily to her feet. Her knees ached. She stumbled forward and braced herself on the bank of the gulch.

"Damn it," she growled as she shook gobs of mud from her hands. "Damn it, damn it, *damn it.*"

It should have worked. Everything was the same, or nearly the same and actually better, and worst of all Dan was here to see her look stupid, to see her fail. All that effort, again, for nothing—not even a glimpse of his face. Dan was half gone already, with that grudge she wouldn't give up. All of it was slipping away—Johnny, Dan, magic, everything.

All at once, Liss found herself back at the beginning of the search: alone and lost with her own stupid dark destroyer of a heart, which burned with the paradoxical truth that nothing would get better unless she *tried,* unless she gave her entire self to it, everything she had, and yet at the same time, that would never, ever be enough to make a difference.

Liss tried counting to four and back but her blood was pounding in her ears, her breath coming in short, quick bursts, and that familiar, burning pain was twisting through her guts. She had to get it together, she had to find some way to force herself forward and make another plan. But wouldn't it be better, somehow, to stay lost in this stupid muddy creek bed forever? To disappear completely—more completely than Johnny and Zephyr and Rickey—just vanished, just *gone.*

"Wow." Dan's voice was flat and inscrutable. *Wow* like that was a huge waste of time? *Wow* like you really fucked that up, Liss? *Wow* like if Johnny wasn't dead before, he sure is now?

Liss couldn't look at her. "I know. Sorry."

"For what? What I meant was—I forgot how it feels. All over your body like that. Like it's inside you or you're part of it or something. I don't know—like it's *really magic.*"

Liss turned back to Dan. Dan was stretching her legs, but she kept half an eye on the mirror. The water was water-colored again and dribbling off into the dirt, but Dan was watching it like it was actually maybe alive.

"It *is* magic, Dan. That's why it feels magical," Liss snipped without intending to be snippy.

But Dan looked back at her with this mischievous, private sliver of a grin. "Exactly."

And suddenly, in that moment, it was the two of them again. Liss and Dan. Who understood each other, who trusted each other when it felt like they had no one else on earth.

Liss allowed herself a small frown. "I was sure it would work. Everything was exactly the same."

"Maybe that's the problem?" Dan mused.

"What do you mean?"

Dan picked the mirror off the ground and tipped the water off into one of the holes left in the mud by her hands. "The auspices of birds change fast. The stars move a little every day. Maybe the perfect place is somewhere else now."

It passed for encouragement, and Liss couldn't tell if Dan really believed it or not.

She decided it might be okay not to care.

SEVEN

Alexa

Alexa had the distinct feeling that Dan had blown her off after school. She decided to do homework at the smoothie place anyway, even if Dan couldn't come, but once she got there she realized it was stupid to spend eight dollars to drink pureed fruit by herself. Instead, Alexa went home and tried to figure out what kind of information she needed from Kim or her dad for her FAFSA application. Of course, that did nothing to make her feel better, because it involved two volatile compounds—money and her parents—that when combined in her presence became explosive.

When Lorelei came home, she asked if Alexa was bummed about something. Alexa blamed it all on FAFSA, and Lorelei promised she'd talk to Kim about money, if that's what was needed.

"You don't need to do that," Alexa answered quickly. "Thanks for offering, I mean."

"Not a problem. I'm not scared of your mom."

"Neither am I." Alexa forced a smile. "It's better if I handle it, that's all."

Lorelei waited a beat for Alexa to change her mind. They'd talked about how she didn't have to do everything herself now, because Lorelei was her ally, but sometimes that didn't make it any easier to accept her help. "Okay. You let me know if you need backup?"

"Definitely," Alexa agreed, even though she knew Kim would never stand for Lorelei's interfering in financial matters. Still, it made her feel a little better that Lorelei had volunteered.

After dinner, the two of them and Domino settled onto the couch to watch a movie on Lorelei's laptop. Lorelei insisted Domino loved action movies as an excuse for always picking them, but Alexa couldn't focus on saving the world right now: her mind kept running to Dan. Alexa knew she was being ridiculous. Dan wasn't required to hang out with her, but it wasn't impossible that she had done something to annoy or upset Dan either.

Alexa frowned at the screen.

It was probably nothing.

But if it was nothing, then why did she still feel this way?

Just then, Domino's ears pricked up and he darted to the windowsill. A few seconds later, headlights shone into the living room and car tires crunched on the gravel outside. Lorelei went to the front window and pulled back the curtain, enough for a glimpse of the yard. "Seriously?" she said under her breath.

Alexa sat up. "What is it?"

"Stay inside." Domino's hackles were raised, and his tail switched like he'd scratch the eyes out of the first person across his path. "You too," Lorelei added, to the cat.

Lorelei slipped out the door before whoever it was had a chance to knock, and once she did, Alexa crept to the window. They never had visitors, save for Dan and their landlord. The plan to infiltrate Black Grass meant Lorelei hadn't been able to make many friends in North Coast, outside the few parents she'd met at Alexa's school and Graciela. They certainly never had visitors that made Lorelei nervous.

Bathed in the car headlights, Lorelei clasped her hands in front of her chest as if she were praying. Alexa couldn't see her face. "What an honor! I wish I had known you were coming. I've been spending so much time at the Center that my house is a mess. Can we talk out here?"

Alexa recognized him from the brochure. Dressed in a polar fleece vest over white linen, his Cool TV Dad hair hanging shaggy around his face, Keith smiled in a way that reminded Alexa of how snakes always looked like they were smiling.

"My Seeker Lorelei." Keith reached out and stroked the back of his hand down her cheek. Alexa grimaced. Maybe it was the bad lighting, but it looked like there was a grayish tinge to his skin. "My heart is full of love for you."

"As mine is for you, my Guide."

"It's due to that love for you that I'm here. I'm worried for your progress. Your advancing has stalled."

"I feel it too. I tried to hide it, because I was ashamed." Lorelei's voice was meek.

"You cannot hide any part of yourself from me, Lorelei. You understand that? Lying disrupts our synergy. When one of us is not advancing toward synergy, none of us are advancing toward synergy. Building a better world takes bold action by every member of our community." Keith ran his tongue over his teeth. "We are nearly at an inflection point. Soon, I'll guide you to speak to our Lord directly, but he can only reach those who really embrace the path of advancement. It's hurtful to me that you might not receive the Lord's gifts."

"I never meant to be hurtful," Lorelei pleaded. "I want to reach the synergy with you. This just demonstrates how badly I need your guidance."

Watching from behind a curtain, Alexa's body was tense and her glasses were slipping down her nose. What even was a *synergy*? Was the Lord some kind of a Christian thing? Lorelei talked a lot about Black Grass, but she'd never mentioned any of this.

The corners of Keith's eyes wrinkled in a way that made him look charitable and caring. "Commit to optimizing yourself. It's time that you joined us, full time, at Black Grass."

"There must be another way. I have told you how deeply I desire to live at Black Grass with my fellow seekers, but I'm legally required to take care of my niece."

Alexa shoved her glasses back up her nose. She needed to stop forgetting that her situation with Lorelei, as good as it might be, was never meant to be permanent. Once she turned eighteen, she wouldn't need a guardian, and although Lorelei never said she planned to wash her hands of Alexa, Alexa couldn't reasonably expect Lorelei to stick by her forever—even though she'd imagined coming home from college for the holidays to the little Dogtown cottage.

Keith placed his hands on Lorelei's shoulders and gazed unblinkingly into her eyes. "This is a pressureful situation for you. But the world is a tangled knot. How do we untangle it?"

"With the clarity to see our deepest energies," Lorelei answered automatically.

Keith nodded. "Remember, the Lord has promised us a better world is coming. He needs you to work harder. Prove you can advance."

Alexa watched, aghast, as Lorelei sank to her knees and bowed her head before Keith. "I will, I promise."

Keith folded his hands over his heart. "I pray the Lord hears you, Seeker Lorelei."

Once Keith's car pulled away, Lorelei locked the door, then peered out the window, twisting the charm on her necklace.

"I'm sorry, Alexa. He wasn't supposed to come down here."

Domino rubbed his jowls protectively against her ankles until Lorelei said, "That's enough," and he stopped.

"Does he really believe all that, about making the world a better place?"

"Unfortunately, I think he does." Lorelei looked out the window a final time and neatened the curtains.

"What's unfortunate about that? Isn't it a good thing?"

"Trying to fix something you don't understand doesn't usually end well. You know what?" Lorelei turned to Alexa. "I think we deserve ice cream after that. Let's go to Crunchies."

"Crunchies is all the way in Gratton. It's kind of late for that?"

"I know." Lorelei winked at her, which didn't feel entirely appropriate. "But I'm in the mood."

Alexa wasn't. She wanted to ask why Keith had come to their house, and whether Alexa was really the only thing stopping Lorelei from moving up to Black Grass like she needed to. She wanted to ask what Lorelei thought would happen when Alexa turned eighteen. But it made her sad to think that she only had a few months left in this cozy little house, so Alexa reached for her cardigan.

"Watch over the house while we're gone, Domino!" Lorelei said as she locked the door.

On the drive to Gratton, Lorelei played her favorite Fleetwood Mac album. She sang along to every song, and when she wasn't singing, she was asking Alexa questions about school and college apps and Dan and whether they were going to the Winter Formal (they were not). She kept it up until they got to the counter at Crunchies.

Lorelei dropped her sample spoon in the little trash can on the counter and said, "I just remembered, while we're out here, I need to check something with the property management company—I'll just drop by and see if Swann is there. Order me a toffee almond fudge cone?" She passed Alexa a ten-dollar bill.

"It's like nine o'clock. Aren't they closed?"

"Swann literally never sleeps, and her office is in Fault Line Tattoo. It's next door. I'll be right back."

Alexa waited in Crunchies as the only employee—probably a kid from North Coast High—wiped down the counters and put lids on the ice cream tubs. Her ice cream was long gone, and Alexa could tell he was about to ask her to leave when Lorelei breezed back in.

"Sorry!" she chirped. "Took a second longer than I thought."

"Is something wrong?" Alexa held out Lorelei's mostly melted cone. She'd had to stick it in a cup.

Lorelei shoved a drippy spoonful into her mouth. "Now that I've got ice cream there isn't!"

Alexa wasn't sure she believed her.

FRIDAY, DECEMBER 12, SENIOR YEAR

Dan

Friday at sundown, North Coasters congregated in the parking lot of the Taubmann Nature Conservancy, a mile north of Marlena. It was two days since Zephyr's disappearance, and a poster-size version of her senior yearbook portrait stood next to a podium with a microphone and two TV cameras.

Someone handed Dan an unlit candle and a paper cup with a hole punched through the bottom to catch the falling wax. Half of North Coast must have been there: virtually the entire populations of Marlena and Dogtown, every little town's mayor, the teachers from North Coast and St. Ignatius, the volunteer fire brigade, even Mad Mags mumbling to herself as she wandered through the crowd. To her horror, Dan spotted her parents talking to their friends from Dogtown Solstice Parade Committee and gave them a wide berth.

Dan had rarely seen Zephyr since high school started. Zephyr had enrolled at St. Ignatius instead of North Coast, but she had gone to the tiny Dogtown-Marlena School, same as Dan and Liss and every other local kid. The school had fewer than one hundred kids, spread between kindergarten and eighth grade. She and Zephyr weren't friends anymore, but that didn't mean Dan didn't know her. Dan would have been at the vigil even if Liss hadn't insisted that the circumstances of Zephyr's disappearance felt a little too familiar.

Dan scanned the parking lot for Liss. There were several groups of girls wearing ultra-down or polar fleece jackets over St. Ignatius's uniform of pleated skirts and sailor shirts with little scarves as ties. A few were wearing jackets from St. Ignatius's softball team; Zephyr had been the captain. Within each group, the girls were parceled into pairs: best friends with arms slung around each other, heads resting on shoulders, holding hands with fingers laced together tight, so they wouldn't be the next girl lost. Dan bristled. Like the girls had been assigned a pair and in pairs they would survive this terrible thing, with both girls intact and perfect and happy on the other side. But there were always girls left alone, asking why her friend let go first, hating everything, most of all herself, and still wondering if she should have held on tighter.

Dan found Liss on the far side of the parking lot. She was nestled into a group of girls, but Dan could tell immediately by the way Liss held herself—arms folded awkwardly over her chest, phone clutched in her right hand, and on her left, fingers counting up to four and back—that they weren't really her friends. They were what she had instead, girls to stand with at an event like this where it would be weird to be alone.

As Dan watched, the girls bunched together to pose for a few frowny-faced selfies (the vigil had its own hashtag), and Liss joined in, trying to play along with the way the other girls' foreheads crinkled up with worry.

What did these girls see when they looked at Liss? A pretty girl, a smart girl, who maybe was a little strange because she locked her car too many times and fiddled with her fingers. They didn't see how being a pretty girl was as much a compulsion as it was a stroke of genetic luck, that what was half the time intelligence was the other half a brain that would never just *shut up*, and that her skin crawled if she tried to lock the car just once.

They didn't know her at all, not the way Dan did.

Liss spotted Dan and untangled herself from the St. Ignatius girls. She met Dan at the hot beverages station that someone had set up in the bed of a pickup truck.

"Can you believe all this?" Liss huffed as Dan served herself a cup of hot chocolate.

"What are you talking about?"

"Everyone's so upset. Even the local news is here, and they only come out to Marlena if it's Fourth of July or there's some kind of apocalyptic storm."

"Oh, that . . . Yeah, I can believe it." Dan plopped marshmallows into her drink. "A girl's missing, Liss. People care."

Liss was hard-eyed, surveying the crowd. "They didn't when it was Johnny."

"Johnny's not a girl. Zephyr's pretty, white, and her family's rich."

"Johnny's mother's a dentist."

"You know what I mean. They're not rich like the Finnemores. And he's Chinese."

Liss glared at her. "What difference does that make?"

Dan wondered if that possibility had ever crossed Liss's mind before: that Johnny's case hadn't gotten more attention because of anything she'd done, but because of things that were beyond her—and his—control. But Dan didn't have the energy to explain to Liss why the world cared more about white girls than anyone else, including brown girls like Dan. She shifted topics. "They don't think she ran away. She left her phone."

It was this particular detail—the leaving of the phone on the driver's seat—that disturbed people the most. It was cited as the top piece of evidence that Zephyr hadn't simply gone, but had been taken against her will, because obviously even if she was going to leave behind her whole life, she would never willingly have left behind her phone. For a teenage girl to physically exist in the world separate from her phone—it was hard to stomach.

There was other evidence against the runaway theory. Zephyr hadn't taken anything from her room, and obviously she had left her car, which Dan thought would be a lot more useful to a runaway than a phone. It couldn't be a Romeo and Juliet thing, because her boyfriend, Brodie, had no idea where she was. He was in attendance at the vigil and was dramatically grief-stricken. In the short time Dan had been there, before any of the speakers had addressed them or they'd sung any of the songs they'd received the photocopied words to, he'd wept openly twice. There were other darryls there to comfort him with bear hugs as he cried: Chas, who was always trying to get his white-boy dreadlocks to take; Rodrigo, who was born in a cabin in the woods and didn't get a birth certificate until he was five; and a red-haired girl-darryl, Willow, who manned the coffee cart that was Marlena's only source of caffeine.

Now, Willow was telling a teacher from St. Ignatius—and anyone else who would listen—about how crazy it was that she'd sold Zephyr coffee every morning and how that made Zephyr like a sister. Willow had been the one who'd introduced Zephyr to Brodie in the first place. "She wouldn't just *run away* and leave him behind," Willow said again.

Liss frowned and muttered to Dan, "Johnny left *his* girlfriend behind. And his phone. That didn't stop everyone from saying he was a runaway."

"We didn't want them asking questions, remember?" Dan said under her breath.

"Still would have been nice if they'd tried a little harder."

Dan wondered who Liss was angry for—Johnny or herself? Liss would have loved to be up there, forcing a tear or two out in front of a crowd, finding out how she looked on TV when the segment aired on the news at eleven.

Liss finished her surveillance of the crowd and turned to Dan. "That one little thing notwithstanding, the similarities are stupid obvious, right?"

"Not really," Dan protested. Liss had sent her approximately ten thousand text messages outlining her theory in the last two days, so Dan had her rebuttal ready. "Yes, they found Zephyr's car by the side of the road with nothing missing or stolen, which is the same way they found Johnny's, but the highway patrol finds like, hundreds of abandoned cars a year out here. That's point one. Point two, there isn't a right-angle crossroad on Highway 1 for miles near where her car was parked. Three, it wasn't the last day of the month. Four, they didn't find any candles or salt or anything like that."

"*That we know of.* And they didn't find that in Johnny's car either, remember? Because we took it all with us."

"So who was she doing the spell with? You think the softball team is some kind of coven now?"

Liss briefly returned her attention back to the pack of girls she'd left. "No. I've been trying to figure out if any of the other girls have anything magical going on, but they're all very . . . regular."

"And five, everyone agrees she was going to meet her boyfriend," Dan said. "You think she pulled over to try a spell real quick in the middle of road, all by herself?"

"You're right," Liss said.

"I am?"

"She could have done it with the darryls. Willow's a crystal hunter, and you never know about people like that."

"Which tells us what, exactly? She's tapped into teenager-kidnapping evil?"

Liss considered this a lot more seriously than Dan had intended it, then raised an eyebrow at her. "I think we should follow them. See where they go after this thing is over."

"We can't *follow* them. What are we even looking for?"

"Anything out of the ordinary. You said your research on Kasyan didn't turn up anything more than mine. We need any lead we can get. And you should stay at my place tonight, and we can ask the Black Book."

"I told Alexa we'd hang out later."

"Well, gosh, Dan, I guess you'll have to think of an excuse to ditch her." Liss's blue eyes were steely. "Alexa can survive one night without you."

"I'm not going to lie to Alexa for you."

Liss cocked a knowing eyebrow at Dan. "Whatever." Then she fished a tissue out of the pocket of her St. Ignatius polar fleece and turned toward the podium. "The speeches are about to begin. Keep an eye out for anything suspicious."

Alexa

The sun was setting. It would probably be an hour or two until Lorelei got home, which meant it was the perfect time to work on *The Quest of the Axials*, which is what she had decided to name her story about a girl warrior-gang after she realized they all carried enchanted battle-axes. But even though she had the map she'd drawn of Flintowerland and her notebook and her favorite pen and her cup of tea, she couldn't concentrate. Dan was supposed to text her to make plans to meet up after the vigil thing, but it was getting late and she still hadn't.

Dan had been weird again at school that day. Or maybe she wasn't being weird at all and Alexa was just paranoid. Well, she was definitely being paranoid. Every time she checked her phone and Dan hadn't texted her, she practically choked on the certainty that Dan was never going to text her again. Dan had probably decided that she was over Alexa, and maybe hadn't even really liked her in the first place anyway.

It sounded crazy, but Dan was only human, and most humans couldn't be trusted.

Alexa took off her glasses and rubbed her eyes.

Out the window, the sun had sunk into the Pacific, and darkness was hemming in the house on all sides—the kind of darkness that existed nowhere in LA, and not even out in the desert in Arizona, where tree cover was hard to come by.

Then Domino, who was sitting on the windowsill as usual waiting for Lorelei to return, jumped to the ground, his hackles raised, and a hiss crackled through the room.

"Dude," Alexa said. "Chill."

Domino did not chill.

Instead, he darted over to Alexa and began skulking back and forth in front of her, his eyes on the front door and his tail switching.

Alexa could hear a car was coming, and glanced out the window. Headlights.

"That's her, you can relax," she said to the cat, and reached out to scratch him behind the ears. She snatched her hand back when he hissed at her.

"Dumb cat," Alexa whispered. "Never liked me."

The ruff of Domino's neck bristled into a kind of mane as the headlights got closer. The car turned into their driveway.

And drove directly into the house.

Thank god for the porch, Alexa was thinking. Of all things, she was thinking thank god for the porch so that the car had hit that, even clearing the columns that supported the porch's roof, and only damaging the railing, because this meant that she hadn't driven into the living room—into the room Alexa had just been sitting in, blanket-wrapped and cozy on the couch. It also meant the landlord was less likely to kill them and that Lorelei was probably fine.

She was probably fine.

The car's nose was wedged into the side of the wooden steps onto the porch, but Alexa could tell Lorelei had managed to turn the engine off. It was making that *tssk tssk tssk* the Subaru made when it was cooling down. The headlights were still on, casting a too-bright light that amplified the darkness around them. Alexa couldn't see into the car, but Lorelei still hadn't gotten out.

She was probably fine, she wasn't even going fast enough for the airbag to go off, Alexa told herself as she ran to the driver's side door. Ignoring the fact that she felt it in the tingling in her fingers, the bristling at the back of her neck: something wasn't right.

"Lorelei," Alexa said—she deliberately kept her voice even and low—as she opened the door. "Are you okay?"

Lorelei was slumped over the steering wheel, her arm slung across the top and her forehead resting on it. Her long hair wasn't tied back, and hung into her face, some stuck in her mouth. The other arm hung limply at her side, but she was clearly breathing, sucking in quick, rattling breaths.

Alexa switched from asking to telling without waiting for Lorelei to answer her question. "You're okay, you're okay," she cooed, as she took Lorelei by the shoulders and gently leaned her back onto the seat. "It's probably just a broken nose. It hurts a lot, but you're okay."

But there was no blood, not anywhere—at least not that Alexa could see in the car's weak overhead light. There was something shuddery, twitchy about Lorelei, as if she was flinching every time Alexa touched her, and even when she didn't. "Did you hit your head? We should go to the hospital."

At this suggestion, Lorelei seemed to shiver. She gripped Alexa's arm, balling the sleeve of her sweater in her fist. "No hospital. Not—not my head."

Then Alexa saw it. The skin on the back of Lorelei's hand where it gripped her sweater was a spiderweb of black. It started at her fingertips, her nails rimmed in something dark, then crawled down the veins between her knuckles, the thin capillaries across the back of her palm, and up into her forearm.

Lorelei hadn't been hurt in the accident.

"Inside," Lorelei heaved. "Get me inside."

She could barely walk, her joints seemed too loose to hold her up, her limbs clacking against each other, and Alexa practically had to carry her up the porch stairs. Inside, Domino was hysterical, running circles around them with his ears back flat, as Alexa half dragged Lorelei into her bedroom.

Lorelei collapsed onto the bed like a marionette with its strings cut.

"You're okay, you're okay," Alexa repeated. Could Lorelei even hear her? Her eyes were open but it was more like she'd forgotten to close them than she was using them to see. She was still breathing and she was still twitching, the way she had been in the car, and if anything it was worse, coming in waves of full-body spasms. She almost kicked Alexa in the head as she pulled off her shoes and socks.

Alexa gasped, a sock dangling from one hand. The black was creeping from Lorelei's toes into her foot, over the knob of her ankle and up into her leg. But Alexa would not let herself panic. Constitutionally, she wasn't a panicker. She'd dealt with adults doing all kinds of irresponsible things—Kim had called her drunk and hysterical from bars, had once gone on a week-long cruise and left her alone in the house with a few boxes of powdered mac and cheese and forty bucks, had brought home boyfriends who punched holes in the walls to make a point. Alexa kept it together. Alexa solved problems. She had learned not to call the cops or paramedics or *anyone* unless someone told you to, which they never did.

But this? Was this just another crazy irresponsible thing adults did?

Lorelei's spasms were getting worse, her spine arching concave then convex and her legs pedaling into the bedclothes. Alexa swore she could see the black stuff spreading up Lorelei's forearms, finding bigger, thicker veins that would carry it into her chest—her heart, her lungs, her brain. Even the air around Lorelei had gone strange—stinging and staticky and charged.

"What should I do? What am I supposed to do?"

Lorelei's hand twisted painfully into a claw to beckon her, and

Alexa went to her side. The blackness was seeping into the skin around her lips and tongue, making her mouth inky.

"Everything's fine," Alexa whispered, but she knew her voice sounded small and shaky and terrified. "You're going to be okay."

"No," Lorelei managed through clenched teeth as another tremor passed through her. Her eyes rolled back so far Alexa could see the spindles of black against the whites.

Maybe she should have called someone—maybe she should now. Could an ambulance even get here in time if she did?

"You don't need to talk. You're okay," Alexa said.

The tendons of Lorelei's neck strained as she struggled to keep her eyes on Alexa. She put a hand to her throat—Alexa's eyes went wide at the swollen blackness of Lorelei's fingers. They were bloated, the joints and knuckles almost indistinguishable. Her fingers were searching for the necklace she always wore, with a charm of an evil eye, but she could barely bend them. Still, when she found the charm, a sense of calm seemed to settle over her, or maybe the spasms were passing, Alexa didn't know. Her skin—all the skin that Alexa could see, at least—was riven with black lines. They fell across her cheeks and forehead, her chest and arms, but it still seemed to be spreading.

Another spasm rolled through Lorelei's corrupted body. She strained against herself, and the hand she'd woven under her necklace snapped the chain. She pulled it free and pressed it into Alexa's hand. The charm was hot against Alexa's skin. It smelled acrid, like burning hair, and as Lorelei pressed it to her, the energy seemed to be draining from her even further.

"I love you," Lorelei said in a way that set free all the panic Alexa had been keeping at bay, because that could not be the last thing Lorelei said, Lorelei could not be dying, just because she wasn't moving anymore, just because her eyes were rolling back without the lids closing and her limbs were all rigid and dark and Alexa wasn't sure if she was breathing at all—she could not be dying, not like this. Tears rolled down Alexa's cheeks as she grabbed tight to Lorelei's mangled hands, the chain of the necklace laced between them.

"No, no—Lorelei, can you hear me? You're going to be okay."

A slow hiss of air was coming from her now, the last air leaving her lungs, and something imploded in Alexa.

A hysterical, furious certainty caught like the flashover of a fire and charged through her. *Lorelei could not die.* Lorelei was too good, had done too much for Alexa when she had no good reason to help her at all, and Alexa loved her more fiercely than she'd ever loved anyone. It was a debt Alexa could never repay, but it meant the world owed her. It meant at least that Lorelei deserved her life, which meant she had to live.

"Don't go, don't leave me." Alexa wasn't sure if she whispered or screamed, but it felt like a prayer. The air was snapping and hissing around her. "You can't die—you can't, Lorelei, please!"

It was senseless and she knew it and she let herself feel sure of it anyway. Death was a fact, not a matter of belief or desire, and it didn't care anything for what she believed. But at the same time, that certainty was the same thing as loving Lorelei, and Alexa knew from all the novels she'd read that love wasn't the kind of fire that could be blown out, just like that.

But Lorelei wasn't breathing anymore, not even in that thin hissy way. She wasn't moving. Her muscles had frozen in a contorted pose, as if she'd been running for something and gotten stuck midstride, but any minute she might move again.

Alexa's tears—she thought they were her tears—darkened Lorelei's blue sheets.

"Don't leave me like this," she whispered. Alexa closed her eyes, her hands still laced with Lorelei's, and her tears not slowing at all. "Don't be dead."

At first, Alexa thought she was imagining it, but the staticky air seemed to tighten and shift around them, picking up into a breeze, then a real wind, blowing papers from Lorelei's bedside table and whipping her hair against her face. From the other room, the front door slammed against its frame—and still, Alexa couldn't let go of Lorelei's hands.

Just as suddenly, the air stilled.

Lorelei shuddered out a breath. Then another.

And another.

EIGHT

Liss

D*an checked her phone for* the twenty-five-millionth time, which Liss had already told her to stop doing because a really good way to be able to see absolutely nothing at night was to shine a bright light directly in your own face. Dan didn't seem to care.

Obviously Dan was waiting for a text from Alexa, because she wore the same rag-doll look whenever that happened, which was pretty ridiculous considering that it wasn't like Alexa was her boyfriend or anything. At Liss's suggestion, Dan had told Alexa that she was feeling down after Zephyr's thing and wanted to chill at home. Dan had said she doubted Alexa would be satisfied at that, but it looked like Liss had been right after all.

They were sitting on a bluff overlooking the gloomy Pacific. A few feet from their position, the dry, blond grass gave way to a steep, sandy slope that two hundred feet below opened out into a locals-only beach in Dogtown.

They'd tailed the darryls in the Range Rover after the vigil broke up. It had not panned out as Liss had hoped, for one because Dogtown Beach wasn't exactly a macabre witches' lair and didn't point to anything in particular about Zephyr's location. For two, the rolling of the waves made it virtually impossible to follow the darryls' conversation, which was being held around a campfire down below at the beach. For three, she and Dan had been crouching in the grass for nearly forty-five minutes, and all the darryls had done was display pretty poor fire-starting skills and smoke several bowls of weed. Willow had just left the three dude-darryls to spray-paint a tribute to Zephyr on the retaining wall along the beach.

"We have to go down there," Liss said. "I can't hear anything from up here, so unless they actually start casting or something this is a total waste of time."

"Go down there and then do what? Ask if they accidentally sacrificed Zephyr to Kasyan and spotted Johnny while they were at it?"

Liss took a moment before she answered to divert the current of anger Dan's words had released. She kept her voice even. "Johnny's alive, so Zephyr might be too. I'm not out here trying to find a dead body."

"Yeah, our luck's not that good," Dan said.

Liss stood and brushed the burrs from her skirt. "I'll go down there on my own if you don't want to come."

It wasn't too dark to see the bitterness in Dan's eyes.

Liss's least favorite thing about St. Ignatius was not the long commute or the mandatory weekly mass, but the stupid skirts they had to wear—no leggings or sweatpants underneath, white or navy tights allowed but discouraged—which left your legs absolutely freezing and meant you had to shave basically every day. It was one thing to prohibit any expression of individuality, but did they have to be so freaking cold at the same time? Still, Liss forced herself to take off her polar fleece and leave it in the car.

Liss picked her way down the unlit steps to the beach. Dan as usual followed her a few paces behind. The fog was thin enough that the half circle of a moon was actually visible in the sky, and its faint blue glow made the sand look like rippling alien terrain. Smoke from the darryls' fire blew toward them from down the beach.

Dan jumped off the last stair onto the sand. "What exactly is your plan?"

Reflexively, Liss rolled her eyes, although her back was to Dan. "There are three dudes down there who've been getting high, and at least one of them has a documented interest in high school girls."

"Oh, *seriously*?"

Liss held herself a little straighter. "Yes, seriously. We're going to flirt."

Dan had always been shit at flirting, as if being in the presence of a boy made her forget all normal modes of human communication. No amount of Liss's coaching had ever corrected it.

"*Gross*," Dan whined. "Aren't they like, twice our age? And they never shower!"

"As if I don't think flirting with the darryls is gross?" Liss hissed under her breath. "It doesn't matter! If we're going to get Johnny back, we have to use every advantage we have."

Liss pulled up her knee socks and smoothed the pleats of her skirt. She didn't want to see the look of disgust on Dan's face. Liss already had to deal with her dad's coworkers making comments about how grown up she was looking when she saw them at wine-soaked dinners, with men in Gratton complimenting her body as she walked to her car, with creepy strangers on Instagram who you couldn't block before they messaged you, and all the other shit older men threw at a teenage girl. If you couldn't escape it, you might as well put it to good use, even if doing that felt gross and wrong.

"No, we don't." Dan's arms were crossed. She looked like she'd rather crawl in a hole and die. "If you don't want to flirt with them, we can just . . . not do it."

Liss felt the blood rush to her cheeks. That was something else

Dan didn't understand—and Liss didn't either. Sometimes she liked that kind of attention, even if at the same time there was something disgusting about it; sometimes she worried she liked it too much. The way men looked at her made her feel like she wasn't a person at all and only a body, like she was actually as worthless as she sometimes felt, but they didn't mind. Sometimes she wanted that feeling so badly it scared her, even though at the same time she despised it.

Liss flipped her blond hair back. She ignored Dan's suggestion. "Do your best, okay? We'll get out of there as fast as we can. It'll be easy, I promise."

As Liss had predicted, it had not been hard to gain seats in the darryls' circle. She'd walked up to them half shivering in her St. Ignatius uniform (that part hadn't been an act), Dan trailing her like a shadow, and told them they'd come from the vigil too. She sat beside Brodie on a driftwood log that served as a bench. He smelled like weed and sticky sweet clove cigarettes, and before long she was leaning against him, just a little. She could practically feel his eyes on her thigh where she'd let her skirt ride up. Part of her cringed at what she was doing—he was so old it was like trying to hit on one of the teachers from her high school—but it helped a little that he was the cutest of the darryls by a long shot, although that was a low bar. Dan sat across the fire, sharing a log with Scratch and Goober or whatever their names were. Willow was a few yards away, outlining an enormous butterfly in spray paint on the retaining wall. Every so often, when the waves fell quiet, Liss could hear her crying.

"It's so crazy," Liss said to Brodie. "What do you think happened to her?"

Brodie fixed his gaze in the distance and let out a long slow breath. She got the sense that he wanted her to watch him contemplating, so she did, pouting her lips a little, while she contemplated how stupid it was to wear a backward baseball cap after dark.

"It's hard to think about it, you know?" he finally said. "Zeph wouldn't run off like that, leaving her phone and everything, so I guess she had to get in someone's car or something. But who would do that, you know?" He adjusted his ball cap with both hands. "I didn't think things like this could happen out here. Girls getting snatched up and all that. Like, they even questioned *me*. It's crazy, you know?"

Liss pouted a little more dramatically, her eyes growing a little wider. "Yeah, I know what you mean." She did know what he meant, and it was hard to respect. So Brodie had come to the tough realization that North Coast wasn't some paradise where he could fuck a high school girl who was "so freaking gorgeous and amazing" without worrying about getting prosecuted for statutory rape or any of the other crimes he'd probably stumbled into. Well, life was like that, wasn't it?

"I just keep thinking I see her. Like, I'm not crazy, I just keep expecting her to show up. Honestly I almost thought you were her. You're wearing that same outfit she always had on."

"Our school uniform?"

"Yeah, you know? I'm checking my phone like she's gonna call me up. This is so much worse than getting dumped. Like I want to try to get her back, but I don't even know where she is. How fucked up is that? She could be with another dude and I wouldn't even know. You know?"

It really was a repulsive way to think about Zephyr, if she had actually been abducted, but Brodie was obviously high out of his mind. Liss looked over to Willow. She'd put the finishing touches on her butterfly and moved on to a large *Z*. Johnny's friends had painted the same wall after he'd disappeared—mostly references to the Golden State Warriors and video games and skating. Liss had come to see Johnny's mural, just once. She'd sat there in the sand, alone, and finally let herself consider, seriously, what she had done, whether their love could be trusted or if he was just under her spell. What if Dan was right, and all the hope and guilt and pain and work she'd put in didn't have to mean anything at all?

"Damn, Willow's still at it?" Brodie mumbled. "She's gonna have some wicked-colored snot tomorrow."

Liss chose to ignore this. "It really is like the worst breakup ever. You keep expecting them to come back, somehow. You feel like you did something wrong and you might not be able to fix it." She leaned a little more of her weight against him. "My boyfriend went missing last year—Johnny Su."

"Shit, I'm sorry." Brodie slipped his arm around her. "You can't think like that. There's nothing you could have done. Whatever's out there—fate, god, all beliefs are cool—it's gonna do what it wants, and we're just here living in it. No control." He made a wave motion with his hand. "Like little boats out on the water."

Liss imagined herself adrift on the frigid Pacific, alone. She wasn't pretending to be sad anymore. "But if that's true . . . that sucks," Liss said in a small voice.

"That's why you gotta live for the moment, man," he agreed. "Make yourself happy."

With his arm around her, she was enveloped in the cloying smell of the cloves he was dragging on, the campfire smoke, his sweat. The heat of his body had stopped her from shivering enough that she could feel the solidity of his chest where she leaned against him.

He didn't know where Zephyr was.

She hadn't been this close to anyone since Johnny disappeared. It had been so long, and she had been so alone, and if the world was as cruel and careless as Brodie made it out to be, then didn't she deserve this?

It was like a compulsion, something in her pulled taut and tense, near to snapping, and if she didn't kiss him in exactly that moment, she might cry or starve or shatter, and he was the only one who could save her, even if he was the worst possible candidate for the job.

"I'm so lonely without him," she said, curling her body closer to his.

He looked down at her with a puppy-dog look. He already had what he wanted and he was only now realizing it. "You're really pretty," he said, almost to himself. Liss gave him an embarrassed little smile, a fragile, precious look of appreciation that made it seem that no one had ever told her that before, when in fact she'd been hearing it her whole life.

She let her eyes search his, her lips parted. It was her kiss-me-now face that let the guy think he was making the first move, and it had a demonstrated track record of success.

He did kiss her, his mouth dry and bitter from the weed and his skin cold. She let him push his tongue into her mouth and slide his hand over her bare thigh below the hem of her skirt but no higher. It was pathetic, but it resolved something inside her when he kissed her like that. It made her feel whole, special, less like a rattling bag of the broken pieces of a good person. He wanted her, and even if he only had her for these few minutes, he would think about her later, remember the time he got lucky enough to kiss a beautiful girl on the beach, and that made her want him even more. She slid her hand down his chest, across his stomach, and the muscles of his wiry frame hardened beneath her palm.

Dan called her name and Liss ignored it. Probably, Dan wanted to lecture her about how this was a really stupid and disgusting idea, but Dan wouldn't understand that Liss *needed* this. It seemed like Dan never did, not with Johnny or any other boy before him. And anyway, Dan could never appreciate that something might be a bad idea and you could decide to do it anyway—not everyone was so eager to run and hide from their own lives.

"Liss!" Dan said again. "Let's go."

"Christ, I thought you girls were here to party," one of the other darryls said, laughing.

"Don't touch me!" Dan yelped.

Now Liss broke away from Brodie. Dan was standing off to the side, away from the fire, as if she'd tried to get as far from Scratch and Goober as she could without actually leaving the beach. Her hair had come undone and was whipping around her face in long black tendrils, and she was clutching herself against the cold wind from the ocean. Her lips were pressed tightly together, her eyes round. Liss recognized the look: Dan was scared.

"What happened?" Liss asked. Brodie's fingers were still in her hair.

"You girls come down to the beach and smoke our weed, can you blame us for thinking you wanted to have a little fun? Brodie's getting his." Liss couldn't remember if this was Scratch or Goober talking.

"I didn't smoke any of your weed," Dan said coldly. "And it shouldn't matter if I had."

"Well, excuse me for thinking you were down," the darryl said.

"Liss, let's go," Dan pleaded.

"What the hell are you doing, Brodie?" Willow had gotten wind of the argument and marched back to the fire, spray paint can still in hand. She was glaring daggers at Brodie and Liss. "What are you going to tell Zephyr when they find her? You couldn't go three days without cheating on her!"

Brodie disentangled himself from Liss. The cold air filled the spaces where his body had been, and she shivered. "It's not like that," he told Willow. "I don't even know what happened. She was just *there*."

"Excuse me, what the fuck?" Liss stood and straightened her skirt and blouse. "I'm not some piece of trash you found lying around."

"Come on." Brodie blew her off. "You know what I mean. It's like Rodrigo said, you girls came to party, right?"

Liss's stomach was on fire, acid rising in her throat.

"Liss, let's go," Dan begged.

"Nah, girls, stay. Willow's mad because she thought Brodie and Zephyr were in love, and that's why Brodie didn't want to give it to her no more." This was the darryl who was not Rodrigo, who had nasty hair mats he was trying to pass off as dreadlocks.

"Yeah, I love her," Brodie said, but there was something in his voice that made Liss think he was still getting used to saying it out loud. "I definitely love Zephyr."

"Yeah man, you *love* high school girls," Rodrigo laughed. "Me too. Only they don't love me back." He made a kissy face at Dan.

Dan's mouth warped in disgust, but she ignored him. "I'm leaving, Liss. You can stay."

"Of course I'm not *staying*," Liss answered, and she and Dan left them on the beach: Brodie with his head in his hands, his two friends laughing their asses off, and Willow, stony-faced, repacking the bowl.

Back at the Range Rover, Liss pulled her polar fleece back on and cranked the heat. "So what happened? Dumb and Dumber didn't know anything, right?"

"You don't even care what they did?"

"Obviously I do, thus the question, what happened?"

"Honestly—" Dan began, then faltered. She began concentrating hard on her cuticles. "Those guys aren't doing any fucking magic," she finally said.

"That's exactly what I thought. Did you hear how Willow said 'when they find her'? So she obviously believes that the police *can* find her. Brodie was really broken up."

"Same with the other darryls. Everyone was really broken up. Just a bunch of really super sad people." Dan's voice was flat and cold.

"It doesn't totally disprove the theory, but I think we need to stay focused on Johnny. Zephyr is someone else's problem."

"Sounds great." Dan pulled up the hood of her sweatshirt. "Can you drive me back to my car now?"

"I thought you were going to spend the night." The familiar craving stirred in Liss's stomach. "What about the Book?"

"I just remembered, my mom is . . . having a thing. In the morning. So I have to go home."

So Dan was mad at her, which took the form of being very quiet. It wasn't fair. Liss had done what was necessary, Dan hadn't gotten actually hurt, and the whole thing was going to be a funny story someday. But Liss did as Dan asked and drove south so she could pick up her car from Taubmann.

As they passed the last house in Dogtown, Dan slumped low in her seat and looked away from her window for what would be the only time in the whole drive. There was only one thing she'd be avoiding, and Liss made sure to take a look.

All the lights were on at Alexa's house, and a car was parked right in the middle of the yard. Liss decided to be pleased with the fact that Dan was hiding. It meant she hadn't come clean to Alexa about any of this, which meant it was still their secret.

Which meant that even if Dan hated her, Dan was still hers.

NINE

Alexa

Somehow the night had passed, which Alexa filled with hours of crying, a bit of throwing up, and punching the wall once or twice, which really freaking hurt. When the dishwater dawn arrived, it felt like it might bring some kind of relief, but nothing had changed. Now it was almost twenty-four hours since the accident. Alexa was fairly certain she hadn't slept—unless she was asleep right now and this was a nightmare, although the chances of that felt slim. Every time she'd stepped out of the increasingly rank bedroom to use the bathroom or to try to force herself to eat something, she'd rushed back to Lorelei, the wings of panic beating in her chest, certain that she would have gone still and cold.

Well, stiller and colder than she already was. She wasn't *ice* cold, but cold enough that when Alexa touched her, she felt like a body, not a person. Cold like a window pane or the seat of her bike when she'd left it outside overnight. Like something that had never been and would never be again and definitely wasn't right now alive.

Now night was falling again, and the moment it began to turn dark outside, Alexa turned on every light in the house, then went back to Lorelei's bedside.

There, she kept only the dim bedside lamp lit. The feeble light made the blackish mottling of her skin less obvious. The wet breaths

Lorelei sucked in sounded like a soaked towel dropped on the floor, and Alexa gagged into her T-shirt.

At least she was still breathing.

It wasn't enough, but Alexa was thankful for it.

Domino hopped up on the pillow beside Lorelei. He leaned down, and Alexa could hear the roughness of his tongue against Lorelei's skin. When he raised his head, a dark patch remained on her cheek where he'd been licking.

"Jesus, that's disgusting," Alexa said, stifling another gag. But then Alexa could almost swear she saw Lorelei's eyelids flutter, heard the mucky sound of her breathing quicken, as if she'd somehow woken from sleep.

Domino glared at her.

"Okay, sorry," Alexa said.

All at once, she was overwhelmed with a memory: when Alexa first came to live in LA, she'd been terrified that she would say or do the wrong thing, she'd break whatever spell Lorelei was under and get sent back to Kim. She stammered out apology after apology, as if she were apologizing for her very existence, until Lorelei had sat her down and told her not to apologize for things that weren't her fault. On top of that, Lorelei had said that she loved having Alexa around and she'd rather celebrate that than have anyone feeling bad about it.

"I'm not sorry like that," Alexa whispered, then pulled Domino off the bed so she could check the affected areas.

The affected areas: hands, feet, arms, legs, left ear but not the right. The flesh gave off a greasy, sweet odor with strong undertones of sour rancidity that smelled straight-up *wrong*, like something you should be wearing a medical mask if exposed to. It was probably the way a zombie apocalypse smelled when it was just getting started, the kind of smell that could take over a world and annihilate it.

At least the blackness wasn't *spreading*, which, of all things, made Alexa feel a little better for not having called an ambulance. Any regular person would have called an ambulance right away, even if it couldn't have gotten there in time to make a difference. It made her ashamed to think of it, but Alexa had learned growing up if you called for an ambulance, the law wasn't far behind, and you didn't call the law unless you were ready for the consequences—the police poking around your house, your mother's boyfriend's rage, victim's advocates or child protective services checking in.

Who could she call now? It was too late for an ambulance. What was she supposed to tell her father, who she barely spoke to—that his sister had been cursed into a fairy-tale coma?

Alexa twisted the charm on Lorelei's evil eye necklace around her neck. She shouldn't call it a curse, although that's how she'd been thinking of it.

The way the room crackled with energy, the heat of the necklace that Lorelei gave to her literally blistering her skin, the wind that felt like it chased evil from the room, as if it were granting the wish she'd made to keep Lorelei alive.

But if that was a wish, it must have gotten stuck halfway, because Lorelei wasn't dead but what she was doing couldn't strictly be called living, either.

A curse, a wish—it sounded ridiculous but it felt right, which was almost weirder.

Domino rubbed his jowls against Alexa's ankles, his tail curled around her shin. In the two and a half years Alexa had lived with Lorelei, the cat had barely warmed to Alexa. He must have sensed that something was wrong.

That wasn't exactly hard to sense.

"I know, babe. I'm worried too," she said to the cat. "But she's going to get better. We need to give it a few days."

But even as she said it, tears were stinging her eyes and she felt her throat getting tight. But what if Lorelei didn't get better? She was still a minor, which meant they could send her back to Arizona if they found her in the middle of nowhere hiding a rotting human body in her house, although there were other places she might end up—like prison, because she felt certain that something she was doing was illegal.

She wouldn't let herself cry, not again. Alexa flung herself out of the chair and went to the kitchen to chug a glass of water. She needed to focus. She needed to keep it together.

She needed to remember to move Lorelei's car to someplace behind the house where it couldn't be seen, or one of many other seemingly endless and surprisingly banal concerns of this waking nightmare. How had Lorelei paid the electricity bill and the rent? How convincingly could Alexa forge her signature? Alexa needed to figure out how to check Lorelei's bank balance, what to say when the phone was for her, what to do if Black Grass called because she hadn't shown up.

At least Alexa was experienced in keeping up appearances while the adults in her life were unavailable for parenting or even regular adulting. Living with Kim had taught her that much: how to pretend everything was normal although your mother had decided she was "too good" to keep her job, then spent her last paycheck on vodka instead of groceries.

Alexa could manage to take care of herself when no one else would. The best way to get through was practical: you did what you had to do to protect yourself, and hopefully there was something left over so you could try to be a little bit happy.

With Lorelei, Alexa had never needed to worry about protecting herself.

Alexa could finally admit to herself that she'd been naïve enough to believe that North Coast and Lorelei could be her future. That she could have a normal life in this little house, a true place where she was safe and wanted and *home*.

Alexa straightened. She wasn't ready to lose all that. Lorelei could get well. Alexa just needed to keep it together, even if that seemed to require superhuman strength. She forced herself to address the pile of unopened mail on the counter, searching for anything that looked like a bill.

Domino *mrow*ed from his seat on the windowsill.

"You got your dinner," Alexa mumbled.

A red envelope slipped free and slid to the floor. The return address wasn't one she knew, but she could identify that handwriting anywhere, with the childish bubbles topping each *i*.

Suddenly, it was if the smell of decomposition vanished, and the stink of her mother's menthol cigarettes and cheap flavored vodka and blond hair dye filled the house instead. Alexa's teeth pressed closed so tightly her jaw ached as she grabbed the letter from where it had been wedged under a cabinet.

She nearly ripped it in two as she tore the envelope open. Inside was one of those glossy printed cards with hideous curlicue writing spelling out *Merry Christmas*—obviously they wouldn't have gone for the more diplomatic *Happy Holidays*. And there they were: Kim, smile slathered in pink lip gloss she was too old for; her husband, Todd, with an enormous cross tattooed on his forearm and his face leathery from the desert sun; and the twins, three years old now but with the same white hair and flat gazes. They were standing by a pool Alexa assumed was someone else's, all of them wearing tank tops in the bright sun. Todd's forehead was glistening under a Santa hat. Kim had said she never wanted a card like that with Alexa— they were expensive, and they didn't need to rub the whole single-mom thing in everyone's faces, especially not her boyfriends'. Her boyfriends shouldn't be thinking of her as a mother at all.

Kim certainly didn't. Or she hadn't, until the twins.

Alexa bit her lip to keep from screaming and flipped the card over to see the inscription to her and Lorelei.

There was nothing there. No special words for the daughter she hadn't seen in months, or for the ex-sister-in-law who'd finally taken Alexa off Kim's hands, like Kim had always wanted.

Now Alexa really did scream—an awkward, strangled howl of rage and heartbreak and the stupid, misguided hope that things could ever get better. The sound erupted from that buried part that held the feelings she wouldn't let herself have. It brought angry, hot tears with it—tears that slid right off the glossy surface of the Christmas card as if they'd never been there at all.

Domino meowed again, more forcefully this time.

"Oh, leave me alone!" Alexa cried.

Get out.

Alexa froze. There was a voice inside her head.

He's coming—get out and hide, now.

Domino switched his tail, his green eyes wide as saucers. His hackles bristled into a ruff, and suddenly Alexa understood.

She grabbed her bag and ran for the back door. Domino darted through before the screen banged closed, and they both hustled into the unlit overgrown brambles behind the house. It wasn't like in fairy tales; bushes weren't meant to be *walked through*. Dry branches tugged at her shirt and scraped her skin, but she pushed on. She filled herself with a kind of pleading—*hide me, let me in, hide me, please*—and finally she found herself in a space where the twigs were less dense, the gnarled branches describing a kind of clearing, deep in the bramble, that was exactly her size. Alexa dropped to her knees and watched the house. Her heart was beating all over her body, a fearful throbbing. Whatever she was doing was crazy, part of her argued, but that part shrank and shrank until it didn't matter at all what the voice of reason wanted to say—something was coming, she felt the warning in her bones.

The lights, hurry.

Inside the house, the lights were on—living room, kitchen. Should she go back in there to turn them off?

No, from here, just try.

And so she did—she imagined the lights snuffed out, gone into hiding like she was hiding in the bushes now. She warned the lights to hide, and as she did, it was as if some force was building in her, something dammed, like holding your breath so long until finally your cheeks hurt. Alexa pushed whatever it was out of her, with a final plea for the light to scatter *now*—

And the house fell dark. More than dark: cold. It looked and felt like a house that had been abandoned, the kind of place where you'd find molding newspapers on the stoop and a fridge full of rot.

Only a few seconds later, the car pulled into their driveway. Its headlights were off, which was kind of pointless since the gravel drive made a stealth arrival impossible. Alexa heard the car door slam, the creak of the porch stairs, a tentative knock.

"What about Lorelei?" she whispered breathlessly. "We left her."

Enough talking! Just think.

Beside her, Domino was a blacker spot in the darkness.

From the other side of the house, the sound of glass shattering, then the whine of the hinges on the front door. Through the kitchen window, Alexa could see the bluish beam of a flashlight scanning the living room and moving toward Lorelei's bedroom.

What does he want? she asked. *Will you look?*

She looked down for Domino, but he was already gone. She

spotted him a moment later, skulking toward the house looking for all the world like a hungry stray. The occasional thud came from inside the house, each sound making Alexa bite her lip a little harder, until she tasted blood and stopped herself.

It felt like an eternity passed before Alexa heard the car's engine start again. This time, the headlights came on: whoever it was had been convinced that no one was home. Still, she waited a few more long minutes after she heard the tires kicking up gravel on the driveway before she made her way out of the bramble and back to the house.

Throughout the house, the lights were flickering back on, but she rushed past the dark shape of Domino sitting on the kitchen counter to Lorelei's bedroom.

Her heart didn't stop racing, even once she was sure that Lorelei was fine—or if not fine, at least that nothing had happened to make her condition worse. Alexa dropped into a chair, head in her hands.

Domino padded into the room after her.

"It was Keith, wasn't it?" Alexa looked at Domino from behind her hands. His head twitched in assent. "If he already thinks she's dead, what else does he want from her?" Suddenly, Alexa's chest got tight as her breathing quickened. The curse, Lorelei's body, the cat—was she hallucinating? Was she losing her mind? "I'm talking to a cat. This isn't really happening, is it? This is—this can't be real."

For all those fantasy books, you have a low tolerance for the unusual, Domino sulked. *Before a panic attack distracts you, you may wish to have a look at the living room.*

Alexa forced herself to take a deep breath, then followed Domino into the living room.

Every book pulled down from the shelves, their covers splayed open and pages bent. The glass of picture frames cracked, the big painting that hung over the couch pulled down and the backing ripped off. The couch cushions strewn around the room, one of them with a deep slash vomiting its stuffing into the mess. Alexa choked when she saw Lorelei's beloved record collection, scattered across the floor, disks of shiny black slipping from their sleeves, scratched and shattered.

But the broad wooden table where she'd spent so many industrious hours sitting beside Lorelei, where Lorelei's precarious pile of papers had always threatened to landslide onto the floor, was bare. Lorelei's computer, the article drafts and notes, the details of her infiltration into Black Grass—all of it was gone.

TEN

Dan

In Spanish on Monday, they went around the room and each student explained what they'd done that weekend.

What *had* Dan done? Cried at a vigil for a missing girl, said no to drugs from nasty men, laid in bed for two whole days feeling miserable and listening to IronWeaks.

She still couldn't get Friday night to leave her: the way they kept repeating "you wanted to party," in a way that obviously encompassed a dozen things Dan didn't particularly associate with parties—less frosted sheet cake and more hungry hands. The disgusting feeling of Rodrigo leaning in to try to kiss her, the unwashed stink of him, the fear and anger singing in her blood as she broke away, and then a lingering shame that she'd gotten upset over something as simple as a kiss. And at the same time, a part of her brain that did not feel very childish kept suggesting what could have happened, but didn't— things that couldn't be walked away from as easily as a mistaken kiss. Her favorite sweatshirt still smelled like their campfire.

But the worst part—*one* of the worst parts—was Liss.

All Dan had wanted was to keep Liss from doing anything stupidly dangerous until she finally accepted that Johnny was gone for good. She'd done her best on Friday, following her to Dogtown Beach when they were practically driving past big neon signs that said BAD IDEA. But she'd done it anyway, so Liss wouldn't have to do it alone.

And what had she gotten but hurt in exchange?

Liss never even asked why Dan had wanted to leave the beach so badly that night, like she hadn't heard what Rodrigo said. Or maybe Liss didn't care.

For all Dan knew, making out with Brodie had been Liss's real goal since they'd seen him looking so tender-eyed at the vigil. It was exactly the kind of thing Liss couldn't let survive. As long as she lived and breathed, she needed the world to be about *her*.

They hadn't even really figured out if Zephyr went missing by magical means or something else. But Liss had decided that was "someone else's problem."

A guy three seats down from Dan started describing a movie he'd seen about zombie football players.

Another worst part was, Dan was pretty sure Alexa knew something was up. Dan hadn't been exactly honest about the fact that she was seeing Liss again. Actually, she hadn't told Alexa at all, had maybe even done what technically counted as lying to cancel their plans on Friday night. Alexa had never texted her back about that.

It was the first weekend they hadn't seen each other since September.

By Saturday night, Dan felt so bad, she'd given up on waiting for a text from Alexa before she cut a bright red line into her hip. It bled more than she'd expected and didn't make her feel better at all—actually it made her feel worse, because it was such an awful and stupid and pathetic thing to do, which on the other hand made it an appropriate thing for Dan to do to herself, but on the *other* other hand it was awful and stupid and pathetic that Dan could even think that way. Her thoughts went in circles until she came back to her anger at the darryls and at Liss, which got her upset all over again, because being angry at them was pointless and hard, because what could she ever do about it? But hating herself was easy, she was right there and she knew she deserved it, even if she couldn't exactly explain why.

So basically, that thought process took up all of Sunday.

The student next to Dan finished reporting the results of her soccer game.

The last worst part was that in spite of everything, Liss badgered her all weekend about the Black Book: they needed to ask it about Kasyan and Johnny, and they couldn't wait any longer. Dan knew that was true, but doing *anything,* even taking a shower, felt impossible, and most of all things involving Liss. She ignored the texts until Liss threatened to show up at Dan's house on Sunday night. Dan agreed to meet Liss in Marlena after school with the Black Book.

Today would be the end of it, Dan had decided. She would give the Black Book back to Liss, and she could do with it whatever she could manage on her own. Liss would get what she wanted and leave Dan alone to close the door on this part of her life: magic, Johnny, Liss. Dan had wanted to help Liss, but enough was enough.

"Daniela?" Ms. Alonso asked. "Cómo estuvo tu fin de semana?"

"Fine," Dan said, reflexively, in English.

Ms. Alonso clicked her tongue disapprovingly. "En español!"

"Lo siento. Fui a la . . . ceremonia . . . de Zephyr," she mumbled.

"De Zephyr Finnemore? Ah, eso es muy triste, no?" Ms. Alonso said, making an exaggerated frown.

Dan's eyes darted to the seat by the door that, last winter, was Johnny's, and that same awful fist of sadness tightened all over again. "Sí."

When the bell rang for lunch, Dan waited for Alexa in their usual spot in the cafeteria, but her stomach was in such a knot, she couldn't touch either the ginger-soy seitan and brown rice her mom had packed or the Pop-Tart she'd grabbed from her secret locker stash.

All morning, Dan had agonized over what to tell Alexa about the weekend when she saw her at lunch. She wanted to tell her how horrible Liss was and about the nasty darryls trying to kiss her and the weird performances of sadness she'd seen at Zephyr's vigil. Most of all she wanted to tell Alexa how she'd been nearly swallowed by blackness all weekend. Even though she was never entirely honest with Alexa about how bad she felt, talking around the edges of her sadness somehow made her feel better.

But she couldn't tell Alexa any of that because she'd lied to her about hanging out with Liss. That could be forgivable on its own, if it weren't for the even bigger problem, which was that Dan couldn't come clean about spending time with Liss without explaining *why*: magic, Johnny, all the horrible, stupid things she'd done.

She had to keep lying. Specifically, she was going to have to lie about seeing Liss that afternoon.

Dan was wondering if she could escape the cafeteria and eat lunch in her car, when Alexa walked up, dropped her backpack on the floor, and slumped into the chair.

"Oh, hey!" Dan chirped. "How's it going?"

Alexa folded her arms on the table and dropped her forehead onto them. "Perfect."

"Perfect?"

"Absolutely," Alexa said into the table.

"Cool. Same." Dan shoved a dry lump of seitan into her mouth. "But I had the most annoying weekend. You would not believe my mom."

Alexa picked her head up, and the words just started spilling out of Dan: "You know my college apps were basically done? Well, on Friday when I got home my mom decided she wanted to go over everything *again.*" Dan hoped Alexa wouldn't realize this sounded nothing like her mom. Graciela only ever nagged Dan about her apps by affirming she trusted Dan to be responsible about her future—a lot more than Dan herself did. Dan rambled on. "Honestly, she was just like, *Let's proofread everything again* and *Did you make sure all the recommendations were requested?* It took literally the whole weekend. She had to reset her password on the College Board website like eight times. And when we were finally done, she insisted on celebrating, so we had to drive like forty minutes to that Ayurvedic Indian place in Rancho Carrera for dinner. She made it into this whole *thing.*"

"A whole thing, huh?" Alexa's voice was flat as she picked at her sandwich. There were dark circles under her eyes. "It sounds kind of nice."

"Well, it just took all weekend, that's all." Dan recalled the actual Great College Application Review, which they had conducted over Thanksgiving. Truthfully, she had enjoyed it. Her parents told her how proud they were that she was applying to such good schools— although anyone could *apply*—and she'd imagined coming home during a break and telling them what she'd learned in Intro to Music Theory or Aesthetic Philosophy. "Have you talked to your mom about where you're applying, or just Lorelei?"

Alexa flinched, her PB&J halfway to her mouth. "My mom doesn't care about that kind of stuff."

"About college? Parents *love* caring about college."

Alexa set her sandwich down and pulled the sleeves of her cardigan over her hands. "Not mine."

Dan knew Alexa's family situation was sensitive; Alexa didn't like to talk about it, so Dan tried not to bring it up. The basics were that Alexa's dad checked out of the family early, her mom drank too much and moved Alexa all around Arizona before marrying some new guy, and then Alexa went to live with her dad's youngest sister, Lorelei. It was complicated and sad in a way Dan wasn't sure she understood. "Maybe if you tried to talk to her about it, she'd get excited. This is like a rite of passage thing for parents. They all geek out on it."

"*Not my mom*, okay, Dan?" Alexa was glaring at her so fiercely Dan nearly dropped her Pop-Tart. "Are you trying to rub my face in it?"

"I—no, absolutely not."

"My mom does not care. She tried to use the college fund from my grandpa to buy herself a boat, and she doesn't even live near a fucking lake. Of course, I want to have a cute heart-to-heart about liberal arts versus state schools, or whatever. But I never will. That's your life, not mine. I have Lorelei and—" Alexa broke off. She ran her fingers under her glasses, and it seemed for a second that she might cry. Her eyelids already looked swollen. "You just have no idea what it's like."

"That's not what I meant. I'm sorry—really sorry," Dan stammered. "You're super lucky to have Lorelei."

"Just forget about it," Alexa muttered. "I have to run an errand for Lorelei with our landlord after school today, so don't wait around."

Alexa crumpled the tinfoil around the remains of her sandwich and left the cafeteria.

After school, Dan sat in her car waiting for Liss by the coffee cart in Marlena—where Willow, thankfully, was not on shift. The Black Book was in Dan's trunk, still sealed in its secret shoebox, but Dan was barely aware of its nearness. She couldn't stop thinking about that vicious look Alexa had leveled at her during lunch. As if Alexa had forgotten entirely why she was supposed to care about Dan at all, like she was just waiting for Dan get out of her way so she could move on with her life. It almost made the lying feel pointless. But then again, that argument worked equally well to justify lying to her, which was somehow easier. Telling her the truth would bring Alexa so close, too close. She'd see Dan for who she truly was.

Dan pulled her bag over from the passenger seat and pawed through one of the pockets. There had to be something in there sharp enough to make bloody scratches in her skin, if not actually a cut. A safety pin, even a paperclip—Dan stopped herself. What good would it do? She'd hurt Alexa, even if she didn't mean to, and hurting herself didn't undo that.

So instead she let the paper cup of her mocha burn the pads of her fingers as she slurped up the whipped cream. She thought about asking for a top-up, even though a whipped cream top-up was not a thing, but she needed *something* else to feel, even if it was only a little greasy.

But the more she replayed the conversation with Alexa in her head, the more it overwhelmed her. Alexa had to know that Dan didn't mean to hurt her; she'd apologized right away. Had Dan done something else, something she wasn't aware of, to set Alexa off?

A sick certainty flooded Dan's chest. It was, as Liss would say, stupid obvious.

Alexa knew Dan was lying to her. She must have figured out that Dan was spending time with Liss, and she was punishing her for it. Probably she was waiting to see how long it took Dan to break and confess what she'd done.

At that moment, Liss yanked the passenger door open, shoved Dan's backpack onto the floor, and collapsed into the car. She was smiling, her blond hair falling into her face, like they were back at the beginning again, when magic was an adventure and Dan hadn't let everything go hopelessly wrong. Liss's eyes were bright. "You brought the Book, right?"

Dan burst into tears.

"Oh my god, are you okay?"

Obviously she was not, with her face buried in her hands and her forehead resting against the steering wheel. "I'm fine," Dan snorked out. "It's nothing, I'm fine."

"Okay," Liss said tentatively. "It just seems like something's bothering you."

Dan glanced at Liss: Her body was pressed against the door, as far from Dan as she could get in the car, and eyebrows were drawn together. She looked more uncomfortable than empathetic.

"The weekend was just kind of hard. I was—" Dan sniffed and rubbed the tears from her cheeks. Why couldn't she just admit what was bothering her, like any regular person would? "I was stressed out."

"Ugh, same. I'm stressed like, all the time." Liss was fidgeting with her fingers again. Up to four and back. "College applications. Finals. Finding my boyfriend before Kasyan eats him or whatever, and my mom is being totally batshit lately. But we're staying focused, right? Once we ask the Black Book, we'll be on track."

"I know that. I mean, I . . ." Dan forced herself to go on. Like Liss always said, she couldn't know when Dan was upset if Dan deliberately hid it from her. "I feel bad about lying to Alexa."

"Wow, tragedy of the century."

Dan tried to ignore this. "I just think she's upset."

"Then apologize to her when this is over and I'm sure she'll forget about it. And if she doesn't, then maybe the whole friendship thing wasn't meant to be. There's that quote—if you can't forgive me at my worst, you don't deserve me at my best."

Dan didn't know what to say. Surely, you couldn't be forgiven for *anything*—but on the other hand, her reasons for lying were at least understandable, if not actually *good.*

"I can't keep doing this much longer," Dan said.

Liss nodded. "We'll be a lot closer to finding him once we're using the Black Book again. It's in the car, right? Let's go to my place, my parents won't be there."

"Jesus, Liss." Her tears were threatening to spill over again. "I'm having a crisis here."

"I can drive if you want to cry on the way."

"Seriously? You really don't get it?"

"No, I don't get it." Liss's body was taut, her eyes wide. "What's your issue? How can Alexa be more important than this? So you lied to her—it happens. People lie all the time. If you two love each other so much, then she'll forgive you and you can go back to your platonic version of *The Notebook* or whatever."

"The thing I'm worried about is her *not* forgiving me," Dan snapped.

"People can forgive anything. Look, you were so mad at me about Johnny that you didn't talk to me for *months*—which I have never given you a hard time about, by the way, and you're welcome for that—and now everything's fine between us. You forgave me, because you wanted to stay friends more than you wanted to stay mad, and I did the same to you. If you and I can get over that, then Alexa can get over a few harmless lies."

Dan couldn't breathe. "Everything's fine between us," she repeated.

"Right. I mean, you never apologized either, but I accepted that and I forgave you anyway."

"*You* forgave *me*?"

"Yes," Liss said. "And it took a while."

Dan's heart was racing now, her tears forgotten. "Honestly, how do you manage to make yourself the victim in every situation?"

"You can't make yourself a victim, Dan. Someone else does that for you."

"*Johnny* is the victim." Dan's voice filled the car. "*We* did that for him."

"Keep your voice down!"

"Johnny is dead," Dan ground out.

"Don't say that!"

"He's dead, Liss," Dan said. "He's dead. We have to move on."

"Shut up!" Liss cried. "He is not. I know he isn't."

"Get out of my car."

"But the Book—"

"Get out of my fucking car!" Dan screamed. "I'm glad you forgave me because I never want to see you again."

FALL OF JUNIOR YEAR

Dan

A month after Johnny and Dan kissed, Liss went from annoyed to outraged that Johnny hadn't made another move on Dan. She cajoled Dan into various stakeouts at school—eating lunch near where his crew usually sat, loitering in the hall where he'd have to pass them on his way to Chemistry—but she wanted more info. Dan complained that there *was* no more info, she'd told Liss everything, and besides, Dan already saw him at work, so it wasn't as if he had no chance to talk to her if he wanted to.

Mortified hardly began to describe Dan's feelings when Liss pulled up his social media again, for the sake of research, or when she shouted his name from across the cafeteria and pretended Dan had done it. Johnny was all Liss wanted to talk about. They'd spent hours discussing The Kiss in the weeks since it had happened, to the point that Dan could barely find the spark she'd felt in those few short moments. The memory of that brief thrill when he pressed her up against the car had been overwritten by the embarrassment of describing it to Liss, of answering Liss's questions about it. Dan could never manage to admit to Liss that mostly the kiss had felt strange, confusing, unfamiliar—she could barely admit it to herself. Who didn't like kissing? Now Dan almost wished the whole thing had never happened. She couldn't help the feeling that all of this was going to end in some humiliation for her, that Liss would push and push and push, but Dan would be the one who finally broke when Johnny spelled out what she already suspected was true: he wasn't interested, he'd never been interested, and he was grossed out that she thought he could have been.

But Liss was insistent, so Dan agreed to let her hang out while she and Johnny closed at Achieve!

It did not go as Dan had imagined.

Liss slunk in, wearing oversized sunglasses. Casually confident, she kissed Dan on the cheek as if they did that all the time, although they did it exactly never, then draped herself elegantly into a desk chair and began tapping something into her phone. Apparently she was practicing some new policy of don't speak until spoken to, and it was highly effective. Neither Dan nor Johnny could take their eyes off her for long as they went about the business of closing.

"Your name's Liss, right?" Johnny finally asked.

Liss shifted her sunglasses down her nose, as if they were the reason she'd barely heard him. Instead of looking ridiculous, as any normal person would wearing sunglasses inside at sundown, she looked sophisticated.

"Yes." She didn't elaborate.

"I'm Johnny."

"I know," she said with a little smile that managed to be at once pretty and dismissive. She went back to her phone. Johnny stood before her, grasping for something else to say for a second too long. Dan smirked with a perverse pride, that Liss had managed to make Johnny small with only two words.

"You like the Misfits?" He eyed the enormous skull on Liss's T-shirt. She'd cut the neck open so the thin fabric draped below her collarbone.

"Would that be surprising for someone wearing a Misfits shirt?" she said, although she had never heard the band until Dan forced her to listen to them after she bought the shirt.

Johnny didn't know what to say.

Dan went into the back to change out of her uniform and returned to find the two of them chatting, Liss still slouched dramatically in the desk chair as if it were a chaise longue, and Johnny fidgeting, aware that Liss was always on the verge of ignoring him.

When she saw Dan, she did.

Liss slipped her phone into her pocket. "Ready?"

"Ready," Dan confirmed, and followed Liss out, leaving Johnny to lock the doors.

"Where are we going?" she asked.

"Doesn't matter. Just look like it's very important."

They walked three blocks to Aroma Café, ordered a pair of co-conut mochas, and stationed themselves at their regular couch at the back.

"Dan, be honest with me. Are you into Johnny or not?"

Dan slurped the whipped cream off the top of her mocha.

"I guess—I mean . . . Honestly? I sort of can't tell."

Liss scrunched up her face. "You can't tell like probably not or like probably yes?"

Dan pressed her lips together. She wanted to say yes—she had the sense that this was the answer she was supposed to have, the feeling she should be feeling—but she wasn't sure if it was true or not. She wasn't sure if she was just scared or not, and if she was, what she was scared of and whether it was a fear worth listening to or a fear worth ignoring. She wasn't sure what Liss wanted her to say. So instead of answering, she asked, "Why does it matter?"

"Just checking." Liss slouched back in her chair. "You're sure you don't want to do the love spell, right?"

"I'm sure," Dan said. "I don't want to talk about that stupid spell anymore, okay?"

"Okay," Liss agreed.

It wasn't until her next shift with Johnny a few days later that Dan understood what Liss was playing at that day at Achieve! At a lull in the shift, Johnny leaned against the wall beside Dan at the back of the room.

"Hey, can I ask you something?"

She wanted to say *You already have,* but that was childish. "Sure."

"Would it be cool if I asked out your friend Liss?" Dan's eyebrows popped. When she didn't answer right away, Johnny added, "Your friend who was here the other day?"

As if Dan—or anyone—might forget Liss. "I know who you're talking about."

"I wanted to check with you, because I know you guys are friends and like, you and me . . ." He gave a sideways kind of smile that meant what exactly? That Dan was a bad kisser and a little too fat? That Johnny had only been looking to hook up with Dan but he wanted Liss as a girlfriend? That he'd only kissed her because of some weed-induced psychosis that was finally clearing? "I'm not trying to make it weird."

Dan soured at how open and hopeful and *good* Johnny looked

as he said this. He truly did not want to make it weird—who ever did?—and he thought he was doing the good-guy thing by asking her before he moved on Liss. She also understood immediately what Johnny didn't: there was no way she could say no. It wasn't the first time a boy had asked her about Liss. It happened at house parties, at school dances, everywhere, because Liss was like a match burning in the dark: you couldn't look away from her, because somehow everyone else looked dimmer in her presence. Liss reveled in that attention in a way Dan couldn't, like she wanted to spend her whole life in the electric moment when a boy wanted her.

"It wouldn't be weird," Dan heard herself say. "It's completely cool. But be careful. She eats guys like you for breakfast."

Johnny eased into his sheepish grin, as if being devoured by Liss was exactly what he was looking for.

ELEVEN

Liss

The Range Rover shuddered as Liss sped from Marlena to Gratton.

What was *wrong* with Dan? Liss had offered her a chance to make things right, and Dan was still bitter that she hadn't ended up with Johnny.

Liss stepped on the accelerator as she pulled out of a turn.

This wasn't the Dan she was used to. Dan was there when Liss needed her. When her mother had offered her fifty dollars to lose five pounds and Liss was so hurt she barely knew what to do, Dan talked her through how to say no. When she needed to go up to Ukiah for an appointment at Planned Parenthood and didn't want to do it alone, Dan skipped school to go with her. When her anxiety had gotten so bad she insisted on taking her car in for service four times in one month, Dan had given her rides everywhere she needed to be.

Dan stood by Liss like a sister—better than a sister, because they'd chosen each other, and that choice was a promise to stand by each other forever.

But now that had changed.

I never want to see you again.

Liss hadn't been lying: She *had* forgiven Dan, and it *had* taken months—months remembering the moment Dan suggested the spell, how she pushed for them to do it even though Liss was busy and if she was honest, less interested in magic now that she was with Johnny. In those damp January days when it seemed like it was always thinking about raining and never really did, and the clouds over the Pacific were so dense and gray it felt like North Coast had been shoved under the bed and forgotten, Liss had felt trapped. Leaving for college felt impossibly far away, and not even a fun fantasy, because imagining it meant imagining SATs and SAT Subject Tests, AP Exams, personal statements, additional extracurriculars, and most importantly preparing herself for the actual rejections she'd be getting. She could already hear her mother sneering, "Oh, *Liss,*" as she received a rejection from one of her dream schools. She didn't know what her father would say. Hopefully something.

Even Dan had driven her crazy that winter. Every weekend she wanted to hang out, every night she texted Liss to say hi, like they hadn't just seen each other at school, or send her little jokes. Apparently she had been oblivious to the fact that Liss was in an actual relationship now, which took effort to maintain, and effort required time and energy, which she did not have an infinite supply of. Even if Dan didn't understand that simple formula, Liss still couldn't comprehend how Dan had failed to see that Liss was so frayed with anxiety, any little thing might break her, and that one such thing could even be Dan herself, if she did not get off Liss's case and just let her *breathe.*

But then Valentine's Day with Johnny came and went, and Liss started feeling a little more stable. And Dan suggested they ask the Black Book for a spell she couldn't resist.

"Wouldn't it be cool if the Book gave us a spell that let us change our future? We've never tried something like that before. Even if it was just something small, that would be so awesome."

"You think it would really give us a spell like that?" Liss asked. "I've read on the witchboards that those spells are crazy difficult."

"The Black Book misses us," Dan said. "I can feel it."

I never want to see you again.

Now Dan was set on keeping the Book from her, when rightfully Liss was entitled to joint custody. After all, they had found it together, just sitting in the Free Box outside Dogtown Grocery. They'd gone because Dan wanted ice cream, although the May afternoon wasn't warm enough for it, and they always checked the Free Box. You never knew what you'd find: a still-viable cactus, decades-old *National Geographic*s, old rubber Halloween masks that they'd worn for a whole day. Technically, Liss had seen the Book first, been the first to grab it, the first to crack its spine open. The pages had been blank then, save for the first few pages: "A Spell for the Making of Naive Witches." Dan just thought the Book was strange, but Liss had sensed something more.

The first time she'd touched the Book, it had felt like the promise of something: a future she didn't have to wait for, the power to have it now. She'd never have another weekend feeling lost and anxious in North Coast, where a Friday-night trip to the beauty section of the CVS in Gratton might be the only notable event.

The Book had been waiting for them. It had given them magic, the power to transform their lives, their very selves.

Now Dan wanted to take that from her.

I never want to see you again.

If Liss hadn't been so angry she would have cried. This was true every day of Liss's life, but it was especially true as she wrenched the Range Rover into a parking space outside Fault Line Tattoo.

The Fault Line Tattoo Shop sat at the end of Gratton's main street, the last storefront before the old rail yard. The peeling paint of the narrow Victorian made the little building look its 125 years. Even the poster declaring Zephyr Finnemore MISSING looked ancient, although she'd only been gone a few days. Liss pulled open the red door. Inside, framed sheets of tattoo flash covered the walls—mermaids and anchors, clipper ships and pinup girls—and a tattoo machine droned from the other room. A burly man, thick arms scrawled with ink, hunched over a magazine behind a glass case of studs and hoops and gauges for piercings. She cocked her head defiantly at him when he raised an eyebrow at her school uniform, and headed for the doorway hung with a crimson velvet curtain in the corner of the room. Above it hung a half-legible sign that once read MADAME SWANN, but the gold glitter glue had begun to crack so that it looked somewhat closer to MA AME SVARN.

"She's with someone," the tattooed man called as Liss pushed aside the curtain.

"Don't care," Liss replied, mostly to herself, as she stomped up the creaking, narrow stairs to the second level of the house.

The smell of the hall half choked Liss. The air swam with hippie incense and holiday spice candles burning on a side table beside a dish of potpourri, but beneath their scent was something moldering that wouldn't be obliterated. Another handmade sign hung on the door:

MADAME SWANN
FUTURE-TELLING, TATTOOING, PROPERTY MANAGEMENT
VISIT MY ETSY SHOP MADAMESWANN14

Liss counted to four and back, four and back, and knocked. She counted to four and back and tried the door.

In a moment, the lock clicked and the door cracked open, and the lithe, long figure of Madame Swann filled the small space.

"May I help you?"

"I'm looking for a book."

"We have an excellent public library."

"I know you sell the kind of book I'm looking for."

Madame Swann's pale hand curled around the edge of the door. Her long, pointed fingernails were painted an opalescent white; her white-gray hair hung in long waves around her face. She swiveled her long neck and leaned forward toward Liss. "I am engaged. You must return another day."

Liss put a hand on the door. "I'm here now. It can't wait."

Madame Swann surveyed Liss, unmoved. Her eyes were a brown so dark they were nearly black—the only dark thing about her. "I don't trifle with lost little sparrows and love spells."

Liss was about to argue when a girl's voice from behind the door said, "I should get going anyway."

Swann swiveled her elegant head back toward the voice and loosened her grip on the door. "Already?"

"I have to grab Lorelei some cold medicine on my way home. I'll have her call you as soon as she's feeling better."

At this, Madame Swann relented. The door fell open, revealing Madame Swann's strange den. The floor was laid with oriental rugs and stacked with pillows—Madame Swann preferred lounging to sitting. Along one wall, curio cabinets held jars of dried plants, rough chunks of crystals, mortars and pestles, candles of all shapes and sizes. Another wall hosted photos of Madame Swann's favorite tattoos. By the window stood a padded tattoo table and a chest of inks, gloves, and tattoo machines. The ceiling was strung with fairy lights, giving the small and cluttered space an undeniable feeling of lightness.

And in the middle of it, slinging her bag over her shoulder, was a girl with a rough-cut black bob and a hard frown.

"What are you doing here?" Alexa said.

Liss's eyes narrowed. "What are *you* doing here?"

"Got lost on my way to church," Alexa said, then pushed past Liss toward the stairs.

Of all the places to run into Dan's new friend.

Dan had assured her that Alexa had no idea about magic or their quest and yet somehow, here she was, having tea with North Coast's only psychic/tattooer/landlord.

And Dan thought she was the one doing the lying.

I never want to see you again.

Liss waited until Alexa's footfalls could no longer be heard on the stairs, then leveled her gaze on Madame Swann.

Madame Swann folded her arms against her ropey body. Her arms were painfully thin: all knobby joints and sinew. "Now that you've scared off my client, are you going to make it worth my time?"

"I'm looking for a Black Book."

"For a black book?" Swann answered. "That's a touch vague."

"It's a book of spells."

Madame Swann's thin eyebrows arched sharply. "Then why didn't you say that you were looking for a book of spells? I might have a few books on folklore, and a few on Wiccan rituals, although there are other shops nearby that cater to Wicca specifically—"

"That's not the kind of book I meant," Liss interrupted. "It's a book of spells that work. You don't have to pretend you don't know what I'm talking about. I already have one and I'm looking for another."

Swann's eyes grew large. "You *have* one and you're looking for a *second*?"

"I guess technically I *had* one. I sort of lost it." *I never want to see you again.* "It was handwritten, but I assume it was a copy of another book."

Swann chirped out a small and pitying laugh. "Little sparrow, I cannot simply sell you a Black Book."

Liss ran her tongue over her lips; her mouth had gone dry. She had been an idiot to wait for Dan, and now an idiot twice over for having assumed that Swann would have another copy—that if she couldn't have *their* book, at least she could have her own. "I'll pay whatever you want."

"You misunderstand me. Black Books almost never come up for sale—although if I had one, I would not sell it to you. The one you had isn't a copy of anything; each book is unique." Swann cocked her head. "Do you know why that is?"

A shiver scampered down Liss's spine. "No."

"A Black Book holds the records of an individual's forays into magic. Some say *the books themselves* are magic."

Liss could see it in her mind: the yellowed pages, stained brown at the edges, and the time-faded lettering that slanted across each page. Full of magic, made from magic, the knowledge of someone powerful and brave and anonymous. Of course it wasn't the kind of thing you could find—it found you.

"By that I mean, these are simply stories and legends that have made Black Books highly collectable!" Swann added. "It goes without saying that magic does not exist."

"If they're so valuable, I'll have to get back the one I had." Liss hoped she'd disguised her visceral and delicious satisfaction. "One more thing: Do you have anything on someone called Kasyan? He's also called Kasyan the Unmerciful. Or the Lord of Last Resort."

"No," Swann answered without hesitation.

"Just . . . no? You don't want to check?" Liss gestured to the bookshelves lining the room. Swann pressed her lips into a tight line before spinning on her heel to make a quick study of the glass-fronted cabinets that held her collection of spell books, grimoires, texts of occult philosophy and practice. Swann tapped a long nail against her teeth, producing a very grating *click-click-click*, then sighed extravagantly and spun back toward her.

"No."

"Nothing at all?"

"I swear on my life and yours that I have nothing that can assist you, little sparrow. I say again that we have an excellent public library." Madame Swann smiled as she took Liss by the shoulder and guided her back to the door. Her long nails pinched even through Liss's polar fleece. "Or you could Google it."

Before Liss could answer, Swann had hustled her across the threshold and shut the door in her face. The deadbolt clunked into place.

Alexa

Alexa hurried down the stairs and out the door of Fault Line Tattoo. Liss's obnoxiously red SUV was parked out front, one tire obnoxiously on the curb. Alexa let out a sigh of relief and headed back to the North Coast High parking lot and her car. Liss might not have any redeeming qualities that Alexa was aware of, but she'd definitely shown up at the right time.

The meeting with Swann should have been simple, but then again Swann was more than a landlord. Lorelei had known her for years, though Alexa had no idea how they'd met. Once a month Swann would come over and she and Lorelei would catch up, during which time—Lorelei implied, never outright asked—Alexa was expected to find somewhere else to be. Lorelei deserved her privacy, so Alexa never asked questions.

Of course, Lorelei's calendar marked one of Swann's visits this week, although it was only the middle of the month and Lorelei had dropped in on Swann a few days earlier. Alexa had posed as Lorelei to text Swann, saying she was sick and needed to move the meeting. Delay it first, cancel it later, was Alexa's strategy. Then Swann wouldn't take no for an answer, which was frankly pushy. Finally, Alexa convinced her to move the meeting to the tattoo shop. Swann had still been expecting Lorelei when Alexa knocked.

"Lorelei sent me to drop off the rent. For the Dogtown house," she'd said. "She wanted to come herself but she's come down with something."

Swann had leveled her black eyes at Alexa—or really, looked down at Alexa, since Swann was quite tall and Alexa quite not-tall—and asked, "Where is she?"

"She's at home. She's super sick. Probably sleeping, I think? Anyway, I brought her check."

Swann had accepted the check but continued looking at Alexa in a way that was entirely unpleasant, with such singular concentration that Alexa worried that she could maybe read her mind, like Domino could, or somehow smell residue of that noxious rotty stink that filled the house.

That was impossible, Alexa told herself as she unlocked her car.

Although what, really, was impossible once you were telepathically talking to a cat?

Swann was sorted, for now. But she would have to be careful— *more* careful.

Alexa put the car into gear and headed back toward Dogtown.

Liss

Liss made it home from Fault Line Tattoo only to find her mother was waiting for her in the kitchen, flipping through a catalog at the massive granite island. Liss could tell that she was ready to spit venom from the way she was clutching her glass of pinot grigio.

Liss pulled a container of leftover pasta from the fridge. Liss's father was in Sacramento, where he spent three nights a week for work. His absence put her mother on edge, but it also meant they were both free from pretending to enjoy family dinners. "Do we have any bread?"

"Bread *and* pasta? Usually it's bread *or* pasta. Have some carrots instead. Are you going to tell me where you've been?"

"Studying at Dan's."

"Was studying at Dan's so important that it was worth missing your appointment with the college consultant this afternoon?"

"That was today? I totally forgot." A knot of anxiety tightened in her stomach. She'd been so excited to meet up with Dan, to lay her hands on the Black Book again, that she had practically run to her car after school had ended. And all that had come to nothing but another stupid fight.

I never want to see you again.

"We paid two hundred dollars for that appointment, and the consultant is booked into the new year. You knew this was your last chance to meet with him for the final edits of your personal statement. The applications are due in a week—"

"I have until the end of the month," Liss protested. "That's like three weeks."

Her mother's jaw was firm, and a tiny muscle near her eye twitched. The lines in her forehead would have been showing, if not for the Botox. "Today is the fifteenth. It's two weeks, and if they're not early, they're late. We had an agreement."

"What agreement?" Liss asked around a mouthful of pasta.

"That I would ground you if that's what's necessary for you to complete these applications on time—"

"By which you mean, early."

"On time. And clearly that is what's necessary."

Liss dropped her fork into the cold pasta. "I didn't agree to anything like that. You can't make things up and say I agreed to them."

"If you could be a tiny bit responsible for the first time in your life, this wouldn't be necessary."

"I *am* responsible, so this *isn't* necessary."

"This is for your own benefit."

"*My* benefit?" Liss knew she should stop herself before she really made her mother mad. Giving into her self-righteousness might feel good for a few seconds, but her mother could make her feel like a worthless nothing with just one cold look. She couldn't win an argument against her—she never had—but still, the unfairness of it ate into her. "I don't even want to go to half these schools. They're only on the list because you want to be able to tell Dad's bosses that I'm applying to their alma maters."

"What is so offensive to you about helping your father? All of this is thanks to his hard work." She gestured around the kitchen, as if Dad's hard work had amounted to dozens of gleaming white cabinets. "That's how the world works. You don't do things just because you want to; you act with purpose."

"So when I want things, it's being selfish, and when you want them, it's acting with purpose. Got it."

"You ungrateful little—how did I end up with such an insolent daughter?" Her mother's nostrils always flared a little piggishly when she was angry. "Go to your room."

"I'm actually grounded?"

"You can tell Dan that she'll be studying alone until you get your applications in. I'm sure she'll understand, unless she's turned into another good-for-nothing druggie for you to embarrass yourself with, like that boy you used to date."

Liss fought against the urge to stomp all the way up the curved staircase, because it was juvenile and also would surefire upset her mother even more, which Liss couldn't risk. It was as if her mother had ripped open her chest and filled it with venom and left her to burn—not with anger or drive or anxiety like Liss often did, but something altogether different and sadder and darker. Something that made her want to unmake herself, consume herself and start again as someone not so terrible, not so worthless, not such a fuck-up. A better daughter, even though she knew intellectually that she was a perfectly fine daughter. She was a good enough daughter. That was the same as awful, wasn't it?

Liss shut the door to her room and locked it.

It was just that her mother was a raging bitch when she got bored, and her boredom was directly proportional to how much attention she got from Liss's father. It was Monday, which meant he'd be gone for three more days before he'd work from his office in Fort Gratton on Friday.

When she saw him on Friday nights, Liss always felt like she'd been rescued. He hadn't forgotten the two of them—"my beautiful girls" he called them—in the too-big house that all his hard work had paid for.

But when he was home, he wasn't really *there*. He spent the Saturdays crammed into a spandex outfit biking North Coast's twisting roads, and Sundays watching any kind of sports and reviewing his work for the next week—alone. He never noticed the tension between his "beautiful girls." Sometimes it was like he never noticed Liss at all, unless she was notifying him of another A.

The applications were piled on Liss's desk along with course catalogs she'd picked up on campus visits, and half a dozen books and reference guides, like *Writing the Personal Statement* or *Cracking the College Admissions Code*. She'd been planning to finish the applications this weekend, but that hadn't panned out. She could still get them done during winter break, while she hid in her room away from all her mother's fussy Christmas stuff. After she knew Johnny was okay and it was safe for her to leave North Coast.

She shouldn't have missed the appointment. She'd planned on telling the consultant the truth, now that she was getting down to the wire: they couldn't go over the draft of her personal statement, because she hadn't been able to write one yet.

It wasn't that she didn't know what it was supposed to be about; she'd gone on a whole community service program last summer specifically so she'd have a "life-changing adventure" to write about. There was even a session on how to convert the experience into a personal statement. She was supposed to say something about how Guatemala was beautiful and inspiring, and she'd been so lucky to have the opportunity to give back to the community, which was not her community but was still really important to her as a global citizen, by building a rural school out of cinderblocks, which was so rewarding because she really valued education, which everyone should have access to, including herself, by being admitted to whatever college the admissions officer reading the statement worked for.

But the truth was, the trip wasn't inspiring at all. She'd been miserable and lonely and distracted the whole time. She missed Dan, even if she was still angry with her for pushing that horrible spell in the first place, and she thought about Johnny constantly. It didn't help that the absence of a reliable internet connection meant she couldn't even do any research into where he'd been taken and how he could be saved. Liss knew building the little one-room school was important, but it was hard to feel proud of it when she'd accidentally let her boyfriend get kidnapped by some kind of demon. Obviously that wasn't something she could put in a statement, which meant she had to lie, but what if they saw through it? The admissions committee, the college consultant, her parents, everyone—what if they cut right through her lies and saw the truth? What if, with her whole life leading up to this, they judged her and found her wanting?

Liss didn't know if she could survive the rejection.

TWELVE

Alexa

*A*lexa *bolted upright—or more* upright—in the chair she was sleeping in at Lorelei's bedside. It was still fully dark outside, and ominous shadows cluttered the room.

Someone was banging on the front door.

Alexa lurched to her feet and grabbed the kitchen knife she'd been keeping nearby since Keith's visit in case of emergencies.

"Open up, Alexa!"

She didn't recognize the voice. It sounded like a woman's—but Alexa's brain was woozy with sleep. Could it be Keith?

Alexa's gaze was fixed on the front windows, but with the curtains drawn and the lights off, she couldn't see anything. Her eyes felt dinner-plate wide.

The banging continued.

But why would Keith knock when there was nothing stopping him from breaking in again?

Alexa tightened her grip on the knife and flipped on the living room light. The room still felt off-kilter and strange. The clock read barely 5:00 a.m.

"Alexa, open the door!"

Domino padded toward her with a casual slink that seemed not at all appropriate for what was happening.

"Should I open it?" she whispered.

I'm a familiar. I don't make decisions.

"That's not helpful!"

Fine, if it means we can go back to bed, I'm in favor.

Alexa opened the door.

Standing on the porch was a tall and slender figure, almost luminously pale in the moonlight.

"Swann?"

Swann came forward, but Alexa blocked the doorway.

"Where is she, Alexa?"

"Who?"

Swann's eyes narrowed. "I'm here for Lorelei. You—oh god, what's that smell?"

Suddenly Swann gave a look of realization and pushed past Alexa into the house.

"She's sick—she's sleeping!" Alexa stumbled over the mess left behind from the break-in to block the way to Lorelei's room. She wedged herself into the doorway and grabbed for the door, but Swann put out a surprisingly strong arm to prevent her from closing it. Swann peered over her head into the dark bedroom. The smell alone was enough that Swann would never be satisfied that nothing was wrong. Alexa shoved back her rising panic. "This is completely inappropriate. I know you own this property but this is our *home*, and you have no right to barge in here—"

"Stop this, Alexa. You must know I'm here to help." Something in Alexa's face must have demonstrated that she knew nothing of the sort, not even close. "Well, I am. Didn't Lorelei tell you? I'm the Overwarden for the whole region, so if something's gone wrong it's my responsibility."

"The what?"

But Swann had already taken advantage of Alexa's hesitation. She

was in the bedroom now, searching for the light. Alexa didn't turn
to watch.

The light clicked on.

Swann gasped.

Alexa nervously tidied the living room, Domino at her heels, while
Swann conducted a stern, closed-door examination of Lorelei.

At least Swann hadn't freaked out when she barged into Lorelei's
room—no screaming or cop-calling. She'd laid a white hand against
her white throat, her shoulders slumping, and quietly said, "Oh,
love, what's happened?" Since then, she'd been concerned but composed, the way TV doctors acted when they faced difficult cases.
The fact that Swann accepted Lorelei's situation as bad in a normal
way, not bad in a defying-the-laws-of-logic way, sparked some hope
that Lorelei's condition was temporary, or even a regular kind of
sickness. Alexa told herself Swann was being helpful, and she *did*
need help, like it or not. But she couldn't entirely quiet the nagging
worry that, precarious as things already were, they'd started to slide
entirely out of her control.

Swann emerged from Lorelei's room, an unreadable expression
on her narrow face. She requested a cup of tea then went to the
bathroom to wash her hands.

"I apologize for showing up like this," Swann said once they were
seated outside. The front steps they sat on were grimy and the porch
partly crushed, but at least the air was breathable. "You set all my
alarm bells ringing yesterday. I thought it best to take the situation
by surprise, which is most easily done before dawn."

Alexa frowned. She prided herself on her ability to work the
sympathies and expectations of adults to her advantage. She'd

thought the meeting had gone convincingly well.

"It's good that I came, because Lorelei's situation is quite dire." Alexa searched for something encouraging in her tone and found nothing. "In truth, I'm not sure an earlier intervention would have helped. Lorelei is very sick. Or, I shouldn't say *sick* because I don't want to suggest she can get better. I'm not sure if she can. She may get worse."

"Okay," Alexa made herself say, letting Swann's words concentrate themselves in her brain. She had known this was possible—probable, even. Although she had dared to hope that if Lorelei was still breathing, there was a chance it would all right. "Okay," she repeated.

Swann leaned forward and gingerly placed a supportive hand on Alexa's knee. "I'm sorry. Lorelei was—*is*—my friend, too. I care very, very much for her."

"What's wrong with her?"

Swann withdrew her hand. "It's a curse, naturally."

"Naturally," Alexa repeated, her voice flat, while her brain caught up to what she'd heard.

A curse.

It was impossible. People didn't just go around *getting cursed* like they were in a freaking fairy tale.

But wasn't that how Alexa had been thinking of it all along, since the very first night? It *felt* like a curse. And science wasn't likely to explain the static in the air as Lorelei's skin blackened, or the strange wind that whipped through the house as she stopped breathing, then started again.

"Okay, so if it's a curse," Alexa said tentatively, "we have to do what, reverse it?"

"This was done very powerfully. I've not seen anything like it in years—perhaps ever—and the damage, you know, is extensive."

Swann gave her a soft look that was not encouraging and fiddled with the handle of her mug of tea. "It *is* strange though."

"That she was cursed?" Alexa ventured.

"No, love, that she's alive at all." Swann tilted her head in an oddly swanlike gesture. "The curse should have worked quickly. Work like this rots you from the inside. That's what the black is: necrosis. It's what's making the smell."

Alexa grimaced. The smell was so stomach-churningly thick Alexa was surprised she couldn't see it.

"I don't have much of a sense of smell, so if I'm getting a whiff, you must truly be suffering. I'll bring something by to help clear it." Swann continued, "To speak plainly, Lorelei should be dead already."

Alexa folded her arms over herself. She didn't know what to say, what to think, what to feel, other than the sick, grasping feeling tangling her guts. Lorelei could be gone. She'd known this was possible from the minute Lorelei rammed her car into the house.

"There must be something we can do," Alexa asked. "Do you think she's in pain? Can she hear me—if I talk to her?"

"I'm sure she can, love." Alexa immediately saw Swann would have answered the same whether it was true or not. "You're right that the best thing to do is keep taking care of her. I'll look into whether there are any spells that might help with her discomfort."

Sure, spells were apparently a real thing, same as curses. Why not?

"I'll put in an urgent request for a healer, and we'll bring someone out to take over Lorelei's position at Black Grass." Swann's mouth puckered with concern. "Although with the Solstice so soon, the Wardens will be stretched thin."

"Why would *The Wardens* care about the Solstice? It's a magazine . . . Oh." Alexa realized she was wrong even as the words were still leaving her mouth. *The Wardens*, whatever it was, was not a magazine.

There was a tight, appraising look on Swann's face. "She didn't tell you?" Swann asked, but it wasn't really a question. It was obvious to them both now that Lorelei had never said a thing about all of *this*.

"No," Alexa admitted.

Swann's face wrinkled into an expression Alexa had seen on adults her whole life when they realized that Alexa's mother had failed in some clear way and they were considering if it was their place to try to intervene. This was how adults looked when they wanted to help you but were worried about the consequences.

"Please tell me."

Swann set down her tea and took a deep breath. "Lorelei wasn't a journalist any more than she was actually a seeker of Black Grass. She was a witch of the Wardens."

"A *what*? You don't mean witch, like, literally. Like with powers and spells and all that?"

"I do." Swann shifted uncomfortably. It didn't seem that this was information Swann had a lot of practice delivering. "Witches exist, and Lorelei was among our number. And yes, powers, spells, communing with animals and the natural world: we engage in a wide range of activities. I know that may be a bit difficult to accept, but perhaps you're beginning to see that the world is far more complex than most people know it to be."

Alexa swallowed hard. She was indeed beginning to see that the world could be full of semi-dead corpses and curses and telepathic cat-communication and who knew how many other things that Alexa had no choice but to call magic. But could *Lorelei* have really lived in that world, instead of the realm of frozen pizza and action movies and road trips in the Subaru that she'd shared with Alexa? Did Alexa know Lorelei at all?

Alexa shoved aside the sting of the revelation. "What exactly do the Wardens do?"

The corners of Swann's mouth quirked. "We keep watch. And intervene when we need to. Mainly we do investigations, monitoring, occasional auditing, that sort of thing. Whatever's necessary to keep people safe."

"Safe from what?"

"From things it would be dangerous to believe in. Things that prey upon the hungry."

Swann's tone made Alexa queasy. "I don't understand."

Swann's light eyebrows knit together. "Humans are amazing in many ways, and one of those ways is our endless desire for what we don't have. We're greedy by nature. We're always hungry for more, better, different. Then we end up with wars and Disneyland and social media influencers, and a lot of other social ills. More importantly, we end up with preachers and mystics and self-taught gurus and self-help whoevers who promise that if you follow them, all your wishes will come true. No more hunger. Unfortunately, in the right circumstances, it can be quite dangerous to have these know-nothings channeling all the energy of that wanting and wishing." Swann leveled her dark gaze at Alexa. "When you gather the threads of desire and *pull*, sometimes the other end of that thread is anchored to something."

Alexa didn't understand—which part of this was a metaphor? "The Wardens . . . watch for when that's happening. That's why Lorelei was at Black Grass. Checking what kind of threads they were pulling at."

"Precisely." Swann paused. "I need to ask you an important question."

Alexa adjusted her glasses. "Anything, if it could help her."

"Has Lorelei . . . moved at all since this happened?"

"She drove home from Black Grass that night."

Swann rested her pointy elbows against her pointy knees. "And since then? Anything?"

The idea of Lorelei moving seemed absurd. "She's just been in bed."

"That's going to be a problem, if this is fatal," Swann said, almost to herself.

"Her not moving is a problem, if she—" Alexa swallowed. "If she dies?"

"Of course, I've forgotten myself. The witches of the Wardens inherit their powers from a witch from the previous generation. This way, we can pass on spell-craft, experience, intuition. It's very important to us that a witch not die without passing her power forward."

Alexa's eyes went wide. "You want her *power*?"

"It sounds callous, I know, but it's part of being a Warden," Swann said gently. "Lorelei became one in the same way. She would want that power preserved. It's an easy process. All she needs to do is give a gift from her deathbed. A comb, a ring, even a glass of water has worked in certain circumstances. It's a very old tradition. Village girls would get turned accidentally all the time when they attended old women whose time had come. It always caused a bit of chaos when they started thinking of spells without any teaching."

"I'll keep you posted if she starts moving."

Swann stood to go. The night had faded into dark blue. She took Alexa by the shoulders. "Lorelei was an excellent witch. She'd been with us since she was nearly your age. We won't take this in stride. We will deal with Black Grass. But the safest thing is for you to keep clear of them. Understood?"

"Understood."

Swann pursed her lips. Alexa tried to stand a little straighter, set her jaw a little firmer, but she probably looked like a tragic case. "May I leave you with a hug?"

Alexa nodded, just once.

Swann wrapped her long, twig-thin arms around Alexa, patted

her back gently. Swann's shoulder was hard and not quite warm under Alexa's cheek. It was such a trivial form of affection, but Alexa was desperate for it.

It took everything in her not to cry.

After Swann left, Alexa tried to go back to her usual post at Lorelei's bedside, but she couldn't bring herself to do it. Instead, she curled into a ball under a blanket on the living room couch as another pale dawn began to break.

So Lorelei was a witch. Sure, why not be a witch? After everything else. Alexa wondered if maybe she'd wandered through some magic portal in a closet and found herself in this different universe. That was always happening in books. Why couldn't it happen to her?

But somehow she was sure it hadn't. She was still in the world she always had been: one where she needed to finish high school all on her own, where her house had been robbed and her cat could talk, where witches and curses and magic were real. Swann had rubbed out the line between fantasy and reality—or no, the line had been drawn wrong in the first place, mistakenly excluding what was real after all. Even if Alexa didn't want to believe in magic, it was right in front of her, making her nauseous and exhausted and miserable, and *not believing* wasn't going to make any of that go away. There was no fantasy doorway she could stumble through to make it all go back to normal.

It was easier to accept that Lorelei was a witch than that she had lied to her, and not just a little. You didn't build a double or triple life on a single lie. The thought of Lorelei spending all day up at Black Grass lying about who she was and what brought her there, only to come home to Alexa and do the same, made Alexa's whole body tight with tears, furious and raw.

Lorelei had already given Alexa more than she'd ever felt entitled to; she wasn't obligated to tell her everything about her life too. But Alexa couldn't help but doubt whether she'd really known Lorelei at all. She wanted to be sure that she had, that she loved Lorelei and Lorelei loved her, but what if that was all made up too.

Alexa didn't want to cry. What a stupid waste of time tears were when you were only feeling sorry for yourself, when they made absolutely no difference, but now they were choking her all the same.

Domino sprung up onto the couch and crawled up Alexa's body, until his front paws were on her chest and his face was inches from hers. In as much as a cat could, he did not appear to be smiling.

She would have told you eventually.

"You don't know that," Alexa mumbled. "She didn't trust me. She probably didn't even *like* me."

Domino glowered at her. *If you keep talking like that, I will scratch you in unpleasant places. After what she's given you, it's an insult to say she doesn't trust you.*

"I know I'm ungrateful." Alexa wiped her nose on her sleeve. "I'd still be miserable in Arizona if it wasn't for her."

Let me rephrase: After what she's trusted you with, it's an insult to say she doesn't trust you. I even had to use trust *twice to express that.*

"Trusted me with what?" Domino crouched down into a sphinx-like position, as if to regard her foolishness from a greater distance. "Yes, I already know I'm incredibly dumb and unobservant, so you can skip that part."

Suddenly Alexa heard Swann's voice playing in her head: *She would want that power preserved. It's an easy process. All she needs to do is give a gift from her deathbed.*

Alexa's hand flew to the evil eye necklace she wore, the one that Lorelei had ripped from her own neck and pressed to her hand that night. She tried to think of something to say, but the best she could do was shake her head at the cat.

Ah, realization: a beautiful thing.

Alexa's blood was rushing in her ears. She was supposed to be happy, right? She'd read enough fantasy novels to have imagined herself as a misbegotten orphan living under the stairs whose life was transformed by magic a million times. But now she didn't *want* her life transformed by magic. She wanted it to go back to the life she'd worked hard to for—a life she'd been happy with, though she hadn't even known it.

"But I can't be a—she's not dead!"

She was dying then. You saw it yourself.

Alexa pressed the charm between her fingers. "But that would mean . . . What did Swann say about spells done by accident? New witches don't even know they're doing them. What if I—"

She couldn't bring herself to say it, remembering the thick crackle of the air in Lorelei's room, the gurgling rasp of her breath and wild roll of her eyes. The charm had burned her when Lorelei pressed it into her hand, and then what? She'd begged for something to stop Lorelei from dying, and that strange wind had blown through the house.

Wasn't that magic?

And if that was magic, then what was happening to Lorelei now—her body seeping and oozing, her legs bloated and black, and Lorelei still not dead, but maybe in some way conscious and living through it—was Alexa's fault.

Something was exploding inside her. Heat, pressure raced through in the veins on the back of her hands, in her temples, down to her toes.

Alexa had to get it together, she had to calm down and breathe, but her mind was full of her mother's voice in her head, telling her that whatever she touched turned to shit, but in this case it was an actual human body that she'd destroyed, the body of someone she loved.

Domino leapt off her and bolted to the front door. *You need air. Outside—now!*

"I'm fine."

Just go.

Her hands curled into fists, Alexa stumbled out into the grayish dawn. The night-chilled air felt better around her, but still she could barely breathe around the sad ruin of her thoughts. She was to blame for all of it—of course, of course she had wanted too much, she had been too happy, she had asked too much of Lorelei and now Lorelei was dead, she was basically dead, and it was all Alexa's fault. She couldn't escape it—she could never escape it—her mother was right about the kind of person she was.

A tremendous force was building inside her. Alexa fell to her knees in the gravel and gasped out a wretched sob.

A bright flash of white blew through her vision, a jagged line of lightning. It felt like it had come from *her*, from somewhere inside her, like the energy of her guilt and misery just *broke free* and knocked her back. Her head smacked against the driveway. As she pushed herself to her knees, she saw what the lightning had connected with: the manzanita bush that had been eking out a meager existence in their front yard was smoking, its once-red bark scorched with black and its leaves charred.

Her palms were smoking.

Don't worry, Domino said from the porch. *Newborn witches are notorious for that kind of thing.*

THIRTEEN

Liss

It was already Tuesday evening and Dan still hadn't texted her, although Liss felt like she'd sent Dan no fewer than half a million messages in the last twenty-four hours. First, she'd kept it casual and bitched about being grounded. When she got no answer, she moved on to reminding Dan that if she, Liss, was grounded, Dan might need to start doing more of the heavy lifting with Project Rescue Johnny. Liss suggested bringing the Black Book over to her house, so they could ask it about Kasyan.

She'd chosen the words of those texts as carefully as if they were spells.

It was like texting a boy when you didn't know if he liked you back, where every little word and emoji pieced together exactly right might crack the code of his affection.

Or maybe, Liss realized, it was like texting a boy who'd already decided he wasn't interested. A boy who'd left you. Who'd moved on.

I never want to see you again.

Now, Liss sat on her bed, staring at her phone. She knew what she had to do. She couldn't afford to lose any more time to Dan's little breakdown.

I'm sorry. I know I messed up, okay? Liss texted.

(The three dots appeared, announced that Dan was typing a reply.)

Sorry about what?

About what I said in the car.

(The dots appeared and disappeared as Dan deleted instead of sending whatever she'd written.)

Liss sighed and texted again.

And about Johnny. About all of it.

She threw that last part in as a bit of insurance against whatever else Dan might still think her guilty of.

I really miss you. You're the most important person in the world to me.

Thanks, Dan finally wrote back.

Liss frowned.

Forgive me? For real this time?

(…)

Liss waited. Dan seemed to be composing some long message, probably she would want to explain all over again why she was mad, and Liss prepared to grind her teeth and accept whatever blame Dan wanted to throw at her. Liss didn't care. Forgiveness was something you worked for, and Dan believed it had to happen before any work could get done. If Dan needed to think the past was behind them, then Liss would take responsibility for Johnny and magic and every paper cut Dan had ever gotten from the pages of the Black Book, if that's what it took.

Her phone finally lit up.

No.

No?

Thanks for apologizing but I don't forgive you.

Liss's stomach turned to ice.

You can't just not forgive me that isn't fair.

Dan didn't reply. Liss imagined for a long, horrible moment that Alexa was in Dan's room curled up in the chair by the window, or beside her drinking coconut mochas at Aroma Café, or in the passenger seat of her car. Dan was reading Liss's texts aloud, or showing them to Alexa, and it was obvious how desperate she was, how she was basically groveling for Dan's help. They would both give pitying little frowns, *Liss is so pathetic and she doesn't even know it.*

Liss's fingers flitted against her thumb.

It was stupid obvious. Why would Dan want Liss when she had Alexa? She'd moved on to a new best friend and left Liss to clean up their mess alone. And if that wasn't bad enough, Liss needed the Black Book.

She'd put off going to Swann's to ask after another copy for so long because she'd been sure that she could win Dan back when the time was right. She didn't want a new Black Book, she wanted the old one. *Theirs.* With its flocked pages speckled with mold, with the crumbling leather of its cover, with its spindly cursive lettering that had taken them weeks to read with ease.

There was only one Black Book. Dan had it, and Liss needed it back. She set her jaw and typed another message.

Your new friend is lying to you. She knows something about Kasyan. Fairy tales.

I never found any fairy tales about Kasyan did you? I saw her at Swann's on Monday and she wasn't there to get a reading.

That doesn't mean she knows about Kasyan.

She's lying about something.

You deserve friends who tell you the truth, Liss added.

The three dots appeared and disappeared, but no reply came.

Dan

Dan lay on her bed and stared up at the collage of posters and magazine pages taped up on the ceiling that sloped over her bed. Rickey leveled his sultry gaze at her, his eyes like hot coals. He was holding the stem of a rose between his teeth.

The picture was ridiculous and hot and Rickey was the prettiest creature who had ever lived.

The album playing through her headphones repeated. It was IronWeaks's last album—the last music Rickey made before he killed himself—and it made the world feel strange and distant. Each song danced through darkness, toying with the question of what living was for, and Rickey's voice answering, maybe nothing at all. His songs could make you feel that in your bones.

No, that wasn't right. Rickey's music was beautiful and passionate and glorious. Then why did the sadness feel like the only thing that mattered? Maybe because it was the sadness that he'd chosen over everything else in the end, over music, over life itself.

Liss's last text was still lighting up her phone. Dan wouldn't reply. She didn't owe Liss anything, forgiveness included. So what if Liss thought Alexa was a liar? Liss thought everyone who didn't do exactly what she wanted them to was an inferior creature.

But it had been days since Dan had talked to Alexa—really *talk* talked. She'd avoided her because of Liss, which felt horrible and weak to admit, and then on Monday she'd said the wrong thing and upset Alexa without even meaning to. Now that she'd definitively resolved to move on from the whole Liss-Johnny mess for good, Dan missed Alexa more than ever. Alexa would make her feel better, fill the void that Liss and magic and Johnny had left behind.

No, that wasn't fair to Alexa. Alexa was more than just a bandage on the Liss-shaped wound in Dan's life, even if being friends with her made Dan feel like she could be okay—that maybe she already was okay and she just didn't know it yet. But other times, that same feeling made Dan want to wrap her hands around her own neck and squeeze. It made her feel pathetic and undeserving and precarious, like her feet were about to be kicked out from beneath her.

Dan's gaze moved to the background of the poster of Rickey. The other members of IronWeaks were there, slouching rockstarishly against a wall. None of them had done anything much after his death. Rickey made their whole lives about his pain, and then he got free of it in the worst way imaginable. Probably they had their own issues, problems they didn't get to sing beautiful, tragic songs about.

Dan grabbed her phone. *Are you feeling better? Want to drive up to the CVS in Gratton?*

It took fifteen minutes, but Alexa replied. *Be at your place in 10.*

Alexa

Alexa watched from her car as Dan climbed out her bedroom window onto the roof, then lowered herself down onto the plastic storage chest that stood near her mother's pottery studio, and jumped to the ground. Dan liked sneaking out, the way characters in TV shows did when they were disobeying their parents. Except Dan wasn't disobeying her parents, who never stopped her from doing anything or got mad at her or told her she was a waste of human space. The only thing they cared about was that Dan make good choices and respect herself, which for some reason Dan thought was the world's greatest burden.

It was probably a bad idea to meet up with Dan tonight. Dan would ask questions she couldn't answer, or Alexa would spontaneously set something on fire or start speaking to an animal, or something would happen to Lorelei while she was gone. Swann had delivered her potions—eyedroppers of scarlet red and green-brown liquids that Alexa dribbled into Lorelei's mouth—and warned her to keep Lore cool. Now the house was so cold Alexa went around in two pairs of sweatpants and just as horribly oppressive, with the smell of Lorelei's decomposition. Alexa felt like she'd lost hold of herself. She'd thrown away the notebooks where she'd been planning her fantasy world. No more Flintowerland, no more *Quest of the Axials*. Domino was dismayed, but what did Alexa need a fantasy for, now? Then she had dissolved into tears thinking about whether it would be more humane to somehow put Lorelei out of her misery than to let her keep living in what was certainly excruciating pain.

Alexa knew that she was being weak, for wanting to see Dan, for wanting an escape—not to mention the last time she'd seen Dan, she'd nearly bitten her head off—but she had grabbed her keys when Dan texted her anyway.

Now, the tension in Alexa's chest coiled itself tighter.

She expected it to loosen upon seeing Dan. Dan was her lifeline back to everything normal, back to before her life had been knocked hopelessly askew.

Alexa hadn't really made any friends in LA. Everywhere she looked she found something to be angry about: the traffic, all the stupid juice bars that tried to meet the city's demand for nasty kale-water. Once, she'd kicked a hole in the plaster of her bedroom wall, and they'd had to rearrange the furniture around it. She didn't know where the anger came from, only that sometimes everything about the world felt wrong. It felt like there was a bomb inside her, and some days it felt like it had already exploded, but she was still holding it in, containing the damage.

Even Lorelei made her angry sometimes. Alexa didn't want to think about those times.

But for the last few months, Dan had centered her with sleepovers and local band shows and leaning over to doodle on her notes in the library and listening to the Smiths because Dan liked them in their separate beds in separate houses at night and skipping around to her favorite tracks until putting "Please, Please, Please, Let Me Get

What I Want" on repeat while they both fell asleep. Slowly, the anger had begun to quiet, concentrating itself into a form that could be taken apart. Alexa didn't know if this was what friendship was like, or something particular to Dan.

It had crossed Alexa's mind that she might be a little in love with Dan. If Dan was interested in girls, she'd never mentioned it. Dan never mentioned being interested in *anyone* like that, other than Rickey IronWeaks, and Alexa wasn't sure that was even really romantic. In any case, love was mostly irrelevant and impractical when it was yours to give and completely unpredictable as a thing to receive. Alexa wasn't stupid enough to mess up their friendship with an unrequited crush.

It was better to have Dan next to her.

It was always better with Dan next to her.

Just then, Dan flung herself into the car as if she was escaping something other than supportive parents who loved her.

"Hey."

"Hey. What're you putting on?"

"Guess," Alexa said. She shoved the CD into the player and soon Johnny Marr was picking out a jangling melody, and Morrissey was moaning that it was really nothing.

Alexa turned the music up and pulled onto the road.

The distance from Dogtown to Fort Gratton didn't feel far enough away from home. The hour's drive was almost exactly as long as the runtime of the Smiths' *Hatful of Hollow*, which was perfect because it meant they could stay lost in the album. Alexa didn't actually feel like talking, and the one place that was always okay was in a car, in the dark, with music.

And if she had felt like talking, what could she have said?

Dan wasn't saying anything either. Something was probably wrong, and it was Alexa's responsibility to find out what and help Dan survive it. It wasn't fair to think of it this way, but she liked taking care of Dan. It made her feel useful, needed, more like *herself*— like a version of herself that she had never gotten to be. A person who could really care about others, because she didn't have to worry so constantly about protecting herself.

Alexa was about to ask when Dan said, "Listen, I'm sorry about yesterday. I didn't mean what it sounded like. Your relationship with your mom is your business."

"No, it was my fault. I overreacted," Alexa said. "But thanks."

"Is something going on?" Dan asked. "You've seemed kind of, I dunno, off lately."

Alexa opened her mouth, then closed it again. If she was going to keep Dan in her life at all, she had to split herself in two. One, truer Alexa, who sat at Lorelei's bedside and worried if the yellowish pus that seeped from the split places in Lorelei's skin was dangerous to touch, who needed to figure out what to do when the inevitable happened. That Alexa would need to leave Dan and North Coast behind someday soon, and would be better off keeping her distance. Then there was another Alexa, who could sit in a dark car and listen to music with her best friend and try to etch into her brain how that moment felt—to remember forever how three and a half months of those moments felt, because soon they'd be gone.

"I had a cold, that's all," Alexa answered.

"Really?" Dan asked.

"Yeah, what else? Honestly, if something was wrong, you're the one I'd tell."

Alexa glanced at Dan. She was watching the road, her feet up against the dash. She seemed satisfied with Alexa's answer.

It was enough, for now.

—————

They stopped at the 7-Eleven outside Gratton and bought too-sweet hot chocolates that burned their tongues, then parked in the empty lot at CVS. They wandered the beauty section, sneakily giving themselves rainbow manicures by cracking open bottles of colors with names like She's Got It! and Green with Envy. They tried on every pair of sunglasses and two pairs of old-person reading glasses and sat in the rickety plastic beach chairs until closing time ejected them, along with Mad Mags, who had also been wandering the aisles, back into the parking lot, where the girls sat in the car listening to a Nick Drake album in the dark.

"Oh, I wanted to ask you," Dan said around a mouthful of Swedish Fish, "what were the stories Lorelei told you about that Kasyan guy?"

"The one the Lizard's looking for?" Alexa's heart sank. Dan had told her she intended to be firm with Liss: Liss could say her piece, but friendship wasn't on the table. That was supposed to be it. "Dan, I don't know, they're just stories. Not even interesting stories."

When she said it, somehow it felt like a lie—which was impossible, because it wasn't. When Alexa was young, every time Lore babysat she had a new tale of some creepy monster or demon—things that skulked in shadows or slumbered in rivers, undying spirits that manifested when the energy was right, bogeys that helped lost travelers or led them further astray. When Alexa got frightened, Lorelei told her being scared wasn't a bad thing, because it meant you knew what to watch out for. Kasyan was a creepy story in a long list of creepy stories—stories Alexa always assumed Lore had made up. The other night, when Liss mentioned Kasyan, that was all Alexa had known.

But that was then.

Kasyan.

The name tugged on something buried in her brain, a thread leading her into the dark. The path was littered with dim memories that Alexa knew were not hers, of things lurking in the shadows that pooled beneath trees at night, girls and boys stolen away, and Kasyan himself, a creature of black smoke, granting wishes designed to unravel around the wisher.

"They can't be *that* boring," Dan was saying. "That defeats the whole point of a story."

"I just—I don't really remember a lot of the details."

Dan dug another Swedish Fish out of the bag. "I'm curious. You said he was like the Big Bad Wolf."

Alexa fiddled with her keys. "The stories were creepy and I kind of tried to forget them."

"Whenever I try to forget something, it's basically a guarantee I'll remember it forever."

"Honestly, I only remember snippets here and there." Alexa scrubbed a hand over her face. She searched her memory for Lorelei's words from all those years ago. "There's one about a woman who wishes for a daughter but after she gives birth, Kasyan takes the baby. I think there's one where he drowns a man in gold coins when he wished for riches." She could see them, suddenly, in her mind: the woman's screams, the weight upon the man's chest— a power that fed on the inexhaustible energy of desire. Alexa cleared her throat. "The morals are always like, never stand with three at a crossroad or something."

"What did you say?" Dan's face was suddenly hard and serious.

"Never stand with three at a crossroad," Alexa repeated. "Why?"

"No reason," Dan said hurriedly. "It's just weird advice. What happens if you stand with three at a crossroad?"

"Depends on when you do it. I don't really remember the details.

Sometimes it's good luck and sometimes it's bad luck, but the point was that messing with luck is risky in general." Alexa tried to laugh. "So, you know, make sure to cross the street in ones and twos."

Dan ignored the joke. "What story was that in?"

"I don't remember."

"Can you ask Lorelei?"

"Why?"

"I'm just curious."

"You said that already. Why are you even asking about all this?"

Dan was silent, fiddling with the empty Swedish Fish bag.

"It's Liss, isn't it? You caved to her after all. Did she tell you to talk to me? Dan, what the actual fuck?"

"Liss doesn't have anything to do with this. I don't just do what she tells me. *I'm actually curious.* Like I think it's pretty weird that you got bedtime stories about a fairy-tale character who isn't even Google-able."

"What are you talking about?"

"Kasyan is like . . . not a thing. I can't find any information about him—no books in the library, basically nothing online. You say there are fairy tales about him, but you and Lorelei are literally the only people who seem to know about them."

"That's not true."

"Yes, it is. We looked everywhere—"

"We?" Alexa's eyes narrowed. "So it *is* Liss."

"That's not the point!"

"Are you hanging out with her again or not? Because you just told me this whole conversation has nothing to do with her, and I really hope that isn't a straight-up lie."

It felt like a very long time before Dan said anything. She was looking out into the parking lot with the intensity of someone struggling not to let themselves cry. "I'm not hanging out with her again," she finally said. "But it's also not true that this has nothing to do with her. I'm helping her look for Johnny. That's all it is. We're not friends again."

"Good," Alexa said before she could help herself.

"What's that supposed to mean?"

"I mean, it's good, you can be friends with her if you want. Don't let me stop you."

"Not, good, *you're doing the right thing by helping find a missing kid*? Why do you care so much if I'm friends with Liss anyway?"

"Yeah, that part's obviously good. And I care because I care about *you*. She made you miserable, that's what you always say, and I'm sorry if it's super offensive that I don't want you to be miserable again."

"Right, thanks, I totally agree, having more than one friend would probably break me entirely, I'm so super fragile. Lucky I have you to protect me."

"That's not what I meant," Alexa said. "You can be friends with her if you want to. But I thought you *didn't* want to. That's what you always told me."

Dan dragged her knuckle against the window, cutting a line through the silvery condensation that filmed the glass. "Let's go home."

On the way home, they didn't speak, but now it felt like there was something to say. The air in the car with thick with it, the energy of their fight vibrating with the tinny beat from the speakers.

Alexa was furious and couldn't figure out what to say to relieve the anger inside her. She knew she had no authority to tell Dan who she should and shouldn't spend her time with, what she should and shouldn't do, but at the same time—clearly she shouldn't waste her time with a private school bitch with entitlement coming out of her ass and a grotesquely expensive candy-apple-colored SUV. Liss didn't respect Dan. Alexa knew that from how Dan talked about her, and it had been dripping off Liss that night she'd been waiting for them at Dan's house. Liss was the kind of person who used people—used people up—and Alexa didn't want that to happen to Dan.

There was nothing wrong with that.

So if nothing was wrong with that, why was Alexa so angry?

She looked over at Dan. She was staring out the window, hiding behind a curtain of black hair.

That familiar storm of anger rocked in her chest—and something else. Rain clouds that hadn't yet broken, lightning that hadn't yet struck.

Alexa accelerated too hard out of a turn.

Now it seemed infuriatingly stupid that she'd ever imagined that she and Dan could go visit each other over fall break in college the next year, that she'd have North Coast to come home to for Thanksgiving. That future couldn't be salvaged, and the sooner Alexa understood that, the better.

No more Lorelei, no more Dan, no more North Coast.

She didn't have time for hurt feelings.

Alexa stepped on the gas.

Dan

Dan stole a glance at the speedometer, then up at Alexa's face in the dark. She was breathing shallow and fast and her jaw was set, like she was grinding her teeth. She was definitely driving too fast, and Dan wasn't sure if she should say anything. What did Alexa have to be upset about anyway? Dan was pretty sure she was the victim here: Alexa basically told her she was too weak to spend time with

Liss without getting hurt. Dan wasn't that easily broken. It was one thing for Dan to say Liss was an evil destroyer of worlds, because she'd *been there*, but Alexa only knew Liss secondhand, from what Dan said about her. She didn't understand Liss the way Dan did or anything about why Dan loved her.

The Toyota hit a bump and the CD skipped in the player.

Used to love her.

None of this mattered, Dan told herself, because she'd already given herself the advice Alexa wanted her to take. She'd cut Liss off before Liss could hurt her all over again. She was done with forgiveness and magic and that irresistible influence that Liss wielded like a precise weapon.

Still, that didn't give Alexa the right to say all that to her face.

Dan was jostled from her thoughts when Alexa hit the next turn. The tires shuddered as they fought to hold the pavement, and Dan gripped the door handle against the force of the curve.

"Aren't you going kind of fast?"

Alexa gave a little sneer in response. Her jaw stayed clenched.

"Seriously though."

"You can drive next time," Alexa said.

"Unless we go over the cliff and there is no next time."

"Calm down."

"You're the one driving like a maniac. People *do* go over the cliff, you know."

Alexa didn't answer.

Fuck you too, Dan thought sullenly. She chewed on a fingernail. The road would even out soon—they were approaching Heart's Desire Beach, halfway between Gratton and Dogtown, where the cliff flattened out into a rough hill and the road ran a bit inland to accommodate the beach.

Dan exhaled as a sign announced the turnoff for parking at

Heart's Desire. Soon they'd pass the trailhead, then one more turn and Alexa's driving would only be deranged, not life-threatening. Dan watched the quicksilver line of the moon on the waves rolling into the beach and tried to tell herself she was nervous for nothing.

Someone was standing at the trailhead

A boy was there, standing as still and glittering as the reflection of the moon on the water. He was staring out into the road like he was waiting for something. The certainty of him crashed into Dan, full force, even before she fully made out the black hair, the hunch in his shoulders, unblinking eyes, and the same ratty jacket he'd thrown on the couch in the Achieve! break room a hundred times.

Johnny.

Dan screamed.

FOURTEEN

Alexa

Dan screamed, and she didn't scream a little bit: she screamed with a life-or-death kind of terror that made Alexa slam her foot on the brake without thinking twice.

Without thinking even once.

The Toyota screeched out in agony, tires whining and the whole chassis shaking. It would have been fine if they'd been going straight, but they hadn't been, and the back tire slipped off the pavement, caught on the dirt, and sent the car into a spin back toward the direction they'd come. Now Alexa was screaming, they were both screaming, and Alexa tried to hold on to the steering wheel as it pulled in the spin. When they finally came to a stop, the car was straddling the double yellow line and Alexa's body was so glutted with adrenaline her first thought was that she couldn't believe she'd gotten behind the wheel when she was so high.

Her second thought was, where the hell was Dan going?

Dan had leapt from the car the instant it came to rest, then started running, leaving the passenger door hanging open. Alexa's heart was beating like a battering ram as she got out of the car and went after her.

"Dan! What are you doing?"

Alexa stumbled after her on the dark road. The Toyota's headlights were pointing in the opposite direction, and without them, the night was shadowed and strange—the huge, unknown darkness of the coast.

"Dan!"

Alexa got as far as the trailhead, always calling after Dan, but she couldn't see anything or anyone in the night, and she doubted Dan could hear her over the crashing of the waves. "What the fuck?" she groaned into the night. The accident had been scary—Alexa's heart was still racing—but you didn't deal with a car accident by running hysterically into the wilderness.

If Dan could hear her, she wasn't answering. Alexa needed to move the car. The roads were nearly empty, but the sharp turns meant it would be nearly impossible for another driver to avoid hitting the Toyota.

Alexa slammed Dan's door closed then slid into the driver's seat. It was a strange feeling, the car pointing sideways on the road like that, as if she was going to drive it directly down onto the beach. It made her uneasy.

She turned the key in the ignition, and the engine produced a wheezy grinding sound. She twisted the key again. This time, the engine added something like a cough to the grinding, but it still didn't turn over. She tried again, gritting her teeth against the sound—she didn't want to hurt the poor Toyota, but even if it was dead, she needed to get it to one side of the road. Without some help she had no hope of pushing it to a turnout.

Alexa smashed a fist against the dash. She knew she'd been going too fast, but she'd done it anyway. Had she forgotten that the margin for error on her life at this point was practically zero? She pulled out her phone and started looking up the number for a tow, but the phone blinked in and out of reception. The connection wasn't strong enough for the search results to load. Now the adrenaline was ebbing into a kind of panic, the sick realization of how totally screwed she was, how badly she wanted to get the hell out of there.

Alexa started to cry.

When she heard the noise, she assumed Dan had come back and wanted to actually help her get out of this mess. She wiped the tears from her cheeks and shrieked.

There was a girl.

Something like a girl.

She was standing at the roadside, in the space between two young redwood trees, and she was *glowing*. Not glowing like she went heavy on highlighter, glowing like she was actually made of moonlight, or one of those bioluminescent sea creatures. She was Alexa's age, and dressed in what looked like yoga pants and a polar fleece—not at all how Alexa imagined ghosts, although why shouldn't they be comfortable?—but her curly hair was limp and almost matted. She had a sharp chin and high cheekbones. Her face might have been more familiar if Alexa studied it more, but she couldn't distract herself from the ghost-girl's eyes.

They were entirely black, like her pupil had expanded to swallow her whole eyeball. They were black in a way that was blacker than the night around them, than the shadows of the trees she stood among. It brought to mind a baby doll Alexa had had when she was six. She'd accidentally pushed the doll's eyes into her plastic head, where they rattled like marbles, the doll's gaze a dark void.

Alexa didn't dare move. She could hardly even breathe.

As a strategy to avoid the ghost-girl, it was totally ineffective, because she was actually walking up to the car now, her movements not jerky or floaty like a ghost's, but sort of trudging and exasperated like any regular girl's would be. A few feet away, the girl stopped. She said something Alexa couldn't hear. When Alexa didn't react, she put her hands on her hips and tried to say it louder.

Being a witch was fucking terrifying.

Alexa forced herself to get out of the car. The girl appeared relieved.

"Um, hello," Alexa said, because some kind of greeting seemed appropriate.

"Is it you?" the girl asked in a weak voice.

Was this a way ghosts greeted witches? "Yes," Alexa said unconfidently.

"But you're so . . . regular." The girl frowned. "Why are *you* helping him?"

"Helping who?"

"Never mind. Just tell me what he needs to know."

Alexa took a step forward. "What who needs to know?"

"Is this like, a riddle? Look, he said he'd let me go once you told me, so please."

"Who would let you go? I don't know anything about—about anything," Alexa said.

The girl's black eyes went wide as a look of horror transformed her face and her voice shifted to something desperate. She stepped backward, retreating into the roadside trees. "Oh no, it isn't you at all! Oh, you have to help me! He has me, and—"

"Who has you?"

But the girl's voice was growing weaker, her glittery silvered figure flickering and fading, and then it winked out entirely.

Alexa plunged into the bushes, up toward the redwoods where she'd first seen the girl, but there was no trace of her, nothing at all. That was strange. It was extremely strange. But Alexa had bigger problems than taking care of some ghost-girl. All she could do was mention it to Swann, in case it was important.

Alexa turned back toward her car and swore under her breath. The Toyota was straddling the lanes right after the turn, and now the headlights had gone out, which meant something electrical.

Alexa stumbled back down toward the road.

She barely heard the truck before it collided with the Toyota.

After the accident—the second accident—everything was a blur. The woman at the wheel of the truck was dazed from the airbag, and Alexa was helping her from the car, and somehow Dan was by her side again, disheveled but pretending she'd been there all along. But the other driver wasn't hurt, just in shock. All three of them were shaking, but the woman remembered what Alexa hadn't: they immediately put on the emergency flashers and waited safely off the road until the highway patrol arrived.

The driver's side door had caved in on impact. Alexa couldn't stop staring at her crushed soda can of a car, even watching it from the corner of her eye as she spoke with the highway patrol. She tried to tell him as little as possible. Accident report, insurance information, proof of registration, claims to file. Had either of them been drinking or smoking? Why had the car spun out in the first place? She didn't know, she'd lost control, she wasn't used to these roads, and Dan nodded along, agreeing.

Even though there was nothing to hide about the accident itself, Alexa could hear Kim's voice warning her that once you involved the law, you lost control. You talked to anyone, you lost control.

Then the tow truck came to haul the car away, and Alexa gathered the CDs Dan had burned for her from where they'd scattered onto the back seat, her textbooks from the trunk, stuffing them into an old tote bag. They'd take it to a mechanic, but Alexa could tell that her little car was a lost cause.

She called Lorelei's cell again and again—no answer. Her aunt was a heavy sleeper, Alexa explained, was it absolutely necessary for her to come? It wasn't, the highway patrol officers admitted, but giving girls rides home wasn't strictly in their purview. At last Graciela showed up. Alexa hadn't even realized Dan had called her.

Graciela hugged Dan close. Alexa had to turn away and bite her lip, until she felt a hand on her back and she turned and buried her face in Graciela's warm shoulder and she splintered entirely, crying so hard she shuddered and choked into Graciela's sweater jacket.

The drive home, Alexa kept waiting for Graciela's anger to fall on them. For all Graciela knew, Alexa had nearly killed Dan in a car accident, every North Coast parent's worst nightmare. She should have made her walk back, although Dogtown was miles away, or at least screamed, the way Kim would have.

"You were so lucky out there. These roads are really dangerous, especially for young drivers. I was worried absolutely sick." The last part Graciela repeated a dozen times, although by the time she knew she should have been worried, they were both already safe.

Alexa said *Yes, ma'am* and *I'm sorry* as often as she was able—any time Graciela paused. In the front seat, Dan didn't say anything at all. Less than that, she didn't even look at Alexa, just chewed her nail with her eyes glued to the window.

Graciela pulled over in front of Alexa's house. When she turned back to look at Alexa, shadows had caught in every line of her face, which was normally so smooth, the kind of face kept young by smiling. Graciela wasn't actually mad at all: she was scared, the same as Alexa was. Scared like they weren't quite out of danger yet and they might still be hurt—like they'd maybe never be entirely out of danger or safe from harm. Alexa braced herself for Graciela to insist on speaking to Lorelei, but instead, she reached awkwardly behind the seat to grab Alexa's hand. "Are you all right, sweetheart?"

Alexa was not, but she knew they both sorely wished she was, so she said, "Just shaken up. I'm so sorry you had to deal with this. I know Lorelei will really appreciate it."

Graciela made a clucking sound. "We look out for each other out here."

Alexa shut the car door, and her eyes met Dan's through the glass of the passenger-side window. Dan hadn't offered any explanation or apology for her scream or the way she'd run off and left Alexa alone, and there was no hint of it in Dan's expression now. What Alexa found instead was dark and brooding and seemed to pierce through her unseeing, as if she was a ghost.

Then Graciela shifted back into drive and they both were gone.

WEDNESDAY, DECEMBER 17, SENIOR YEAR

Dan

Dan's mom spent Wednesday morning fawning over her. There was no way Dan was going to school, but she got up early because Graciela made chilaquiles with eggs for breakfast, and she even grilled up a plate of bacon on the side. Dan and her dad were speechless. Had Graciela been hiding *bacon* in the freezer this whole time?

Yes, she had been, for special occasions. A little something extra to help Dan recover from her "tough night."

Dan's tough night: that's what her parents called it. As if it would be bad luck to call it what it was—a car accident. Or maybe that's not what it was, because Dan hadn't been in the car when it happened, and actually, she hadn't even been close enough to see it, although her parents didn't know that. Maybe it was bad luck to talk about near misses, about things that almost went a lot worse than they did. That sounded like the kind of thing Graciela would believe.

Dan's father cleared his throat. "Your mom and I want to talk to you, Dan."

Dan set down her second helping of bacon to quickly check

that her sleeves were pulled down and none of the thin little scars were visible.

Her parents exchanged uncertain glances, then her dad pressed on. "When we got your call, we were a little surprised because we thought you were in your room. I don't know if we just didn't hear you leaving, but you shouldn't be going out like that without telling us. You know, a girl from Marlena went missing last week."

"Zephyr Finnemore. This wasn't anything like that." As Dan spoke, she realized the opposite was true. Zephyr had been out on the roads at night and stopped in the middle of nowhere for no one knew why. It wasn't so far off from what had happened to them. "I was with Alexa the whole time."

"Be that as it may, given that situation, it's time to make sure we're being really responsible and thinking about the consequences of our actions."

Her dad fiddled with his wedding ring. Dan gaped at him. Was he *disciplining* her? Dan's parents' correctives were usually along the lines of telling her they knew Dan was disappointed in herself because everyone knew she could do better—verbal acrobatics that made nothing anyone's fault. Dan couldn't remember a single time when they'd come out and told her she'd done something wrong.

Graciela picked up where he left off. "We've always valued giving you your space and letting you grow into this beautiful person, Daniela. But for us to respect you, we need you to respect us."

"Are you grounding me for getting in a car accident? I wasn't even driving."

Her mom's brow wrinkled. "Ground you? Oh, no. We would never limit you like that."

"But you need to let me or your mom know where you're going at night," her dad said.

Graciela gave him a stern look and added, "But if you can't tell us exactly where, letting us know that you're going out is enough. We understand you have your own life."

"Oh. Okay." Dan picked up her fork again. Why was she nearly disappointed? "That's it?"

"That's it!" Graciela brightened. She reached across the table and cupped Dan's cheek. "We love you so much, honey."

Back in her room, Dan fell onto her bed and played last night over in her head.

There wasn't a doubt in Dan's mind that the boy on the beach was Johnny, but she wasn't sure how to reconcile that with the fact that the boy hadn't actually been *real*.

She had bolted after him, but the silvery light he'd been catching flickered into darkness as he disappeared down the steep path to the beach. Dan didn't hesitate. She barreled after him, stumbling down the rough stairs cut into the dirt, nearly twisting both her ankles half a dozen times. But Johnny was a dark thing in a mess of things just as dark, and Dan's eyes couldn't keep hold of him.

She caught up to him on the black sand of the beach at the water-line. The skinny half-there shape of him, a gray face made of shining smoke, or moonlight.

"Johnny," she breathed. "How do we find you?"

He looked right at her. His eyes: maybe she couldn't see them properly, or it was the bad light, but they looked black, as they had the day he'd been taken. No iris, no white, darker than the sky on a new-moon night. Dark as nothing at all. He seemed almost afraid of her.

"It's me," she said. "Dan."

Something like recognition flickered in his face.

"You're the one?" he said.

She hadn't figured out how to reply before he was fading, the vapory glow of him vanishing, blown out to sea. "Johnny, don't go! I am, I'm the one—tell me how to find you!"

She stumbled down the beach, screaming his name and begging him to come home. The ocean ate her words and she screamed them again. She called for him until her throat burned, until her Converse were filled with salt water and black sand.

She was midway back up the trail when she heard the accident.

You're the one . . .

Was it a question or a statement, asking or telling?

And the one *what*? She wanted to think he was asking if she'd be the one to save him, or telling him she already was—like in that Chosen One fantasy trope that Alexa had educated her about. She didn't feel particularly heroic or day-save-y. The hero was being played by Liss. She was the one who had worked tirelessly and with unshakeable faith and no care for her personal safety.

Dan wasn't like that. She'd only been trying to stop Liss from doing something stupid on her own, and maybe a small part of her could admit that she was looking for closure on what had passed between them. But reopening the door on that friendship hadn't been tender. It had hurt. The very unheroic truth was that Dan had only imagined as far as *trying* to help Johnny; she'd never honestly considered the possibility that it might actually work.

Seeing him on the beach—or whatever part of him appeared to her—changed that.

You're the one.

If she wasn't the hero, there was one other available role: villain.

She didn't want to remember how disappointed she had been to see Johnny's car pull up at the crossroads that night, how Liss gave him a kiss and invited him to watch. It felt worse than if Liss had slapped her, worse than any of the rude things Liss had said in the past, worse than feeling Liss's eyes gloss over the cuts on her arms without seeing them. Dan still didn't understand why Liss had given a share of their most secret, precious thing—magic—to Johnny, who wouldn't get it and if he *did*, he wouldn't care, and anyway it wasn't his. It wasn't Liss's or even Dan's to share. It was *theirs*.

Or it had been.

Did Johnny know how hard she'd wished that he'd just *go away* and leave her and Liss alone so that things could go back to the way they used to be?

Dan flinched—her cuticle was bleeding and she hadn't even realized she'd started picking it.

A wish like that didn't mean anything, Dan quickly reminded herself, even if she'd been thinking it that night at the crossroads. You couldn't just make a wish in your own head without any spellwork to intensify it, and she hadn't even considered the specifics. That measly, ill-considered, and unspoken wish on its own was as dangerous as the dribble from a cracked squirt gun. It was no way responsible for the disaster that followed, no matter how hard she'd wished it (which had been painfully hard, as if her ribs had seized upon the desire to have Johnny just be *gone* so tightly that her breath had gotten shallow).

Dan took a deep breath. Maybe he meant it as a question. Was she the one who could get herself together and help fix this awful mess? For the first time, she felt like the answer to that question could be yes. Even if it hurt to face what she'd done, she could choose that pain over living with the guilt.

Together, she and Liss would find Johnny. They would bring him home. Everything would go back to the way it was before.

Luck had not been on their side so far, Dan knew. But that was why they had magic.

Dan grabbed her phone and typed out the text: *I'm coming over after school and I'm bringing the Book.*

FIFTEEN

Liss

"You're grounded for real?" Dan asked as Liss hustled her into the bathroom that adjoined her bedroom. In addition to grounding her, Liss's mom had been bad with boundaries lately, and Liss didn't want her walking in on them without any warning.

"She'll get over it," Liss said. Right now, she didn't care about her mother or the fact that her college applications were no closer to finished than they'd been last week. Dan was here, at Liss's house for the first time in months. Liss locked the bathroom door then turned back to Dan. Or rather, to the beat-up shoebox Dan was holding.

Liss's heartbeat picked up, as if her very blood was calling to it.

The Black Book.

It was here, at last, and suddenly Liss was overwhelmed with the feeling that they were reunited lovers who hadn't yet kissed.

No, she didn't feel like that because that would be perverse. She'd been thinking about Johnny, her true lost love. Liss forced herself to take a deep breath. She was exhausted, that was all, and her brain was playing tricks on her.

Dan put the shoebox on the counter. "So let me tell you about Johnny."

"Right." Liss pulled herself together. "You really saw him?"

Liss perched on the edge of the bathtub while Dan explained what happened. She counted up to four and back. Liss expected to be jealous of Dan—she had been, when Dan had first texted her.

Johnny had just *appeared* to Dan in a glittery nighttime beach-vision, without her having to invest months in actually doing anything to bring about that situation. But now Liss was trying so hard to ignore the gnawing hunger growing in the pit of her stomach that she'd forgotten entirely to be jealous.

"So did he say anything that could help us?" Liss asked.

Dan scrunched her face up. "No, not really."

"Not really or no?" Liss's eyes roved back to the shoebox.

"I couldn't really hear what he said. He seemed surprised to see me, but would he be waiting for someone at Heart's Desire?"

Liss's attention snapped back to Dan. "This was at Heart's Desire Beach?"

"I said that already. Do you know something about the auspices there?"

"No," Liss lied. "All I know is that it's a good place for drowning. Are we ready for the Book?"

They sat on the bathroom floor, Liss's back against the tub, Dan's against the vanity, and the shoebox between them, DAN + LISS TOP SECRET written on the top.

Liss tossed the lid aside. Inside, each item was wrapped in newspaper—candles, bundles of dried plants and grasses, egg-shells and crystals, the animal bones they'd spent months slowly collecting. Liss reached to the bottom, careful not to disturb any-thing breakable, until she found what she was looking for.

A shiver of electricity pulsed through her, tingling in her chest and fingertips. She eased the blocky mass free of the other items, then set it on the floor and folded back the newspaper.

There it was: an old and unassuming book, with the same warp in its black cover, the same loose pages and crack in the spine. Its presence fizzed the air with an electric charge. Liss let her eyes close and inhaled deeply. She had missed that scent: a musty sweetness that stayed on your hands, so that hours later you'd catch the scent of it later and remember, all over again, that sense of power you had when you held it.

Liss's smile was a small and famished thing.

Dan had a dreamy expression on her face too. "It's a magician's diary," Liss told her. She wondered if, now that they knew what it was, they would feel the history of it or find traces of its author.

"Why didn't we realize that? It's stupid obvious." Dan snorted a little laugh.

And then because Dan had snorted, Liss was laughing, and then Dan was laughing with her, and for one crystal-clear minute, everything was exactly the way it was before, when magic was a game, or even before they knew about magic at all—when it was just Liss and Dan laughing until their stomachs hurt on the bathroom floor.

Dan must have felt it too because she leaned back against the cabinet. "If this works, it'll be like we turned back time. Like the whole last year didn't happen at all."

"That's what you want?"

"Isn't that what you want? Then everything will be just like it was, before all *this*."

It brought a bitter taste in Liss's mouth. Dan had to know that it was impossible, even with magic, to erase the past. "That's what this is all about," Liss said instead. "Ready?"

Dan nodded and placed her hands on the Book's cover. "We need a spell to find Johnny."

"A spell to find Johnny," Liss said, doing the same.

A spell to find him, Liss repeated in her head. She tried to make her heart beat to the rhythm of his name: *Johnny, Johnny, Johnny.*

Liss looked at Dan; her eyes were half closed, her gaze on the Book. Liss could still see that sick look Dan had given her at the crossroads that night when Johnny had gotten out of the car after her. Liss had told herself a thousand times that she'd only let Johnny come because she wanted to share the part of herself that did magic with him. But that wasn't the whole truth. She'd also wanted to prove that he loved her enough that he'd be down for something as wild as magic. It was like daring him to break up with her, by forcing him to see that magic, like Liss, was more than he could handle. She'd barely given thought to how Dan would feel about it.

Dan's mouth was moving subtly, and her forehead creased in concentration. Liss reminded herself to refocus.

It felt familiar to have Dan here, but it would never be the same as before. Before Dan punished Liss with whole months of silence, and before the crossroads. Before the day Liss had convinced Dan to let her hang around at Achieve! Before the Black Book and before they'd transformed themselves into something beyond the girls they were, when they were simply best friends.

How far back did Dan want to go to find the *before all this*? So many mistakes had led the three of them to that crossroads. Those mistakes were a fundamental part of them now. Dan was wrong: you couldn't undo the past.

You just had to push on.

Dan opened her eyes. She seemed to think they'd spent long enough on the asking, and Liss was willing to trust her. Liss nodded and together they opened the cover. First Dan, then Liss turning one or several or a whole chunk of pages, whatever felt right. Liss forgot whatever she'd been thinking and let herself savor the feeling of the paper, the way it sent prickles from her fingertips to her scalp, then down to the base of her spine. It never ceased to amaze her that a book could feel like a whisper in the ear, a touch at the back of your neck, a sigh. Something you wanted to give yourself over to.

Liss turned the page and stopped.

They had found the spell.

THURSDAY, DECEMBER 18, SENIOR YEAR

Alexa

The following evening, Domino's green eyes tracked Alexa from the arm of the couch as she paced in the living room. Her phone was pressed to her ear.

"What do you mean you hit a roadblock? What kind of roadblock can stop people with literal magical powers?" Alexa was failing to keep the anger and desperation from her voice, but she'd already had to do some combination of begging and threat-making ("Maybe I should take Lorelei back to Arizona!") to get Swann to tell her what the Wardens were doing about Lorelei, Keith, and Black Grass.

"A hiccup in the plan, that's all," Swann admitted begrudgingly. "Another Warden has arrived in North Coast for the Black Grass case, but it seems they're closed to new seekers."

Alexa stopped. "They're what?"

"They're not accepting new seekers right now. Apparently they're at capacity after overwhelming interest in their methods. We're on a waitlist."

"You're telling me your magic can't beat a *waitlist*?"

"We are assessing our options, I assure you, love." Alexa had by now figured out that when Swann called her *love*, she either meant it as a form of genuine comfort or as a suggestion that she move on from the present topic. "How is Lorelei?"

Alexa did not want to move on.

"Well, I think she's pretty shitty, Swann, because she's dying and you and the Wardens are going to let Keith get away with it."

Probably she should not have hung up on Swann.

Alexa threw her phone onto the couch and turned to Domino. "I'm going over there."

To Swann's?

Alexa shook her head. "To Black Grass."

He pushed himself into a seated position, his black paws kneading the padding of the couch. *Are you sure that's wise?*

"Absolutely," Alexa said without missing a beat. Her cheeks were flushed, and her heart had picked up. She was never impulsive like this. She planned and was careful and tried generally to avoid disaster, rather than ride headlong into it. But she'd been that way because she'd always thought there was hope for her to have a life like everyone else.

Alexa didn't have that hope anymore. She had no one and nothing left to stop her.

What I meant was that is definitely not wise. Domino glowered at her. *It's incredibly dangerous.*

"It wasn't too dangerous for Lorelei."

Domino flicked his tail by way of response, which Alexa assumed meant *And look how that turned out for her.*

"Nothing will happen to me," Alexa told him. "And if it does, so what? It's not like anyone cares."

What about Dan?

Alexa wanted to think Dan would miss her, but they hadn't talked since their fight the other night. Dan wasn't worried about her, even after an accident that could have killed them both (if Dan had been anywhere nearby). Graciela had called Lorelei a half-dozen times since then, wanting to check if Alexa was okay and suggesting that the girls take a defensive driving course together. Dan's *mom*, who Alexa barely knew, cared more about her than Dan did.

"That's not the kind of comment I keep you fed for," she finally said, and sank onto the couch.

Alexa still couldn't think about the accident without being filled with nausea, not as much over how close she'd come to serious injury as how stupidly close she'd come to drawing the attention of the authorities exactly where she didn't want it. She realized this position was counterintuitive: avoiding the cops only mattered if she was alive, rather than squashed in a road accident. Still, she didn't want to lose control of her situation any more than she already had. That's what she'd risked to hang out with Dan that night, and it had been completely not worth it.

"Anyway, it's silly to worry that something will happen to me when something already has." She looked at Domino. "Keith needs to be stopped before he curses someone else."

The Wardens will—

"Will they actually, though? Because as far as I can tell they're not doing anything at all, while he's out there being the king of his commune! Don't you think Lorelei deserves revenge?"

Domino flipped his ears back.

"So you agree. Everyone knows cats love revenge."

And what will you do if this goes wrong?

Alexa chewed her lip for a moment. "The same thing I'll do if it goes right. Leave. I can't stay in North Coast. Someone will realize something's fishy eventually. I'm not going back to Arizona. And I'm not staying in one of those group homes. College can wait."

Domino skulked forward and rubbed his jowls against Alexa's shoulder.

"Don't get all sentimental," she told him.

Ignoring her, he headbutted her again. *Where will you go?*

"I haven't decided yet. Leaving town is phase two of the plan." Alexa smoothed out the crumpled pamphlet with Keith Lewandowski's face on it. "Phase one is revenge, which I am starting tonight with reconnaissance."

It was as good a beginning as any. Alexa didn't know what was going on at Black Grass or how Keith had cursed Lorelei. She had no idea what she could do to make him hurt the way he'd hurt them. It had to be more than screaming and crying at him but probably less than murder, both of which she imagined but only one of which she had the capacity for. But she was a witch, she was furious, and she had nothing to lose. That seemed like enough to rely on for now.

Alexa grabbed her sneakers, under Domino's judgmental stare. He switched his tail back and forth as she dug up a flashlight and dropped it into her backpack. *I have a bad feeling about this.*

"You're my familiar, not my mother."

She fished Lorelei's keys out of the bowl of change and receipts next to the door. Domino jumped down from the couch and curled his lithe ink-colored body between her legs and stationed himself in front of the door. "Honestly, I can't be taking a black cat everywhere now that I'm a witch."

Domino switched his tail exactly once.

"Fine, you can come," Alexa relented. "But only because you're sneaky and you have good night vision."

Domino followed her out the door.

Dan

"Heading to Alexa's?" Graciela looked up from her *New Yorker* as Dan trudged down the stairs.

"Liss's actually."

"Oh, Liss's again?" Graciela gave a hint of a smile. "Sleeping over?"

"Probably."

"Don't drive back here if it's too late, but text if you decide to stay. And don't forget about school tomorrow."

"Okay," Dan said, edging toward the door. The house felt too close around her. She couldn't wait to get out onto Highway 1, heading out of Dogtown and toward Marlena, then on to the place Liss had picked for the spell.

"Before you go, I wanted to ask you," Graciela said, leaving her magazine and leaning against the kitchen counter. "How's Alexa been doing?"

"What do you mean?"

"After your rough night, how's she been doing? I've been trying to get a hold of Lorelei, but I can't reach her and I'm sure she must be as nervous as we are about the situation with Zephyr."

"Really? Alexa's fine. She's—" How *was* Alexa? Dan had to know how Alexa was, she always did. She'd been so focused on the Black Book and Johnny and Liss in the two days since the car accident, she'd barely talked to Alexa at all. Maybe Alexa still wasn't over their fight before the crash. Then again, maybe Dan wasn't either. "I'm sure she told Lorelei about the accident, if that's what you're worried about. They tell each other everything."

"If you see Lorelei, could you ask her to call me? I'd like to get you girls into one of those defensive driving courses."

"I don't think I'm going to see Lorelei at Liss's house."

Graciela clicked her tongue at Dan. It was a sound that always made Dan feel a little guilty.

"I'll ask her the next time I see her," Dan corrected herself.

"Thanks, honey." Graciela gave her a kiss on her forehead. "Love you."

Dan rolled her eyes and headed for the door.

Liss

When Dan texted that she was there, Liss grabbed her stuff and walked out the front door, through the gate, and straight to where Dan's little hatchback was parked down the street. The fact that she was grounded meant that someone should have stopped her, but neither parent was up for the job: her dad was in Sacramento, and her mom was off doing whatever it was lonely mothers did at night. The odds were on her side that her mother would never notice Liss wasn't there.

They headed north, letting the black bend of the road carry them back toward Dogtown. Liss reviewed the notes on her phone. She had a nagging feeling that something was amiss. But the auspices were good—better than good, she assured herself, although she hadn't had time that afternoon to double-check them.

Liss pushed the thought out of her head. Everything would be fine. They would find Johnny, and the stalled engine of her life would start moving forward again. Dan rounded a switchback, then another.

"The turn's up here," Liss said.

Dan turned off the highway onto the dark, unpaved road. Her headlights cast a hazy glow that didn't do much to illuminate the way ahead.

The road snaked up the back of the hill, and soon the blackness of the Pacific was out of sight, lost in the closer darkness of the cypress and pine trees. Near the top of the ridge, Liss said, "Stop anywhere you can leave the car."

They got out of the car and took stock of the area. Nearby, a cattle gate was attached to an old wood-and-barbed-wire fence, and behind it was a track so poorly traveled it was barely visible in the moonlight. The gate was locked, and to emphasize this point, it had NO UNAUTHORIZED VEHICLES and PRIVATE PROPERTY NO TRESPASSING signs that reflected the beam of Liss's phone flashlight.

Dan fitted her headlamp over her hair. "I've never been up here. Whose land is this?"

"It's owned by an LLC," Liss answered. "That's all the information I could find. We're headed to a clearing down the hill."

Dan nodded, and Liss was struck by how much Dan seemed to trust her in that moment. She didn't question her or complain or admit she was a little freaked out (as Liss was, maybe more than a little). She just said okay.

Liss hadn't realized that this was part of what she'd missed, in missing Dan. How Dan was game for any of Liss's ideas, and she'd trusted Liss not to let her get hurt—at least not too badly.

"What are you smiling at?" Dan asked.

Liss had been worthy of that trust, hadn't she?

"Nothing," she said. "Let's go."

Liss climbed between the rusty bars of the cattle gate. Dan followed her, and together, they set off into the darkness.

Alexa

Alexa drove south from Dogtown toward Black Grass, until she found the inland-traveling road she'd picked out on the map. As expected, it had no name, and wasn't even paved after the first five hundred feet. At least it didn't seem to be anyone's driveway, and after bumping up it for ten minutes, Alexa had spotted nothing that looked like a Murder Shack. When she reckoned she'd driven far enough, she pulled the car into a shadowy patch as far off the road as she could.

Alexa left her phone in the car and locked it. Suddenly she remembered that girl who went missing from Liss's school—Zephyr—and a shiver radiated from her spine. If something went wrong tonight, Alexa's car would be found the same way, except there was no one to report her missing. Maybe no one who would miss her at all.

Domino, pacing at her feet, gave a stern meow.

Alexa oriented herself in the dark. The dinky beam of her flashlight lit up so little of the night that she simply clicked it off again. She should have checked the batteries. But the moon was nearing full, and the cloud cover was spotty enough to let some of its blue light through, and she had a cat with her, which had to count for some kind of night-vision bonus points. All around her, as Alexa's eyes adjusted, a world of darkest blue and black revealed itself, the bright scatter of stars between the clouds, the click and twitch of the insects of the night, the nervous footfalls of the small nocturnal beasts. The night was alive, a dark, blossoming flower. Alexa inhaled its wet, fresh scent. She fished Lorelei's evil-eye necklace from under her sweatshirt and pressed her lips to it, then set off toward Black Grass.

———

Aside from the barbed-wire fence she'd had to wriggle under at the outset, the hike hadn't been difficult. After fifteen minutes of stumbling across a kind of field in the dark—literal black grass, Alexa thought—the lights of the campus came into view. Its perimeter was circled by a wooden fence with plenty of space between the boards. Not exactly what Alexa had expected from the intimidating gate that cut the campus's driveway off from Highway 1.

Alexa couldn't risk tripping an alarm or getting caught on video, so she tried to step quietly as she moved around its edge. She looked between the slats for anything that might be helpful, but for the most part, she saw—nothing. The campus looked somewhat like a rustic resort, with whitewashed bungalows with potted flowers at every door, clotheslines and hammocks strung up between trees, and a bench set up with half-played game of chess. It wasn't exactly the awful prison she'd imagined.

On top of that, prisons usually had people in them. Alexa couldn't see a single one of Black Grass's seekers.

Domino came slinking from the underbrush; he'd run ahead to scout.

Where is everyone? Alexa thought to him with a horrible feeling in her stomach. What if Lorelei wasn't the only one who'd been cursed?

Come on, Domino answered. *It's evening meditation.*

A few yards from the fence, Alexa positioned herself behind the forked trunk of a tree and peered through the gaps in the fence. The seekers were gathered in an open space in front of the largest bungalow—Keith's, no doubt. Maybe forty of them sat cross-legged on the ground, hands folded in their laps and heads bowed.

It looked exactly like the meditation they'd been taught in North Coast High's gym class. The only difference was that instead of Mr. Haskell reminding them to breathe in and out, here Keith was moving among the seekers, leading their breathing but also touching them. He placed his palms on their foreheads and cheeks, pressed his hands to their hearts and the midpoints of their backs, all with a horrible little smile on his face, like he was entertained by a private joke. A bolt of rage lurched inside Alexa. She knew the joke he was laughing at, and it was Lorelei: Lorelei dying, Lorelei dead, and here he was *smiling* about it, acting like a healer when he was at best a con artist and at worst—something else. Something Alexa didn't have a word for yet.

She was going to make him pay.

I'm going closer, Alexa thought to Domino. She could feel his green eyes glaring at her although it was too dark to see them. *While Keith is out here we can look at his bungalow.*

Maybe it was dangerous to get closer, but it was dangerous to be there at all, and Alexa was past the point of caring. In the dark, Domino was probably switching his tail at her in judgment.

She crept closer to the fence, keeping half an eye on Keith, who was keeping both self-satisfied eyes on his obedient followers. As Alexa snuck closer to Keith's bungalow, she lost sight of the meditation session. Not a big deal: breaking into the bungalow was her new prize. The fence wasn't so tall that she couldn't climb it. She could even try to leap from it onto the bungalow's roof, which seemed like the kind of cool thing she would do if this was a movie, although she couldn't figure out a practical reason to do it now. She put a hand on the fence and pressed, testing to see if it could hold her weight.

Domino hissed at her from somewhere near her feet. When she

looked down, she only saw an inky spot of darkness. He hissed again.

Move back. It isn't safe.

There's no one around.

Domino's tone darkened. *Do you truly think it's only what you can see that can hurt you? Don't you feel it?*

Suddenly the rage monster wasn't straining against anything anymore—suddenly she was scared. She felt reckless now, lucky that she hadn't been *more* reckless and actually scaled the fence without a plan.

Domino was right—she *could* feel it, whatever *it* was. There was a crackling in the air, a frisson like static electricity prickling through the wind. Something was happening.

She had nearly made it back to her earlier vantage point when the wailing began.

The seekers were crying.

Or moaning. Or *something*.

They'd left their peaceful cross-legged positions. Some were standing, some kneeling, they were pulling at their hair and tears were streaming down their faces, their mouths hanging open in a kind of howl. Alexa's heart raced.

Were they in pain? What was Keith doing to them?

But then she saw that not all of them were crying. Others appeared to have paired up and were hugging—even kissing. One couple had grabbed a blanket and was on the ground doing something that looked like a very sexual and emotional massage. The more she watched, the less sure she was that the ones who were crying were actually sad. Some of them seemed just overwhelmed, and others were sort of smiling. One weeping woman had crawled—actually crawled on the ground—up to Keith and was kissing his feet, which were encased in those weird shoes that separated each toe. But a grimace had replaced his satisfied smile. Whatever the seekers were doing, Keith had evaluated it and found them wanting.

The wailing went on and on. One weeping man ripped his shirt, then another wrestled him into a very aggressive hug, and the couples were doing increasingly . . . private things. Several people were gasping for air and shaking all over.

Lore had mentioned the lame health food, all the meditating to "iterate past their desires," whatever that meant, and everyone's obsession with pleasing Keith. She hadn't said anything about *this*. The thought made Alexa sick. Surely the Wardens can't have expected her to do whatever *this* was—and Lorelei wouldn't have been willing to join it, would she? It was impossible to imagine her rolling in the dirt wearing a crazed look of glee, or slapping herself in the face.

But when he came to their house, Keith had said Lorelei was rising through the ranks quickly, and had a chance to prove herself deserving of their Lord. Was this what he'd wanted her to do?

And what actually *was* this thing the seekers were doing—in addition to being super disturbing? It was like the seekers had overwhelmed their own capacity for self-control, and emotion was exploding out of them. There was enough energy released by it that the air crackled with it, raising the hairs on Alexa's arms and at the back of her neck.

Meanwhile, despite the woman prostrate at his feet, Keith was getting frustrated. He ran his hands through his long hair and over his patchy goatee and then finally disappeared into his bungalow.

Is it safe for you to go after him? she asked Domino.

Safer for me to try, he answered. *Focus on me and you should be able to hear.*

Focus on you? How?

You'll figure it out. He was already slinking toward Keith's bungalow. *How do you think I always know what you're thinking?*

Alexa grimaced at Domino's vanishing form. How much time had he spent skulking around her brain; how many of her weird thoughts had he seen?

I do have a life of my own.

I was thinking that privately!

She focused on Domino as he easily leapt to the top of the fence—the chime of his voice in her head, the green coins of his eyes, the roll of his shoulders as he stalked prey.

Suddenly she could feel him balancing as he padded along the top of the fence posts, the unfamiliar sharpness of things in the dark. She felt him take a graceful leap from the fence to the narrow windowsill of the only lit room of Keith's bungalow.

The curtains were closed, and Domino's sharp ears came in handy.

". . . but something is blocking the synergy," Keith was saying.

"Maybe the fact that it's just some shit you made up?" a female voice said. There was something almost familiar about it—or no, there wasn't.

"I have asked you repeatedly not to disrespect the synergy."

"Fuck your synergy."

"I'm trying to troubleshoot here. You can at least help me source ideas."

"My idea is for you to crawl in a hole and die."

"That is really unhelpful! You are part of this team now. You need to start acting like it."

A sound lanced through Alexa's concentration. She was back in her own mind again, listening for something out there in the dark. No, it was nothing. She took a deep breath and tried to focus on Domino.

But there it was again. It was clear it wasn't just some leaf rustle or animal howl. It was human, and it was behind her.

We have to go. Get back here now.

Don't wait for me, Domino told her, and she didn't.

SIXTEEN

Liss

"*A little bit to the* north." Liss scrutinized the compass she held in one hand. In the other, she held a round stone wrapped in scarlet fabric, dangling like a pendulum from a leather lanyard. A *veliron*, the Black Book called it when it gave them directions to make it.

Dan tried to keep the flashlight focused on the compass and veliron as they stepped a few feet north in the clearing. "Here?"

"I think so. I'd be a lot more sure if I actually knew what this rock did. It looks like one of those necklaces the weirdos from the commune in Jenner wear."

"But you checked the auspices for this place today, so with that plus the veliron, we should be fine."

Liss pushed her hair out of her eyes. "I've almost got it, okay?"

"Okay," Dan assured her.

Liss was relieved when the stupid veliron finally stopped spinning, which had taken basically forever. They were on the north side of the small clearing, beyond which a dark line of trees obscured the view down the hill. Dan got busy mashing down the tall grass so they'd actually have room to do the spell.

Liss took a drink of water. She'd had too long to think, spent too long staring at that rock on a string, too long trying to ignore Dan's little comments about shouldn't they have found the place already? But something did feel off, and it could be the auspices. It shouldn't have taken them so long to find the spot. The few clouds had cleared, and she could see the faraway pinpricks of stars, as if the sky were taunting her with all its moving parts.

Liss counted up to four and back, up to four and back.

It didn't matter now. They were here. The Black Book didn't lead them astray.

Except, of course, that once.

"Liss?" Dan raised an eyebrow. "Ready?"

Liss balled her hands into fists. "Absolutely."

Because Liss had done the auspices, Dan initiated the spell. Usually the Black Book gave them spells that could simply be doubled: two voices casting together. This spell was different: one person needed to speak the incantation, while the other manipulated the materials. Dan had copied the unintelligible syllables of the spell onto a few sheets of binder paper that she was carefully arranging before her while Liss set up the materials. She poured some rubbing alcohol (the spell had called for spirits) into a metal bowl, then submerged the feathers and tried not to gag as she squeezed a few drops of chicken blood from a sandwich baggie into the mix. She had a clipping of fabric from the neck of a sweatshirt that had been—still *was*—Johnny's. The spell called for his hair, but it seemed ridiculous to require the hair of a missing person for a spell to find them. Usually when people left, they took their hair with them. Lighter, candle, and the veliron, all laid out and ready at hand. Beside her, she weighted down the edges of the map of North Coast.

Dan began the incantation. The syllables were hard-edged and strange to Liss's ear, but Dan didn't stumble. Liss was close behind with the materials: drop the sweatshirt fragment into the alcohol mix, then soak the veliron too. Next she lit the candle and passed it in three circles around the bowl. Finally, she pulled the spirit-dampened veliron from the mix and held it by the lanyard over the map. Next came the scary part: Liss touched the candle to the alcohol in the bowl. It lit with a *fwump* and a burst of blue flame. Liss snatched her hand back and blew out the candle. Really, this spell was awfully dangerous, mixing alcohol and fire like that, but the flames stayed cupped in the metal bowl, burning down the feather and blood along with the traces of Johnny on the sweatshirt. Dan had stuttered a little when the fire caught, but she seemed to have found the thread of the incantation again.

Liss watched the veliron spin over the map. It was as if it was pulled by a magnet, moving by an unseen force. She was waiting for the spirit to fall on the map, a clear and quick-vanishing dot to guide them to Johnny. Was the map even big enough? What if they'd gone somewhere totally different, somewhere far away, somewhere unmapped or unmappable? She stole another look at Dan. Her eyes were half-closed, sweat beading on her forehead. She was getting tired.

"Come on, come on . . ." Liss whispered.

She scanned the map again. The veliron began to spin more quickly on its lanyard. "You can go a little longer," she whispered to Dan, as she caught a corner of the map against the breeze that had suddenly kicked up. Something burning in the bowl cracked and popped, and a single drop of rubbing alcohol fell from the stone onto the map.

Liss flung the veliron aside and pressed her face to the paper, looking frantically for the spot marked by the clear drop of liquid. She's seen it fall—where had it landed?

The breeze was intensifying, tugging her hair free of her bun, until suddenly it burst into a gust that lashed her from all angles. Liss had the crazed sensation that she was being *tied up* somehow by ropes of wind, as if the wind wanted to pin her into place, the same way it had pinned the map against the dry grass. Liss fought against it, lunging for the map. She had to find the spot marking Johnny's location—

But then she wasn't looking at the map at all, but at the dark grass underneath. The wind had whisked embers out of the bowl. The air still swirled around them. First pinprick burns riddled the paper, then in seconds they bloomed into a single red and black abyss, eating up the topographic swirls of the mountains and down the arteries of the rivers. The fire gnawed through the old map like it would destroy the whole of North Coast, and soon the paper was obliterated altogether. Liss clung pointlessly to the scraps—the legend, part of the blue border of the Pacific Ocean.

"Did you see it, Dan? I didn't get it." Liss was frantic. "Shit, the whole map's wrecked."

Then she saw Dan.

At some point Dan had stopped the incantation. Or no—she'd frozen, her lips stuck on a word half said and her eyes screwed up tight. Her notebook paper was crumpled in her fists, her body rigid and still, the wind whipping her hair around her face. It was as if one minute she'd been doing the spell and the next she'd just *stopped*, like a toy run out of batteries. In front of her, the bowl of fire still snapped and burned, responding to the rush of the air.

"Dan?" Liss whispered, then cleared her throat. "The spell's over."

Liss crawled toward her. Dan was trembling all over, and there was a low moan coming from her throat, like the sound had gotten stuck there. "Dan, open your eyes!"

Liss put her hand on Dan's shoulder.

The sound in Dan's throat broke free—a wild, inhuman sound that the wind rushed up from behind her to carry away. Dan didn't struggle against it, as Liss had. She let it shove her forward, and she fell—directly into the bowl of blue flame.

"Dan!" Liss screamed.

But the fire was already spreading, urged on by the wind. The dry grass that Dan had carefully tamped down before the spell was smoking, fingers of flame lacing through it. Before Liss knew it, the world started to burn.

Alexa

Alexa cut across the middle of the flat top of the hill to avoid whatever was happening on its north side. Whoever it was wasn't exactly trying to escape notice, not with a flashlight pointing all directions like that. By the same reasoning, they didn't seem part of Black Grass. It was probably a darryl or some stoner kids. She reconsidered heading back to the car, now that the noise wasn't a threat after all, but she'd agreed to meet Domino there.

Then that *sound*—a guttural scream with serrated edges. Alexa felt it in her chest, like a hot knife. The flashlight was bobbing like crazy now. A chill ran down Alexa's spine. Whatever they were doing, it wasn't any of her business.

"*Dan!*"

Alexa was running before she thought about what she'd heard. It was that scream and Dan's name that played in her brain as she bounded through the grass, struggling to keep her feet under her. What was happening up there—was that the orange glow of a fire? The wind shifted and brought the smell of smoke to her.

Alexa ran faster.

Liss

Liss did not know what to do.

The fire had spread so much in just a few seconds—Dan still wasn't awake, and it was the best Liss could do to drag her away from the worst of it, but then she'd stupidly left the backpack with the fire extinguisher where she'd been sitting for the spell, and now it was completely out of reach—the backpack itself was *actually on fire*. Then the stink of something sulfur hit her, and Dan's lovely long, dark hair was burning. Liss grit her teeth and stamped it out with her foot, then tried to hook her arms under Dan's shoulders, but she couldn't, she just couldn't. Dan was lying in a field of burning grass and Liss was too stupid and weak to help her.

Liss reached for Dan again but something flung them both back and flattened her to the ground. For a split second there was a tremendous *pressure* in the air, sucking and pulling, and the terrifying sensation that she couldn't *breathe*—and then once again she could.

Just like that the fire was gone. Liss was coughing and clutching Dan, and the grass was dark and slowly smoking where the fire used to be, and everything felt tired and frantic at the same time. The fire just *went out*, like it collapsed into itself the way horror-movie demons did, leaving behind a pile of blackened bones. It wasn't possible—none of it was possible—but Liss couldn't think about that now.

Dan was breathing. She still wasn't awake but her eyes were open and she stank like a cheap curling iron. Dan would be furious about her hair when she woke up.

If she woke up.

If Liss could get her out of here.

Liss heard something coming through the grass, but she was beyond caring. "Whoever's there—help! We need help!"

"Is she okay?"

She knew that voice, even gasping and panicked as it was.

Liss looked up at Alexa and she could have sworn, for a second, that smoke was coming from her too.

Alexa

What had she done?

There were foreign words on her tongue that had come to her from nowhere. They tasted dry as chalk, felt like sand in her teeth, and with them she had opened herself, *thrown* herself against the fire. She barely knew what that meant, only that it was enough, and the fire had died like a candle under a snuffer. She cared even less with Dan lying on the ground catatonic like she was.

"What do we do?" Liss was asking again, as if Alexa might know. "How did you do that? Never mind—I don't care. Is she okay?"

Alexa never imagined she'd see Liss frantic like this, and she fought to keep the panic from her own voice. "I don't know. She's breathing."

"There's an urgent care in Gratton—or the hospital! The hospital is better, but it's so far." Liss looked up at her, helpless. "She can't die," Liss added with sudden terror.

But then Dan's eyes started moving, and the awful frozen expression on her face relaxed. A second later she was rolling onto her side, coughing and spitting and rubbing her eyes.

"Don't rub them." Alexa grabbed Dan's wrist. "It's from the smoke."

Alexa found a bottle of water and poured it directly into Dan's eyes. Water ran down her face like tears.

Liss

Liss wasn't religious, but at that moment she could not stop thanking god. Thank god for Alexa. Thank god Dan seemed okay. Thank god they hadn't set all of North Coast on fire. She didn't care what Alexa was doing in the same patch of wilderness as they were in the middle of the night.

Dan was groggy, and not anywhere near as scared as Liss still felt. Adrenaline whizzed through Liss's blood like a drug that wouldn't wear off.

Which is why she almost didn't notice the cat.

A black house cat had not wandered so much as galloped out of the grass and was pacing alongside Alexa, who was staring down at him with great concern.

"Is that your . . . cat?" Liss asked.

"Shit," Alexa whispered, almost like she was speaking to the cat directly, then her head snapped up, as if she'd been caught doing something she shouldn't be. "We have to go, right now. Where's the car?"

"I think Dan needs a second."

"We don't have a second. They're coming, now. We have a few minutes' head start. Where is the car?" Alexa demanded.

"Who's coming? There's no one up here," Liss said.

"Black Grass," Alexa said. "You didn't know you're on their land?"

"Shit," Liss hissed in agreement. "Dan, do you think you can stand? Because you're going to need to try to run."

Alexa

Back at Dan's house, Alexa and Liss were left alone in Dan's room as she showered. She had promised them she felt fine, only her eyes stung a little. Now, Alexa sat on the floor against the bed, trying to quiet the sick feeling in her gut. Liss was looking very small and skinny and pale curled up in the armchair, directly on top of Dan's clothes. She'd been fidgeting with her hands nonstop; it hadn't stopped them from shaking.

"What did you do?" Liss finally asked in a flat voice.

Alexa pushed her glasses up her nose. "I didn't do anything. The fire went out right when I got there. It must have been the wind or something."

Liss shook her head. "I saw it. I *felt* what you did. And the cat?"

Alexa didn't take the invitation to explain. Liss looked at her for a long minute with her lips pressed between her teeth. Then she dropped her eyes. "Don't tell me if you don't want to. I don't care. You saved her, that's all that matters. I couldn't do it. I couldn't do *anything*. If something happened to Dan like . . ."

"Like what happened to Johnny?"

Liss took a very deliberate breath that meant *yes*. "Look, I don't think she remembers anything. You can tell her you used the fire extinguisher. As for why you were up there in the first place, you need a better excuse than getting lost on your way to church."

"I don't need an excuse," Alexa said, because it seemed like the kind of thing a non-liar would say.

"I don't care. Tell her the truth if you want. But if you want a lie she'll believe, tell her there's a guy. Secret boyfriend. Dan won't ask for all the details."

"It would have to be a girlfriend," Alexa corrected her.

Liss waved her hand. "Whatever, secret girlfriend then. Just tell her you were sneaking around because you wanted to meet her somewhere alone."

There was something about Liss as she said this, like it was a secret weapon, a weakness of Dan's that she was wrong to expose, that made Alexa sad for all of them, and somehow jealous that Liss knew Dan well enough to hurt her like that.

Alexa pushed her glasses up her nose again, although they hadn't fallen. It was a good excuse. She could avoid Dan as long as she stayed in North Coast, maybe even say she'd run away with this girl when the time came. Could she do it? Alexa could still see Dan coughing by the remains of the fire, feel the desperate relief that she was okay. She wished there was a way to leave without leaving her behind.

That was the awful problem: even after everything had gotten so beyond-belief screwed up, Alexa wanted Dan to know her, the real her, and with every passing minute that seemed increasingly impossible. It was stupid to try to save a friendship she was only going to have to leave behind. But Alexa didn't want to push Dan away any more than she already had to.

"How can I tell a lie I don't want her to believe?" Alexa said.

Liss studied her with a stern look. "Okay," she finally said.

Before Alexa could ask Liss what she meant, Dan appeared in the doorway, her eyes bloodshot and her wet hair dripping onto her T-shirt. "You guys haven't managed to kill each other yet?"

"Actually, we're best friends now. It's a regular three-musketeers situation over here," Liss said.

It was amazing how easily she did it—how Liss had been tense and scared one minute, then back to the same snarky, unshakable bitch just when Dan walked into the room. Alexa knew Liss was pretending although she couldn't see any sign of it. All of a sudden she felt a rush of gratitude, because as freaked out as she might have been inside, Liss was acting normal for Dan.

"Well," Dan said. "Well, good."

"And the last thing tonight needs is a body to dispose of," Liss added with an eye roll.

How often did Liss pretend? Alexa wondered.

"I was just saying how lucky we were that Alexa managed to get the fire extinguisher so fast. Half of North Coast would be ashes by now without her," Liss said coolly. "It's a crazy coincidence that she was up there killing time before she picked her aunt up." Liss looked at Alexa and gave a little smile. This was a gift, Alexa knew—Liss was lying to Dan so Alexa didn't have to—and the kindness of it made tears sting her eyes, even though she could practically see Liss willing her to keep it together. "Dan told me she works up there or something, right?"

Alexa raised a hand halfway to her glasses but stopped herself. "Lorelei and I are sharing a car now, so she can't drive it to work. I was just, you know, having a wander while I waited for her. The timing was crazy."

"We were really lucky you were there." Dan crawled onto her bed and examined the ends of her hair.

"How bad is it?" Alexa asked.

Dan freed a lock of hair that stopped abruptly at her collarbone. It was at least six inches shorter than the rest of her hair. "I think that's the worst."

"Maybe you can layer it, you know, so it blends? I can go with you after school tomorrow to get it cut."

"Dan, we should tell her," Liss cut in.

"Tell me what?" Alexa asked.

"Liss," Dan said in a low tone. "No."

"She already saw us," Liss said. "You really want to act like everything's fine?"

"Everything *is* fine." Dan gave Liss a hard and pleading look.

Liss held her gaze. "We all know that's not true. All three of us smell like an ashtray and you just burned off half your hair. Alexa probably has, you know, some very legitimate questions about how we nearly became teenage arsonists. And we could use her help." When Dan didn't answer for a long time, Liss added, "I can tell her if you don't feel up to it."

Dan cut her off. "No. If we're going to tell her, I'll do it." Dan took a ragged breath to fortify herself, and Alexa thought that Dan sat a little taller. Whatever she was about to say, Dan was trying to be strong. "This will sound kind of crazy, I'm asking you to hear me out before you make any judgments. Earlier, what you saw us doing was . . ." Dan lowered her eyes, as if she couldn't bear to see Alexa's reaction to what she was about to say. "It was a spell. The truth is, me and Liss, we're kind of . . . witches."

SEVENTEEN

Alexa

"**Y**ou're what?" *Alexa blurted out.* What dying witch had given *them* a gift? Was Dan hiding a rotting body in her garage? They had to be playing at some dumbed-down TV show imitation, not living with a putrefying undead corpse and unintentionally communing with ghosts. "You guys *cannot* be witches. Like pointy hats and broomsticks and black cats? That stuff is made up."

Liss cleared her throat, but Alexa didn't look at her.

"It's a little more complicated than that," Dan ventured. "It turns out magic is, um, actually real and there's kind of a lot of it up here in North Coast."

"For historical and geological reasons," Liss chimed in.

"Right. So there's a lot of magic but it's not all exactly *good* magic."

"It's not really a good/bad thing—more like a dangerous/not dangerous thing," Liss corrected.

"Whatever." Dan went on, "Some of that magic is dangerous. Which is bad."

"Okay, I'm with you," Alexa said tentatively. "I mean, it sounds super weird, but I'm listening."

"Do you remember Johnny—Liss's boyfriend?"

"The one who's missing."

"Everyone thinks he's missing. But we know what happened to him." Dan composed herself. "It was our fault. There was a spell that went bad and he got . . . taken."

"Taken? By who?"

"Kasyan," Dan said quietly. "Technically, he was taken by Kasyan's henchwoman-thing."

"*Mora* took Johnny?" Alexa kicked herself; she'd let the words out before she even knew what they meant.

Dan's eyebrows popped. "So you know about Mora too?"

"No! I mean, just what you said. Kasyan's bad, Mora's his henchwoman-thing, but they're not real."

"You're wrong," Liss said with such casual authority that it was impossible to disagree with her. "We don't know much about him, but the fact is Kasyan is real. We think he's somewhere in North Coast. Johnny's with him, and he's going to die if we don't get him back soon."

"That's the spell you caught us doing. We were trying to locate Johnny." Dan leaned back and studied the look on Alexa's face. "Maybe I shouldn't have said anything. You probably think we made this all up."

"No," Alexa said. "Not really. Tell me what happened, from the beginning."

Dan gave Liss another heavy look, but this one, Alexa could read. It asked, *Are you sure about this?*

Liss shot Dan an ironic smile. "Like I said: three musketeers."

Dan

Dan told Alexa that it was February, right after an info night about college applications that had freaked them out with talk of safety schools and reaches. They'd looked for a way to make the future feel nearer and surer. The Black Book responded, as it usually did, with a spell that sounded perfect.

What Dan didn't say was: It was Valentine's Day, which was a very stupid holiday. Who needed a special day to celebrate having a boyfriend or girlfriend? When you were in a relationship, your whole life was a celebration of that fact. For the last two years, she and Liss had gotten ice cream and made fun of the other couples from school spending money they didn't have on flowers that were already dead. This year, Johnny had planned a whole romantic evening for Liss.

Dan tried to be excited for Liss, but the harder she tried the more she felt tired and hopeless. When she got home from school, her mom had left a present outside her door, as she always did on Valentine's Day. It was always the same incredibly dismal thing: funny socks.

Dan laid on her bed and listened to Rickey IronWeaks until she cried. Then she told herself she was stupid for crying and then well, she *was* stupid so she might as well just fucking cry, although who even cried over something like this? So your best friend and her boyfriend went out on Valentine's Day, obviously they did, it had nothing to do with you at all, actually it had so little to do with you that you could completely disappear right now, like vanish or die or something, and nobody would care.

She couldn't stop the thoughts until she dug out the razor blade hidden in a breath mint tin from the back of the bottom drawer of her desk. She kept it there so it would be harder for her to get when she wanted it—although she *could* still get it whenever she wanted it, so that wasn't really a working strategy. Once she was done, she wasn't crying anymore. She only felt numb.

No matter what happened with Johnny, she and Liss would always have magic. Their bond *was* magic, and she could use magic to get it back. Dan would think of a spell to ask the Book for that Liss wouldn't be able to resist.

It was called Volunin's Frame, Dan told Alexa. Although Liss was strictly speaking too busy to be doing much magic, with Johnny and the pressure her parents were putting on her, she agreed to it. It was the kind of spell you said yes to. It was written like a brainteaser. You needed a spot where two roads crossed at a right angle, and you needed to be there the last day of the month. The spell often failed, for reasons the Book called idiosyncratic, which they took to mean were basically random. If it went right, they would find themselves in a game of chance, which of course the Book provided no details on. What they stood to win was a wish, and not just any wish: a wish big enough to transform your future. "Beware the risks," the Black Book said, which was pretty generic as far as warnings went. At the time it had seemed low stakes: probably the spell would fail, but if it went right, who knew the limit?

It did not go as planned.

First, Liss brought Johnny, Dan said. That complicated things, like where was he supposed to stand and was he going to laugh at them and break their concentration and in all honesty, Dan was actually a little annoyed that Liss hadn't even given her a heads-up, if she couldn't be bothered to ask. They agreed Johnny would wait in his car and was strictly forbidden from taking pictures.

What Dan did not say was: when she saw Johnny's car instead of Liss's Range Rover pull up on Escondido Road, she thought she might actually throw up. She even started sweating, the way you do right before you're sick. They parked in front of her and then made out for a really unnecessary amount of time. The longer it went on the harder she wished Johnny was gone—away, anywhere but here with her and Liss.

When they all finally got out of their cars, Liss kept running the back of her hand over her mouth, as if she were wiping off his spit, when there wasn't anything there anymore, she had wiped it away already, and was she actually just trying to draw Dan's attention to the fact that Johnny's spit, and therefore also tongue and lips, had been all over hers a minute ago? Because Dan was already acutely aware of that fact.

With the two of them there, she was more alone than when she was by herself.

Dan pulled Liss aside. "What's he doing here?"

"I thought he could come watch," Liss said.

"What does he think he's watching?"

"I told him it's a Wicca thing. Besides, if the spell goes like we expect, then he shouldn't see anything. It's mostly in our heads."

"If you *had* to bring him you could have at least told me. We could have done it another time."

"Yeah, the last day of next month. What's the issue? He doesn't care."

"I care, okay?" Dan snapped. "It's weird having someone else here. We've never done that before. I thought this was *our* thing, you know?"

Liss's expression melted into something condescending and sweet. "Aw! It *is* our thing. But Johnny's here too now, and obviously, we can't just tell him to leave."

The understanding in Liss's voice sliced Dan in two. Liss knew— she had to know, was too smart not to—how badly she'd hurt Dan. How badly she was still hurting her.

But Liss didn't care.

"Fine," Dan said. "Let's get this over with."

"That's the spirit."

Dan didn't say that the whole time they were setting the spell, Johnny was all she could think about, Johnny and Liss, Liss and Johnny, wishing that he would just go away, just gone. She hated the feeling that he was watching the two of them doing this. Last summer was forever ago, their September kiss from another lifetime. It felt sometimes like it had all happened to Liss, and not to Dan at all.

Dan cursed Johnny under her breath.

Dan told Alexa how they set the spell. Liss insisted they use a guardian line drawn in salt where they'd stand. Just outside the salt perimeter lay the three vertebrae from a swan that Dan had ordered online.

Thankfully the roads weren't busy, because they had to set up right where they crossed. Dan glared at Johnny, who was perched on the trunk of his Volvo messing with his phone, and suggested he might make himself useful and keep an eye out for any cars that might squash them.

Liss rolled her eyes. "He doesn't think any of this is real."

"Is that supposed to be reassuring?" Dan said.

The two of them stood shoulder to shoulder inside the salt circle, said the words, said them again. Dan felt her focus narrowing, closing in on the spell, the air simmering, the goose bumps on her skin. They began the incantation a third and final time when Johnny interrupted.

"Yo, this actually looks pretty cool. Can I get in on it?"

They dropped their hands and the magic faded.

"You were going to wait in the car, babe. We agreed," Liss said. Dan could tell now she was annoyed too.

"Come on, I can say whatever you were saying. I'm a fast learner," he answered, and kissed Liss on the cheek.

Liss smiled. "Dan? What do you think?"

"I don't care," she said. "I don't care anymore."

The three of them crammed inside the line, saying the third

incantation. The hair on the back of Dan's neck stood up, and it might have been coincidence, but it felt like the wind picked up.

All at once, a woman was there.

She was hunched as an old woman might be, but there was something tightly coiled about the way she held herself, so that it was more like her body was hiding something than that she had a natural stoop. Her rough, anemic skin reminded Dan of an old rope line abandoned on a dock. She wore what appeared to be a matching jogging suit from the 1980s, a visually offensive mashup of pale pink and teal. On top of that, her neck was circled by some type of fur scarf that seemed to be strung together from the pelts of small woodland creatures—rabbits, squirrels, mice—with their little feet and heads still attached. Her hair was colorless and nestlike, but beneath it her face had a pointed look, the features sharp and gathered too close together, and her eyes were a disconcerting black, with no white at all.

Dan exchanged a horrified glance with Liss. They'd never summoned a person—or something this personlike—before.

"Oh, *awesome*," Johnny breathed.

The woman looked at each of them in turn with wet eyes. Her skinny lip twitched in and out of a sneer, and when it did, they could see something darkish and very not teeth-looking in her mouth. Dan had always thought that the expression *her blood ran cold* was a metaphor, but now she realized that could literally happen.

She was *terrified*.

The woman stooped and scooped up the three vertebrae and rattled them around in her grimy hand like dice.

"The game is Likho," she said in a rough and phlegmy voice. She picked a vertebra out of her hand and held it pointy side up between two thick, yellow nails. "Evens," she said, then reversed the bone so the pointy side was down. "Odds." Her track suit rustled as she tapped her sternum.

Then she hiked up the legs of her tracksuit and squatted back on her heels. The three of them followed suit, kneeling in the street. She rattled the bones in her knob-knuckled hand again, then cast them into the triangle.

One pointy side up, two pointy side down.

The woman grinned, and they could see her teeth for real. Drippy little stubs of things, narrow and sharp and red-brown. They could smell them too; Dan was struggling not to gag. "Odds. For me."

"Our turn?" Liss asked, and the woman nodded. "We play as a team."

"You know how this game works?" Dan hissed at her.

"I think it's like odds and evens. She got more odds than evens that round, so she won. I'll roll for us first."

"This is crazy, babe," Johnny whispered. Liss's expression devolved into grave annoyance as he kissed her on the cheek, for luck. Dan caught her eye and nodded her encouragement.

Liss closed the bones in her hands, rolled them against her palms, then cast: all three, pointy side up.

The woman grumbled something unintelligible in response, collected the bones, and cast again. Evens took her cast as well.

"Dan goes next," Liss said, although Johnny was next in line, between them.

Dan took a breath to steady her nerves and gathered the bones. She tried to focus on something else, something good, but all she could think of was how the spell had failed, and even when they got out of there, it wasn't going to do anything to help her and Liss, because now Johnny was here, Johnny was ruining everything. He was rocking on his heels like this was going to be a sick story to tell his friends.

She cast the bones: odds.

The woman celebrated with another gruesome grin and without hesitation cast the bones herself. Odds again.

"It's three to two. We have to roll evens to tie now," Liss breathed. Her voice buzzed with anxiety. "We *cannot* lose."

"What happens if we lose?" Johnny asked.

Liss swallowed hard. "Whatever it is, it'll be bad, okay?" She rubbed a hand across her forehead and gave them both a desperate, fearful look. "I don't like this."

Johnny put an arm around her. His other hand held the bones. "I got this. Trust me."

Johnny looked at the woman straight in her inky dark eyes, breathed on the bones for luck, then rubbed them in his palms.

Dan didn't breathe. She was pretty sure Liss didn't either. The only one who carried on was Johnny, like what he was doing wasn't dangerous at all. He was having an adventure, buoyed along by that same Johnny confidence he always had. He wore the same look when he skateboarded in the street: it wasn't exactly safe, but he was pretty sure that it was all going to be cool anyway.

He cast the bones.

Dan heard Liss let her breath out before she looked down, and she thought for a second that that meant they'd tied. But Liss's eyes were wide, her mouth hanging open a little, and Johnny's brow was wrinkled the way it was when he got to a Spanish phrase he couldn't translate.

Dan looked down.

All three bones lay odd-side up.

The woman screeched.

She lunged at them from across the field of play. Dan screamed, and they all fell back, scrambling to their feet. The woman sprang up too, surprisingly sprightly, and making a sound disturbingly like a growl.

Liss held on to Johnny's arm. They stood in a little huddle inside the guardian line. At some point a cold February wind had picked up, and it seemed to press them closer together. Liss's hair came loose—a blond smear across the night.

"What do you want?" Dan managed to ask.

The woman's face cracked into a bark of gruesome pleasure. She licked her thin lips—then her teeth. "Now I take."

"Take what?" Johnny's voice had a staccato edge of panic.

"One of you!" she cackled.

"Hell no! We'll play again. Double or nothing!" he said.

"No!" both girls cried at once. Dan's heart was beating almost out of her chest. There must be some way to reverse it. The Black Book lay out of reach, beyond the guardian line. Somehow it was splayed open, fingers of wind leafing through its pages.

The woman edged a toe toward the line and hissed as she tried to cross the salt.

"We're safe in here," Liss said. "Maybe we can wait her out."

Dan looked down. Already the wind had thinned the line, sweeping the salt out into the night.

But then the woman's neck started to—uncoil. That was the only way to describe it. It came loose from itself like a tumbled coil of rope and unwound, in the undulating wave of a swan's neck or an elephant's trunk.

"The fuck?" Dan heard Johnny say.

Dan couldn't say anything at all.

The woman's head bobbed toward them, easily crossing the line, her face coming close to each of them in turn, sniffing them out and something more—sniffing *for* something, testing for something. She was evaluating them—but for what? As she slithered toward and away from Dan, she could hear the intake of air, smell the woman's rank breath. She knew if she stepped outside the line, she'd be the one who was taken.

Once she'd examined them all, her head waggled back and forth in front of them on its long, prehensile neck. She was weighing them, deciding which to pick.

Then her neck swiveled to a stop. She bore those horror-show teeth in a smile.

Dan's mouth went dry.

Johnny.

"No," Liss gasped, but Johnny didn't say anything at all, for the woman's head had already snaked closer to him, and she was whispering in his ear. He dropped his arm from Liss and stepped out of the line, kicking open the circle of salt as he did.

"No!" Liss screamed. "Johnny, stop!"

But his eyes were already blown-out black like the woman's were. He couldn't hear Liss as she begged him not to go. His face was expressionless and vacant, as the woman hobbled through the now-broken line to his side. She patted him on the stomach, then, with surprising flexibility, wedged a foot against his hip and swung herself up so that she was crouched on his shoulders like a bird on a branch. She was nearly Johnny's height, but he didn't sway under her weight. His back was stiff and nail-straight.

She muttered something to him and he began to walk.

Just like that, the sickening tower of them was gone into the night.

Dan didn't tell Alexa how badly she'd wished it would be Johnny or that part of her flooded with relief that it had been him and not her or Liss. Not that she had wished him harm, not at all, but how else could she feel, when she realized she'd been spared whatever terrible fate awaited him?

Liss was gaping at the dark and terrible night, her eyes white and round. "He's gone," Liss whispered.

And Dan realized what her wish had done.

EIGHTEEN

Dan

"*What the actual fuck?*" *Alexa* said when Dan was done. "That's horror-movie-level messed up."

"Horror movies usually have happier endings than this," Dan said.

"We are *not* in a horror movie," Liss protested. "We're in, like, a very disturbing rom-com, and we're going to get our happy ending if we have to pry it from Kasyan's cold, dead hands."

"His hands are always cold," Alexa corrected. "I mean, in Lore's stories. Because he's not, you know, human," she quickly added.

"So this is why we need your help," Liss added. "You and Lorelei are the only people we can find who know anything about Kasyan. He's real, and he has Johnny, but we've got almost nothing to go on. I'm not exactly excited to try tonight's spell again."

Alexa's forehead wrinkled. She was silent for what felt like a very long time, all of which Dan spent imagining various scenarios in which Alexa told her she was delusional or awful or otherwise undeserving of help. Then Alexa said, "I'll tell you what I know—what I can remember right now, but it's just bits and pieces of things. And I don't want Lorelei hearing anything about this, so we're never meeting up at my house, okay?"

"Absolutely," Dan said. "Liss?"

"Fine by me."

"Some stories say he's a saint gone bad, who got kicked out of heaven. Sort of like how Satan is a fallen angel."

"I don't love that comparison," Liss said.

"That's not the only theory. In other stories he's more like a mythic figure. People say he chains the winds, he has eyelids so long they reach the ground, and he can kill a field of crops with one glance."

"Gross! Does he have to like, move the eyelids aside to do that?" Dan asked.

"Yes." The unhesitating tone of Alexa's answer chastened Dan: that would be a terrifying thing to see. Something about the way Alexa had pulled her cardigan close around her suggested she was thinking the same thing. "He can take many forms. That's just one he particularly enjoys."

"You've heard all the stories, so give us your opinion," Liss said. "What is he? Saint, not-saint, tiny devil, other magical entity?"

"I guess you would call Kasyan a trickster demon," Alexa began. "He's not as evil as a demon-from-hell kind of demon, if that makes sense. Like, he's not out there eating babies or anything."

"That's a relief," Dan muttered.

"Kasyan grants wishes, but only if he feels like it." Alexa's brow tightened, which forced her glasses to slip down her nose, and when she spoke again it was with a new certainty, despite the faraway look in her eyes. "Kasyan doesn't care about good and evil, which makes him unpredictable. He feeds off burning desires, I guess you'd call them. Things people want badly enough they'd do anything to get them, even if they don't really understand why. Kasyan is who you beg to when appealing to the good spirits or gods or whatever failed, and you're desperate. That's where the name Lord of Last Resort comes from. The thing that makes him really dangerous is, what he loves most is turning a wish against you: giving you your greatest desire and turning it into a punishment." A chill flowered up Dan's spine. "That's where the second name comes from: Kasyan the Unmerciful."

"I guess we wanted to control our futures," Liss suggested.

"That's a pretty big favor to ask. But we didn't get the favor, and she took Johnny anyway."

Alexa grimaced. "Other things went wrong too. You did it on a leap day."

"What's wrong with that?" Dan said. "The spell said it had to be the last day of the month."

"If it had been any other month, or any other February, I don't know what would have happened. But leap day is Kasyan's Day. Once every four years."

"So if we had waited until March, Johnny would still be here?" Liss asked. "That's the worst fucking luck."

"I don't know," Alexa said. "It could have happened anyway. That's bad luck to start with: you had three at the crossroads. The problem with that is it invites a fourth."

"You told me you didn't know why it was bad luck to have three at a crossroads," Dan said.

"I didn't," Alexa said. "I mean, I'm just remembering this stuff now."

Dan held Alexa's gaze a second too long. There was something *off* about how she'd said it—how she'd said any of this about Kasyan, almost like she herself was hearing the information for the first time.

"But why Johnny?" Liss demanded. "Why did he have to be the one?"

Alexa shook her head. "I don't know."

Liss's face puckered, unsatisfied at Alexa's answer, and she looked to Dan. "You think about that too, don't you? Why she chose Johnny and not me or you?"

Dan cleared her throat. "Of course I do. But we might never know why it was him, and I'm not going to say I wish it had been one of us instead."

Liss's silence was an awful, clotted thing between them. Dan wanted to say something to make it better, but what? Anything she might say risked exposing the awful thing she'd done to Johnny.

Finally Liss dropped her eyes and said in a low voice, "This is all my fault. He shouldn't have been there at all. He shouldn't have been *with me* at all."

"Don't say that, Liss. You guys were in love. If we had known how dangerous it was, we wouldn't have done it. You can't blame yourself." Dan's heart twisted. At least Liss could be forgiven for bringing Johnny along; Dan would never be so lucky. "We're going to make everything right. Like it never even happened."

Liss let out a heavy sigh. She still wouldn't meet Dan's eyes. "But it did," she eventually said. "It's late. I should get home."

"Do you have my keys?" Dan was exhausted, but she began to disentangle herself from her bed. They had taken Dan's car, so Liss had no way to get home without her. And there was something so cutting and dismissing in Liss's voice that made her want to tell Liss a thousand times more, the way she'd tried to tell herself, that their mistakes should just be forgotten. If you repeated it enough, maybe one day you'd feel it was true.

"After what you went through tonight you're not driving," Alexa said. "I'll take her home."

Dan hesitated. "Really?"

"Are you kidding? You'll drive right off the road," she said.

Dan frowned a little at Liss, a warning to be on her best behavior. Liss smirked at her in reply. "Okay, I get it," Dan said. "Three musketeers."

Alexa

In Alexa's car, Liss flipped through her CDs. "I can't believe there's no adapter in here. Did Dan burn you literally every single one of these? I didn't even know she had a CD burner."

"She got one, for this," Alexa said.

"Oh," Liss said, a note of surprise in her voice. She set the CDs down as they climbed the hill between Dogtown and Marlena. They rounded the turn and passed Black Grass's gate. Alexa shivered.

"I know," Liss said, misreading her reaction. "Magic's not the kind of thing most people would just *believe* if they'd never seen it before. But maybe you're not most people."

"Maybe not," Alexa said.

Liss fell silent in a way that left the door open for talking—for confession. Alexa reminded herself that she hated the Lizard on principle. Liss was rude and self-obsessed and had been nothing but a terrible friend to Dan. Liss might have borne witness to a tragedy, but that didn't mean she was a great person to go spilling secrets to.

Even if she might already suspect some part of the truth.

Alexa turned up the music, and they didn't say much until they turned onto Liss's street.

"Please don't say anything to Dan, okay?" Alexa said as Liss unbuckled her seat belt.

"You can trust me," Liss answered.

Alexa let out a strained laugh.

"What was that for?"

"It would be nice if that were true," Alexa said. "No offense."

"Fair. If you can't trust me, know that I don't want to mess this up either. I need you. Dan needs you," Liss added a little begrudgingly. "She's lucky to have a friend like you. You know that, right? Thanks for the ride."

Alexa watched as Liss let herself into the hulking, unlit house.

Domino was waiting for Alexa on the buckled porch when she pulled up to the house. He was practically frowning as Alexa unlocked the door, releasing a cloud of Lorelei's noxious stench.

I know it was a long walk back, but you're all in one piece, she thought to him with a heavy sigh, then tossed him a kitty treat by way of apology. *My little familiar.*

I may be your familiar, but that's no reason to indulge in pet names.

But you're also my pet. Alexa bent to scratch under his chin, and his eyes vanished into slits. *Black cats and witches. What else, flying broomstick? Warts?*

A witch never jokes about warts, Domino scolded.

Alexa pushed open the door to Lorelei's room. Lorelei lay still, the same as ever, her breathing a wet rattle. The smell was getting worse—fetid and rotten, and undercurrents of something greasy. Alexa tried not to imagine little particles of almost-deadness coming in through her nose and filtering down into her lungs. She administered an eyedropper full of one of Swann's potions then settled into the chair at Lorelei's bedside.

"You won't believe the night I had, Lore," she sighed. "Dan and Liss told me this crazy story about Mora kidnapping their friend and taking him to Kasyan. They believe Kasyan's hiding somewhere in North Coast." Very carefully, Alexa touched Lorelei's cold hand.

Lorelei didn't say anything.

"The whole time Dan was telling her story, I kept thinking how lucky they were to have had each other when it happened. They had to live through something terrible, but at least they didn't have to do it alone. Even if they're not friends anymore, there will always be someone else who understands."

The jealousy and loneliness had been singing in Alexa's blood so powerfully that she almost told Dan and Liss everything. Maybe she should have; after all, they'd trusted her with something unbelievable first. But Alexa couldn't help but feel that if she told them what happened to Lorelei—what happened to *her*—it would make all of it real in a way there was no going back from. That was ridiculous, because it was already, very obviously real: a minute ago she'd dripped a blood-colored potion into the mouth of a living corpse. But it also felt like something she wasn't yet brave enough to accept. Instead she'd pulled on the thread of witch-knowledge that connected to Kasyan and found something that might help all three of them.

"I miss you, Lore," Alexa said, then clicked off the light and returned to the living room and stood in front of the piles of books Keith had tumbled from the shelves.

Domino sprang up onto the dining table.

What do we have about Kasyan? she asked.

NINETEEN

Dan

It was the last day of school before winter break. North Coast High's cafeteria had a feverish, barely contained energy to it in the hours before vacation. Dan observed it from her corner as she picked at her lunch and waited for Alexa to turn up.

She was exhausted. Part of her had hoped that coming clean to Alexa would alleviate the guilt—not entirely, just a little—but last night, as she lay in bed listening to IronWeaks, she couldn't sleep. She didn't want Alexa to forgive what she'd done or accept who she was. She didn't want Alexa to help them with Kasyan or make nice with Liss. She wanted everything to stay how it had been between her and Alexa, and once Alexa was drawn into this mess, that would be impossible.

Dan didn't want to lose her.

When Alexa slid into a seat across from Dan, her face was drawn and there were dark circles under her eyes behind her unusually smudgy glasses. She looked as out of pace with the amped-up atmosphere of the cafeteria as Dan felt.

Dan wanted to warn her that she didn't need to get mixed up in this just because Liss had pressured her, but Alexa cut her off.

"I have a lead—someone who probably knows something about your, uh, issue. Text Liss and tell her to meet us at Aroma Café after school."

Which is how Dan ended up following Alexa and Liss down Fort Gratton's Main Street that afternoon. It wasn't even five o'clock, and already the sun was sitting right on the water. It was nearly the shortest day of the year.

Alexa pushed open the door of an old Victorian storefront.

"You're taking us to a tattoo shop?" Dan asked.

Alexa waved to the burly, inked receptionist of Fault Line Tattoo. He seemed to know her. When had Alexa made friends with someone like that? When she'd met Alexa, the only places in Gratton she'd been to were North Coast High and the public library. Dan had been the one to introduce Alexa to the Teen Oasis, Aroma Café, and SmoothieTown, the same places where she'd hung out with Liss. It felt strange, although Dan knew it shouldn't, to think that Alexa could have a life in North Coast without her.

She and Liss followed Alexa to the back of the shop and up a creaking flight of stairs to a door. The name was familiar—a local woman who did tattoos and read tarot and palms on the side. Alexa rapped on the door and called out, "Swann? It's Alexa."

There was a rustling from inside, then the door swung open to reveal a long-limbed and pale woman, all elbows and edges, draped in a dramatic floor-length kimono. Recognizing Alexa, the woman's face shifted from businesslike to more maternal and sympathetic. "Alexa, is everything all right? How is—" She spotted Dan and Liss. "Oh, you're here for a reading?"

"Can we talk?" Alexa asked.

Swann insisted on brewing them tea as they situated themselves among the pillows and ottomans on the floor. "I'm a friend of Alexa's aunt," Swann said as she prepared an electric kettle. "How is Lorelei?"

"She's the same as ever." Dan watched Alexa fidget with her cuticle. There was something off about the way she'd answered, as if she meant more than her words had said.

"I see," Swann chirped. "No news is good news."

"Not if things are already bad," Liss muttered. She'd been in a mood since they crossed Fault Line's threshold. How totally typical of Liss to be rude to someone trying to help her.

"What was that?" Swann asked.

"In my experience, if things are bad, then no news is also bad news," Liss said.

"I suppose that's not untrue." Swann poured their tea. "Now, are we looking for fortune telling? Love spells?"

"Do we look like we're here for love spells?" Liss said.

"Liss, *don't*," Dan grumbled, and raised the tea to her lips. Thanks to her mom, Dan had encountered a lot of really unpleasant tea that claimed all kinds of physical and emotional benefits at the expense of any reasonable flavor. This was worse than all of them. Combined. A lot worse. She took the smallest possible swallow and struggled not to gag. "Delicious," she managed.

"Swann, these are my friends. You can trust them," Alexa said with gravity, and again Dan had the sensation that there was a second conversation going on between them, freighted with meanings that she couldn't hear. "They're looking for information about Kasyan."

Swann arched an eyebrow at Liss. "I see your book report is still underway."

"It's more of a long-term research project," Liss said blithely. "Possibly with an experimental component."

"Actually, I've gotten interested in Kasyan too," Alexa went on. "I was hoping you could tell us what you know about him."

Swann set down her mug and folded her slender limbs into the cushions. "Happily. There are many wonderful folktales about Kasyan I can share."

"We're not interested in stories," Alexa said firmly. "We're looking for real information. You know what I mean."

Swann cocked her head to the side, her jaw tight. "Kasyan is a figure from folktales. If that's not *real information* to you, I can refer you to a lively debate in folkloric studies about epistemology."

"Do people actually buy that?" Liss said. "I don't know what epistemology is, but we know Kasyan's real, so you can just cut to the good part."

Dan shot Liss a corrective glare and summoned her most polite, talking-to-adults voice. "What she meant is, stories are always helpful and we are super appreciative that you're willing to share some. But we were hoping for some more concrete information. We think Kasyan's in North Coast. We're looking for his exact location. We wouldn't ask if it wasn't for a really good reason."

"Kasyan—in North Coast? What's next, ghosts and zombies?" Swann gave a small chuckle that was too lighthearted. "This is a fantasy. I don't know what else to tell you."

"Really, Swann?" Alexa asked. "You know I'd ask Lorelei if I could, but I can't. And it turns out all the books—everything, really—she had about Kasyan was lost. Recently."

"I see. That's unfortunate, but what's lost is lost. Alexa, rest assured that Kasyan is not your concern. It's simple as that."

Alexa's eyes flashed at Swann. "Dan and Liss are witches," she said coldly. Dan's heart skipped a beat to hear her say it out loud, and to a virtual stranger, like it wasn't a secret at all. Her eyes shot to Liss, who'd gone from annoyed to annoyed and vaguely horrified. But Swann didn't even flinch. Alexa went on, "Mora abducted their friend for Kasyan."

"The girl?" Swan's voice was flinty. "The recent one—the girl from Marlena?

"No, not her," Alexa said. "Their friend Johnny. It was leap day of last year. They did a spell: three of them at a crossroads."

Impossibly, Swann's already porcelain skin paled even further. "They did *what*?"

"They didn't know better. Their luck was bad," Alexa said.

"Clearly!" Swann replied. "This is exactly why we can't have any average nobody playing around with these things."

The color rose in Liss's cheeks. "Excuse me, *any average nobody* couldn't manage to do what we have."

"You'd be surprised. Anyone can do anything badly," Swann said. "And you wonder why I won't sell dangerous material to anyone who walks in my door. You understand that you could have died."

"Our friend getting *kidnapped by a demon* really drove that point home to us," Liss said.

Swann folded her twig-thin arms. "I won't help you down a path that will end in absolute disaster."

"You thought *this* would be helpful?" Liss glowered at Alexa.

"This wasn't quite what I had in mind." Alexa's eyes stayed fixed on Swann. "Could you guys wait for me downstairs?"

Liss sneered at Swann. "That tea is disgusting."

Alexa

"That girl is not very polite," Swann said as they waited for the door to close behind Dan. "She's been in here before, asking for spell books. I didn't encourage her behavior, but I see that has not stopped her."

"They aren't really witches, are they?" Alexa set her undrinkable tea down. "They said they did some kind of spell on themselves, but you said witches get their power when another witch dies."

Swann crossed her long legs. "I said that's how the *Warden* witches are usually turned. It's not the only way. Certain rituals do exist. We don't promote that kind of thing. Naive witches are . . . difficult to deal with."

"Naive witches?"

"Witches who are self-made." Swann's face soured in displeasure. "They have no training. They're erratic in magic, their technique is terrible, as are their manners. They can be very exasperating. Happily, the rituals are very difficult to execute correctly and almost always fail. So to answer your question, no, they are not really witches."

"That makes sense," Alexa said. There was a steady certainty in the pit of Alexa's stomach that Swann was entirely wrong about her friends. "I shouldn't have brought them here, and I'm sorry for that. But look, I think I know what Black Grass is doing."

Swann regarded her, neither pleased nor displeased.

Alexa continued. "Black Grass is after Kasyan. Last night Dan and Liss told me about Kasyan, so I tried to look for stuff about him in Lorelei's books. You know what I found?"

"Nothing good, I imagine," Swann sighed.

"Nothing. At all. The books were *gone*. Things were such a mess I hadn't realized it before, but maybe a dozen books are missing. I remember the letter *K* was in all Lorelei's notes for her investigation— I thought that meant Keith, but it didn't. Those notes are gone too. Don't you see? Keith stole everything Lorelei had on Kasyan. It can't be a coincidence. *That's* the thread of meaning that Black Grass is pulling on—what Lorelei was supposed to be watching. If Black Grass is worshipping Kasyan, then Kasyan probably gave Keith the power to curse Lorelei. Don't you think?"

Alexa had thought Swann would be impressed by her discovery, but instead her expression was brittle. "You promised me you would leave this to the Wardens."

"But I can help. I actually . . . Lorelei sort of . . ." Alexa tried to press on. If Swann knew Alexa had Lorelei's powers, then they'd have no reason not to work together. But as Alexa fumbled for words, Swann's lips were grimly pursed, as if she was simply waiting for Alexa to finish so she could dismiss her. A puzzle piece clicked into place in Alexa's brain. "But . . . you knew all this already," she said slowly. "The Wardens have known Kasyan is in North Coast all along."

A light flush bloomed in Swann's pale cheeks. She shifted uncomfortably against the throw pillows. "Alexa, this is none of your concern. Kasyan is incredibly dangerous. You need to drop this."

A flare of anger shot through Alexa's chest. The Wardens had known exactly the danger Lorelei was in when they sent her to Black Grass, and now that the worst had happened, they hadn't done a thing to fix it—at least nothing Alexa, the person who cared most about Lorelei in the world, could see, and nothing that was making her suffering any easier. The Wardens had used Lorelei, with no care for the price, and even if Lorelei had let them do it, that didn't make it right. Alexa ground her teeth. She couldn't believe she had nearly just told Swann that she'd inherited Lorelei's powers. The Wardens didn't deserve the gift Lorelei had passed to her. "What am I supposed to do instead—let Keith get away with it? Let Lorelei die?"

"We are taking steps that I cannot share with you. I know you don't understand how the Wardens operate, but perhaps when this is all resolved you could apply to join and—"

"And do *what*? Put my name on a cult's new-member waitlist and sit back while they knock off North Coast's population one by one? I don't need to join your dumb organization to do that. I bet you don't even really want her to get better. Why hasn't anyone come to help her yet, after everything Lorelei sacrificed for the Wardens?"

Swann's fists were clenched and tense tendons corded her long neck. "The Solstice is an incredibly busy time for us. You have no idea how many flare-ups we've seen in California in the last few weeks. The Wardens are doing the best we can. *I* am doing the best I can. You know I care deeply for Lorelei."

"You *care deeply* for her power," Alexa spat. "That's all the Wardens really want. You probably don't even care about stopping Keith or Kasyan, not like Dan and Liss and me do."

"The Wardens have kept the world safe from Kasyan for over a hundred fifty years." Swann's voice was cold and sharp. "Since what happened at Icaria, we have struggled to ensure that accurate information about Kasyan is almost impossible to come by, certainly nothing that could lead to his liberation. I will not stand by while you denigrate this organization because you and your little friends feel entitled to that knowledge. You *are not* entitled to it."

"Kasyan ruined our lives," Alexa said. "I think we're entitled to know why."

With that, the air seemed to go out of the room. Swann didn't respond, but neither could she look directly at Alexa. "At least tell me what happened in Icaria," Alexa said.

Swann tapped a fingernail against her teeth, the *click-click-click* counting off seconds until, Alexa assumed, Swann would tell her to leave. But finally, Swann spoke. "It was a gold-rush town, a few miles up the coast. Well, 'town' always was an overstatement. It's abandoned now and has been for a very long time."

Although Swann had relented, Alexa still couldn't keep an edge of anger from her voice. "Is what Kasyan did there so much worse than what he's done to Lorelei and Johnny?"

Swann shook her head. "That's not even a question. Lorelei and

Johnny are two people. Two is too many, but still. Icaria was a *catastrophe.*

"Kasyan manipulates desires by working on technicalities. He pushes things to extremes. We suspect that one, or more likely several, of the gold prospectors was desperate for a successful claim. Everyone back then wanted a bigger windfall than anyone else's. One way to satisfy the conditions for that wish is for all the other claims to fail. Or the prospectors who'd claimed them to fail." Swann pulled her kimono around her. "So they died: dozens of them at least, probably closer to two hundred. Their bodies became corrupted. Typical Kasyan. First the fingernails and tongues turned black. Then they were coughing up sticky black gobs. It came weeping from their eyes and noses in drips like crude oil. Teeth loosened, then fell out altogether, and black seeped from the sockets. In two or three weeks, they were dead. It made things worse that men kept showing up to stake claims even after the town had ceased to function."

Alexa swallowed hard. "Kasyan did all that?"

Swann gave her a tight-lipped smile. "Well, a person's insides don't just liquefy unprovoked. Ultimately a Warden made it to Icaria to challenge Kasyan. He managed to put him somewhere he wouldn't cause any trouble for a long time. Very bravely, I would add."

"And if he hadn't? Would the black stuff from Icaria have spread?"

"We don't know. Kasyan is fickle. One thing I can say is that he has had nothing to do for the last century and a half other than nurse a grudge. If he's released, North Coast will be a very dangerous place to be indeed. It could be Icaria all over again, or worse."

"The Warden should have killed him."

Swann arched a whitish brow at her. "This is what worries me, Alexa. You think Kasyan's the kind of thing that can be killed."

TWENTY

Alexa

Alexa caught up with Dan and Liss outside Fault Line Tattoo. They were watching one of those "North Coast characters," Mad Mags, deliver a speech about patience in the general direction of the Pacific Ocean.

"You'd think she'd get tired of saying the same thing all the time," Liss was saying. "Who does she think she's waiting for?"

"Don't be insensitive," Dan scolded.

Liss swished her blond hair over one shoulder. "I *am* being sensitive. You think she's not tired of it?"

"Sorry about Swann," Alexa said. "Listen, what do you know about a ghost town called Icaria?"

Alexa was still relating the gruesome details of Icaria's downfall when Liss had a route mapped out on her phone. Icaria was an hour and a half north, in Lost Coast State Park. "Then I'd say a two-hour hike from the highway, depending on the conditions," Liss said.

Dan peered at Liss's phone. "That might be an access road," she said. The two of them were huddled together, shoulder to shoulder, and neither had thought to show Alexa the map or even thank her for what she'd told them. *Don't be disappointed,* Alexa reminded herself. This was probably how it was supposed to be all along: Dan and Liss, together forever, and Alexa on her own.

"Icaria will be perfect for a spell," Liss said.

Dan was still examining the map. "The vibes there are probably intense."

"I'm sorry, the what now?" Alexa winced. "Vibes?"

"The magic-y feeling of a place?" Dan looked up at her. "I don't really know how to explain it."

Alexa did not need an explanation. A line in her mind had been tripped, triggering that knowledge she'd inherited from Lorelei. The girls were talking about the *fortunes* of Icaria—the magical valence of a place, the weight of its past and future and its current auspices. Given what had happened in Icaria, it was clear its fortunes were powerful, but that power was the result of suffering, death, and betrayed hope. "Vibes" made it sound like Icaria was just a ghost town with good selfie lighting.

Alexa was beginning to see why Swann thought naive witches were exasperating.

"I get it," Alexa said.

"We should leave early tomorrow. We don't want to be out there after sundown," Liss said. "So we should ask the Black Book for a spell tonight."

"A spell for what?" Alexa asked.

Dan and Liss exchanged a look that read: *She doesn't know what we know, she isn't one of us.* "There's a procedure for finding a spell in the Black Book. You have to ask it in a particular way and it gives you the spell you need," Dan said. "So we need to ask it for a spell to rescue Johnny."

"And that's something the Book would know?" There was something . . . off about that thing. Not that she'd seen it. She didn't particularly want to. The point of books was that they were predictable—*readable.* They didn't tease you with special access via ritualistic communication.

"Why wouldn't it?" Liss said.

"Why *would* it? Asking the Book what to do isn't the same as having a plan." Alexa wondered if they had ever considered that before. "Which we could come up with."

Dan's eyes went wide. "We?"

"Am I not invited?"

"I mean," Dan faltered, then shot a glance at Liss, who didn't do anything particular in reply. "We can do this on our own."

"Cool, thanks," Alexa said. "I'm feeling super included."

"I didn't mean it like that! It's just that this isn't your problem."

"You wanted my help and I'm giving it to you." Alexa crossed her arms. "You made it my problem."

"This isn't some fantasy! It's is actually dangerous," Dan said. "We're witches, and—"

"And you couldn't even protect yourselves from half the shit you've called down," Alexa snapped. "Swann's right. It seems like being witches is what's gotten you in trouble in the first place, so I can't imagine I could do much worse."

"Let her see the Black Book," Liss said. "If you want a taste of magic, watch us ask it for the spell. We can decide about if you're coming tomorrow after that. But I'm in favor. It'll be safer if there's three of us."

"Yeah, because the last time we did that, one of us got abducted by a nightmare creature." Dan dug her keys out of her backpack. "The Book's at my house. I'll meet you there."

Dan

Dan yanked the shoebox out from under her bed. She watched Alexa notice the writing on the lid—DAN + LISS TOP SECRET—and her cheeks grew hot.

"Impressive security measures," Alexa joked as they sat themselves in a circle on the carpet.

Liss eyed Alexa. "Don't make me regret inviting you."

"Come on, I was just—"

Dan set the Book on the floor between them. Alexa shifted uncomfortably, her eyes fixed on the Book.

"You were just . . . ?" Liss raised an eyebrow.

Alexa pulled her cardigan around her and crossed her arms. "Does it always feel this way?"

"What way?" Dan asked.

Alexa drew back from the Book as much as she could without actually leaving the circle. She adjusted her glasses. "Just a little nauseating. I mean, I was skeptical but yeah, that thing is magic."

"Maybe you're just having a reaction because you're not a witch," Dan suggested.

"We weren't either the first time we used the Book," Liss said. "Are we ready? I don't want her puke gumming up the pages."

Everything felt strange, having Alexa there. The energy in the room felt off-kilter, like they were three planets that would not align. Dan could hardly keep focused on the kind of spell they were looking for—a spell to rescue Johnny from Kasyan.

When Liss opened the Book, Alexa hissed out a tightly held breath. Dan turned her page—nothing—and then it was Liss again. Now, Alexa looked legitimately sick, her face wan and a little sweaty. It was gratifying, somehow, that Alexa was incompatible with magic. There was no way she'd want to come with them to Icaria now. Instead she'd be waiting back in Dogtown when they returned, keeping watch over a life that was normal, not terrifying, not ravaged by guilt.

Dan chose a page, then glanced back at Alexa, so it was Liss who realized it first.

"That's it. That's our spell." Liss wore a satisfied grin.

Alexa glared at the page, her brow pulled tight. "No, it's not."

"Liss and I get a feeling when the spell is right. That's how we know," Dan said. "I don't know how to explain—"

"Yeah, you can't explain your feelings, I get it." Alexa pushed herself up off the floor and sat on Dan's bed, which was about as far as she could get from the Book without leaving the room. "But you can't do that spell."

"It looks complicated, but we've done much more difficult ones," Liss said as she copied out the spell into her notebook. "Dan and I actually have a lot of experience with this stuff."

"It's not that it's complicated, it's just—wrong."

"See, this is why I don't think you should come tomorrow," Dan said. "It's one thing to be curious about magic, but what we're involved with right now isn't entry level. We can't risk you getting upset in the middle of the incantation or something."

"I'm coming with you." Alexa's voice was cold. "But if you do that spell tomorrow, you'll get yourselves killed."

"This is ridiculous. What else are we supposed to do?" Liss asked.

"Doing nothing would be better."

Liss shot Dan a look. "I thought we were clear that Project Rescue Johnny was about *not* doing nothing?"

"If that's how you feel, then don't come," Dan said.

"Maybe you shouldn't go either!"

"We don't have a choice—you do," Dan argued. "You don't need to get involved in all this. You can just go home and pretend none of this ever happened.

Alexa pushed herself off the bed and grabbed her bag. "Make up your mind, Dan. Do you need me or not?"

Dan flinched as Alexa slammed the door behind her.

Alexa

Alexa heard the front door open and shut as she walked to her car, but she didn't look back.

"Dan, I don't want to talk about this—"

"I'll let her know."

Alexa turned to see Liss standing behind her, her face a shadow under the light of her hair. She was fiddling with her fingers again.

"What's wrong with the spell?" Liss asked.

"You tell me. You're the expert."

"I know it might look like I have a death wish. Actually, I don't. I need Johnny back. Dan does too. We're too close to slow down now. Give me a good reason not to do that spell tomorrow and we won't. But until then, it's all we have, and I don't care that it isn't particularly safe."

Alexa's hand was bunched into a fist around her car keys so tightly the metal bit into her skin. "Give me the night to think about it."

Liss nodded. "I'll be at your place by eight thirty tomorrow."

"Fine."

Liss did not turn and walk away. Instead, she crossed her arms against the dampness of the fog and cleared her throat. "How are you?"

"What do you mean, how am I?"

"Like how are you doing, what is the state of your affairs, are you about to go jump off a cliff?"

"Don't worry about me." Alexa's voice was flat. "I know you think this spell stuff is freaky, but I can handle myself around some pretty fucked-up things."

"Yeah, I got that," Liss answered. "That's not what I meant. Something's going on with you. You look like you haven't slept in a week—or showered. You obviously aren't talking to Dan about it, and you clearly have no other friends. So I'm asking."

"Nothing," Alexa tucked her hair behind her ears. She hadn't realized how greasy it was. "Everything's fine."

"Liar," Liss said simply.

Alexa opened her mouth to deny it, but closed it again. To her horror, the prickle of oncoming tears stung her eyes. She was not going to cry in front of the Lizard. "Why do you care?"

Liss rolled her eyes. "Because caring about you is such an incomprehensible thing for someone to do?" Alexa could do nothing but swallow hard against that, and Liss hastily added, "I meant that rhetorically. I just care, okay? The whole point of witch-gang is that we stick together."

"I'm not—"

"Whatever." Liss gave her a pointed look. "Tomorrow, eight thirty."

"I'll be ready."

Alexa

Alexa paced in her living room, navigating around sneakers and dirty dishes and broken records and unstuffed pillows she'd never cleaned up from Keith's rampage.

Domino surveyed her from his perch on the back of the couch. *And why exactly are you going to Icaria?*

"Kasyan's been there—or at least used his power there, so the fortunes will be good for any magic related to him. But the spell Dan and Liss want to do there is all wrong. It uses an equinoctial structure." Domino seemed to smirk at her, insofar as a cat could. Alexa turned on her heel to look at him. "Yes, that was witch-knowledge. But the important thing is, you can't do an equinoctial spell the day before Winter Solstice without something going seriously wrong. Those spells are for the Equinoxes—it's in the name! Of course, that creepy Black Book didn't include that detail."

Domino's ears twitched. *What Black Book?*

"It's supposedly a magician's diary. They ask it for a spell to do a certain thing, and it gives them . . . something." Alexa collapsed onto the couch, took off her glasses, and scrubbed a hand over her face.

Just thinking of the Book now, she could practically feel the cold wave of nausea that overcame her when she first saw it. It was more than unpleasantness: the Book was undoubtedly the emanation of some power, and in Dan's bedroom it had directed that power toward Alexa, sending out tendrils that she could feel examining her. Those tendrils had not liked what they found. She and the Black Book were like poles of a magnet, repelling each other.

The Book was easy to distrust, but Dan and Liss had come to a different conclusion. They took its spells at face value, because the spells always worked. They hadn't realized that wasn't a good thing when *working* meant disappearing Johnny or burning down all of North Coast or worse.

Alexa rubbed her temples. "Naive witches," she groaned. "They're going to get themselves killed."

You won't let them.

Alexa shoved her glasses back on so she could properly glare at Domino. "Of course I won't—I can't. But how am I supposed to stop them? Liss said she needs one good reason and she won't do the spell, but what can I say? Like, 'Hi guys, I'm actually a witch too and here's a crash course in equinoctial versus solstitial spells?'"

Do you want to do that? Not the lecture part, the first part.

Alexa let her head fall back against the couch. She knew Domino was staring at her with those sage-green eyes, waiting for an answer to his totally normal and not at all soul-crushing question, which was definitely not bringing tears to her eyes. The cat, like most cats, had only two modes: aggressively hissy or calmly reserved. But sometimes, Alexa wished he could be just a little affectionate when she needed it.

As if he'd read her mind—he definitely had—Domino crawled into her lap. Just the weight of him there was comforting. He nuzzled her cheek, wiping away the tears that slipped through her lashes.

Then why can't you tell them?

Because they would never believe her—although they had witnessed unbelievable things. Because she had bigger concerns, like how the Wardens hadn't sent anyone to care for Lorelei or how she would exact her revenge against Keith and Kasyan—although Dan and Liss wanted to destroy Kasyan too. Because once she had that revenge she would leave North Coast, even if she would miss it painfully—although if Dan and Liss fell victim to a miscast spell, there would be nothing left here to miss.

"Dan and Liss have enough problems." Alexa spoke deliberately. "They don't need to get involved in mine, and I don't need them to. I've been handling things on my own my whole life. This is no different."

It was a reminder she needed herself to hear, and it was true. At least part of it was true.

Alexa pictured herself, a tiny girl, standing before a huge black mass, a pale face with long sharp teeth and a gaze that could wither whatever it landed upon. Swann had said he couldn't be killed. That would make facing him extremely challenging.

And terrifying.

And possibly fatal.

But it had been done before. A Warden had trapped Kasyan to protect North Coast.

Suddenly, Alexa sat up, forcing Domino to squirm off her lap.

"Does Lorelei have a history of the Wardens anywhere? A record of who they are and what they worked on?"

Alexa followed Domino as he padded toward Lorelei's bedroom.

Dan

Dan was running: her heels striking the dark pavement, the heavy mist of the fog beading on her skin. Rickey's luscious voice soared through her headphones and carved the pit of sadness inside her a little bit deeper. Her legs ached with each stride, but she tried to focus on that steady rhythm, one foot in front of the other. She'd run two miles down the coast road before turning back for home, wishing that dumb repetition would dull out her thoughts.

It hadn't.

Dan couldn't stop thinking about Alexa.

Dan was sick with the feeling that had been building since they stepped foot in Swann's, that had overcome her when she saw Alexa recoil from the Book: Alexa needed to be kept separate from the part of her life tainted by magic.

Alexa, who was good and true and solid. It already felt like magic, how Alexa cared when Dan was down and managed to text her precisely when she couldn't be alone with her thoughts anymore. Sometimes, before she fell asleep, Dan would tell Alexa she was going to bed and Alexa would say she was too and Dan would text good night and Alexa would text it back, and then, with her throat tight and her lip held between her teeth, Dan would write

Thanks, before she turned out the light. But then she'd turn it back on to see if Alexa had written back.

Alexa made her want to stop cutting.

She hadn't actually stopped, but that was beside the point. Dan was waiting for a moment when stopping would just happen to her. There had to be a time when the darkness would leave her altogether. Just like that, cutting would be in the past, just like once Johnny was saved it would be like she never made that wish. She could really be the person she was always pretending to be: someone good, who didn't hurt herself or anyone else deliberately.

But she had been waiting for that moment for so long. What if it never came? Could she carry on like this forever? Pretending was exhausting. She'd spent so long doing it that she was starting to wonder if it was a solution at all.

Rickey's voice snarled something angry and beautiful in Dan's ears as she ran down the hill that curved into Dogtown, the little town's lights growing closer.

Worse, none of it was fair to Alexa. Alexa always tried to be a good friend—truly *tried,* which had never even really occurred to Dan before Alexa—but that didn't make any of this her responsibility. She wasn't the answer to any of Dan's problems. She was more than that.

Dan would not let Alexa get hurt by all this. Alexa deserved to live in a world where she could read the fantasy books she loved without worrying that they were actually nonfiction. If anything happened to Alexa in Icaria, Dan knew she'd drive herself crazy trying to make it right, the same way Liss had with Johnny.

Dan rounded the final turn into Dogtown. Ahead, the first house had its outside light on. Dan pulled out her headphones and walked up Alexa's driveway.

———

Alexa slipped out onto the porch and closed the door behind her. "What are you doing here?"

There was something about the house that felt unfamiliar from Dan's other visits. It definitely smelled like the garbage hadn't been taken out anytime recently.

"I was on a run, and I—" Dan fumbled at the way Alexa was looking at her—like an intruder. "Are you busy? I can go."

"No," Alexa crossed her arms. "Lorelei's sleeping off a cold. We can talk out here."

Dan noticed the planks of the porch were buckled and one of the supports broken nearly in half. "The wood's rotted," Alexa said. She didn't invite Dan to sit. "What's up?"

"The Dogtown Solstice Parade's on Sunday. My mom wants me to work at a table selling her pottery, but there's usually a good view of the parade. Do you want to come?"

"Parades aren't really my thing."

"It's just been a while since we hung out," Dan said.

Alexa eyed her. "The last time we hung out, you ran off screaming while my car got destroyed."

"I told you, it was Johnny. I had to go after him." Dan shivered and crossed her arms as the sweat on her running gear cooled.

"I know." Alexa adjusted her glasses. "But an apology would have been nice."

"I did apologize."

"You said you didn't have a choice. It's not the same thing."

"Okay, I really am sorry. I shouldn't have done that." Dan bit her lip. She *was* sorry, but she didn't see what else she should have done.

"You didn't even ask if I was okay. You just forgot about me. Do you have any idea how it feels to be *alone* like that?"

Dan opened her mouth to say that she absolutely did, but the fraying in Alexa's voice made her doubt herself. Lorelei hadn't answered the phone that night, Dan remembered. Dan had called her mom because she'd been tired of waiting. She'd never doubted that her mom would come.

"I should have been there for you. I don't know what I was thinking."

"That's not true either, Dan." Alexa's voice was small. She wouldn't look at Dan. "You were thinking about all this stuff with Liss. Like once she's back in your life, I don't matter anymore."

"That's not fair. I have to—"

"Forget about me until this magic stuff is over? You think I'll be here forever, waiting for you when you're done with Liss. You know, she's really not as bad as you made her sound."

"No, that's not it at all." Dan clutched her headphones. "I didn't mean to hurt you. I really am sorry that I did. I'm trying to do the right thing, but I don't always know what it is."

"I know that," Alexa said in a way that still didn't feel like forgiveness.

"Please don't come to Icaria tomorrow," Dan asked. "I know you want to and Liss said it was okay, but you should stay as far away from all this magic stuff as you can. It sounded cool to me at first too but now . . . if I could erase all of that, I would. I don't want you to feel like you have to get involved in this for us."

Alexa scowled. "I'm already involved."

"I'm saying this for your own good," Dan pleaded.

"How do you know what's good for me? I told you I have my own reasons for wanting to go."

"This isn't for tourists," Dan said. "Magic is *dangerous.*"

"I *know*," Alexa snapped. "I wish I didn't."

A chill shivered up Dan's spine as a look of genuine fear shattered Alexa's composure. "You're serious," Dan said.

"From Lorelei's stories and that kind of thing. That's what I mean."

"I don't believe you," Dan whispered.

"Whatever." Alexa nearly managed to sound dismissive, but there was something lonesome and exhausted in it instead. She looked back at the house, arms crossed. "We're going to wake up Lorelei. I'll see you tomorrow."

Dan pushed her hair back and unwound her headphones. "Okay," she forced herself to say. If Alexa wanted her to go, she'd be gone. But she couldn't shake the feeling that somehow she was leaving Alexa all over again—alone, exactly what Alexa said she didn't want to be.

Alexa

Dan was walking away. Good. *Good.* It was dangerous to have her at the house, so close to Lorelei, to Domino, to the fragile wreck of her life.

It was good that she was going because Alexa had almost told her everything. She could practically taste the words—how badly she wanted to say them, how tired she was of the special isolation that misery stranded you in.

Almost telling Dan and watching her walk away made it all worse somehow. She couldn't be mad at Dan for not understanding, for not helping, when Alexa had never given her the chance.

Dan's sneakers crunched on the gravel as she queued up a song for the walk home.

Alexa gripped the porch railing.

She was strong enough. She could hold it together, alone.

Dan turned back.

"Do you really want me to go?"

The evening air seemed to freeze around them. Alexa felt herself splinter.

"No," she choked out. "There's something I need to tell you. About Lorelei."

"I don't understand," Dan said, sitting beside Alexa on the porch steps. "You mean she's— Is she dead?"

"It's complicated. The curse stopped before it killed her, but she's not exactly alive," Alexa managed. The air stung with the smell of a candle snuffed out, and Alexa wondered if this was the magical scent of a witch giving up completely. She faced Dan. "You can't tell anyone about this—*anyone.*"

"I won't."

"Promise me you won't." Alexa's breathing was coming in shallow bursts. "Without Lorelei, I'll have to go back to Arizona and I can't do that. I can't—"

"I promise, Alexa. You can trust me."

Dan put her hand on Alexa's back and just like that, Alexa wasn't holding it together anymore. Hot tears rolled down her face, and she couldn't stop herself from gasping, "Why did this have to happen? After everything else, why this? Living up here with Lorelei was the first time I've been happy in *ever.* You don't know what it's like. You have parents who love you and I—"

"You're not going back." Dan interrupted her with such firmness that Alexa didn't need to say any more. Dan pulled her into a hug, and Alexa let herself collapse against Dan's shoulder, her tears mingling with the sweat still drying on Dan's skin. "I won't let you. I don't know what you did to Liss in the last two days, but *she* would never let you and she gets her way. North Coast is your home. You belong here, with us." Dan pulled back and met Alexa's eyes. "This is where you're going to stay."

Alexa was too exhausted not to believe her, for now at least. She let herself live in that fantasy a little longer: friends who would protect her, in a place she loved, Domino nuzzling her ankle.

Alexa decided they needed to tell Liss—witch-gang and all that—and once she arrived, the girls stood around Lorelei's bed. Lorelei's dark eyes were the only part of her that still looked somewhat like her old self, even if they were still and the corners were crusted with dried pus. Her flesh was mushy and brown, seeping various yellow-ish liquids, splitting at the seams. With other humans in the room, Lorelei looked much, much deader than Alexa had thought.

"Remind me never to get cursed," Liss mumbled as they went back into the living room, away from the stench.

"Keith Levandowski did this," Alexa said. "The leader of Black Grass."

"Why would he want to kill Lorelei?" Dan asked. "She was one of them."

"Not exactly. She was only posing as seeker," Alexa began. "She was doing an investigation into Black Grass when she was—when it happened. She told me it was for a magazine, but actually she was in this sort of magical FBI called the Wardens. I think Keith must have found out and punished her for it."

Liss held up a Black Grass pamphlet with Keith's smirking face. "You're telling me *this* guy did *that*?"

"Not alone. It was Kasyan's power working *through* Keith, I think. I've been trying to figure out what's going on. That's why I was up there last night when you did your spell. I was spying on Black Grass, with Domino."

"Your cat?" Dan asked.

"He's not just a cat. He's a familiar." Alexa took a deep breath and shoved her glasses up her nose. "He was Lorelei's and now he's mine."

"Only witches have familiars," Liss said slowly.

Alexa nearly lost her nerve. No matter what Dan promised, life demonstrated over and over again that people could not be trusted. Kim always said that betraying your fellow man was a basic human activity, just like eating and sleeping.

There would always be a part of her fighting to keep them at a distance, but right now, she could resolve not to let that part win. It was a strength she'd won incrementally, first when Lorelei took her in, and then when they came up to North Coast and she met Dan, and now Liss, who was somehow just as bad as Dan had said she was without really being bad at all. None of them were perfect, but they were trying.

Alexa took a deep breath. "You're naive witches, but that's not the only kind. Witches who inherit their power from another witch inherit their familiars too. When Lorelei was dying, she gave me hers."

Dan's eyes grew wide. "You're a witch?"

Alexa nodded. "All it takes is a gift from a witch on her deathbed. Lorelei gave me this necklace that she always wore. But she—she managed to live, I guess."

"Did she leave you her Black Book?" Liss asked. "How do you know what you're doing?"

"When you become a witch by inheritance, it comes with, um, a certain level of knowledge. I know a lot of what the witches who came before me knew. And it's . . . kind of a lot." Alexa said.

"Like you've taken AP Witchcraft and we're still in entry level," Dan said.

Alexa smiled. "Basically. If Lore had a Book, Keith probably stole it. He broke into our house not too long after what happened. He took everything we had on Kasyan too."

Liss was still fiddling with the Black Grass pamphlet. "We need to know whatever the deal is that Keith has struck with Kasyan."

"I don't know how they're working together, but I might I know why," Alexa said. "I think Keith is trying to set Kasyan free."

Alexa's dining room table was spread with information about Black Grass: a mix of official promotional materials and Lorelei's remaining notes. Everyone agreed that it was a definite point in favor of Alexa's theory that Keith had left untouched all of Lorelei's research on his organization and taken only things related to Kasyan.

"Black Grass's Center opened on May first this year," Alexa said.

"Keith bought the land in March," Liss added. "I remember my parents talking about it. A big Silicon Valley guy buying a chunk of land in North Coast. People noticed. He built the whole place up with his own money virtually overnight."

"Keith's story is that he founded Black Grass when he heard a calling. He was driving down Highway 1 and literally heard a voice telling him to stop near Dogtown." Alexa read from the pamphlet. *"Our Lord promised me exclusive access to unparalleled fulfillment. We seek a better future for the world."*

"How do you *access fulfillment*?" Liss said.

Alexa shot her a side-eye. "Join a cult and the answers will be yours."

Dan was chewing on a fingernail. "Keith wasn't just hearing voices.

It had to be Kasyan. That seems a lot more likely than a tech bro discovering a forgotten demon who's locked up in the middle of nowhere, right? We could barely find anything about Kasyan, and we were really looking."

"That's no accident," Alexa added. "It's the Wardens. Swann basically told me they've been eliminating information about Kasyan for years."

"So Kasyan speaks to Keith sometime in March and he sets up Black Grass. Johnny was taken at the end of February," Dan continued. "What if Kasyan used Johnny, somehow, to put all this in motion?"

"It makes sense," Alexa said. She almost didn't dare to look at Liss. When she did, Liss's lips were pressed into a thin line, and her brow was pulled low. Liss's pulse flickered in her neck.

"So Kasyan's been waiting this whole time for someone stupid enough to do that exact spell on that exact day." Liss's voice was taut.

"We didn't know," Dan ventured. "It was an accident."

Liss smashed a fist against the table. "We should have known. How did we think nothing would ever go wrong? We were so fucking stupid, Dan." She was trembling. "I think about it and try to forget it and then I end up going over it again anyway until I feel like I might explode. I keep trying to make it better and it just keeps getting worse. *What we did* keeps getting worse. We're just as bad as Keith or Kasyan."

Alexa held her breath, watching Liss, then Dan. Alexa waited for Dan to speak but she was barely moving, save for the tears welling in her eyes.

"You're not as bad as them," Alexa said. "Not even close."

Liss ran a hand through her hair. "You don't know. You don't know how this feels."

Alexa felt the blunt, bright truth of it: you could know that trusting other people was dangerous and decide to do it anyway.

"I do know. Lorelei's like this ... because of me. She was dying right there, and it was happening so fast. I was desperate." Alexa thought of how over the last few days she'd watched Lorelei's lips dry and blacken, and the skin over her jawbone fall away to expose stringy, greenish muscles underneath, and how still she'd sat by Lorelei's bed every evening and told her about her day, told her everything about Dan and Liss, the break-in and the car accident, in case Lorelei could still hear her. Lorelei had always been the person she wanted to talk to. That hadn't changed. Alexa wondered if it ever would. "She gave me her power, and I must have done some kind of spell, because then she just *wasn't* dying anymore. Or she's still dying, but more slowly. I should have just let her go. Can you imagine how much pain she must be in? I don't even know if her mind is still working—I can't tell if I hope it is or not. But it's like Dan said yesterday, you wouldn't have done it if you'd known what would happen."

Liss was looking at Alexa with her mouth open and her eyes round. She was horrified, probably, at what Alexa had admitted, and regret curdled Alexa's stomach: she had said too much. But then suddenly her face was buried in Liss's blond hair, her glasses crushed against Liss's shoulders, and Liss's arms were fiercely tight around her. And then Dan was there with them, the three of them in a hug.

"What happened to Lorelei isn't your fault, Alexa," Dan said. "The same goes for you, Liss. Kasyan is a trickster. He's taken things from us and made us blame ourselves. But we're making it right, or as close to it as we can," Dan said. "Tomorrow, the three of us, Icaria: one way or the other, it's the beginning of the end."

Alexa broke away. "About that—I have a plan. We're going to get answers the Black Book doesn't want us to have."

TWENTY-ONE

Liss

She *heard her parents fighting* before she closed the front door. Liss had been hoping to sneak in unnoticed after Alexa's, so she waited in the hall—perfectly still, perfectly silent, her keys pressed into her palm—and listened.

"How *dare* you!" her mother squealed in a pitch that always made Liss's heart beat faster.

"I'm not *daring* anything. I have to spend the weekend in Sacramento for *work*," her dad emphasized.

"I know what you're up to down there."

"Of course you know, I just told you that I'll be working. Do you think I *like* spending so much time away from you and Liss? *I love you.*" This last part, he groaned in an unloving and angry way.

"Then I'll go with you."

"I won't be able to spend time with you because I will be *working*." Liss clutched her keys so hard the metal teeth dug into her flesh. Her father was already hopelessly exasperated. "And someone needs to be here with Liss."

"Maybe we should all move to Sacramento and then you'll never be able to get away from us."

"We agreed not to move until Liss is in college."

"That might never happen." Her mother paused, Liss knew, for a swig of wine. "You have no idea what's going on with your daughter." A lump rose in Liss's throat as she crept closer to the kitchen.

"I had to ground her until she finishes her applications. And where is she right now?"

"She's probably with her friends."

"She can't be with her friends because she is *grounded*. She's so irresponsible it drives me crazy. First this runaway druggie boyfriend, now this thing with the applications. We're lucky she didn't go after him, did you ever think of that?"

Liss needed to make it upstairs to her room. She could pretend she'd been at home since school ended. It would obviously be a lie, but they might go along with it to avoid another fight.

"Are you saying our daughter doesn't want to apply to college?" Liss's chest grew tight at the concern in his voice.

"That's what it looks like! She's procrastinated until the last minute. She hasn't even shown me a draft of her personal statement yet."

"Writing's never been her strong suit," her father added.

Her father's words, out of everything, were the ones that hit Liss like a punch to the gut. He barely took an interest in anything she did, but she'd never gotten less than an A in English—even the semester Johnny went missing.

She didn't need to hear this. She would go to her room.

But then her phone rang.

Liss cursed silently and frantically searched the pockets of polar fleece for her phone, but it didn't matter. Her parents were in front of her now, hard-eyed and angry.

"Hi, I'm going up to my room—"

"Oh no you aren't," her mother cut in.

"Is this true about your applications?" The disappointment in her father's face made Liss feel like she was shrinking down into nothing. Less than nothing.

"It isn't true that writing's not my strong suit. I'm pretty good at it. My SAT verbal was in the ninety-second percentile."

"Don't be a wiseass," he said. "Where were you?"

"At the library."

"It's past ten o'clock at night. If she says you're grounded, that means you are at school or at home—not at the library, not with your friends."

"I have to work on a group project tomorrow!" Liss protested. She couldn't let this interrupt the trip to Icaria.

Her father's gaze was steely. "You are here, nowhere else. That personal statement better be in your mother's hands by the time I'm back on Sunday night."

Her mother nearly dropped her wineglass. "We agreed you weren't going."

"You're putting words in my mouth," her father spat as her mother stormed back into the kitchen and Liss had played the role they needed her to in their fight.

Up in her room, she traded her uniform for sweatpants, and only sometimes heard her father's voice raised ("I'm a lawyer, I know what I said!"). Liss sat at her desk and stared into the blank document on her computer. *It's just an essay.*

There was an energy in her that wouldn't still, even as her fingers counted up to four and back. She would not think of Dan or Alexa, poor Lorelei's deeply disgusting body, or Johnny's abduction. She would not think about Icaria's dark past, or Mora's shardlike teeth, or Kasyan, whatever he might be. Liss's will had never failed her before, and now she would turn it to this, the most important essay she would ever write and the only thing standing between her and an un-grounded Saturday doing magic in a cursed ghost town.

My junior year I unleashed a demon. I spent my senior year trying to fix it, Liss typed. *Please let me into your college.*

Liss pressed delete and the line vanished.

It was amazing that something as simple as a white rectangle could ruin someone's entire life.

Downstairs the door slammed and one of the BMWs—probably her father's—pulled away. A minute later, that theory was confirmed by footfalls on the stairs.

"So *now* you're hard at work?" Liss's mother stood in the doorway to Liss's bedroom clutching an overfull glass of wine.

Liss closed the laptop and stood to face her mother in the doorway. "You're supposed to knock."

"Your father's gone." From the sharpness in her tone and the way she was sucking down her wine, her mother was more than halfway to nasty-drunk. Liss hated being alone with her when she was like this, and she only got this way when Liss was alone with her.

Her mother started in. "You have no appreciation for what your father and I have done for you."

Liss didn't say anything. It stung, but in the same way the last ten thousand cuts her mother had given her stung. You sucked in the pain, didn't let yourself feel it, and you didn't give her the satisfaction of seeing you hurt.

"We've given you so much, and sometimes I think it's all been an absolute waste."

"It's not my fault that you passed on an abortion when you had a chance."

"Don't be disgusting, Elisabeth." She took a big swallow of wine. "Your father's gone."

"You're being dramatic," Liss said, but her mother's words made her nervous. He wasn't *gone* gone. He'd said a dozen times he was going to work, but that was before her mom had really lost it. He wouldn't leave Liss alone here, even if he already did it a few days a week. Liss had to say something she knew was true intellectually, because she didn't feel it, not even a little. "If Dad's unhappy, I feel bad for him. I feel bad for both of you. But it isn't my fault."

"That's a nasty, hurtful thing to say."

"You say nasty, hurtful things to me all the time!"

Liss's mother lunged forward and slapped her hard across the face.

"Shut up!" her mother screamed, then pulled her hand back and brought it across Liss's face again and then again, until Liss at last remembered she could step back. She stumbled away from her mother, back toward the desk.

Her mother was spewing words, but Liss could hardly hear her. The shock made the world white and quiet—her cheek was numb, then hot as it blossomed into real pain.

Liss had never been hit like that.

Her mother started back at her, panting, like all that spinning and yoga she did hadn't adequately prepared her for the exertion of slapping her daughter. There was a horrible look in her eyes: she wanted to take Liss apart completely, and she'd do it with her words or her fists or whatever she could.

"Fuck you," Liss said, her voice ragged. "I hate you. You're a pathetic drunk—"

"Do *not* talk to me like that." She moved toward Liss and raised her hand again, but Liss moved first. She caught her mother by the wrist and pulled her forward. She stumbled into the desk, knocking the laptop onto the floor and dumping her wine onto the carpet.

Liss didn't wait. She dashed down the stairs, grabbed her jacket, and shoved her feet into sneakers. She stumbled out of her house, through the gate, and onto the empty street. She felt like an explosion of needles, and somehow the pain wasn't even focused in her cheek and her jaw, where her mother's hand had fallen, but was all over her body: her skin, her lungs, her stomach, her heart, every one of her muscles was scorched with it. The night was cold and dark and the fog was close and damp against her skin and it did nothing for the pain.

Liss ran. She ran down Kingfisher Drive to where it dead-ended in a clear swathe of sand, and then she ran into the beach, the dried-out shells of tiny crustaceans crunching under her sneakers. She ran, although the wind off the ocean stung her eyes, although her mother would never have followed her. She ran down the beach, away from the lights of Marlena, until her legs gave out and she tripped in the sand. She wanted to go until she collapsed, because her heart was racing from the damage her mother had inflicted on it, and if she didn't do something with that energy she would explode. She heaved herself up again, but she was gasping for air.

Liss realized she was crying.

She was crying hot, giant tears that were coming so fast they weren't really tears at all but streams, and she was shaking and there was a great gob of mucus in her throat and she was making this horrible, pathetic moaning-wailing sound that she'd never heard herself make before, not even when Johnny went missing, not ever. She sank to her knees in the sand.

Her parents *hated* her, just like everybody else did.

It was an crushing, undeniable truth painful enough to splinter her ribs.

She blew a slug of snot from her nose directly onto the sand, which was disgusting and she just didn't care. She wanted—no, *needed* someone. Someone who would make her feel less like she was starving to death at the bottom of a pit. She pulled out her phone to call Dan but stopped herself. Dan's house practically reeked of her parents' love for her. Dan wouldn't understand this kind of sadness. For someone who always acted like misery was her own special thing, Dan was terrible at recognizing it in others.

Then there was Alexa. Liss had tried, that afternoon, to be kind to her. Maybe Alexa would do the same for her now. Alexa's mom was such a problem Alexa couldn't even live with her, so maybe she'd get it. Liss had almost pressed *Call* before she realized how awfully pathetic it was. Alexa had made it perfectly clear she thought Liss was some kind of monster.

She was right.

Anyone could see it—her parents, the only two friends she had in the world. It didn't matter how hard she tried to be good, she couldn't escape what she was: self-obsessed, destructive, unlovable.

The only person who had ever been convinced otherwise was Johnny, and it had been a lie.

She had stood on a beach like this, one she picked for the name— Heart's Desire Beach. October had just begun, and the water was ice-cold against her ankles where the tide broke. She had felt like she was standing on the edge of the world as she cast the spell to make Johnny fall in love with her.

The Black Book had given it to them for Dan, but Dan had refused it. Dan worried that they didn't know what it would do, but Liss didn't care. For weeks, she had it copied into her notebook— "An Incantation for Love"—and it had nagged at her. A spell that would finally satisfy her hunger. She couldn't resist it.

The stupidest thing was, she did it when she already had him in her sights. She had already seen the interest in his eyes while she hung around at Achieve!, he was already messaging her silly GIFs and videos. But it was the night before their first date and she had been nervous. She wanted him to want her, and the Book had given her something that meant she didn't have to take any chances.

The spell was so simple, simpler than any other they'd done, and it definitely could be done alone. She stood with her feet in the ocean and the sheet of notebook paper in her teeth as she washed the long-handled bell in the salt water. She read the incantation's words, then rang the bell and said his name, then again. She hesitated before the final time but forced her hands to move, forced herself to speak, and then there was a dull sense of relief, a silence inside her, an assurance that Johnny would be hers as long as she wanted him.

It had been the loneliest moment of her life.

Until this one.

Liss sobbed into the sand, her hair whipping her face in the freezing wind.

Mora should have spared Johnny and taken her instead.

"Hey!" a voice called. "You good?"

Liss whipped her head around. "Who's there?"

"Over here!" A flashlight clicked on a few dozen feet away. "I was going to warn you about the rocks if you keep jogging that way— Oh, you're that girl from Zephyr's school. Liz?" Liss squinted until the flashlight's owner turned the beam on himself.

"Brodie?" Liss picked herself up and smeared away her tears. "What are you doing out here in the dark?"

"You're the one in the dark. I was coming out of a meditation when you jogged up and took a spill."

"Yeah, I'll be more careful. I thought you lived around Dogtown."

Brodie ducked his head and gave an embarrassed smile that, in the flashlight beam, made him look closer to Liss's age than his own. "Just camped out here for a minute. I thought the beach would be nice, but it gets real cold at night. I'm kind of between places right now."

"Same," she said.

He pointed the flashlight toward a sheltered place by the cliffs and a bright orange tent. "I've got a six-pack. Wanna chill?"

Liss arranged her face into something less pathetic. The firestorm inside her resolved, just a little, as that energy found another target. Chilling with Brodie was exactly what she needed.

———

Up at the tent, they sat in the sand. Liss winced as he opened a bottle of beer with his teeth and handed it to her.

"Thanks."

They knocked the necks of the bottles together in a toast. Liss took a swig. The beer was exactly the same temperature as the chilly beach air.

"So what's a girl like you doing wandering the beach at night?"

The beer was bitter and it made Liss's voice small and rough. "You don't know what kind of girl I am."

"I guess not." He liked that answer, she could tell. "What kind of girl are you?"

She took a long swallow of her beer. It was already half gone, and the alcohol was loosening the strings that bound Liss tight.

There were a dozen truthful answers to his question, and none of them could be said without crying. It didn't matter. She didn't need Brodie to know who she was and she didn't want him to. What she needed was something else to feel, a place to hide from this crushing self-disgust. He could give her that.

She set her beer bottle in the sand. In the feeble light of the lantern, she could see his face was weathered and he was watching her, a little hungry and a little wary.

"Why don't you find out?" Liss said.

His mouth pulled into a quick O of surprise, but he recovered quickly. "C'mere."

She moved closer to him. He slipped his arm around her and tilted her chin up with his knuckle, so their faces were only a few inches apart. He smelled like sour beer, greasy hair, and sweat, and Liss thought she might gag if he didn't kiss her exactly then.

But he did.

Liss squeezed her eyes shut, willing herself to get lost in it—waiting for that upsurge of intensity that made her want his hands all over her, her hands everywhere on him, the beginning of that vacant feeling where you were only a body and nothing else. Brodie's tongue chased Liss's around her mouth, his lips sloppy and over both of hers at once. She hadn't noticed it earlier, but Brodie kissed the way toothless babies gummed pureed carrots.

Liss wanted him to go further, even though she already knew she'd never tell anyone about this, that every time she remembered it she'd hate herself for it, that she would have lectured anyone else about how unsafe it was to trust strange men on the beach. It was pathetic that getting groped by a man nearly twice her age on the beach was the only way she knew how to take care of herself.

But if she was awful and this was awful too, then it was at least appropriate.

Brodie paused. "This okay?"

Liss opened her eyes, which were stinging and swollen from her tears. It was the correct question, but the answer was stupid obvious: nothing about this was okay. Before she could answer, he edged back from her.

"Look, don't take this the wrong way, but crying girls freak me out," Brodie said.

Liss raised a hand to her cheek. It came away wet. "Sorry, I'll stop."

She reached for him again, but he rubbed the back of his neck. "I'm just looking to have a good time, you know?"

"We *are* having a good time," Liss pleaded, although she hated herself for saying it. "Don't stop."

Brodie grimaced awkwardly and grabbed two more beers. "To be straight with you, I'm a romantic guy, and crying's a boner-killer." He passed a beer to Liss. "Let's just be cool."

Not even Brodie wanted her like this.

"Does it look like I know how to be cool?" Liss whispered as she wiped her tears on the back of her hand. "I'm a fucking mess."

"Hey now." He moved to put his arm around her, then reconsidered when she snorked up a glob of snot. "You know what always makes me feel better?"

"If you say meditating, I'm leaving."

Liss followed Brodie's flashlight to an outcropping of rocks at the tide line. He handed her one of the empty beer bottles from the six-pack he held and pointed at the rock.

At first, Liss fumbled, but then she felt the satisfying crack of glass shattering, and the pleasure of destroying something that wasn't herself. She broke bottles against the rocks until the sand glittered with glass, catching the thin moonlight like shattered bits of dead stars, and though she knew the comfort it gave her wouldn't last, it helped a little, at least for now.

TWENTY-TWO

Dan

When the red Range Rover pulled up outside Dan's house Saturday morning, Dan was ready, which was basically never true of Dan in the morning. Yesterday had been hard, but it felt like a good kind of hard. For the first time in a long time, when Dan had turned the lights out to go to sleep, she hadn't wanted to listen to IronWeaks. She didn't need Rickey's sadness to dampen what felt undeniably like excitement.

Alexa was already sitting shotgun, so Dan slid into the back seat. The windshield wipers were on against the cold drizzle. Liss tossed her the cord for the music as she navigated north out of Dogtown. "Alexa wanted it, but I told her you have seniority."

Alexa twisted around in her seat as Dan scrolled through her music. Alexa's eyes were puffy, but Dan was relieved to see that under her glasses, she was wearing her signature cat eyeliner again. "Did you find a geode?"

"My mom had a bunch in her studio," Dan said. "I got a hammer too."

"That's everything, right?" Liss said to Alexa. Liss was glaring at the road from behind her oversized sunglasses, which the weather did not at all require; then again, Liss wasn't a morning person.

"That's everything," Alexa confirmed.

"Kasyan better watch out," Liss said in a flat voice. "Witch-gang is armed with basic household items, and we're coming for him. Not even this shit weather can stop us."

Dan and Alexa laughed, but Liss just adjusted her sunglasses and acted like she hadn't made a joke at all.

All of a sudden, Dan felt *good*, in spite of everything. The three of them, together, felt right. Maybe things didn't need to be back to the way they were before. They were each fucked up and desperate and tragic in their own way, but together, they could begin to make some kind of sense. As if Liss teasing Alexa for liking the music that Dan had picked was evidence that magic could come within an inch of destroying your life and you could survive it—they *had* survived it. Dan could almost imagine a future where all this was gone but not forgotten, a time the three of them could look back on together with pride instead of shame, and the thought made her heart feel too large for her chest.

They stopped at the 7-Eleven outside Fort Gratton for additional supplies. In the parking lot, Dan ate a s'mores Pop-Tart edges-first while she and Alexa waited for Liss. The sugar made her heart throb, and she remembered the night she had come here with Johnny, the single kiss that set all of this in motion.

"That's the missing girl from Liss's school?" Alexa pointed at a flyer taped to the store's window: the poster of Zephyr that community volunteers had stuck up all over North Coast. "I never met her, did I?"

"I don't think so. Why?"

"She looks kind of familiar."

"Her face has been everywhere for like two weeks."

"Her story's kind of like Johnny's, isn't it?" Alexa asked. "They just found her car abandoned by the side of the road."

"That's where the similarities stop, we think," Dan said.

Alexa was still staring at the poster. "It's a weird coincidence, is all."

Liss emerged from the store with two sugar-free Red Bulls. She cracked one open and guzzled it in practically one go.

"Didn't sleep last night?" Alexa asked her.

"I'm fine." Liss tossed the empty can into the trash. "Let's go."

They sped through Gratton, which was still asleep in the rain, then up Highway 1, where the wind off the Pacific rattled the car and Liss kicked the windshield wipers into overdrive. North of Gratton, the towns were few and far between. Eventually, the settlements were so small you couldn't tell by looking at them if they were inhabited or not: just a few broken-down barns with moss growing on their caved-in roofs, a pile of rusted car parts, a propane tank or trailer hidden among the redwoods or coastal pines. The land became green and wild. Dan watched the reception on her phone waver, then disappear completely.

The spell they were planning was Alexa's idea. Or it might be more accurate to say it came from Alexa. Alexa was basically a living, breathing library of Black Books. Last night she had made it clear she was serious that doing the spell their Book turned up would kill them.

Dan believed Alexa, but still, it was hard to take in. The Book had been their only conduit to magic for so long. They'd spent who even knew how many hours with the thing. It was unthinkable that it could be trying to kill them. But Dan conceded that even if the Book's spells always did something, that wasn't the same as working. Actually, they had no idea how it worked or why, only that it had led them to some pretty catastrophic failures recently and Alexa hated being physically near it.

"Just because it's the only way you've ever accessed magic doesn't mean it's the only way that *exists*," Alexa had argued. "Other witches can train you."

"Are you offering?" Liss had asked.

It helped that Alexa's idea was a killer.

Alexa had spent nearly five minutes pacing the small, stinking house, her face set in serious concentration and Domino at her heels, every so often muttering comments like, "We'd never catch one in time." Alexa had looked more like a mad genius than a witch, in her oversized cardigan and round glasses and her hands weaving through the air. When she finally yelped "That's it!" Dan and Liss were legitimately unsure if she was addressing them.

When Alexa was done explaining the spell, there was no doubt in Dan's mind: they didn't need the Black Book, because Alexa was definitely a mad genius, and also a witch.

"We just passed the vista point," Alexa said, tracing their path on the road atlas. "The turn should be coming up on the right."

Liss almost missed it anyway, like she hadn't heard the warning. She cut the wheel so hard that Dan and Alexa were both flung against their seat belts. A few dozen yards in, the paved road turned to gravel and slippery mud, and veered inland and uphill. Soon, the scrubby windblown vegetation that lined the headland gave way to straight, soft-barked redwoods growing clustered in rings and tall Douglas firs, their trunks speckled with tufts of electric-green moss. Tendrils of fog wound through the trees, snagging on branches.

"This is looking more *Hobbit*-y than demon-y so far," Alexa said.

"We're not there yet," Liss said. "Although I don't know how much farther we can take the car."

Liss was right. Soon after, what little was left of the road was blocked entirely by a fallen redwood.

"Now our hike begins," Alexa said as Liss pulled the car to a stop.

The fallen tree had an ugly gash running down it that split the trunk in two, and what should have been reddish wood was blackened and dark. Dan leaned forward from the back seat for a better view. "Is it some kind of lichen?"

Alexa squinted at the tree. "It looks off to me."

Alexa got out of the car and immediately pulled the neck of her shirt up over her nose. She grabbed a stick and tentatively prodded the tree trunk. Suddenly the black stuff rose into the air, and Alexa yelped and ducked: a cloud of black flies. Alexa swatted them away, although it made little difference, and peered into the crevasse of the trunk. She was coughing as she came back to the car. "Something's dead in there—some kind of animal, I can't tell. Maybe a couple of animals."

Dan shuddered as she got out of the car. "This is a good idea, right? I mean—what if he's here? What if we're walking straight into Kasyan's lair?"

Liss slammed the door closed and set about locking the car repeatedly, the way she always did, although this time it seemed to take longer than usual. Dan hadn't realized that hidden behind her sunglasses, Liss's eyes were veined with pink. "That's the whole point of looking for him, Dan," Liss said—not cruelly, but not exactly with kindness either.

The hike was long, and not made any more pleasant by the rain. Dan immediately felt soaked, in spite of her waterproof layers. The road narrowed into something overgrown that was barely a road at all, and then just a dirt track, and thick mud clung to Dan's boots. The hike took them up to the top of a ridge, after which the towering, pin-straight redwoods and firs cleared to a plateau of smaller bishop pines, the cypress that grew everywhere in North Coast, and smooth-barked manzanitas, then through another uphill slog over another ridge. At the top, the girls stopped for water and to check their map. The rain had finally eased off, and they pulled down the hoods of their jackets. Hundreds of feet below them, the slate-gray

Pacific and the relative safety of Highway 1 seemed impossibly far.

"We're close," Liss said, scrutinizing the map.

As they headed down the far side of the ridge, the nature around them began to change. The first thing Dan noticed was the silence. Now that the rain had stopped, they should have heard bird calls, animal grumbles, but instead she heard—nothing. The ground was littered with fallen branches and dull, rust-colored pine needles, and where it wasn't, there were standing pools of water that were placid and lifeless; not even a bug skittered across the surface.

It wasn't until Alexa asked, "What's with these trees?" that Dan noticed how undersized the trees had become: the pines and cypresses that should have been dozens of feet tall were barely a foot or two above Dan's head. Some of them were as short as shrubs, yet clearly they were trees, with stunted, contorted trunks and gnarled, sinewy branches. The forest was a gray bramble. Many of the misshapen trees were ash-colored, with dead sun-bleached needles, but strangely other driftwood-gray branches hosted a few living green twigs—as if the rest of the tree had died so those little twigs could survive. Rippling olive-gray or whitish skins of lichen were clinging to the bark. Elsewhere, nearer the ground, the lichens were bulbous and white, studded with bright red, glistening dots.

"It's a pygmy forest," Liss said. "These trees are the same as the ones we were just hiking through, and they're probably decades old. They come out stunted like this when there aren't enough nutrients here for them to grow to their full size." She glanced back at them. "What? I did a report in seventh grade. Extra credit."

"Why build a town in a dead zone?" Dan said.

"Was it a dead zone before Kasyan?" Alexa said.

It was a place easy to get lost in. As they went on, the path began to wind, zigzag, and at least once looped over itself. There was no other way to go, but Dan was getting nervous. As it stood, they couldn't see the horizon line over the last ridge they'd crested, and that ridge looked almost indistinguishable from the next. Dan felt dizzy: for the first time in her life in North Coast, she wasn't sure which way the ocean was.

"If we don't find it soon, we should turn back," Dan finally said. The sun, still hidden behind the thick cloud cover, wasn't going to help orient them at all, and the thickets of pygmy plants were too dense, too short to provide any landmarks. "I don't want to get lost."

Alexa was up ahead, looking at a grouping of oddly shaped rocks. "You guys, I think we're here."

Liss glanced at the nothing around them. "This can't be it."

"It's a grave marker." Alexa tentatively touched the inscription cut into the worn stone. "This is all that's left of Icaria."

There were no decrepit old buildings, no overgrown road, no ramshackle sign marking the town that once was. All that remained of Icaria was the small graveyard, fewer than twenty markers and nowhere near the number that had perished here. Instead of grass, strange scaly patches of bluish white lichen topped the bare dirt. Dan shuddered to think of the old skeletons just a few feet down in the hard-packed earth, scarred by Kasyan's touch.

The spell took a long time to complete, the three of them sitting knee to knee in a triangle while they each took turns at a different component. Dan wasn't sure if it was that the spell hadn't come from the Black Book or that three of them were casting rather than two, but the magic felt different: more anchored and stable, less like a wild thing about to slip free.

When Liss brought the hammer down on the geode, cracking it in two and revealing its crystalline center, the air stilled around them. Dan pulled her jacket tighter around herself.

"Did it work?" Liss asked cautiously.

"I think . . ." Alexa began. The way her face lost all color and her mouth was hanging open, she didn't need to finish. Dan's stomach was already in her throat as turned toward what Alexa was staring at.

There was a man—what looked like a man—in the graveyard. He was moving slow and stumbling among the grave markers, like he was unused to walking. He wore a thick beard touched with gray and a heavy black mustache that, in neater times, might have been waxed into curls at the end, and he was dressed in a way that reminded Dan of those tourist places where you could have your picture taken in gold-rush-era outfits—hat and vest and pocket watch.

"We actually did it," Alexa murmured. "We summoned a freaking ghost."

"He looks so *real*," Liss said, and she was right. He was far from rosy-cheeked, but he looked more like he'd had a hard night than been dead for nearly one hundred and fifty years. He looked as substantial as someone with an actual body, which made it all the more disconcerting when his leg passed cleanly through a gnarled, stunted cypress tree.

"Can he hear us?" Dan whispered.

"Hopefully," Alexa said grimly as she rose from her crouch. "Are you the Warden?" she called to him.

When the man turned his face to them, Dan couldn't breathe. Where his eyes should have been there was instead blackness: the utter, pure black of negation. His eyes were twin voids, and it hurt Dan's brain to look at them. She had seen eyes like that before, on Johnny, as Mora took him.

"Where have you called me?" he said in a voice like the rustle of dry leaves.

"To Icaria," Alexa said.

The ghost made as if to spit on the ground, but nothing left his lips. "Icaria is a cursed place."

"We know. We're sorry to disturb you but we need your help. You defeated Kasyan when he tried to destroy Icaria—"

"Kasyan did not try to destroy Icaria," the Warden corrected. "He didn't care for it at all. He only wanted the people. Wardens destroyed this place."

"Why?" Alexa asked.

The Warden drifted among the graves, passing his fingertips through the crooked stones. "So he would have nothing to come back to." Something about him seemed to flicker. "Tell me, do you have news of Maggie Kelly—my sweetheart? She was waiting for me. I was to deal with Icaria, and she promised to wait for me. She was going to make me an honest man."

"It's been a long time since you were last here." Alexa was trying to be delicate, even though Liss rolled her eyes at the ghost's digression. "Like one hundred and fifty years."

The ghost clutched his hat to his chest, his shoulders caved. "It wasn't my fault—I missed her so badly. She was my love, and she'd promised to wait for me." His voice broke, then he let out an otherworldly howl of sadness, like a scream echoing from the bottom of a well. Dan shivered. "I should never have thought of her in his presence. I should have hidden it from him, but I couldn't help imagining coming back to her. He told me he would keep her waiting as long as it took. Forever, he said. He reminded me of it every day. Although there weren't days down there. No sun, no days."

"I don't follow," Liss cut in. It was incredibly *Liss* to be rude to a grieving ghost, Dan thought. "Are you talking about Kasyan?"

"What was that? Who spoke?"

"I'm, uh, Liss." It was weird to hear Liss introduce herself to a blind ghost. "Another witch working on this project."

"Two women? You both sound very young," he said.

"You've been dead for more than a century—literally everyone on earth is younger than you. And we're three young women here, technically," Liss snapped. "Was it Kasyan who told you that Maggie would wait forever?"

The Warden turned his hat in his hands, his brow drawn with lines. He nodded. "Once he knew I loved her, used it against me—against both of us. Now I'll never see her again."

Dan spoke behind her hand to the girls. "He's saying Kasyan cursed this woman he loved and then killed him, right?"

Alexa nodded. "And not fast either."

Dan cleared her throat. "Um, sir, you sacrificed so much to fight Kasyan. We deeply respect that. But we have a bit of a situation with him now. He kidnapped one of our friends, and this sort of cult thing is trying to set him free."

The Warden's mouth pulled into a look of horror. "Set him free? That's a diabolical thing to do."

"We're trying to make sure Kasyan stays locked up for good. But we have to get our friend back too. Seeing as you're the one who trapped him in the first place, we were hoping you could tell us how you did it and where he is."

The Warden shook his head and replaced his hat. "It's too dangerous. You could easily free Kasyan yourselves in this rescue attempt. It cannot be worth that risk."

"How long did Kasyan have you before you died?" Liss's hands were clenched into fists. "Do you even know? No days and nights down there, you said. Must have made it hard to keep track."

A look of pain flashed across the Warden's face. "I believe I lasted just over three months."

"Johnny has been surviving down there for two hundred ninety-five days. That's ten months, and he's not dead yet." Liss's voice was firm, but there was a bloodless, sick look to her as she spoke. She looked, Dan realized, miserable.

"Ten months," the Warden repeated.

"Tell us about the spell," Liss said.

The Warden hesitated long enough that Dan feared he'd refuse them. "I'll tell you what I can recall, but the details are hard to keep hold of. It's been a long time."

"Anything you remember would help," Dan said.

"I had been studying Kasyan for some time. The Wardens had given me the duty of watching him. I came to Icaria looking for him amidst all that death. When I found him he looked like any regular man. He had been living in Icaria, watching his handiwork as it unfolded. Somehow I drew him down the coast. About a day's journey by horse south of here, but I needed somewhere remote, away from the miners and prospectors and the Pomo settlements. A place where no one could cross Kasyan's path by chance. There is a beach where, when the tide was low, one can follow the waterline north along the base of the cliffs. When the tide is at anything but its lowest, the way is impassable. I led Kasyan there, into a cave that tunneled beneath the cliff. We fought." His brow fell, his thick eyebrows nearly touching his lashes. "By the time it was over and I had him in his chains, I was weak. Too weak. And bleeding, from the spell. The way out was flooded. There was only one way to seal the cave." He scrubbed a hand across his brow, then his voice fell into a quiet rasp. "I remember the last time I saw the light of day. It's a strange feeling, wanting to live, but wishing you could die more quickly."

"I'm sorry for what happened to you." Dan forced her eyes to meet his vacant black ones. "You shouldn't have lost your love, and you shouldn't have had to die like that."

"Thank you," the Warden said, his shoulders sagging.

"Do you know what beach it was?"

"My Maggie—she knew the beach. She was the one who suggested the idea. She would have made a fine Warden. I promised to begin teaching her, once Kasyan was dealt with."

"That's a start." By the tone in Liss's voice, she clearly had little patience for a gentle approach. "What can you remember about the spells you used?"

"There are two spells. One to chain Kasyan, and another to seal the cave—an extra precaution. To chain him, blood was needed."

"What kind?" Alexa asked.

Alexa flinched when the Warden focused his unblinking black-hole eyes on her. "Human. You must avoid spilling any blood once you've entered the cave. If you can manage it, his chains should hold. But do not think that will keep you safe from him."

"And the spell for the cave?" Liss pressed. "This was the most important magical day of your life. You can't just *not remember*."

"Has anyone ever told you that you're very unpleasant?" He scowled at Liss. "I wish I could tell you, but the best I can do is tell you where to find it. The spell was in my Black Book."

Dan heard Liss draw a sharp breath. "Your what?"

"My notebook. But it was with me in the cave, with Kasyan, so there it stays, along with my bones," the Warden added. "Kasyan won't be able to do the spell himself. It's not designed for his type of power, and the amount of energy it requires is enormous."

"We have a Black Book," Liss ventured. "That's where we found the spell. The one that let Kasyan take our friend."

The Warden's frown deepened.

Liss went on. "There were three of us at a crossroads on Kasyan's Day, so the odds were against us. The spell went weird, somehow, and that crone-woman who works with Kasyan appeared."

"Mora? That woman is a magpie," he scowled. "She's little more than a servant to him. The spell was designed to hold Kasyan, not her. She is harmless without him. Mainly she's a scavenger—you know how birds like that are."

All three of them shook their heads, which the ghost ignored.

"Anyway, we played this game, Likho, with her, which is sort of like evens and odds—"

"I know the game," the Warden interrupted. "What was the wish?"

"What wish?" Liss asked.

Dan had to be very deliberate about continuing to breathe.

"The conditions of Kasyan's capture don't fully contain his power. But even on Kasyan's Day, Mora cannot simply wander around kidnapping the unlucky. Kasyan's power relies on desperation and desire and willing sacrifice: wishes, prayers, things like that. Mora could only have taken your friend if someone wished it. Presumably you knew that when you played."

"But we lost the game," Dan said, her voice small.

The Warden shrugged. "Kasyan's games are more complicated than winning and losing. What made you think you knew the rules?"

As they hiked back in silence, with each passing step Dan clung tighter to the possibility that Liss would ignore what the ghost said about the wish, or maybe she'd think that there was no way to know what went wrong with Mora's game. Maybe Liss herself had hoped it was Johnny who was taken. But the lower the sun fell in the sky, the more desperate that possibility felt, and so the harder Dan wished for it, because if Liss and Alexa knew what she'd done, then what?

But when they got back to the car, Liss turned to Dan.

"Why did you do it?"

"Do what?"

Liss's voice was honed to a knife's edge. "The wish."

"What are you talking about?" It sounded feeble and incriminating.

"The *wish*, Dan! Don't act like you don't know. You heard him—someone had to have wished that Johnny would be gone or disappear or *something* for Mora to take him."

"Liss, watch yourself," Alexa said, but her eyes were fixed on Dan, waiting for an answer.

It was a sensation like falling, slipping into an abyss and that abyss was the truth of what she had done and who she was. There would be no going back from it: she would lose both of them for this, but there was no way to deny it now.

"I didn't mean for it to happen."

Alexa stepped back. "Dan, you can't be serious."

"It was an accident. It was just a *thought* I had, before we even started doing the spell," Dan tried to explain. "I didn't know anything about Kasyan—neither of us did."

"Why?" Liss said. "You wanted Johnny so bad that you had to destroy him? Or did you wish that he'd leave me so you could have him all to yourself?"

"It wasn't like that." Dan was shaking. "It wasn't some evil plan."

"You should have had him take me instead."

"But then *I* couldn't have had you, Liss!" Dan cried. "It was never about Johnny. It was about *you*."

"What are you talking about?" Liss glared at her, genuinely confused.

"You're exactly the same, even now. You've never once thought about how much you hurt me."

"Hurt you *how*?"

This was why Liss's friendship was an unhealing wound, and

Dan felt it now like physical pain. Liss was still blind to Dan's sadness. She never saw how badly Dan wanted her best friend by her side, instead of at her boyfriend's. Even now, Liss was annoyed that Dan's feelings had interrupted her anger.

"You abandoned me for him," Dan forced herself to say. "You started dating, and it was like I barely existed. You were my best friend. I had no one else. I was miserable and you didn't even see it. Can you blame me for wanting him gone?" Dan smeared tears across her cheeks. "It wasn't the kind of wish that was supposed to come true."

Liss gave her a look that could shatter ice.

"Get in the car," she finally said. "Before I leave you here."

TWENTY-THREE

Liss

Liss didn't speak as she drove away from Icaria. She threw no one the cord for the music. Her hands curled so tight around the steering wheel, she couldn't even release them long enough to count to four and back. She worried if she pried her grip away, she'd lose control completely—of the car, of herself. Her jaw hurt from how hard it was clenched.

Dan didn't say anything either. At first, she was making whimpering noises, and when Liss dared to look at her in the rearview mirror, her face was tear-streaked and she was wiping her nose on her sleeve. Fury sparked in Liss at how unabashedly wrecked Dan looked. Like once this last secret was out, she'd let it all go, without caring who saw her misery. It wasn't fair, Liss snarled to herself, that Dan didn't have to be strong anymore, not when Liss wanted to sob too.

God, she wanted to sob. Instead, Liss devoted her attention to keeping the car steady between the yellow and white lines of the road through each curve and turn on the way back home.

By the time Liss pulled into Dan's driveway, they were still silent. Dan sniffed and hesitated before she left the car.

Alexa turned back to Dan. "Are you okay?"

"I'm fine." Dan tucked her hair behind her ear and looked

cautiously at Liss. "I'm sorry. I promise, I didn't mean to do it."

Liss felt something thick rising in her throat. She swallowed hard against it and turned back to the windshield until Dan had gone.

Outside Alexa's place, they sat in the car.

"I don't know if I can let Dan be a part of this anymore," Liss said.

"Liss, don't. It was an accident, and you know she feels terrible. I think she's been punishing herself over it for a long time."

Liss couldn't look directly at the chain of reasoning spawned by that thought: they cared about each other so much it destroyed them. Instead, she said, "Is that supposed to be enough?"

"It's something," Alexa said.

"Don't act like you know how this feels. I swear, if you're about to tell me I have to forgive her, get out of my car."

"I'm not. That's not how forgiveness works. But you can give her a chance to earn it. You can't really think she meant to do it deliberately."

"No," Liss conceded. "Dan's not that kind of monster. I just—I can't even look at her right now, let alone talk to her. I need some time."

"I don't think we have that," Alexa said carefully. "Tomorrow's the Winter Solstice."

"Yeah, it's the Solstice Parade."

"And it's a full moon. That combination means we'll have some of the most extreme tides all year."

"*Shit.*" Liss hissed, rubbing a hand over her eyes. "Which is what we need to get to the Warden's beach."

Alexa pushed her glasses up her nose. "Whatever Keith is doing, he's doing it tomorrow. We need to figure out where that beach is, soon."

———

Liss dropped Alexa off, then sped all the way back to Marlena. The only sound she wanted to hear was the reckless roar of the Range Rover's engine. She wanted it louder than her thoughts, and she pushed the car stupidly hard coming out of the turns. She regretted it when she pulled up to her house: through the fence, she could see her mother's BMW in the driveway.

Her foot still on the brake, Liss squeezed her eyes shut as hard as she could and contorted her face into a soundless scream.

Liss should have been furious at Dan. She was within her rights to feel that familiar scorching rage. But she didn't. Maybe she'd been burning from the inside out for so long that there was nothing left for the fire. She was a bag of dry ashes.

She pulled away from the gate, drove down to the beach, and left the car in the small lot. The sand was thick from the rain, and a dull blue sunset was draining away what little light the day had had. The wind was howling in off the waves in frigid, wet gusts. Liss was exhausted and hungry and shivering, but that was nothing compared to how pathetically alone she felt.

She forced herself toward the rocky outcropping where the cliff rose out of the sand.

She would make him want her, and he would make her forget. She would absolutely not tell him what was wrong. She wouldn't let him see her cry this time. They'd have sex in the sand. Their skin would be clammy and chilled. The sand would smell like the old kelp and the empty shells of dead crabs that washed up on the beach, and feel terrible against her skin. It wasn't even fully dark, and dog walkers or all-weather joggers or anybody would probably be able to see them. She could already smell the sourness of his body and the sweetness of the nasty clove cigarettes he smoked.

Liss hadn't even done it yet and already it made her want to cry, but she wouldn't let herself turn back.

He was going to make her feel good, she told herself, even if it felt like a punishment.

The rocks came into view. She searched for the pathetic little camp, the obnoxious orange tent.

Brodie wasn't there.

Of course he'd moved on: it was a terrible place to camp, probably completely intolerable even for a darryl now that it was raining.

Liss felt like she was collapsing in on herself. Why did she feel like she was the horrible one, when Dan had done this horrible thing? This was Dan's fault and yet the more Liss tried to make that matter, the more she recalled all the things she'd done to push them to that point. She had dragged Johnny to the crossroads that night. She had cast a spell for Johnny's love and rung the bell to seal it. She had insisted they become witches with that first, reckless spell.

She had hurt Dan.

She had hurt Dan without even knowing it. Liss remembered missing Dan all summer and fall, and her efforts to win her into Project Rescue Johnny. She'd pressed against Dan's resistance, but she hadn't understood what she was fighting against. Liss didn't know what she had done to Dan, how exactly she'd inflicted the wounds. For a second that felt unfair, but that didn't matter. So much of what had happened wasn't fair, and it had happened anyway.

Liss wanted to hate Dan, but she couldn't.

Liss took a deep breath. Thank god Brodie wasn't on the beach. He wasn't who she really needed right now.

She went back to her car.

Dan

Up in Dan's room, IronWeaks was blasting. Dan set the razor blade on her nightstand and waited for that numbness to flood her. She shouldn't have cut on her forearm, where it would be almost impossible to hide, but that didn't feel like it mattered anymore. She was a nightmare of a person, and everyone might as well see it.

In any case, there was no one left who would care. Liss was so angry on the drive back that she'd literally been shaking, and Alexa probably wouldn't speak to her again, knowing what she'd done to Johnny.

Are you the one? Johnny had asked her on the beach. Now everyone knew: she was the one who did this to him.

Blood ran down her wrist and filled the crevices of her palm with red.

Dan had been stupid to think that helping rescue Johnny could put things right. Nothing had that power. But somehow she'd felt better for trying, even though their chances of success had always been slim. It felt better than carving pointless lines into her skin and better than hating Liss. Especially with all three of them working together, it had felt almost like hope.

It hadn't been hope at all, but its opposite.

Blood was pooling in her hand, but the numbness still hadn't come. Maybe one more would do it. Already, she'd never cut this much before, Dan realized, and the thought turned her stomach. It was sick that she did this to herself. She should stop. She wanted to stop. But one more might make the difference between feeling this and feeling nothing. She could make herself do it.

When would it feel like enough?

She had the razor blade in her hand when the door to her room flew open.

"What are you doing here?" Dan gasped. She hadn't heard the creak of the stairs over the music, and now there was no time to hide any of it: the blood, the wounds it seeped from, not even the razor blade.

Liss could see it all.

"Graciela let me in. I wanted to talk—oh my god, you're bleeding!" Panic ripped through Liss's voice. "What happened? There's so much blood."

"It's nothing!" Dan grabbed a T-shirt from her bed and wrapped it around her arm. Liss's face shifted from wide-eyed shock to horror. Dan wished she had somewhere to hide the razor blade where Liss wouldn't see it, but she was still pinching it between two fingers and Liss was staring right at it.

"It's not nothing," Liss said, breathless.

"Can you close the door?" Dan whispered. "My parents are downstairs."

When Liss's back was turned, Dan wiped up as much of the blood on her arm as she could and scuttled the razor blade away under a book. Her heart was racing as she turned off her music.

Dan expected Liss to sit in her regular chair, but instead she came and sat beside her on the bed. Her voice was ragged. "Are you doing . . . what I think you're doing?"

Tension tightened in Dan's stomach, then up through her throat. "It's nothing serious." By which Dan meant she wasn't trying to die, which didn't feel like something she could say out loud. "I'm fine. Honestly."

"Oh, fuck that. You are *not.*" Liss pressed the heels of her hands against her eyes and made a strangled kind of sound. Dan realized Liss was crying—actually crying, not pretending to or forcing it. "Neither one of us is fine. We can't keep going like this. What's wrong? Just tell me what's wrong."

Watching Liss cry, whatever rationalization Dan had come up for herself vanished. Dan had resented Liss for so long for not trying harder to find out why she was unhappy. She'd imagined dozens of conversations where Liss pushed past "I'm fine." But she had never wondered what would happen if Liss pushed and she still couldn't open up.

"Is it because of Johnny? Because of—of me? Dan, talk to me. Please."

"No, that's not it. It's not because of you or Johnny," Dan managed. "I started before I even knew him."

"I had no idea. I should have stopped you." Liss held her face in her hands for a moment, her eyes pressed shut. Dan had thought that too: if someone caught her, she'd stop. But now Liss was sitting right next to her and Dan had to admit that wasn't true. She realized with a jolt of fear that part of her wished she was doing it even now. There was a voice in her head, rocked with panic, that just wanted for Liss to leave and let her deal with her stupid, hateful pain the way she'd taught herself to. It was the same part of her that always worried about getting caught, because on top of the embarrassment, it would mean she'd have to give up cutting, which sometimes felt like it was the only thing holding her together.

She wanted to be a person who didn't do this. who could deal with her darkness. Instead she'd just become a person who couldn't stop hurting herself.

"It's not that simple," Dan said.

Liss looked up at her. A tear fell from her chin. "Then tell me how it is."

"I don't know if I can explain it."

"*Dan.*"

"But I'll try." Dan swallowed hard. "Sometimes, I just feel so *bad*. Like being alive is suffocating me. Like *I'm* suffocating me. I'd rather feel anything else than keep feeling like that."

"When you're so desperate to feel okay again that you'd do almost anything."

Dan nodded.

"I think I know what that feels like," Liss said. "But doesn't it hurt?"

Dan looked down at her arm, wrapped in the T-shirt. It had started to throb. What came after was the worst part: after a few moments of bloody relief, you were left with a cut that ached for days, scabs for a month, scars you would have to hide or lie about forever. It did hurt, and Dan was so tired of pain. "That's the whole point. Sometimes everything hurts and it feels like there's no difference. Sometimes it feels like I deserve it."

"You don't deserve it!" Liss snapped. "Look at me Dan: You *do not deserve* to feel like that. You deserve to be happy. And don't tell me you don't, because you're a bad or messed-up person or whatever, because I know you better than anyone else on Earth, and you're not an impartial judge."

Dan crumpled. "How can you say that? After what I did?"

Liss let out a deep breath. "I'm saying that knowing what you did."

"Really?"

"You didn't mean for any of this to happen. It would be crazy to hold an accident against you for the rest of your life. Crazy in a way that I am not," Liss clarified.

"Thank you," Dan managed.

"Is it true, what you said earlier? That I hurt you?"

Dan didn't know what to say. It was true that Liss had hurt her and afterward she'd wished Johnny gone, but saying it that way made it seem like it was Liss's fault, when it obviously was Dan's.

"You meant before what happened to Johnny, I did something to hurt you. I didn't mean to." Liss ran her hand through her hair and swallowed hard. "Sometimes, I worry . . . it's too easy for me to treat people badly and not even realize it. Like in the moment, nothing's as important as the way I feel, and it doesn't matter who I hurt to make myself feel better. That sounds terrible. It *is* terrible. It does matter that I hurt you. I'm so sorry, Dan. You're my best friend, and that probably means you got it twice as bad as anyone else. If you don't want to be friends, I understand. You put up with me for so long."

"The whole problem is that I *like* putting up with you," Dan said.

"You're the only one, then." A fresh wave of tears streaked Liss's face, even as she tried to smile at this.

"What is it?" Dan's brow furrowed. "Something else is wrong."

Liss took a steadying breath. After a moment she raised her eyes to meet Dan's, and there was a dark grief flashing in the blue. "Do you remember the love spell we asked the Black Book for? The one you didn't want to try, because you didn't know what it would do?"

Dan nodded.

"I cast it, for Johnny. The stupidest part is, I already knew he liked me. We were about to go on our first date and I just . . . I needed him to be mine, I needed to be sure. So I forced him to love me. I did it deliberately—it wasn't an accident like your wish—which makes it a thousand times worse. If I could do it over again—"

"We can't," Dan cut her off. "I thought the point of rescuing Johnny was to undo what we did. But that isn't right. That means avoiding what we've done, and why. But now I think the best we can do is try to make amends and get some justice for Johnny."

"If we do, do you think Johnny will forgive me?"

"I want that too," Dan said carefully, "but I don't think it's fair to expect it of him. If we can forgive each other, maybe we can try to forgive ourselves too."

It wasn't enough. Maybe it never would be.

But it was a start.

TWENTY-FOUR

Dan

"It's open!" Dan called out when Alexa knocked the next morning. "We're in the kitchen!"

"Who's we?" Alexa yelled back as she closed the front door. "I thought your mom was doing Solstice Parade stuff . . . Oh!"

"Good morning to you too," Liss said without looking up from the coffee maker she was trying to decipher.

Dan knew she should explain to Alexa how Liss had ended up in Dan's kitchen, with her hair unbrushed and yesterday's makeup under her eyes, and wearing a clearly borrowed shirt. That meant telling Alexa the full story about Johnny, and confessing to her about cutting, which seemed almost more difficult.

Difficult, but not impossible.

Alexa deserved the truth about who Dan was, even if there were parts of that truth that embarrassed or scared Dan herself. And more importantly, Dan deserved that honesty too. She had been lying to herself for so long, letting her secrets fester, but it was easier to move forward when you brought things into the light. That's what she'd had realized last night, as she and Liss stayed up talking for hours. There were too many things that had gone unspoken between them over the years of their friendship. Dan had been sure she knew everything about Liss, but it turned out that Dan hadn't been the only one with secrets.

Alexa propped herself up on a stool at the counter. "Is this a peace treaty or a cease-fire?"

Dan turned the heat down on the eggs. "I have a lot to tell you, but I'll explain later, I promise. Everything's good now," Dan assured her. "Except the coffee might never be ready."

Liss poked at the coffee maker's buttons. "Do I look like a freaking *wizard* with a *wand* who can just make coffee magically appear?" Liss whined.

Dan and Alexa grinned at Liss.

"What? This is *complicated!*" she cried.

Then all three of them burst out laughing. It was a laughter weighted with exhaustion and fear, but also the particular kind of joy that could come from living through awful things and choosing to laugh anyway, and it filled Dan with the warm, fluttering feeling of hope.

They drank Liss's too-strong coffee and ate eggs that were at least definitely scrambled, with hot sauce and chunks of avocado.

"What's the deal with this parade?" Alexa asked. "I spotted a lot of creative face paint walking over here. And at least one guy on stilts."

"Dogtown's event of the year," Liss said around a mouthful. "It's what it sounds like. A parade for the Solstice."

"You say that like it's a thing that happens in every town."

"It's a North Coast thing," Dan explained. "Anyone can join. The idea is to thank the spirits or whatever for the last year and then cleanse yourself for the next."

"The cleansing part involves running into the ocean naked at Dogtown Beach." Liss leaned toward Alexa and cocked an eyebrow. "Dan's parents always take the plunge."

Dan rolled her eyes at them. "My mom's on the organizing

committee. I promised her I'd work at a table for her pottery during the parade."

"You do know that's prime Kasyan-fighting time," Liss said.

"I can't get out of it," Dan said. "Until we figure out more about when and where and how Kasyan-fighting is going to happen, I will be spending prime Kasyan-fighting time selling pottery."

"We could ask the Black Book again," Liss suggested.

"Even though it's been trying to kill you?" Alexa scraped up the last bit of her eggs. "You've asked it a ton of different ways how to find Johnny. Somehow it has a blind spot at the one thing you really need it to do."

"What other ideas do we have?" Liss argued. "It's our last resort."

"A last resort?" The words caught on something in Dan's brain. She set down her fork. "That's kind of how the Book feels, isn't it? Like you're desperate, and you'd sacrifice anything for one last chance to get that thing you want."

"That's not the Book, that's just how magic feels," Liss said.

"No, it's not," Alexa said. "I've never felt magic like that."

Liss rubbed her forehead with the heel of her hand. "You make it sound like the Book's as bad as Kasyan."

A queasy pulse of dread washed over Dan.

"What?" Liss faltered. "It's not, is it?"

Dan turned to Alexa. "The Warden who fought Kasyan—do you know his name?"

"It was in the record book Lorelei had. Something Russian. He lived in the Russian settlement down at Fort Ross. Ivan Ivanovich— Volin?"

"Volunin?" Dan said.

"How'd you know that?"

Dan was already running up to her room. When she came back down she flung the Book onto the kitchen island. She flipped open the front cover. On the first page, a familiar script spelled out *Black Book*.

And beneath it, the letters *IIV*.

"They're Roman numerals," Liss said.

"That's not how Roman numerals work," Dan said. "They're initials. IIV: Ivan Ivanovich Volunin. The spell that started all of this was called Volunin's Frame. Somehow, this is his book. Either the original or a copy."

"He died with his Book in Kasyan's prison," Alexa said. "That means . . ."

All three of them stared at the Book. A few short moments ago it had seemed at least familiar, if not harmless; now it felt altogether less innocent.

A divot formed between Liss's brows, and then the muscles around her mouth tightened. "You're saying Kasyan's been using the Book to mess with us this whole time," Liss said slowly.

"That's what I'm proposing," Dan answered.

A dark look crossed Liss's face. She pushed back from the island, paced across the kitchen and living room and back before she managed to say, "We're idiots. We're absolute fucking idiots for falling for it."

"Falling for what?"

"For *what*? For the Book, obviously!" Liss ran a hand through her hair. "It's a handwritten magical diary, and we convinced ourselves we just found it by chance in the Free Box."

"It's magic," Dan hurried to say. "Anyone would have fallen for it."

"But they didn't. *We* did. The Book's been Kasyan's since the very beginning. Don't you see what that means?"

"The first spell," Dan said slowly. "'For the Making of Naive Witches.'"

Liss nodded. "When we turned ourselves into witches, we turned ourselves into his tools too. All the magic we've ever done is his. We set all of this in motion, just like he wanted us to." She turned to Alexa. "I thought you were exaggerating about the Book trying to kill us, but Kasyan must want us out of the way for whatever he's planning next."

For a moment, none of them spoke. That black-hole feeling was opening in Dan's chest, the concentrated mass of all the things that had gone wrong to bring them to this place: the whirlwind that first night in Liss's bedroom, the love spell Liss worked on Johnny, the fateful night at the crossroads, and the months of hiding that followed it. In a panicked flash, she felt herself being drawn back into that dark, guilt-ridden place. She couldn't go back there.

So this time, she was going to resist.

Dan took a steadying breath. "I didn't become a witch just so some demon could use me and toss me aside. If Kasyan is the reason we have this power, then it will be his fault when we use it against him, right?"

Liss's forehead was drawn tight as she glared at the Black Book, her shoulders tense. For an instant Dan worried she was going to give up. But then she straightened her back and met Dan's gaze with clear eyes. "The Book is too dangerous for us or anyone else to use again. We should burn it."

"We can't just burn it," Alexa interjected. "If it's really Kasyan's tool, it's not really *material* like that. If we did manage to burn it, it would release a huge amount of energy. If that energy didn't have somewhere to go . . ."

"It would be like setting off a bomb," Dan said.

"Exactly." Alexa pushed her glasses up her nose. "And I hate to say this, but if Kasyan has the spell that locked him up, he probably knows the spell to free himself. There's a way to sort of . . . negate spells. Like they contain their opposite. I can't really explain it, it's just..."

"Mysterious ancient witch stuff," Liss provided. Alexa smirked at her. "If Kasyan knows the spell to free himself, he must have given it to Keith. He's talked to him directly before, when he told him to set up Black Grass."

"Keith's been in North Coast for months. Why not do it on the Summer Solstice or the Equinox?" Dan asked. "Maybe he's still waiting for Kasyan to tell him where to do it."

Alexa froze. "*Shit.* The night of the car accident, after you ran after Johnny, I saw something too. There was a girl on the side of the road right where the accident happened—sort of like a ghost."

"You sort of saw a ghost and you're only mentioning it now?" Liss asked.

"It wasn't the weirdest thing that happened to me that week, okay? I don't even know if she was a ghost. She was all shimmery and silver, but she was dressed in like, a polar fleece and leggings."

Dan jumped up and started searching through a stack of mail on the counter. She pulled out a newspaper and slapped it down in front of Alexa. "Was this her?"

Zephyr Finnemore's face stared back at Alexa from the front page. "I knew she looked familiar."

"You think Zephyr's ghost was looking for Johnny?" Liss said. "Zephyr's *dead*?"

"I don't think so," Alexa said. "She wanted me to tell her 'what he needs to know.' She said he had promised to let her go once I told her. I don't think she meant let her go peacefully on to the afterlife."

"That night Johnny said something to me too," Dan added. Before Liss could interrupt, she pushed on. "He said, 'You're the one?' but he sounded sort of surprised to see me. I didn't mention it because I thought he meant that he knew what I'd done, but he must have been looking for Zephyr. If we hadn't been there, they would have been virtually face-to-face."

Liss nodded. "If Johnny was looking for Zephyr, that means Kasyan doesn't have her. So who does?"

"Keith," Alexa said. "It has to be him. There's no way he could figure out how to free Kasyan on his own. They must be using Zephyr and Johnny to communicate."

"Like a fucked-up game of telephone," Dan said. "We saw them days ago. They must have connected since then."

"Then we are completely screwed." Liss balled her hands into fists. "If Volunin didn't know where he trapped Kasyan, the best we could hope was that Kasyan didn't know how to direct Keith there either. But Johnny knows North Coast, and so does Zephyr."

"So Keith knows the where," Dan said. "He's waiting for the right when."

"Which is low tide today." Alexa tapped at her phone. "That's at 7:13 tonight. We have seven hours, forty-five minutes."

Dan grimaced. "Maybe we are a little bit completely screwed."

Liss

They spent the next few hours at Dan's clawing through every North Coast outdoor recreation guidebook her parents had, which was two decades' worth of worn trail maps and water-stained coastal access listings, enough to store in a plastic tub. When Graciela called to remind Dan to head over to the pottery table, they were no closer to finding Kasyan's prison. At Liss's calculation, exactly four hours and thirty-seven minutes remained until peak low tide.

"But actually we would need to arrive *before* 7:13. We should be turning back from wherever Kasyan is at 7:13, for maximum safety," Liss told the girls as they lugged the tub of maps out to the pottery table. "So realistically we need to figure this out yesterday."

"We're all on full alert, Liss," Dan said as she flopped into a plastic chair behind the table. "Right, Alexa?"

But Alexa was watching the parade. "This is . . . different."

"That's the holiday season in North Coast for you," Liss said. "No one's putting up nativity scenes out here."

Liss had to admit, the Solstice Parade was a lot to take in if you hadn't seen it before, and Graciela's pottery table had a front-row view. It was never clear who was parading and who was just a North Coaster dressed for a fancy occasion. Every local, darryl, weirdo, normie, hippie, organic farmer, and spiritualist turned out for the parade, and brought their kids too. A man in oversized sunglasses roller-skated by, playing snare drum with a Halloween-store bone, followed by a troupe of gray-haired belly-dancing ladies in white bra-tops and bells looped around their ankles. Liss spotted old Mad Mags following, waving her hands to the music. Behind them, a contingent from the bird refuge wheeled giant papier-mâché puppets of blackbirds and gulls with flapping wings. Next up, a pair of dudes wearing feather-covered speedos came by, one spinning poi through the air and the other doing tricks with a light-up hoop.

Liss ignored them and grabbed another guidebook, but as the afternoon wore on, even she had to admit they'd exhausted the maps. There were hundreds of beaches, and they had nothing to go on. All three of them were anxious now. Dan had run out of nails to bite and moved on to her cuticles, while Alexa's knee had never stopped bobbing as she frowned at the parade. Liss had fixated on the timer on her phone, which she'd set to a countdown until low tide.

Two hours, forty-one minutes.

Dan picked through the popcorn topped with brewer's yeast

that Graciela had brought them for yeast-less kernels. ("Why couldn't she just *not* put brewer's yeast on it? Isn't that easier?" Dan griped.) Alexa repeatedly reorganized the pottery they hadn't sold, which was all of it.

Two hours, thirty-nine minutes. Two hours, thirty-eight.

"What do you think will happen when—if Keith frees him?" Dan asked.

"Maybe the Wardens will deal with him," Alexa said. "I hope they at least stop Keith from taking over the world or something."

"Kasyan might go somewhere with more people to menace," Liss offered. "Hopefully these little middle-of-nowhere towns will be too small for him. I don't want to imagine Kasyan wrecking Marlena or Gratton or Dogtown or any of *this*." She gestured at the parade. A group of folks marched by playing drums made from trash cans and buckets, carrying signs that read DRUM CIRCLES FOR WORLD PEACE. Behind them, a bunch of little kids marched in flower crowns and butterfly wings.

"No. He'll stay here. I have a feeling," Dan said darkly. "We have what he wants in North Coast. Everybody here's a dreamer. That's the exact thing Kasyan likes to destroy. It was that same when Volunin was around."

"Volunin seemed like a romantic," Alexa said. "The way he talked about that woman—Maggie—and wanting to teach her to be a Warden and everything."

Liss looked up from her phone. "He said she was waiting for him. She was going to wait forever." Something notched into place in Liss's brain. She scanned the crowd. "What if she still is?"

Liss grabbed a map and set off running, weaving through the crowd. Liss caught her near the path down to Dogtown Beach, already full of half-naked North Coasters getting ready to take the plunge. She'd woven some flowers into her mess of matted hair and stuck a few into the bodice of the same dress Kasyan's magic had kept her in for one hundred and fifty years.

"Mags!" Liss called. "Maggie—Maggie Kelly!"

Mad Mags fell silent, her head cocked.

Liss pulled her out of the flow of the parade. "Your name is Maggie Kelly, isn't it? You're waiting for Ivan?"

Mags opened her mouth, but no words came out for long enough that Liss was beginning to think she'd been an idiot about the whole thing. This was their final, desperate chance. Still, part of Liss hoped she was wrong: that Mags was not being made to live forever by Kasyan, trapped in unending longing for her dead lover, and that she'd come by her crazy the way most people did—naturally.

"I called him Vanya," Mags finally said. Her voice was gravelly now, so different from the singsong she typically used. "Have you seen him?"

"In a way," Liss said. "He said you knew about the work he was doing."

"Kasyan," Mags said.

Liss nodded, though hearing Mags say the name sent a chill down her spine. "I'm trying to help him, but I need to know where Ivan wanted to trap Kasyan."

"Will you bring Vanya home to me?"

Liss looked at Mags, those round, watchful eyes Liss had always thought were childlike. They weren't childlike at all. They were tired, the irises ringed with milky gray and the whites flecked with brown. Her sun-leathered skin was wrinkled as a crumpled paper bag. A century and a half later, she had never given up hope that her love would come home. Never stopped watching, never rested. Never been allowed to change or move on. Trapped.

"No," Liss said. "He died in the cave with Kasyan a long time ago. But he still loves you very much, and he wants you to know he's at peace. He wants you to move on if you can."

Mags let out a small sigh. "Better that he died all those years ago than to suffer. It's been so long."

"I'm so sorry," Liss said. "You both deserved better. Can you show me where he went?"

Mags beckoned for the map. She dragged a shingle-like fingernail down the jagged line of California's coast, then settled on an inlet. She brought her face close to the map and peered at the text.

"They call it Heart's Desire Beach now," Mags said. "Head north. Watch the tide. It'll kill you, if Kasyan doesn't."

TWENTY-FIVE

Dan

They moved as fast as they could, but with the chaos of the Solstice Parade approaching the beach, that wasn't as fast as they wanted. They hauled Graciela's pottery back to Dan's house without breaking any of it, and grabbed the Black Book and then their leftover Icaria gear from Liss's car.

Dan felt like the gears in her brain had ground to a stop, jammed by the enormity of what they were planning to do. Take on a cult. Fight a demon. Spend way more time in an easily flooded cave in an active earthquake zone than anyone in their right mind would.

But then they were half running, half walking to Alexa's house, because hers was the only car not hemmed in by Solstice Parade traffic and barricades. They were in the car and on the road to Heart's Desire. As Alexa drove, Liss rattled off disheartening facts about the tidal patterns and the exact number of minutes remaining until low tide (one hour, fifty-eight minutes). Liss had found information about a hiking trail that led north from Heart's Desire. The tides and the wave patterns made rescue of stranded hikers impossible, so the parks department warned people to avoid the area. Liss finished reading the post aloud, then fell silent. The sun sat on the water like an uncooked egg yolk while Dan's heart hammered in her chest.

"We'll be fine," she said, almost to herself, in the passenger seat.

"What's that?" Alexa asked.

But before Dan could answer, they pulled up to the trailhead parking. A battered school bus, *Dream Peace* spray-painted on the side, was occupying four parking spots.

"They drove here in a freaking hippie bus," Liss grumbled as they got out of the car. "Where's the originality?"

"Quiet," Alexa said. "I think I can hear them."

They crept toward the overlook of the beach. The sun dying out in the Pacific cast the beach in golden light and indigo shadows, the clouds a toxic pink in the distance. Black Grass's seekers were lying in the sand, their bodies arrayed in an almost-completed circle facing the ocean. Some rested their heads on other followers' bellies, others were holding hands, still others snuggling in pairs, but all of them were touching in some manner. Keith was moving among them, laying his hands on foreheads and shoulders, whispering into ears.

"It's a transcendental meditation," Alexa whispered. "I saw him do the same thing the other night."

At the break in the circle, another figure was kneeling between a few cheap tiki torches, whose flames snapped in the wind. She was in a long white dress that was appropriately cultish. Her long curly hair whipped around her in the wind; she kept pulling it from her mouth with her bound hands.

"That's her," Liss breathed. "Zephyr."

Keith had made his way around the circle and stood behind Zephyr. Dan thought she could see Zephyr shivering. Keith said something to her then gave her a shove, and she lay down in a strip of sand designated for her, so that the seekers nearest to her left and right were touching her shoulders.

As she did, it was as if a circuit had been completed. The seekers, who had been lying quietly and still, began to writhe: some were moaning miserably, others grinding their bodies against the sand, still others (those who had been snuggling) began to kiss and grope. Dan's mouth dropped open. "No one warned me that there was a sex part to this," Dan said, looking to Alexa. "Are they going to free him with an *orgy*?"

Instead of answering, Alexa's face shifted into a look of horror, and Dan looked back to the beach.

The bodies of the seekers were crackling with gray-violet electricity, flashes of lightning emerging from the friction at their points of contact or the caverns of their gasping mouths. Energy chased itself around the circle—until it arrived at Zephyr.

"He's charging her like a battery," Liss whispered.

"I think I heard him talking to her the night I was there," Alexa said. "He called this the synergy. He was complaining that the seekers had released all this energy, but it just dissipated. I guess he figured out how to direct it. That must be why he didn't let her go."

By the time the seekers stopped moving, Zephyr's whole body glowed that otherworldly gray-violet. The bodies circled on the sand were still and silent again, but a different kind of stillness, one that made Dan cold all over.

"Do you think they're . . . dead?" Dan asked.

"If they're not, they'll be a lot worse off if we can't stop Keith," Liss said.

Keith had already fitted himself and Zephyr with headlamps and was hauling her off the ground. Her bound hands already made her unsteady on her feet. Keith fastened a rope to her wrists. Keith yanked her toward him, but she pulled back, wrenching her arms away from him. The tension caught him in the shoulder, and even from a distance, it was clear he wasn't happy. He closed the few feet between them and without any warning, slapped her across the face. Liss flinched. The next time he tugged on the rope, Zephyr stumbled after him toward the jagged rocks of Heart's Desire's northern edge.

The girls followed.

———

Down on the beach, it was dark enough to feel treacherous. Liss went for her headlamp. Dan held out a hand to stop her.

"It's getting dark," Liss said.

"He'll see us," Dan said. "We should go without light as long as we can. Until we're far enough along that he won't have time to deal with us if he wants to time the tide correctly."

Liss nodded, but she didn't seem reassured.

The way was perilous, doubly so in the fading light that made all the shadows blend together. Where the cliff began, the beach gave way to a narrow promontory of jumbled rocks, tumbled smooth by the waves and slick with sea water, algae, and leathery kelp. The waves still pushed high enough to flood their sneakers with icy water almost immediately. If they waited too long to try to return here, the waves would slam them right into the cliff, then drag them out into the ocean. A wrong step or a wrong wave could do it even now. Dan, leading the way, already could barely see the next footfall, and she nearly lost her balance stepping into a pool that soaked her past her knee; she would have fallen altogether if Alexa had not shot out her arm to steady her.

At least the churning water was loud enough to cover the sound of their stumbling.

Up ahead, the headlamps and Zephyr's purplish glow vanished around a curve in the cliffs, then reappeared. They weren't moving fast—not as fast as Keith would likely want—given Zephyr's stupid dress and bound hands.

To everyone's relief, after what felt like way too long, the submerged promontory opened to a maze of granite slabs that were mostly above the waterline. The girls hung close to the shadows of the cliff's edge. It was getting too dark to make out any of the coast's features—black rocks on black water on black sky. But in the bright swoop of Keith's headlamp, Dan spotted their next obstacle. The cliff jutted out into the ocean, forming a sharp point that cut off their route. A narrow keyhole passage was the only way through the rock. Thankfully, Liss had found a post about it on her phone during the drive: the passage was only four feet high, maybe two feet wide, and at least eight feet long. The main issue was that, toward the center, the rock pinched so severely that to pass you had to edge sideways on your knees such that your neck slid through the narrowest spot.

On a good day, it was an easy place to get killed.

Now, they watched the beams of light disappear into the rock, and crept toward the keyhole's entrance. Inside was impossibly narrow and dark. They would have to get through as fast as they could, because Keith would be hurrying now. Dan reminded herself to be brave.

"I'll go first. I'll tell you on the other side if you can use your lights."

Alexa and Liss nodded.

Dan eased herself into the small passage.

It was worse than she'd imagined inside. The rock was dripping with seawater, and jagged edges snagged her hair and clothes, and scraped her skin. The small space made the sound of the waves echo enormously into a constant roar. She tried not to think about the press of the rock against her chest, how close it was to her face in the dark, how a dislodged stone or a sudden tremor could trap her there until the tide came back in.

And then she felt the place where the rock pinched further. She felt for the space her neck would slide through, then swallowed hard and carefully sunk to her knees.

The rock pressed against her back and her chest and her neck and her knees. What if it got so close she'd have to struggle to breathe?

Dan gasped in a breath and felt the rock push back. Her pulse spiked.

No, she told herself. She forced her focus to Johnny. Zephyr. Lorelei. They needed saving, and they couldn't save themselves, so she was going to help them if it killed her.

Dan pushed on through the tunnel of rock, until she wormed her first leg free, then her shoulder, then stumbled out onto a narrow crescent of stony beach. She scanned the area, but Keith and Zephyr must have already moved on: no headlamps in sight. Dan clicked hers on, then pressed her face back to the keyhole. "It's not that bad," she called back to them.

Dan was watching Alexa worm her way through the passage, her headlamp on for safety, when pain exploded through her shoulder. Something in her neck cracked and she went down hard, face forward, on the sawtooth rocks.

She rolled over just in time to see Keith pull his leg back and land a kick in her gut.

Dan didn't even manage to scream.

She had never felt pain like this before—bewildering, starbursting—and she knew it hadn't even fully arrived yet, but was still getting worse. She curled herself into a ball as best she could against Keith's blows. She was dimly aware of her arms trying to make some kind of attempt at crawling away, and another separate part of her brain reminded her that that never worked in movies.

And suddenly Keith stopped. Dan froze too, as if moving would set him off again.

Alexa was there, her headlamp blazing like the white beacon of an angel.

"... to help you," Dan made out Alexa saying. "We're not following you. Kasyan called us to your aid. Why else would we be here?"

Before her, Keith's eyes were red-rimmed and wild, his face pouchy and bloated. "The Lord speaks only to me."

"He spoke to us too. He sent us to help you." Alexa was managing to keep her voice even. She hadn't even looked at Dan. "We're here for you."

Keith's mouth pulled into an sneer of confusion. "I wasn't circled in on this plan."

"The Lord, um, circles each of us in differently," Alexa said. "We know about the spell—spilling blood and all that. We heard it from him."

Just then, Liss pulled free of the keyhole and rushed to Dan. "How bad are you hurt?"

Dan managed to get up to a seated position and gingerly tested her shoulder. It was sore, and her neck ached, but the rock he'd hit her with had thankfully missed her head. As for her stomach, she wasn't sure. Keith was wearing those shoes that separated each toe, which had softened his blows a little. "I'm fine—I mean, I'm hurt but I can keep going."

Keith was still considering Alexa, his jaw working as if he were chewing on his tongue. "If you're lying, the Lord will discover you soon. Five is auspicious, better than two. Let's move."

When Alexa turned to Liss and Dan, Dan could have sworn she saw fire in her eyes.

Alexa

Alexa hung back as Keith grabbed the rope tied to Zephyr's wrists and led them on.

Her mouth tasted of bile, and she was sure she smelled like smoke. Every square inch of her body was trembling just from being near him. His white cargo shorts were streaked with grime from the keyhole (honestly, what was the point of white cargo shorts?), his white veneers were too big and bright for his mouth.

She could kill him right there on the rocks. She wasn't sure exactly how but the roiling fire in her blood meant her magic would find a way, right now, if she let it. She flexed her hands, cracking her knuckles. Getting revenge on Keith for what he did to Lorelei had always been her goal, after all, and without Keith, Kasyan would stay in his cave, maybe forever.

That meant leaving Johnny in there with him.

When Alexa heard Keith turn on Dan, she had screamed. She screamed the whole time she was pushing herself through that horrible mini-cave thing. She had a dozen bruises and her glasses were scratched, and her heartbeat was nearly at actual explosion-level intensity when she finally made it out.

She hadn't cared about Keith then at all, only about Dan. It wouldn't be fair to her or to Liss, and definitely not to Johnny, if she got her revenge on Keith before they made it to Kasyan.

Some quieter part of her whispered that it wouldn't be fair to Keith either. Lorelei always said Keith was more vain and self-obsessed than evil—that was back before Alexa knew Keith was literally the conduit for a demon. That was how Alexa had known what to say to convince him to let them join him: people like that were too ready to believe the story was about them. Why wouldn't Kasyan send three high school girls to him, like cherries on top of whatever else Keith had been promised?

But whatever Keith was after, he wasn't getting a fair deal either— he just didn't know it yet. Already he was acting possessed, as twitchy and rattled as a meth-head. Keith might be terrible, criminal, and dangerously stupid, but Alexa trusted that he would get what was coming to him. She couldn't sell out Dan, Liss, and Johnny just to make sure it was by her own hand.

She took a deep breath, willed her magic to submission, and

focused her attention from Keith to Zephyr, stumbling behind Keith over the rocks. The purple-gray electricity racing over her skin was beautiful, transfixing even. It was bright enough that Alexa could see it snaking across her body through her wet, wholly unsuitable dress. But Zephyr's face, when Alexa had seen it, was horrifying. Her jaw hung slack, and her eyes had a terrible faraway look, and her pupils were too large, like everything she was seeing was out of focus. Whatever had made Zephyr *Zephyr* was missing— whether it had been pushed out by all that electricity, or was hidden somewhere deep, Alexa didn't know. She hoped it hadn't been stolen for good.

They passed under an arch of rock and then traversed another half-submerged promontory. Alexa was the last to creep around the cliff's edge, her feet freezing as the waves slapped against the rocks. When she made it to the other side, they hadn't gone ahead.

Her breathing hitched.

Before them was a low black opening in the cliff. The tide surged against their legs, pushing salt water through the maze of cracks and crevices at the cave's dark mouth.

"Onward!" Keith commanded them.

Liss

Liss had never thought about it before, but a cave at night was pretty much the darkest place you could be—dark like Volunin's eyes had been dark, dark like there could be rocks inches from your face and you'd never see them. The headlamps' beams seemed only to concentrate the dark outside their sweep. Liss was glad she'd insisted on fresh batteries for everyone before Icaria.

At least they'd never lose Zephyr. She was lit up like a neon sign, with purple sparks chasing themselves over her skin. Liss hoped Zephyr felt better than she looked, which was really not good. Liss suspected that they would need to run at some point if they all wanted to get out of here alive, and this wasn't exactly easy terrain for a jog, especially after you'd been held captive by a deranged cult leader. Everywhere, still, there was freezing seawater. It still rushed under their feet with the pulse of the tide, and the rocks were still slick with Liss didn't want to know what. The ceiling was low enough that Keith, the tallest of them, had to duck occasionally.

If they were lucky, maybe he'd knock himself out.

The farther they went, the shallower Liss's breathing got as she tried to avoid thinking about how deep into the cliff they'd traveled. Or how frequently earthquakes struck North Coast's fault line, or the eventual inundation of the cave, or how if the passage got any narrower it would be hard for them to turn around. Her mind ran through all the different ways they could be trapped until she was too anxious even to count to four and back because she wasn't even really anxious anymore: she was *scared*. It wasn't only the claustrophobia. They were basically trapped already: nowhere else to go, no plan, nothing they could do but follow Keith wherever he led. That was basically doing nothing at all. Liss's chest practically seized with the force of that powerlessness.

Just when she thought she might stop breathing entirely, their way sloped abruptly upward—as did the ceiling, thankfully—and opened out onto a chamber. It was high enough that they all could stand comfortably, and despite the rough walls, the cavern was clearly not a natural formation. For one, the ground was more or less even. For two, the place positively *reeked* with magic. Liss had always been convinced her magical Scooby sense was a lot weaker than Dan's and now clearly Alexa's, but even she could feel it. The air should have been musty and stale, but instead it crackled with magic, the same way the purple lightning was crackling over Zephyr's skin.

Zephyr could feel it too. She'd dropped to her knees as soon as they arrived, and now she looked like she was struggling not to vomit.

A few seconds later she lost her struggle all over the cavern's floor. Even her puke sparkled with magical energy.

Keith didn't waste time letting her recover. He heaved Zephyr to her feet and set about preparing the spell. As Liss watched him, all she could think was how little she understood of what was happening, how poorly she had planned for this. Maybe being a control freak wasn't categorically great, but that was who she was: she came up with plans and she put them into action. She'd been channeling that obsessive need for control to free Johnny for months, only to realize she'd just been another one of Kasyan's victims all along. Now she was standing here helpless while Keith did his thing, which at that moment was shoving Zephyr against the far wall of the cave. When she shuddered, he ordered her not to move.

Liss grimaced. Here she was feeling helpless, when *Zephyr* was the helpless one. Zephyr was a victim who'd done nothing to deserve getting involved in this disaster that might well end her life. Liss was closer to an accomplice. She needed Keith to use Zephyr as a stick of dynamite, because she needed that rock broken open to get to Johnny. She had once called Zephyr someone else's problem, but she was Liss's problem now. Rescuing Johnny couldn't be worth it if Zephyr didn't survive it too.

And that was something, Liss realized, she could control.

"Will she be okay after the spell?" Liss asked.

Keith didn't pause his work. "Who?"

"Zephyr."

"That was the plan. I need her for the next step." He cocked his head. "But with the three of you here, we have redundancy."

"What are you talking about?" Alexa said.

"He means, it's okay if Zephyr dies, because he can use us for the next part of the spell," Liss said. She was pretty sure she was about to make the biggest mistake of her life, and that she couldn't live with herself if she didn't. "Let me do it instead."

"Liss!" Dan cried.

"Transfer that purple energy stuff to me, just like you put it in her." Keith eyed Liss. He was twitching like a zombie at the earliest stages of zombification. "Zephyr's just some girl. I'm that, plus a witch. You grabbed her on the side of the road, but Kasyan *chose* me to be here. For this."

"She's right," Alexa added. Her eyes behind her glasses were so wide, the whites were visible all around her irises. Liss hoped Alexa saw what she was doing. "We don't want to displease him."

Keith jerked his head in what seemed like an agreement. Beside Liss, Dan crushed her fist against her mouth but didn't entirely stifle her gasp.

"Let's do it," Keith said.

Before Liss could think about it anymore, Keith cut Zephyr's bonds and the two girls were holding hands. Keith was muttering something that felt too strange and far away for Liss to hear. No sooner had Liss noticed a stinging sensation all over her body than it exploded inside her, white hot and racing, the inside of stars, catastrophe and ecstasy, everything too much—too much—too much. Her skin was crackling with electricity.

Zephyr's face loomed across from her. How weird that Zephyr was the lucid one now.

"Liss?" Zephyr said, then static filled Liss's ears.

Dan

Liss's pale skin was lit bright enough to make Dan's head throb—
even more than it was already throbbing.

Fucking hell, Liss. What have you done?

Zephyr staggered and fell into Alexa's arms, but her legs stayed
under her. That eerie, vacant look had left her along with that
buzzing, purple-gray energy. Instead, her face pulled into a taut
mask of terror.

"You'll be okay," Alexa was saying to her. "When you get out, head
south as fast as you can." She pulled her phone from her pocket and
pressed it into Zephyr's hand, then nudged her in the direction of the
passage to the beach.

Keith was already ignoring them, his attention on Liss now. He
was anointing her face and palms with some kind of oil. Dan's stomach turned as he began an incantation. Liss's whole body shuddered
against the rocks.

Keith clearly didn't have the practice she and Liss did at spellwork, nor Alexa's powerful gift for it. Keith's expression had hardened; sweat dotted his brow as he focused on his graceless words.

Suddenly Liss's back arched so extremely that it had to be painful, and she was pressing her hands against the wall. The purple energy stuff was gathering there, rippling toward her hands in pulses
from all over her body as Liss submitted to his spell.

Dan thought she could see that familiar fierce look in Liss's eyes.
The cave wall shattered.

With a splintering, crystalline crack, the wall of rock collapsed.
The air clouded thick with dust that cleared to reveal a heap of
purple-tinged rubble and a gaping hole into what lay beyond.

Liss was on her knees panting and shaking, buried past her ankles in the rubble, but she was obviously *alive*. Dan wanted to rush to her side, but she knew that wasn't what Liss wanted. Instead, she caught Alexa's eye, then looked at Keith. He had his hands pressed palm to palm in a prayer, preparing himself to enter his Lord's prison.

It was too perfect.

Alexa bent and grabbed the rope that had bound Zephyr's hands, keeping half an eye on Dan as she soundlessly counted *one, two, three.*

Together, they lunged for Keith. Dan tackled him and he went down hard on his back with an awful crack. Alexa had the rope looped around his wrists and yanked into a firm knot before he could figure out how to resist them.

"No one's spilling blood in there," Dan said as she reached into the pocket of his cargo shorts and grabbed his knife. "We know that's the key to breaking the spell. Kasyan's staying right where he is, forever."

And then the wind began to blow.

TWENTY-SIX

Dan

The wind rushed out of Kasyan's prison with such force that it was hard to stand—Keith fell twice without his arms to steady him. In a matter of moments, most of the dust from the shattering of the rock had been blown down the passage to the beach—all that didn't end up in their eyes and mouths and noses. The wind was so strong it was hard for Dan to *breathe*.

Alexa yanked Keith's rope. They clambered over the rubble and headed into the cavern.

With just the beams of their headlamps, it was hard to see how large the cavern was. It had a seemingly endless perimeter of blackness, which Dan tried very hard not to be terrified by. She reminded herself that there were (probably) no monsters here, other than the ones they were already aware of. The cave's granite surfaces sparkled with white and ochre crystals, and when the wind flagged long enough for them to catch a whiff, it smelled of eggy sulfur. Weirder still, the cave was full of junk—*human* junk. Broken chairs, rotting books, dirty throw pillows, a ratty mold-speckled loveseat that looked like it had been left on the curb two decades ago.

"What is all this shit?" Liss asked. "When Volunin said Mora was a scavenger, I didn't think he meant literally."

Dan's headlamp caught an old army cot. Johnny's jacket was draped across it. She wondered where Volunin's bones were.

"Where are they?" Alexa asked.

"My Lord!" Keith was wailing. "They tricked me! These girls

promised that you called to them and they tricked me!"

"We should have gagged him," Liss muttered.

Just like that, the wind died.

Which was definitely more terrifying than the wind had been.

"Help me and I'll free you as I promised! I earned my wish!" Keith screamed.

"Shut up!" Alexa hissed, yanking on the rope.

"There he is," Liss said. "Kasyan."

Liss was pointing to an elevated spot at the back of the cave where a dim greenish light illuminated an indistinct figure seated on a rock. Around him, Mora's scavengings were arranged like offerings: a pile of lawn flamingos, a shiny chrome bumper, a bushel of plastic flowers, and what looked like a pinball machine.

"Are we ready?" Dan said.

"Does it matter?" Liss answered, and she led them toward Kasyan's strange altar.

As they came closer, they could make him out: a lean man, bare-chested with skin so pale that in the darkness of the cave, he appeared a glowing white, like one of those cave-dwelling salamanders whose coloring had been lost and whose eyes had evolved away. His hips and chest were draped with chains that anchored him to the rock. They seemed to be made from rock themselves.

Dan saw that Kasyan's eyes had not evolved away. On the contrary, they were twin black pools, with neither white nor iris nor pupil visible in the ink, dark enough to bring to mind oblivion. His hair, likewise black, hung down raggedly around his face, which gave the impression of being something very close to a skull, with pale lips and sunken cheeks. His eyelids, thankfully, were a regular length, unlike in Alexa's stories, although he lacked eyebrows or lashes.

In his white hands, he toyed with a book.

Volunin's true Black Book.

"You've come to free me." His voice was strange, grating and at the same time harmonious, like someone had rung the wrong set of bells at once.

"No," Liss said. "We came for Johnny. It's time for him to go home. Where is he?"

"Free me, and he goes free too," Kasyan said.

Johnny and Mora emerged from the darkness of the cave. This time, Mora was wearing a heavily beaded dress, like she'd prepared for company, and her long and ropey neck was unwound and ranging toward them. She was perched on Johnny's shoulders, her claw-like feet pinching his flesh, as she had been the last time they'd seen her. Then, Johnny's posture had been rigid, his eyes blank and unseeing. Now, he was awake.

Johnny was rail-thin and ashen. His black hair no longer fell in slashes across his forehead but was greasy and long enough to touch his shoulders. His face was grooved like he'd aged ten years in as many months, and half-moons of purple smeared under his eyes. She'd expected him to be terrified, but instead he just looked exhausted.

When he saw them, he stumbled under Mora's weight. She dug her heels in deeper and he flinched. "No, no—get out of here! Go, while you can!"

Kasyan gave them a smile cruel enough to blunt a scalpel. "And if you don't free me, Mora will kill him."

Mora screeched with glee, her pointed features pinching closer together. She inched a talonlike fingernail toward Johnny's ear.

"No!" all three of them cried.

Kasyan lifted a hand and Mora froze.

"You were using Johnny to talk to Keith," Dan stammered. "You don't need that anymore—let him go."

Kasyan's pale lip twitched as he considered her. "I don't need him for that? He's already been unreliable for months. Communication like that just consumes a person's vitality." Kasyan shifted his weight under the chains into a languid pose. His eyes flashed as a sliver of a smile crept across his face. "He did quite a lot of wishing to go home. All the time. Not a lot of imagination, but he was just desperate. *I want to go home!*" Kasyan said it in Johnny's voice—or what Dan imagined Johnny would sound like when he cried. Kasyan sighed, although breathing did not seem strictly necessary to him. "There were times he thought he found his way to escape, only to be disappointed. Just. Like. That." Kasyan snapped his fingers and something rumbled deep in the cavern, out of range of their headlamps, and the sound of falling rock followed. Johnny flinched.

"You *tortured* him," Liss growled.

"Desire is a complicated thing. It leaves you open. I merely explored his desires. Exactly as you did, Liss." Liss flinched. She was for the first time in her life at a loss for words. "Perhaps Johnny would not be here if he had wanted the *right* thing. The right girl." Kasyan's black eyes flitted to Dan. "Don't you think so, Dan? If only he'd chosen you instead. He hurt you so badly, you sent him to me."

He was obviously trying to upset them, but why did Kasyan think that at a time like this, she'd care if Johnny liked her or not? There was no love triangle among them—there never had been, as far as Dan was concerned. All she had really wanted was Liss's friendship. As for Johnny, she realized, she'd never really wanted anything from him at all. Kasyan was supposed to be able to see their desires; why had he gotten hers wrong? "Let Johnny go and he can make that choice for himself."

"I promised Keith a wish for his assistance in my liberation. He thinks that together we're going to make the world a better place." Kasyan grinned, the pallid flesh of his lips pulling back to expose a mouth like a black abyss. "You three aren't so foolish. I'll extend that offer to any of you. Just a little spilled blood."

"We don't want your wishes," Liss cut in.

"Really?" Kasyan set the Black Book on the rock beside him. And suddenly Kasyan was gone, folding in on his own inky darkness and then opening himself into a new form.

A sandy-haired man in a suit rattled the chains as he strained them to lean toward Liss. "Now, Liss, you know how important getting into the right college is for your future. Let's get you accepted to Columbia, or maybe Princeton? Harvard?"

"Is that your dad?" Alexa said.

"That's a pretty insulting offer," Liss answered. "I'm already a straight-A student, and I'm not a fucking cheater."

"You should consider it," he pressed. "The fact is, I've never really been proud to be your father. If you were admitted to the right school, I'd finally have a real reason to love you. I'd even go through with leaving your mother if you wanted me to. You'd never have to see her again. How about that?"

Dan looked at Liss. She wasn't moving, not even blinking. For a second, Dan worried, what if—

Liss spoke through clenched teeth. "Leave me and my family alone, you manipulative piece of shit."

But Kasyan was already unraveling himself again, re-forming himself into an olive-skinned woman with long chestnut hair, the fine crinkle of laugh lines around her eyes. She gave Alexa a smile so full of love that Dan's throat grew tight.

"Hey, kid. How's our little family-thing holding up without me?"

"Lore?" Alexa whimpered.

"Stop!" Dan shouted. "You can't do that to her!"

Alexa turned to her. "It's okay. I can handle it."

"I don't know about that, kid," Lorelei-Kasyan said. "Kasyan's pretty powerful. He's the only reason I'm still alive, you know. He granted your wish once—remember, you asked to let me live?"

"He didn't grant my wish," Alexa said. "This isn't what I wanted."

"Things turned out pretty badly, right? Let him fix it now, that's all. Me and you could move back to LA like we talked about, and it'll be like none of this ever happened. Just help me get out of these chains, huh?"

"I cursed her!" Keith suddenly cried, falling on his knees before Alexa. His eyes were bulging and manic. "It was my idea—with my Lord's assistance! I needed to kill her. Spill my blood for it! You know you want to. Get your revenge on me and Kasyan will give her back to you."

"Alexa . . ." Dan began, but Alexa shot her a look so hard it silenced her.

"Why did you do it?" Alexa asked Keith. "Why try to kill her?"

"I had to. She was going to ruin the plan." The words spilled out of Keith. "She was sneaking around. She couldn't be trusted. And then she saw the girl—Zephyr. She wanted me to let her go. But I needed Zephyr—Kasyan told me I needed someone young. They have the best energy. I tried to get her to bring you to me! I wanted it to be you." Dan thought she smelled something burning. There was a ghastly, beatific look on Keith's face. "Punish me. Spill my blood to make me pay."

"No," Alexa finally said. "Lorelei's gone. You took her from me and you don't even understand why. You've just been Kasyan's pawn all along. Sending you to prison is going to have to be enough."

"Just ask him to heal me, Alexa. Don't you think I deserve that much?" Lorelei-Kasyan was crying now. "I'm in so much pain. After everything I've done for you, just do this one thing for me. How can you let me rot, when I'm the only person who ever loved you?"

Alexa stared Lorelei-Kasyan down. "You're not Lorelei, and

I won't talk to you like you are. I don't believe you can fix what you've done to her. And you're wrong: she's not the only person who loves me."

For a second, Lorelei-Kasyan's face contorted into a howl of rage, and then the face and body melted away. He was transforming, blackening and folding in on himself again. A sick dread rose in Dan's gut. Who would he choose for her? What did he think she really wanted? He had been wrong a minute ago about Johnny, but that was nothing compared to what he was doing now.

What *did* she really want?

Pulling against the chains, Kasyan's unsettled form seemed to be growing bigger, coming closer to Dan.

"I've got a wish!" someone screamed from behind them.

Dan turned to see Zephyr, her hair loose and wild and her white dress caked in grime. She was holding a fireplace poker she must have found among Mora's scavengings.

"You were supposed to run!" Liss cried.

"Not while he's still out there," she said, swinging the iron poker.

The girls lunged for her, but Zephyr had four years on St. Ignatius's softball team behind her swing, and it landed true: directly on Keith's temple with a nightmarish crunch and he fell, unmoving, at the foot of Kasyan's throne.

"I wish you'd rot in hell!" Zephyr cried as the poker clattered to the ground.

Blood poured from the crack in Keith's skull.

Everything moved at once.

Kasyan's chains burst and fell to the floor. As they did, he shifted back into true form.

Dan didn't know why she'd assumed the human form he'd first

taken was his natural shape. It made a lot more sense for him to be what he was.

Darkness.

He hovered in the air: a shifting, wind-hounded vortex of tendrils of black smoke, crackling with white lightning.

The instant that Mora leapt from Johnny's back, Liss grabbed for him. He fell into her, sinking his face into her shoulder.

But Dan barely paused to look at Johnny. She was searching the cave, looking for Kasyan, but all around was darkness.

"What do we do?" Alexa cried.

"I have an idea," Dan said. She grabbed the true Black Book from where it lay on the rocks by Kasyan's broken chains, and thrust it at Liss. "Get back to the beach. Find the spell to seal the cave and get ready. Now!"

Liss grabbed the book in one hand and Johnny's arm in the other and ran for the passage to the beach. Alexa was beside her, pulling Zephyr along.

Behind them, Dan was left alone in the cave, hoping the blackness that was Kasyan wouldn't beat them there.

She was a witch.

Witches were magic, and magic was power.

Dan focused on that power now—the heavy, skin-prickling rush of it, its wildness. She imagined it wakening something in her veins and arteries, making the hair of her arms stand up. She called magic to her, to fortify her, and when she felt it come, she imagined seizing it in her fists.

"*Kasyan!*" Dan pushed everything into that scream: all the fear and horror, how fiercely she wanted for them all to be safe again. She needed to sound desperate. Luckily, she was. "Kasyan, wait! You promised me a wish!"

Across the cave, Liss and Alexa's headlamps were no longer visible; they'd entered the tunnel to the beach. Panic thrummed in her chest—she was all alone down here, with Keith, who was making a terrible gurgling sound and clutching his head—but instead of fighting it, she let the panic into her voice too. She called Kasyan again and again, her voice pitching high and shaky. "Kasyan, please! You're my last chance."

And then he was there.

Or not a *him*, exactly. Now Kasyan was a kind of black airborne jellyfish, throbbing with that purplish luminescence. A voice emanated from it. "The other girl freed me." It was strange that something without a face or even a human form could be so overwhelmingly smug.

"But you didn't grant her wish. I would have done it. I didn't have the chance." Dan allowed her voice to waver. "It's hard for me to stand up to them. Liss especially. That's why I didn't do it sooner. You wouldn't be free now without Johnny, and you know Johnny wouldn't have been down here without me."

Kasyan's ghostly form floated nearer. The way it shifted was transfixing, as if stirred by a wind Dan couldn't feel. "What is it you want?"

"Don't you know?"

"You're unusually difficult to read."

"Maybe that's because . . . sometimes I feel like I don't want anything. It scares me. Sometimes it's like there's nothing in the world that can make me feel anything but miserable. And I'm just so tired of that." There were tears in her eyes. She really was tired, and they were so close to the end of it all.

"You want happiness."

"But how do I get there? It's like happiness just exists on a whole different planet from the one I'm on. I thought you could see people's desires. I was hoping you could tell me what would . . . fix me. Tell me what I should be wishing for."

Kasyan drifted still closer to her, and now his inky tendrils were twisting in on themselves, weaving together until his black mass was something like a human form.

It snatched the breath from Dan's chest.

The kohl-rimmed eyes and pouty lips and cheekbones as sharp as North Coast's cliffs, limbs thin as a wire.

He was playing with a rose, pressing the pad of his finger against a thorn—exactly like in the IronWeaks poster she had taped over her bed.

Rickey.

Dan couldn't speak or breathe or blink, not when Rickey-Kasyan was *looking right at her* with his heavy-lidded eyes. In all her favorite pictures of him, even when his eyes were looking at the camera, they were really focused elsewhere, on that bleak and tortured place inside. Now those eyes were turned on her, like they could see right into her own closely guarded version of that place. Rickey had made that seem beautiful and poetic and tragic and inescapable all at once. Rickey bit his lip, just a little, and Dan couldn't help it: her body flushed with heat.

"What I want is . . . Rickey?" Dan managed to ask.

There was a tender, sad smile on Rickey-Kasyan's face as he slowly shook his head, which should not have come off as so diabolically sexy. "Rickey's dead," he said softly. His voice was like rich chocolate, like a candle flame, like getting lost in the in the woods at night.

His voice was still so familiar and velvety, part of Dan wanted to crawl inside it. She had spent hours with that voice. It had sung to her while she cried, when she cut, and it had sung to her until she was brought to do those things. It had kept her company at her darkest moments, and it had led her to those moments, too. She had let it.

The hair on the back of Dan's neck stood on end.

"He killed himself," she said slowly.

Rickey-Kasyan took a slouchy step closer to her, but the closer he got, the more his glamour dulled. His beautiful eyes looked sunken, his sad smile more like a sneer. His torso was bare and scattered with moles Dan had never noticed before, and the thinness of his chest and the jutting angles of his hip bones above his jeans were almost painful to see. He was near enough that she could touch him, but the possibility revolted her. Rickey wasn't someone she wanted to touch or kiss. He wasn't, she realized, a person at all to her. He was an indefinable, romantic sadness, and that made him a dangerous thing.

Dan shoved her hands into the pockets of her windbreaker.

"You don't need to fight it, Dan," Rickey-Kasyan said. "That sadness is part of you. It's who you really are. We're the same that way."

"I can't keep going like this," she made herself say. "I don't want to be miserable anymore."

"There is another way," Rickey-Kasyan said. He arched his eyebrow invitingly at her, his lips a little bit pouty.

Dan's heart fluttered as she inched forward, closing what little distance remained between them. "What other way?"

"Do what I did."

This, Dan understood now, was the idea Rickey's music had always danced around the edges of, long before he killed himself. It was an idea she carried inside herself too, and now she was going to face it.

Slowly, Dan pulled Keith's knife from her pocket.

"There's nothing wrong with giving up." Rickey-Kasyan's long lashes reflected in the knife's blade. He was always so tragically beautiful, even before he'd made himself a tragedy. "You can disappear forever, just like I did."

Dan's palm sweat against the handle of the knife. She tightened her grip. Last night's cuts were stinging and sore on her arm.

"Rickey gave up," Dan said. "But I'm choosing to fight."

She plunged the knife between Kasyan's ribs as hard as she could, then wrenched the knife up to the side. The pupils of his gorgeous, dead eyes blew out wide and his mouth fell open, black vapor pouring from his throat.

Dan didn't wait to see if Kasyan was dead.

She knew he wasn't.

She ran.

Alexa

On the beach, Alexa shivered against the wind. A few feet away, sheltered by some rocks, Zephyr and Johnny were devouring the granola bars from Liss's backpack, though Johnny was gagging on his. Liss paced in the sand, staring at the mouth of the cave.

"What's taking so long?" Liss said.

Alexa tried to sound confident. "She'll make it out."

At least they had enough time to find Volunin's spell to seal the cave in his original Black Book. It turned out the real Book was a lot easier to use than Kasyan's knockoff.

A light flickered in the passage.

"That's her headlamp!" Alexa said. "Get ready."

Dan

Dan plunged through the dark cave as fast as she could, thankful for all those horrible runs she had made herself go on. She concentrated on keeping her footing on the slick rocks. She couldn't fall, she couldn't stumble, she couldn't slow.

He had to be behind her. A knife wound wasn't enough to kill Kasyan, that much was obvious, but she'd gambled on the guess that if he took a human form, he might be injured enough to buy her a little time.

She trusted Liss and Alexa would be ready.

Because if Kasyan was behind her, he was furious.

Alexa

Alexa and Liss stood at the mouth of the cave, their hands joined, and already whispering the words when Dan came bombing out of the cave, gasping for breath. Alexa grabbed her hand, pulling her into line with them.

Stacked in front of them were the Black Books—the one that Liss and Dan had tended for so long, and the real one, that held Volunin's power. The energy they contained would have to be enough to seal the mouth of the cave.

Alexa raised her voice, shouting the words of the spell, their voices a chorus. Magic rippled through them, from Alexa's palms into Dan's and Liss's, the three of them a channel, a bond, three stars in constellation. Alexa focused on the Books, envisioning their power bursting free.

A thin vein of smoke was rising from the books.

Alexa pushed harder, sweating now, the effort of magic like a horrible deep-sea pressure inside her bones, inside her teeth, inside of everywhere. She pulled on every thread inside her—Lorelei and Swann, Volunin and Maggie, generations of witches who had come before, who had fought and sacrificed so that Kasyan would be contained.

She clutched Dan and Liss's hands harder and they squeezed back, and the three of them lifted their voices louder.

He was almost there—a dim figure was moving in the dark.

Kasyan would not go free.

Not while the three of them had life left in them.

Alexa thought of laughing with Dan on their drives into Gratton, of Liss protecting her secrets when they were still strangers, of watching sunsets in LA with Lorelei and Domino nuzzling her feet, of how the people you love can somehow become the only place of stillness in the wild and beautiful world that all of them shared and none of them understood.

Alexa pushed her voice into a roar.

A light flashed, magnesium-white and brilliant. The Books exploded into flame and the girls stumbled back into the waves. With the release of the Books' energy, the rocks began to grind against one another, sending tremors through the sand.

They kept chanting.

The fissure in the cliff that had led into Kasyan's prison was closing, beginning at the top and working its way down, the passage becoming smaller with each moment, the earth groaning and shaking against the force of the spell.

But Kasyan was closer now. He held a physical form, and Alexa could make out his white hands and pale face. He was staggering, then bounding toward the narrowing gap in the rock.

Alexa raised her voice higher still, summoning every last bit of energy, all of her magic. She would burn all of it out, for this.

Their magic was stronger than him. *They* were stronger than him—stronger than all they had been through, strong enough to move the earth against itself. The cave entrance narrowed: a slit, a sliver, the rock colliding into itself. Kasyan was so close, Alexa could see the utter darkness of his eyes as he lunged toward them, desperate and furious.

The spell was complete.

The cave was sealed, a white hand protruding from a black seam in the rock.

TWENTY-SEVEN

Dan

They ran.

Or they ran where the terrain allowed it, when everyone was able, because they weren't home yet, not now that the tide was rising. They stumbled through the suck and heave of the waves, over the jagged and slippery rocks, with barely enough light to share among the five of them.

Bringing up the rear of their line, Dan breathed deep against her fear. Her feet had been soaked by the glacial, dark water of the Pacific so long and thoroughly that they were clumsy unfeeling bricks. The muscles in her legs wobbled, and given the way she'd missed a few steps, Dan worried they might give out completely.

She kept seeing Kasyan's hand in that rock. He wasn't chained in the same way Volunin had chained him, only stopped by the sealing of the cave. Who knew if he could escape that way? Alexa had burned the hand into crumbling ash, using a freaky white fire she summoned with the remaining energy from the destruction of the Black Books.

Was it enough?

Dan pushed the thought away. She could worry about Kasyan later, so long as there was a later.

First, they had to get home.

It was the only thing that would make everything they'd suffered worth it. Johnny and Zephyr could reclaim the lives they'd almost lost. Alexa could begin to mourn Lorelei. And for her and Liss, it was the chance to live with all this in the past, as people who had made horrendous mistakes and done their best to make things right.

Only if they made it back alive.

Up ahead, Liss was leading them back, and Dan wondered how she felt to have Johnny just a few feet behind her, after all the months she spent missing him. She must be desperate to hold him or kiss him or even just ask if he was okay, but Dan could tell from the beam of Liss's headlamp that she didn't turn back to him. Instead, she pushed them forward, against the press of the ocean itself, and Dan knew Liss was just as scared as she was.

At the final promontory, the waves swelled to their knees. The ocean pressed them against the cliff then tried to pull them from it, but Dan could see the curve of Heart's Desire Beach with its black sand up ahead. First Liss made it back onto the safety of the beach, then Johnny collapsed into her arms. Zephyr followed, falling to her knees in the sand, with Alexa just behind.

Dan's gut flooded with relief. They had done it. *They had actually done it.*

She didn't see the wave coming until Liss screamed.

The hump of water rolling toward her was at least twice as high as the waves they'd been dealing with, big enough that it would smash her against the cliff and take her back out to sea. Dan scrambled, her frozen feet unsteady against the rocks and her legs near to giving out. The water pushed higher around her. The beach was just a few paces away. She could make it—she had come so far and she was *so close.*

Her feet went out from under her. Salt water slammed into her nose and eyes. Everything was black, icy, and she was being *pulled*, and she couldn't tell if it was the tide or something else.

But then hands were grabbing her by the armpits and heaving her out of the waves and up onto the beach. Dan opened her eyes, stinging with salt, and Liss and Alexa were there, their limbs tangled together. Behind her, the wave slammed into the cliff, and the sand-thickened water surged against them.

They had saved her just in time.

For a moment, it was just the three of them: Liss and Alexa and Dan. They were shivering and soaked and crusted with sand, but here they were, back safe on the beach, staring at each other with the absolute certainty that they'd nearly lost everything.

"We are never doing anything like this ever again," Liss said.

Then she burst into tears.

They called 911. Liss came up with a story: the three of them were going to hang out at Heart's Desire to avoid the lame Solstice Parade scene, but they'd found that weird cult from outside Marlena doing its own pagan ritual—except this one involved two missing teens. They'd followed Keith down the beach, which they totally didn't real-ize was probably very dangerous. Zephyr told the officers that Keith was acting deranged and talking about sacrificing her and Johnny to some god he made up. They'd struggled, and Keith slipped on some algae and got pulled away in the tide. It happened so fast, there was nothing they could do to help—plus he was basically trying to kill them at the same time, so it was a challenging situation. Johnny couldn't manage anything more than a nod in corroboration; he'd barely spoken since they'd gotten back to the beach, and Liss hadn't let go of his hand.

Dan, huddled beside Alexa in a silvery thermal blanket, watched officers from the Highway Patrol and the county sheriff's office point flashlights at the cliff the girls and Johnny had just navigated. They shook their heads; it wasn't passable at all. They weren't optimistic about evidence recovery.

Fortunately, Black Grass's seekers didn't remember what happened. They sat bewildered in the sand, talking past the officers' questions. It was supposed to be the most important meditation of their lives, and now Keith, their Guide, was swept out to sea— disappeared. How would they speak to the Lord now? Had their Guide advanced without them?

"*Honestly*," Alexa whispered. Dan fished her hand out from the thermal blanket, found Alexa's, and squeezed.

"We're doing a full investigation," an officer assured the seekers. He was doing an impressive job of keeping a straight face. "But this looks like a death by misadventure. I'm going to need to take down everyone's names."

Then a cry pierced the commotion on the beach, and Johnny's mom was running toward them—toward her son. She wrapped her arms around the frail shape of him and wept into his hair. Then everyone was crying all over again, even some of the officers, and soon Zephyr's parents were there, and she and Johnny were packed off into ambulances.

Finally Alexa, Liss, and Dan got back in the car and followed the snaking road back to Dogtown.

LATER

Alexa

Lorelei was dead.

Whatever part of Kasyan had kept her breathing for those painful weeks had stopped when they trapped him in the rock. Domino was sitting in the window when Alexa got home, waiting to tell her.

Never forget, I love you, kid.

Domino's voice in her head was exactly like Lorelei's, the way it sounded like a wink, felt like a sigh—like all the trust and protection and love that Lorelei had shared with her.

Alexa bundled Domino into her arms and cried into his silky fur for a long time.

Then she called Swann, took the cat, and went to Dan's house. She stayed for the next eight months.

Swann staged Lorelei's death as some kind of accident. The police never asked Alexa any questions about it, which made it clear that the Wardens had avoided a proper investigation using some unnatural influence. It was also discovered that a rather large life insurance policy had been taken out on Lorelei, which Alexa was to be the beneficiary of. It was enough to get her through college, maybe with a little left over depending on where she went. Alexa cried all over again when she found out, not because of the money, but because it meant that Lorelei was still taking care of her, even now that she was gone.

Alexa went down to LA for the funeral with Swann, who greeted the majority of Lorelei's friends as fellow Wardens. It was a real loss, Swann had said on the flight, that Lorelei had passed without handing down her powers, but if Alexa wanted to join the Wardens, she'd be more than welcome. It was still hard to think about how Lorelei had lied to keep that part of her life from Alexa, but then she felt the secret crackle of magic in her fingertips—a reminder that Lorelei hadn't kept it from her, only that she hadn't managed to tell her before she died.

At the funeral, Alexa's dad wore a patchy beard and smelled like booze, which Alexa wasn't sure was due to his sister's death or a regular habit. As usual, their conversations were full of meaningless platitudes like "Look at you, all grown up!" that hinted he felt a little bad for not being there and wanted assurance that he hadn't entirely screwed up her life. She always replied with something like "Yep, that is how time works," in the hopes of reminding him that if her life *wasn't* entirely screwed up it was absolutely no thanks to him. He seemed relieved to be rid of her when he clapped her on the back and said, "Keep doin' what you're doin', sweetie," before heading for his car.

The whole experience was so exhausting Alexa barely wanted to leave her (extremely comfortable) hotel bed. When she did, LA felt unfamiliar. Too many people, the weather too nice, too many memories that felt like they belonged to an ancient version of herself.

It was only a few days, but she missed the dangerous and empty roads, the clammy fog clinging to her skin. She missed Dan and Liss—and Zephyr.

At first, Zephyr had just needed a friend who had been there, when *there* meant inside a demon's lair, where Zephyr had killed a man who would have destroyed them all. But Dan and Liss had been there too, and Zephyr didn't text them virtually all day, nonstop. It made Alexa's heart feel funny, like it was sneaking toward happiness when her back was turned.

Then Zephyr kissed her, and that settled that.

It was strange and new and surprisingly, a little scary. It wasn't that Alexa hadn't wanted a girlfriend before, just that she had tried not to dwell on it, because thinking about what you wanted and didn't have felt like a dead end. But now that she was with Zephyr—someone who she liked so much it was almost hard to breathe in her presence, who smelled good and put up with her rambling about Flintowerland and *Quest of the Axials,* and who kissed her with lips so deliciously soft and hungry—Alexa wondered if there wasn't another reason she hadn't let herself think too hard about romance.

Being with Zephyr was amazing, but how long could it possibly last? She'd seen her mother be left and do the leaving so many times, and losing Lorelei was almost more than Alexa could bear. She couldn't stand to imagine the lifespan of Zephyr-and-Alexa; she could practically feel the cracks spidering where her heart was preparing itself to break.

"You think I'm going to break up with you?" Zephyr said when Alexa confessed how she felt. They were lying side by side, sharing a pillow in what used to be the guest room at Dan's house, but was now Alexa's.

"I don't know," Alexa mumbled. The pillow pushed her glasses off-center, and she couldn't fix them without getting up, which she didn't want to do. "When I'm with you, no, not at all. I forget about all of that and it's just—us. But then later, I get worried, I guess."

"I get that. I think it's normal to be nervous," Zephyr said. With her curly hair clouded behind her on the pillow and her blue eyes searching Alexa's, she looked like an absolute vision; she always did. "Sometimes it still feels weird that I'm dating a girl. But then it feels even weirder that I haven't been dating girls for my entire life. When I was with Brodie—which is so gross to even think about now—I kept trying to convince myself he had something that guys my age didn't. I thought none of them had ever really made me feel anything because they were too immature." Zephyr smiled. "But you made me realize I'd been looking for the wrong thing all along, when I should have been looking for you."

Alexa's heart felt impossibly full and fragile at the same time. She bit her lip. "You can still break up with me if you want. You don't have to not break up with me just because I said that."

"I'm not breaking up with you." Zephyr traced the line of Alexa's jaw with a finger. "I'm like, completely in love with you, Alexa."

"You're—you're what?"

Zephyr grinned. Her fingers teased the baby hairs at the back of Alexa's neck. "I love you, Alexa. I don't want to think about breaking up with you or hurting you, not ever."

A tear ran from the corner of Alexa's eye onto the pillow, but she didn't care, because Zephyr was kissing her, wrapping her arms around her, pulling her close and all of it felt like coming home.

Zephyr pulled away. "It's okay if you don't say it back. My feelings aren't totally hurt or anything."

"You kissed me before I could!" Alexa kissed her again, gently this time, her nose brushing against Zephyr's and her eyelashes fluttering against her cheeks. "I love you too, Zephyr Finnemore."

Liss

After a long hospital stay, Johnny came home quietly. The story of Zephyr's kidnapping drew a lot of media attention and kept Johnny out of the spotlight. He claimed he didn't remember much of what had happened over the last ten months and never said otherwise until the doctors diagnosed him with a form of amnesia stemming from his trauma.

Liss didn't believe it. There was a difference between forgetting and not wanting to remember.

Liss finally got to visit him two weeks after he was released from the hospital. Johnny had no phone, so his mom was the only way to contact him. She had promised to let Liss know when he was ready for visitors, and Liss had to respect that.

Liss had only been to the Sus' house a handful of times; no comforting feeling of returning to simpler times greeted her when Dr. Su opened the door. The house was crowded with boxes and rolls of tape.

"You're moving?" Liss asked.

"I'm joining a dental practice near Davis."

"That's hours away."

Dr. Su offered half a shrug. "We think he'd do better somewhere inland. He has issues with the ocean. And the wind. And darkness. There are trauma specialists there." Dr. Su removed her glasses and rubbed her temple. "I can't wait to leave this place."

Liss couldn't argue with that.

She held her breath as she walked the hall to Johnny's room.

He was sitting on the floor in front of a crate of records, but nothing was playing on the turntable.

"Hey," she said quietly, because she had to say something. "How are you feeling?"

His eyebrows scrunched up. His hair had been cut short, but he ducked his head like he could still hide behind it. He wouldn't meet her eyes. "Happy to be home," he finally said, his tone flat.

She couldn't bear looking at him like that, so she scanned the room instead. It was still dusty from his absence, and unassembled boxes rested against a wall. His desk chair had been pushed aside, and under the desk lay a pillow and a blanket.

He saw her staring. "It's the only way I can sleep."

"For now," she said, kneeling next to him. "You'll get better. It just takes time."

His voice fell into a whisper. "You don't know what it's like."

He sounded so miserable that her heart perked up in a familiar way at the challenge. She would do anything, give anything. She had promised herself that she would always try one more time for Johnny. She reached for his hand. It was balled into a fist. "I can help."

He flinched at her touch. His hand didn't relax in hers at all. "Can you? Really?"

Seeing him like that, his knees pulled up to his chest and his T-shirt loose on his malnourished frame, made her feel young and afraid. She remembered Kasyan's cruel smile, her terror at the un-ending darkness of his eyes, the liquid relief she felt to see his pale hand trapped in that rock. She felt Johnny's name on her lips that night she cast the spell that set all of this in motion. Johnny had had a hole blasted in his life and no matter how badly she wanted it or how many plans she came up with, she couldn't fix that.

She let his hand go.

"I don't know. But you're not alone. You never were. I was always coming for you." She swallowed hard. "I love you, Johnny."

He looked at her like he didn't know what that meant; maybe,

Liss thought, neither did she. "I'm sorry," he eventually said. "The doctors say I'm still processing."

Liss stood to leave. "You have nothing to apologize for. I'm here whenever you want to talk," she said, although something told her she would never see him again. "I'm so sorry, Johnny, for everything."

Liss got in the red Range Rover and drove into Fort Gratton's downtown. She parked near a corner of Main Street where a cluster of dried flowers and candles and peace signs woven from twigs were gathered in front of a laminated picture of an old woman. There was a ballot initiative to install a permanent plaque, but for now a sign read:

IN MEMORY OF
MAGGIE "MAD MAGS" KELLY
NORTH COASTER AND FRIEND

Liss paused at the memorial. Mad Mags died the night of the Solstice too, watching the Pacific from Dogtown Beach. No one could remember a North Coast without her, and no one knew how to reach any of her family, although only three of them knew this was because she was nearly two hundred years old. The whole community had mourned her loss, and Dogtown had already declared that next year's Solstice Parade would be held in Mags's honor. Liss hoped she'd found some peace, and her love Ivan, now that her ordeal with Kasyan had ended.

Leaving the memorial, Liss made her way to the last Victorian on the block, shoved open the red door, and waved a greeting at the tattooed receptionist before heading up the back stairs.

When Swann saw Liss standing there, she leaned against the

doorjamb and folded her thin arms. "You again."

"Me again," Liss said. Apparently the bad impression she'd made on Swann hadn't faded.

"What can I help you with today?"

Liss raised her chin and took a deep breath. "I want to join the Wardens."

Swann cocked her head. "And what makes you think you'd be suitable for the Wardens?"

"I miss doing magic," she began.

"That's not what the Wardens are about."

"You didn't let me finish!" Liss steadied herself. Swann wasn't her enemy, and more importantly, she needed to speak from the heart. "I know that the Wardens aren't running around doing whatever magic they feel like. That's not what I want either. I spent months using magic selfishly, and I'm not an idiot—I can see where that got me. I don't need magic for myself anymore. I want to make sure no one else goes through what Johnny did, or worse. I want to help people, and the Wardens can help me do that."

Swann regarded her, lips pursed.

"And the whole facing-down-Kasyan thing has to count for something, right?"

Swann shook her head. "You think you have experience, but you're still a naive witch. Most Warden witches start out with inherited knowledge. There will be a very great deal to learn."

"I'm an excellent student."

"You will have to be relentless."

Liss grinned. "I wouldn't have it any other way."

Swann moved aside and welcomed Liss into her den.

Dan

Dan slammed the front door, bounded up the stairs to her attic room, and shut the door behind her.

"Dan!" Alexa called from downstairs. "They're going to be here in like fifteen minutes!"

"I know," she yelled back. "I can get ready fast."

Dan looked at the dress lying on her bed, then back to the mirror. Her eyes were a little puffy from crying, but she could distract from that with eyeliner and mascara. She cried all the time in therapy, almost every week for months. She'd considered rescheduling her appointment this afternoon, but when she had asked her mom to help her find a therapist in January, Dan promised herself that she would do her best, even if it was hard.

And it *was* hard. Really hard. It turned out that she had learned some bad coping mechanisms to deal with some even worse emotions. It was important to stop cutting, but it was even more important to look directly at why she'd started doing it in the first place.

So she hadn't canceled, even though today was senior prom.

Dan took a deep breath and eyed the dress again. She and Alexa and Liss had spent hours looking at literally thousands of dresses online to find one she loved. It was black, with sparkly silver stars all over, and it had a skirt perfect for twirling. But the dress was sleeveless, which meant it would be impossible to hide the hatch of whitening scars on her arm like she usually did.

They had spent the whole of today's session on it: what to say if people asked, how to deal if they didn't ask but obviously saw anyway. One thing Dan was sure of: she was done with lying about it. Maybe she wasn't *fine* and maybe she never would be—but maybe fine was boring and the braver thing to do was work every day on at least being okay.

Sometimes, she was even good. It was a feeling she deserved, and more than that, she had earned.

If other people saw her scars and saw someone who was weak or sick or fucked up, that was their problem.

Because when she pulled the dress on and looked at herself against the white wall behind her—she'd torn down all the posters of Rickey and IronWeaks; she hadn't listened to them since that night—what Dan saw was pretty amazing.

"They're here!" Graciela called up.

She looked out the window to see Liss's red Range Rover parked in front of the house. (A new UC Santa Barbara sticker was on the back window. Liss promised her parents she'd apply to transfer to Berkeley the next year. She promised herself she'd see if she liked UCSB first.)

Dan wriggled into her heels and grabbed her phone.

"Aren't you beautiful?*" Graciela beamed* as Dan came down the stairs. "That dress!"

"Love the stars," Zephyr said, her hand already laced with Alexa's. Alexa was looking very *Grease* in a black '50s-style halter dress with a poofy skirt, and Zephyr had gone for something sleeker in purple.

"Look, we match!" Alexa chirped, flipping up the hem of her skirt to show a purple petticoat. They'd gotten each other coordinated corsages, too.

"You don't match, you *go*. Matching is lame, which is why I stopped you from doing it," Liss said, who looked extremely chic in a forest green jumpsuit. She had flowers woven into her hair and wore a fierce red lipstick.

Dan broke into a smile. They looked brilliant.

"Oh, you girls," Graciela said as Dan's dad juggled everyone's phones for pictures. "So much power and beauty in one place!"

Dan cringed. "Mom, honestly! It's just prom."

"I see everyone went for dark colors," Dan's dad said as he snapped a picture.

"The theme is fancy witches, Dad," Dan said, as they shifted to a new pose.

"Your prom's theme is fancy witches?" he asked.

"It's more like a personal theme," Dan answered, and all of them grinned. "Just for the four of us."

Acknowledgments

There are too many people I've depended on and celebrated with and learned from since I began this journey to thank everyone here. I've wanted to write a book since before I knew how to write. Thank you to everyone who has encouraged me since then.

Ruta Rimas, thank you for understanding my girls and making sure their story had a home. I'm very grateful to the team at Razorbill and Penguin Random House: Casey McIntyre, for believing in this book; Jayne Ziemba, for watching over it; Abigail Powers, for copyediting; Dana Li, for designing a far better cover than I ever dared imagine, and Rebecca Aidlin, for the interior design; everyone at marketing and publicity, especially Christina Colangelo, Bri Lockhart, Bree Martinez, and Felicity Vallence; and Gretchen Durning for keeping track of everything along the way.

I am hardly the first to claim to have the best agent ever, but in my case it's actually true. Jennifer Udden, I'm not sure why you took a chance on me, but when you did, I found a tireless champion, friend, occasional ice-skating buddy, and much more. Thank you.

Melissa Eastlake, my critique partner, you've taught me more about craft than any writing instructor I've ever had. Thank you for responding to my ten thousand whiny emails with care and encouragement.

Blake Miller, Joe Klaver, Michael Thompson, Steven Moore, and Zander Furnas, I don't know where I would be without you, but probably not in freaking Michigan, so thanks for nothing. Just kidding. Thank you for always having my back, for celebrating my successes and failures, and for making fun of me. I love you guys. Devi Mays, thank you for pointing out when I am being too extremely Capricorn. I'm grateful Hannah Begley and Pippa Kelly gave me a reason to get to know West Marin, which is the inspiration for North Coast. Thank you to Morgan Whitcomb for a friendship that feels like home. Ashraya Gupta, you've read practically every word I've written since I turned nineteen, and incredibly most of the time you even seemed to enjoy it. Thank you for always being there and for laughing at all of my jokes, even the ones no one else hears.

Alissa de Vogel, I love you more than anything and trust you more than anyone. I'm so lucky to have you as a sister. Thank you to my parents. It kind of goes without saying that I wouldn't be who I am without you. You have never doubted I could achieve whatever I dedicated myself to, even when I didn't see it myself. I love you.

Finally, I'm so grateful to every reader who gave this book a chance. I hope you find the witch gang you need.